# Rachel's Prayer

**Country Road Chronicles**

*Rorey's Secret*
*Rachel's Prayer*


**Related books by Leisha Kelly**

*Julia's Hope*
*Emma's Gift*
*Katie's Dream*

# Rachel's Prayer

## A Novel

## Leisha Kelly

**Revell**

Grand Rapids, Michigan

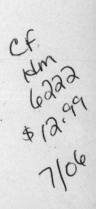

Published by Fleming H. Revell
a division of Baker Publishing Group
P.O. Box 6287, Grand Rapids, MI 49516-6287

Printed in the United States of America

Library of Congress Cataloging-in-Publication Data
Kelly, Leisha.
    Rachel's prayer : a novel / Leisha Kelly.
        p.    cm. — (Country road chronicles ; bk. 2)
    ISBN 10: 0-8007-5986-9 (pbk.)
    ISBN 978-0-8007-5986-5 (pbk.)
    1. World War, 1939–1945—United States—Fiction. 2. Domestic fiction. I. Title.
PS3611.E45R33 2006
813'.6—dc22                                        20006007957

Dedicated to our veterans
and servicemen and women.
Thank you, and may God bless.

# 1

## January 18, 1942

Robert was leaving tomorrow. I was trying to be brave and happy for his sake, but it was hard not to worry. It wasn't that he was too young. My son was twenty, a strong young man capable of thinking things through and doing well on his own. It was the war that frightened me. Like a demon reaching its shadowy arms in all directions, it pulled the whole world into its grasp.

Plain as yesterday in my mind was the bright December morning when I was heating water for washing while Robert tinkered at our battery radio, trying to fix the temperamental thing again. It was a Monday, and we'd been without the radio all weekend. We hadn't even been to church because Samuel and Robert had miserable colds. The girls were getting ready for school and singing the song they were supposed to perform for the school's annual program. Robert got the radio working. And then all the singing stopped. My wash water was forgotten. And nothing has been quite the same since.

The attack on Pearl Harbor we heard about on the radio that morning was a slap that left us reeling. Such hideous, blatant evil demanded response. We all understood that. We knew that our nation must step firmly and forcefully into the war we hadn't asked for, and that it would require commitment, even sacrifice, from all of us.

I shouldn't have been surprised when Robert told us he was going to enlist. He'd registered with the selective service and told us plainly that he would be proud to serve when called. But he didn't wait to be called. And now he would be on tomorrow's train.

At least he wouldn't be alone. Willy Hammond was going too. They'd been best friends since they were ten, and they'd talked it over and made their decision together. Several other boys from our southern Illinois area would also be getting on that train. But it was especially important to Robert to have Willy beside him.

I stirred the batter for the lemon cake I was making, but my mind was still on that terrible news report we'd heard more than a month ago. Sarah and Katie had both sunk in their chairs and cried silent tears. I might have, if I hadn't been so numb. I remember running to the wood shop to get Samuel and then being unable to tell him why I wanted him to come to the house. He and Franky Hammond had run inside, wondering what could have happened to get me so upset. And Samuel went white as a sheet when he heard. Frank started praying right away. But it was Robert out of all of us to be bare-fisted angry.

I guess I knew then how much the war would touch us. Seeing our son pacing, slapping the back of a chair, fiery-eyed, I knew he'd go. And he wouldn't be the only one. Two of the older Hammond boys were already in the service. Willy and Frank would be next, I figured. And I was right about their feelings. They went with Robert not long after that to talk to the marine recruiter when he came to town.

The recruiter had been happy to sign up Robert and Willy. But eighteen-year-old Franky would be staying home. At first he'd only confided in me what happened. But then his brothers started asking him questions, and it all came out. His limp, of course. But the recruiter had asked him to fill out a form anyway, and it didn't take the man long to realize that Franky couldn't read it.

"So?" Robert had asked them then. "He can shoot a rifle and repair an engine. Ain't that what you're looking for?"

But Frank had the limp and the reading problem, and they'd also determined him to be underweight. Any one of those things could keep him from service. So he was turned away. What might have been relief to many was galling frustration to Frank. It seemed to me he'd been extra quiet ever since.

But not everybody was quiet today. Most the Hammond clan had been over for lunch. All but Lizbeth's family and, of course, Joe and Kirk, who were already far away with the army. The place was still bustling as I tried to get us ready to go into Dearing tonight. The cake I was making was for a party put on by the Porters to see off the young men who'd be leaving on tomorrow's train. It had started out as a birthday party for their son, Thomas, because he'd be to Fort Dix by his actual birthday next week. They wanted to do something special for him. But the Porters, who did so much for our community anyway, had decided to include all our brave young men in the party. And everybody appreciated them for it.

We'd be leaving early because of the chance of snow. Pastor and Juanita Jones had invited us to their home for a bite to eat before the party, and to stay the night afterward if the snow looked taxing, just to be sure we wouldn't have trouble on our country roads.

I knew it was selfish of me, but I almost wished the gray sky outside would hurry up and spit the snow it threatened, in quantities enough to slow the train and let me keep my little boy home a while longer. But he wasn't little. He was far taller than me, taller even than his father, and he was anxious to get started on the grand adventure of duty.

*Oh, Lord, how I wanted the war to stay far away, oceans away, where it couldn't touch us! But now it wrenches at my heart!*

George Hammond, our nearest neighbor, stepped into the kitchen behind me and plunked himself into a straight-backed chair without a word. I wished he'd talk a little more about this. It might set my mind at ease about the state of his thinking. But he just sat, staring straight ahead and doing his best to ignore the sounds of his family in the house.

George had lost his wife ten years ago, and since then Samuel and I had done all we could to help the family. His children had become almost like our own, they were at our house so often.

Sarah came in, brushing the little bit of snow off her overshoes, and hung her coat in the closet by the back door. "Whiskers doesn't seem to want to eat, Mom," she told me. "I'm worried about him."

I sighed, hardly wanting to think right now about the family dog, who seemed to be showing his age more and more lately. "Honey, he'll be all right. Sometimes dogs are like that. Is he curled up in the hay?"

"Dad let him in the shop with him and Frank," she told me. "It's warmer in there. I think Dad's worried too."

I started pouring the cake batter into a buttered pan, not sure what to tell her about the dog she loved so much. Sarah was sixteen but still seemed younger to me

10

sometimes, especially when she talked about Whiskers.
I hoped he wasn't really sick. For Samuel to let him into
the shop when he and Franky were working was unusual,
because Whiskers was a big dog and not all that prone
to sitting still. At least not until now.

"Are they about done with the shelves?" I asked her.

"Almost," Sarah answered. "Dad said they'll be in
pretty quick. They're gonna load the shelves in the truck
first. They're the nicest ones yet, Mom. Thomas Porter
is gonna love his initials carved on the top. It's a funny
birthday present for his mom to get him, though, especially with him going away."

"Well, I guess the young man loves books. And his
mother wanted to get him something special."

She nodded. "That would be special. When I have my
own family, I want Dad and Frank's furniture all over my
house. You need some help with anything?"

Before I could answer her, George's oldest son, Sam,
came into the kitchen. "Pa, we're gonna have to be goin',
but we'll see you tomorrow, all right?"

"Yep," George answered from his chair by the kitchen
table.

"Don't you be worryin', okay, Pa?" Sam continued.
"William's a strong man now. He'll make it all right."

Sam and Thelma's son, Georgie, came running into
the kitchen with a whoop and a jump. At five and a half
now, he was hardly ever quiet, and I was glad the cake
wasn't any further along when he started jumping some
more.

His three-year-old sister, Rosemary, followed him,
singing her own version of Jingle Bells. "Dingo Beh.
Dingo Beh . . ."

"You kids ain't never heard a' quiet, have you?" George
grouched at his grandchildren, but they didn't seem to
notice.

Thelma came in the room, trying to juggle baby Doro-

11

thy and two or three coats. Two-year-old Albert followed
her with his thumb in his mouth, dragging his little coat
behind him.

"Katie's bringing the rest of our wraps," Thelma told
her husband. "Thought we best get the kids started into
their coats."

Bundling up little ones for the weather could always
be a bit of a challenge, especially with Dorothy starting
to fuss, and Georgie and Rosemary trying to scoot in
circles around the table. So I went ahead and put my
cake in the oven and tried to help as Katie brought hats
and mittens and scarves, along with Sam and Thelma's
coats. Everybody's boots and overshoes were lined up
to the right of our back door, and Sam collected those
that belonged to his family and got started getting little
feet into them.

Albert was the only quiet one. He stood patiently still
as I fastened his coat, and he lifted one foot at a time
obligingly when his father brought his little four-buckle
galoshes. He looked up at me with his big brown eyes
full of understanding and gave me a good-bye wave. But
he didn't say a word because he didn't talk yet. Albert
hardly ever made a sound.

As soon as they were gone, George Hammond shook
his head. "I know they's family, but them young'uns wear
me out."

I thought it a strange comment from a grandfather
who had ten children of his own, but I didn't answer him.
Willy had come in the kitchen along with ten-year-old
Emma Grace to tell their older brother's family good-bye.
Harry and Bert, who'd been playing checkers again, had
followed them, but only Emma Grace, the youngest of
the bunch, stayed in the room very long.

"Can I help you with anything?" she asked me when
Sam and Thelma were gone. Emmie loved to work in

the kitchen and was becoming a pretty good cook, even at her young age.

"Do you want to mix the frosting or help me with the casserole?" I asked her.

"The casserole," she answered immediately. "I think I already know how to do some frostings."

"I'll do the frosting," Sarah offered. So I got her my recipe and left her to it. But I told Emmie step-by-step directions aloud. That's what she liked me to do every time she helped in my kitchen. She struggled at reading a recipe book but would remember what I told her amazingly well. I had no idea how many recipes she'd memorized already. She did a lot of cooking at home now, as I understood it. Her father and brothers weren't much interested in trying their hand in the kitchen. And with Lizbeth having a family of her own, the only other girl home was Rorey, who made herself scarce when she could.

Like now. Where might Rorey have gotten herself to? So far as I could tell, she hadn't even told Sam and Thelma good-bye. But that wasn't so unlike Rorey. She was preoccupied with her own thinking much of the time.

I wished George Hammond would take a little more of a hand with Rorey. She was pretty well grown, seventeen a month ago, but the way I saw it, she still needed guidance. She'd taken a liking all over again to a boy who had caused plenty of problems before, and even though he was leaving along with Robert and Willy on tomorrow's train, it still concerned me.

But George didn't care who his daughter chose to be with. He'd even said that she could marry as young as she wanted to, it was all right with him. He was so distant from his kids and even his grandkids anymore. I wished he would go in the other room a while with Willy, but he just sat at the kitchen table in silence as we worked.

13

Maybe he was worrying, and that's what had him so quiet. I could certainly understand that very well. But I still hoped he'd manage to talk with Willy a little before tomorrow's train.

Samuel came in with Franky, and I offered them coffee. Frank was young but a good partner to my husband in their woodworking business. And good help with the farms too. Our families still did most of our farm work together, just as we'd been doing ever since Mrs. Hammond died. It seemed to be easier for George that way.

Samuel leaned over and kissed my cheek. "Starting to snow," he said. "How soon can we leave?"

"We have to wait till the cake's done," I answered, sneaking a peek between the kitchen window curtains to see if I could tell how fast it was coming down.

"Probably a good thing Pastor and Juanita said we could stay over tonight," he continued.

"I don't like it," George answered him. "Don't like leavin' the stock on a cold night."

"I told you," Samuel replied patiently, "Mr. Mueller will be coming to check on them. And he'll milk in the morning too, if he doesn't see us back by then."

"Gettin' snowed in's better'n bein' snowed out," George protested. "If it turns off bad, we might not get back by nightfall tomorrow. We'll miss the evenin' milkin', an' there won't be nobody to feed none a' the critters."

Samuel wasn't at all disturbed by that idea. "Charlie Hunter said he could bring me through in his sleigh if worst comes to worst, but I don't expect it."

"I better stay here just the same," George said, holding his ground. "Just to be on the safe side. We don't wanna lose no stock, Samuel. They're too important to us."

Samuel nodded. "I know they're important. But your boy's more important than the stock, and you promised him you'd come to town with us. I don't think we'll get a bad storm. The weather doesn't have that kind of feel about it."

"You never know," George said with a shake of his head.

"If you think somebody oughta stay, Pa, better that it be me," Frank offered. "I can take care a' things."

"If you're down t' earth long enough," George scoffed.

I turned and looked when he said that. There was just no call for it. Franky could be quite a thinker sometimes, but he wasn't terribly absentminded and certainly not slothful. I was sure Franky understood how unfair his father's judgment of him was. But as usual, he didn't answer back.

"No need either of you staying here," Samuel told them. "I don't think there'll be that much snow. We'll be able to get back just fine."

Samuel leaned to kiss me again like he'd forgotten he'd done it the first time. Then he and Frank each gulped a cup of coffee and went to put out plenty of feed and start the milking, even though it was a little early. Robert pulled on his coat and stepped outside to join them.

It wasn't long before Rorey came downstairs. She was a bit bigger than Sarah and Katie but not so much that she couldn't fit some of their clothes. And she'd been looking in their closet and picked out a sweater she asked if she could borrow. It matched her best dress better than any sweater she had, and she wanted to look as good as she could for the party. Sarah agreed graciously enough, but I noticed she had a funny look on her face. She was never very happy with Rorey's efforts to impress the boys. Especially that Turrey boy.

I hastened everyone at getting their things together that they wanted to wear for the party. George said he wasn't changing clothes, that he didn't care how he looked and nobody else should either—just being there was good enough. He protested going into town two or three more times before the cake got done. But I knew he wasn't that worried about the animals. Surely it was the thought of the train that bothered him, like it bothered me. I began to consider that maybe the only difference between him and me was that I wasn't voicing any of my feelings about it.

But then, my feelings were different than his. Wild horses couldn't keep me away from the depot tomorrow. Yet I knew it would be difficult not to cry in front of my son. Samuel and I had talked about it several times, and he had as many concerns as I did. Yet Samuel managed to show only his pride in Robert's decision to serve our country. I prayed that I would stand as strong for my son tomorrow and then continue to stand strong for the rest of my family. Even more than that, I prayed for Robert's safety. And Willy's. And every other boy we knew. And the boys we didn't know.

As I double-checked Robert's and Willy's bags, Katie and Sarah were busy washing up all the dishes we'd used. I decided to empty the cookie jar into a paper bag and send the cookies along with the boys tomorrow. I suddenly wished we'd made twice as many.

Pretty soon the cake and the casserole were ready to come out of the oven. Samuel was ready to go, so we decided to wrap the warm cake in a towel, let it cool on the way, and add the icing once we got to the Jones's house. We would have plenty of time, as early as we were leaving. Samuel wanted to make sure we got into Dearing while we still had light and before the snow could accumulate. Apparently he was more confident about getting home than he was about getting to town.

The Hammonds didn't have an automobile or a sleigh, so they rode with us rather than get their wagon and pair of horses out in the weather. It was quite a squeeze, fitting George and six of his children in the truck with the five of us and Thomas Porter's bookshelves.

I brought quilts to help keep everybody warm on the way since most of us would be riding bundled together in the open back end. It wasn't snowing hard. The fields were kind of pretty with their sprinkling of white.

Samuel wanted me to sit up front with him, but I insisted that Willy and his father have the privilege, hoping that being squeezed together like that would prompt George to say something to Willy. Robert had told me that in the whole time since they'd decided to enlist, Willy's father had never once said a word directly to Willy about it.

I don't know if they talked. I only know that the bunch in back wasn't quiet at all, except for Franky. Maybe it was easier to stay warm with the chatter and even some singing going on.

"This party's gonna be special," Rorey announced. "I brought flaxseed for hair gel, Sarah. I wanna fix my hair to look the best. Mrs. Pastor won't have no trouble with me boilin' it up at her house, will she? I was fixin' to start already, but it's better I didn't so's I can finish all at one time with the gel still fresh."

Sarah barely acknowledged Rorey's words. I'd once thought the two girls would be friends for life, they'd taken to each other so well when they were little. But in recent years, they'd seemed to grow apart. After the Hammonds' barn fire, they'd never been as close as they'd been before, and that was understandable, I supposed. But they kept getting more and more different. Once, Sarah and Rorey had spent all their time together, even after Katie came to us. But now it was more usually Sarah and Katie together, while Rorey was busy with something or other of her own.

I prayed for all the kids, the Hammonds and ours. Life had changed so much as they'd gotten older. Even Emmie was not such a little girl anymore. And with the world the way it was, I was a little afraid of the things they'd have to face.

Franky was staring out over the dormant fields. I'm not sure how his thoughts were turning right then, but he spoke sudden words that gave me comfort.

"The earth is the Lord's, and the fullness thereof; the world, and they that dwell therein."

I knew he was quoting from the Bible, but no one asked him the reason for his chosen verse, and he didn't explain himself.

I thought of the many miles between our farm and the war that was being fought. Miles of earth and ocean, all held in the hand of God. And then I was glad I'd wanted Franky's father to ride up front. I was glad he wasn't back here in the wind to see his son's eyes stretch across the distance as though he saw something the rest of us did not. I was glad he hadn't heard Franky's words. He would only have criticized them.

# 2

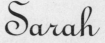

Pastor and Mrs. Jones met us at their front door. The casserole Mom had made to contribute to dinner went right in the oven to warm up again, and the pastor ushered most of us to chairs in the sitting room to get warmed up too. It hadn't snowed enough to make the roads difficult, and it was already stopping, but the wind was cold. I was glad to be inside a while.

Rorey asked Mrs. Jones right away if she could use a pan and a little water to boil her flaxseed to make the gel for her hair. Mrs. Jones was very obliging. She even said we could use some of her perfume for the party if we wanted to. Rorey said it would be the biggest party Dearing had seen in years. I didn't know about that. But I could tell there were a lot of different feelings in the house tonight. Willy was excited, but his father was grumpier than I'd seen him in a while. Robert seemed as deep in thought as Frank gets sometimes. And Emma Grace stuck as close as she could to either me or to Katie, like it was comfort to her somehow.

It was a little strange to sit down for dinner at the

pastor's house. They folded their little table out, added two extra leaves, and squeezed all of us around it. Robert was suddenly talking more than he ever had before with the pastor in the same room, and he ate like he figured he might be missing that good food before long. Willy ate heartily too, like he always did.

My mother was doting on people, fetching things though it wasn't even her house. I remembered her telling me one time that keeping her hands busy kept her brain from getting overworked. So I figured she was fretting about Robert going away, and I sure couldn't blame her for that. It was bothering me a little too.

But Dad didn't have time to fret because Mr. Hammond kept asking him about the sow with the scrape on her side, or ice on the cattle troughs, or some such stuff. Pastor was talking about the war a little bit, but I don't think Mr. Hammond wanted to hear it. He'd always had a hard time dealing with things, ever since I could remember. So much that my mom and dad had to take a large part helping to raise his kids after Mrs. Hammond died. Now the whole bunch of them felt like family. And it just seemed natural for Worthams and Hammonds to do things together. Even go to war, I guess.

But Robert was the only Wortham boy, and Willy would be the third Hammond to go. Kirk left last September. Joe had been in the service a lot longer than that. He was an officer, and people said George Hammond ought to be proud.

Mrs. Jones had made us ham and beans with cornbread. That was just about everybody's favorite. But I noticed Frank wasn't eating much. I watched him a little, wishing he'd say something, but he was even quieter than usual and spent more time staring down at his plate than eating anything.

I wondered if it bothered him that he'd be the oldest Hammond boy home now, though maybe it wasn't right to say he was home, since he spent more time in the wood shop than he ever spent at the Hammond farm. He even slept out in the wood shop a lot, on a little cot he'd made and set up in a side room. Except for helping with the farm work, Frank hadn't been home regular since he was fifteen, though it was so close. And strangely enough, his pa liked it that way.

So maybe Harry was the oldest boy home at fifteen. Bert was thirteen, and I knew they'd be doing a lot of the farm work in Willy's stead come spring. But I was sure Frank would be home more too. And doing more than his share.

Probably Lizbeth would be there a lot, just to check on things the way she often did already. She was next oldest after Sam and married to Ben Porter, Thomas Porter's cousin. I thought sure Ben and Lizbeth and their little one, Mary Jane, would be at the party tonight. I hoped so, because it was nice to have Lizbeth around. Maybe she could cheer up Frank. And calm Rorey down a little. That girl was getting too excited for her own good.

More than anybody else, Rorey was hurrying through her dinner so she'd have plenty of time to make herself pretty for the party. It bothered me that she wasn't thinking about her brother near so much as she was thinking about Lester Turrey. Somehow she'd taken the notion that he was head over heels for her and likely to propose before tomorrow's train to keep her waiting for him while he was gone.

I hoped it wasn't true. I didn't like Lester Turrey. Not one bit. I never had, and I was pretty well determined that I never would.

My brother had a girlfriend, Rachel Gray, and she'd be at the party. They'd already promised to wait for each other, but he'd told me he wasn't going to propose, not till the day he got back. I hoped Lester didn't propose either. Not ever.

"Sarah, you're gonna help me fix my hair, ain't you?" Rorey called across the table, setting her fork down with a little clunk.

"I thought I ought to help Mrs. Jones clean up."

"But I already boiled the flaxseed," she went on. "We can't wait very long. It's plenty cool by now to use, and it hadn't ought to set too long."

"You can go ahead," Mom told me. "I'll help Juanita. You go too, Katie."

From the corner of the table next to Emmie Grace, Katie looked over at me. I wondered if she was thinking like I was. We didn't have boyfriends to fix ourselves up for, but even if we did have, they'd be less important tonight than Robert or Willy. I was glad for Katie because she was sensible. She was just a little younger than me, a relative on my dad's side. My folks took her in when she was six, and she'd been with us ever since. I liked that because Katie was as good as any sister could be. And she had as much trouble understanding Rorey as I did.

Tonight Rorey was in a tizzy. She took off for the kitchen without taking her plate, so when I got up I reached to take hers along with mine. She was getting the pan of flaxseed and the cheesecloth she'd left by the stove, along with a few matches Mrs. Jones had said she could use. She went straight for the dressing table in the bedroom, and I followed her reluctantly. Katie and I would at least put on our Sunday clothes and make sure our hair was nice. But I didn't feel like making any fuss over appearance, despite Rorey's intentions.

She started in right away squeezing the flaxseed through her cloth and talking about Lester. "Won't it be grand, Sarah, if he gets down on his knees?" she exclaimed. "He can't afford no ring yet, I know, but we can always get one of those sometime later."

I made a face. "If he's planning that at all, maybe

he's thinking like Robert, that he'd rather do it when he comes home."

"No. We've been friends so long, I think he'll want to make sure a' things tonight. Then we can have the weddin' soon as he gets home. And till then, I'll write him every day."

I shook my head. "I wish you'd quit talking like this."

"Why?" Rorey asked me all innocent. "You know we've been likin' each other a real long time."

"Off and on, sure. But that doesn't mean it's particularly good for you. Or that he's thinking like you are about this."

Rorey strained the last bit she could of the flax gel and rubbed some at the hair framing her forehead. "You're just jealous, that's all. 'Cause you don't have a beau. You wanna start settin' the waves in back for me?"

"I don't know why you bother," I huffed at her. "Your hair's wavy enough already."

"No, it's not. And anyway, I want the best finger waves in town tonight."

Katie came in just then, and I saw Rorey's eyes turn toward Katie's beautiful curls. But Rorey didn't say anything about Katie's hair. She never did. She never really talked to her much at all.

"You know, Sarah, Lester's brother Eugene's kinda taken with you," Rorey told me. "You oughta dance with him tonight."

"I wouldn't dance with Eugene Turrey if you paid me," I snapped without thinking.

"Why not? Just 'cause he's Lester's brother? Honestly, I woulda thought you'd forgive and forget the past a lot easier than that. Even if somebody done somethin' that don't suit you, that's no reason to hate their whole family."

My problem with Lester was more than some little

thing that didn't "suit" me, and she well knew it. His foolishness once, along with hers, had caused a fire that almost got my father killed, and Lester'd been even slower than Rorey to own up for it and say he was sorry. But besides that, he was mean, hateful to Rorey's brother Frank, and rough as an old cob. I didn't mind *all* the Turreys. Not the girls, anyway. But the problem with Eugene and with Lester's other brothers was that they were too much like Lester.

"I don't hate anybody," I told Rorey. "I just don't like their trouble."

"Yeah. You sound like Franky—too good to say you hate 'em, but that sure don't mean you'll treat 'em very nice. All Eugene wants is one dance."

"I don't have to dance to be nice. And Frank doesn't have to let himself be walked on, neither. He's not been mean to them one time, Rorey, and you know it."

"Whatever you say." She kept at spreading the flax gel in her hair and setting the waves as best she could. I wondered if she knew how mad she made me. I wondered if she did it on purpose. "You want some curl?" she asked me suddenly. "I boiled enough flax for you if you want."

I looked in Mrs. Jones's dresser-top mirror at my long straight hair, just like my mother's, fine and brown. I supposed it needed cutting. I supposed I ought to accept Rorey's offer to help me curl it some for the party. But I didn't feel like obliging her in anything right then. "I like my hair the way it is," I told her, glancing for a moment at Katie across the room. "Katie said she'd help me put it up in back."

"Oh, Sarah, that's so old on you. Don't you wanna look nice for the boys?"

"I don't care if I do or not. I just want Robert and William to have a good time."

"Well, it's okay if you have a good time too."

"I think everybody will," Katie broke in. "Except it'll be kind of strange thinking about saying good-bye tomorrow." She had laid out her dress on the bed and kicked off her shoes to run the polish rag over them again. I knew Rorey wouldn't ask if *she* wanted to use the flaxseed gel. Katie had Shirley Temple curls. All natural.

I polished at my shoes a little bit too, even though they didn't really need it because Dad had shined everybody's earlier. I made sure my wool stockings were pulled up in place. Then I changed my dress lickety-split and straightened the pin on the collar. For warmth, I added the pink pearl-buttoned sweater that Mom let me wear since Rorey had borrowed mine. I guessed that would be about all I'd do, except for putting my hair up like I'd said. Katie was already combing hers, though it didn't look like it needed it.

"You mind lightin' the matches for me, Sarah?" Rorey asked. "I need to fetch a little more water."

She went out of the room with a towel in her hands, and Katie walked over to the dressing table. "I'll strike the matches. I was thinking I might use a little of Mrs. Jones's perfume, since she said it's okay. But I don't think I want to do much of anything else. What do you think, Sarah? Do I need to fix up some more?"

"Oh, Katie. You never need anything. You're cute as a lamb."

"You're the one that's extra pretty, Sarah. The boys watch you an awful lot. I don't think Rorey'd think half as much about her appearance if it weren't for that."

I scoffed. "Rorey thinks I'm plain. Just ask her. She's always telling me I need to do something or other."

"She's just jealous. And she doesn't want you to know."

I shook my head but didn't say anything else. Katie struck three matches on the bottom of Mrs. Jones's pottery jewel box, let them burn just a little, and then blew

25

them out and set them down one by one on the plate Rorey'd left.

"How do you think my eyes would look lined like Rorey's going to do?"

"I don't know. Your eyes are dark already. With pretty lashes. You don't need nothing."

Rorey came hurrying back with her bowl of water, primping at her hair. "What do you think? Will the curls stay?"

"They can't go anywhere stuck together like that," I teased her. "Sure hope you got all the seeds out so they don't start dropping off on the dance floor."

She ignored me. Carefully she used the burnt match ends to line around her eyes so they'd stand out better in the evening light. And then she took a crumpled piece of red crepe paper from her pocket and dunked it in the water.

"What's that for?"

"Sarah, don't you know anything? Esther Mueller showed me. It's for just a little color."

I thought "a little color" was a little understatement. The wet crepe paper rubbed against Rorey's cheek left a whole lot more color than she would've needed. But she was satisfied once she'd smoothed the smear around the edges some.

While she was doing that, Katie helped me put my hair up in a twist, and she put on her sweater. Pretty soon we were all ready to go.

"Don't you look lovely?" Mrs. Jones said when we came out in the sitting room. But I knew she was just being polite. We didn't look much different than we did on Sundays, except for Rorey's dolling up. She'd put a ribbon in her hair on the right above her ear. It matched her dress perfectly. I guess she did look pretty nice.

Everybody else had gotten ready too, and some of the boys were already bundled up waiting for us. Mrs. Pastor had to quick pull off her apron, and then she grabbed a hat and started helping everybody get their coats.

"Your scarf's gonna muss your hair," Harry told Rorey.

"I'm wearin' it around my neck, not on my head tonight," she replied.

"Won't your ears get awful cold?" Emmie Grace asked her.

My mother expressed the same concern, but Rorey was headstrong. She bundled up like the rest of us except that she left her head bare. Her father just looked at her sideways a little. "If you get sick a' the cold, girl, it ain't nobody's fault but your own."

Those words didn't bother Rorey the slightest bit, and pretty soon we were all walking down the street toward the community building. Dad and Pastor Jones were carrying the cakes that Mom and Mrs. Jones had made for the party. Dad would go back later for the truck and Thomas's bookshelves. We didn't want to bring them now because it was supposed to be a surprise.

"You s'pose the cows'll be all right tonight?" Mr. Hammond suddenly asked again as we were walking.

"Yes, George," Dad told him patiently. "There won't be any problems. Mr. Mueller'll be by to check on them before long."

"I hope he remembers to get 'em fresh water if it's froze up. Surely is by now."

"He'll remember. They'd be all right till morning anyhow. They've been through plenty of cold nights before this."

"Not without us close. I don't like bein' away so long."

Dad sighed, but he didn't bother to say anything more.

Mr. Hammond didn't say anything else the whole way either. I thought the way he looked might bother Lizbeth

27

when she saw him tonight. He was walking stiff like he had been the last few days, though he wouldn't say there was anything wrong even when my mother asked him. He didn't try to clean himself up very well lately, either. It seemed to me that he wasn't thinking like he should or he wouldn't keep asking about the cows. He'd known for days how we were going to do things tonight. I figured Lizbeth would worry. But Rorey didn't even seem to notice.

"We're not running late, are we?"

"What's the matter?" Willy teased her. "You 'fraid Lester'll leave 'fore you get there?"

"I just wanna be there for the first dance."

Harry rolled his eyes really funny at her, and I tried not to laugh at him.

"Are you gonna dance with anybody, Harry?" Emma Grace asked innocently.

"Are you kiddin'?" he answered, making quite a face. "There ain't a girl in this county to look twice at."

"You just don't know how to look," Robert said solemnly, and Willy nodded.

"You're all young enough, you don't need to concern yourself with that kind of thing tonight," Mom told them. "We'll just have a good time with friends and then get some sleep. Tomorrow's a big day."

I looked at her when she said it. I wondered if she was a little sad, but nobody could tell it in her voice or on her face. I knew she'd miss Robert. How could she not? But she acted like everything was just fine. I thought my mother must be one of the strongest people in the world not to be showing her feelings about this.

The wind was getting colder. It seemed to pierce right through my coat, and I knew there was a threat of more snow. But that didn't stop folks from coming out. A lot of people were already gathered at the community hall. We saw Charlie and Millie Hunter and a couple of other

28

friends from church on their way in. And then I saw three of the Turrey boys by the front door. I don't know why, but I looked for Frank's reaction instead of Rorey's, but he didn't even seem to notice.

Emma Grace eased closer beside me again. "Am I too young to dance tonight?" she asked in a whisper.

"Not for fun. Especially with your pa or your brothers. But you're for sure too young to think much on other boys."

"What about you? Is there a boy you think about?"

"Tonight I just want to think about the ones that are leaving. They might be gone a long time."

"Robert's a good big brother," Emmie affirmed with a nod. She hesitated for just a moment. "I guess Willy is too."

I thought for a minute about the way she'd said that. Willy could sure give people a hard time when he felt like it, especially his younger brothers and sisters. So Emmie was speaking generously. And I thought I'd share something to make her feel better about him. "I've heard that with some brothers, the more they love you, the more they tease."

"Then he must love us a whole lot," she replied in a quiet voice.

"Yeah," I acknowledged, not sure what else to say.

While we were talking, Rorey started waving like crazy, hurrying toward Lester.

"People love more than they let on sometimes," I told Emmie. "We just need to make sure we let 'em know how we feel before they go."

"I will, Sarah," Emmie said, looking at me kind of straight. "Are you worried?"

"I don't know. I guess not. I guess God's with us all the time, so there's nothing to be worried about."

Eugene Turrey was waving at me, but I ignored him. Lester and Rorey went inside holding hands right in front of everybody. I wondered if Robert would be bold enough to do that with Rachel Gray.

The inside of the community hall was all decorated with streamers. A big table was set up at one end where Mom and Mrs. Jones took the cakes we'd brought. The Porters were using the same giant punch bowl that Lizbeth had borrowed for her wedding. That bowl was such a pretty thing, and there were pitchers and pails of punch under the table—enough to keep it full many times over.

Everybody took their coats and hats and things off and set them in the area marked for them with a cardboard sign. Then I just went and sat in a chair, watching people hugging here and there. I thought of the friends and brothers going away, and I didn't feel like talking to anybody.

The music started, and it was slow and pretty. Elmer McKay and his friends from Mcleansboro were playing. Rorey told me once that they knew hundreds of songs. They could play just about anything anybody could think of.

"Wanna dance, pumpkin?" I looked up and saw my father's smile. He was looking playful and serious all at the same time.

"Okay, I guess," I told him. I didn't really feel like it right then, but I couldn't tell him no.

"Everything'll be all right, Sarah," he said. "Robert and William are strong and smart."

"Doesn't it bother you?" I dared ask him. "Even a little? They'll be so far away."

"Sure it does. Quite a bit if I get to thinking about it. But they're doing their duty. I'd be doing the same thing if I were younger. We can pray. Every day. And write too. That'll help."

We went kind of slow across the dance floor. I just held my daddy, glad he wasn't younger and it wasn't him

30

going. It'd been bad enough, the times we'd almost lost him—once when he broke through the pond ice, and then in that awful fire. I couldn't picture loving anybody more than I loved my father. Maybe right then was the first time I realized that if I ever got to thinking on a boy, that boy would have to be an awful lot like him.

Not too many other folks were dancing yet. Lester and Rorey were, of course. They seemed to want everybody to know how much they thought of each other. I guess it shouldn't have aggravated me so, but it did.

But then I saw my brother Robert dancing with Emma Grace. That made me smile. Robert was like Dad. A real good man. He'd been a tease when we were younger. But not in a bad way. My eyes filled with tears just thinking about the things we'd heard on the radio, and Robert maybe going across the ocean to face hateful men who didn't care how many people they hurt. It made my gut ache. And even though I usually liked dancing with Daddy, I was glad when the song ended.

Someone said the snow had started again. And I hoped it snowed so hard the train couldn't come.

# 3

## Frank

The place was fillin' up with people. I sat over in the corner with Pastor Jones. That was the best place for me, where I could watch most everything goin' on. 'Course, Rorey was still with Lester. I didn't figure they'd turn loose a' one another the whole night. Willy danced with a Mueller girl, and Robert switched and danced with his mama while Mr. Wortham give Kate a turn. Sarah Jean left the dance floor with Emma Grace and went and got some punch.

"Anybody you have in mind to dance with?" the pastor asked me all of a sudden.

"No, sir."

"Want some punch then?"

"No, sir."

Pastor was quiet a minute. "You know," he finally told me, "I realize there'll be some changes for your family with William away for a while. Do you suppose your father'll need some extra help?"

"He's still got me an' Harry an' Bert. An' Mr. Wortham. We'll manage all right."

"Mr. Wortham will have more to shoulder without Robert around. And I hear you've got a lot of work of your own in the wood shop. How's that been?"

"Mrs. Chafey wants a step stool. An' I'm makin' a hope chest for Pearl Daugherty. There ain't so much right now. Be good if there was more, 'cause we could use the cash. But we'll make it fine."

I looked over to the table where the pastor's wife was helpin' Mrs. Porter cut the cakes. Lizbeth and Ben come in the door about then, and I was glad to see them. Looked like they'd brought some snowflakes in on their shoulders.

"Do you still give the money you earn to your father, Frank?" Pastor was asking.

I turned my head his way, not sure why he'd inquire on somethin' like that, especially when I wasn't keen on talking right then. But he was the pastor. I figured he had a reason. "No, sir, I don't. Not direct, at least. Mostly I just buy what's needed."

"A lot of working young men would be saving for their futures, if they have any way they can manage it. To get a place to settle down and start a family of their own."

"I got no special plans 'side from the business."

"I know that, Frank, and I don't mean to imply that you should."

"You meanin' somethin' else particular then?" I asked him straight out. The pastor and me had a pretty good understandin' by now, and we could talk about most anythin'.

"It just seems that most of your money's going to your family. Or to the church. I thought I'd mention that you have a right to set aside some."

I shook my head. "Couldn't much do that an' see my brothers an' sisters do without."

The pastor frowned. "I thought your father was doing a little better with things on the farm."

33

"He ain't doin' better with his money. But I'm not meaning nothin' against him."

Truth was, Pa drank away some of the farm money. Not all of it, thank the Lord, and I wasn't anxious to talk about Pa's drinkin'. I'd told the pastor about it one time, but it only made Pa sore at me. He did better for a while after the pastor talked to him. But then later he took the drinkin' back up, just like all the other times, when he figured nobody'd know. This time he was hidin' it as good as he knew how. I didn't think anybody knew for sure he'd started up again 'cept me an' Willy. An' Willy'd told me to leave him alone about it. Just help him with things and let it go. He said there weren't nothin' else we could do. But it didn't seem right to hide things from the pastor if he was asking.

"You think it would help if I talk to him again?" Pastor said with a sigh.

"No, sir."

"Why not?"

"'Cause Pa's headstrong," I tried to explain. "He wants what he wants. Ain't no convincin' him what he don't want. It's just the way he is. He ain't gonna change." I shook my head at myself talking so much. But maybe it needed to be said, at least to Pastor Jones.

"Any man can change with the Lord's help," he told me.

"Sure. If he wants it," I agreed. "But Pa don't. He wants to lose his thinkin' in a bottle a' Buck Fraley's brew now and then. But it ain't so bad as it could be, Pastor. 'Least he's got it about him to hide it from Emma Grace an' the rest. He don't get drunk 'less he's alone, an' he ain't been hurtin' nobody but hisself."

Pastor give another long sigh. "I'm not so sure about that."

"Well, it don't seem to do no good to talk at him over it. Prayin's the only thing I know to do."

34

"Then you wouldn't mind me praying on this a bit?"

"No, sir. I wouldn't never mind that." I rose to my feet, knowing I'd given my pa cause to be sore at me again. Pa had respect for the pastor most of the time, but he didn't much like me bein' so straight-out honest with him. "I b'lieve I best go an' greet Lizbeth over there."

Pastor nodded. "Does Mr. Wortham know your father's drinking again?"

"No, sir. 'Least I don't think so. It ain't come up in our conversation."

"Maybe you should tell him, so he can keep an eye on things."

"He keeps an eye on things anyhow. He's always bein' a help. An' he's likely to find out sooner or later."

"I think it'd be better for him to know sooner, don't you?"

"I don't know. The Word says true love covers a multitude a' sins. Don't seem right to go to him against my pa. I only told you 'cause you're the pastor an' I figured you'd keep on askin' me things."

"I would think Mr. Wortham would ask about it."

"He does. Sometimes. So maybe he sees more'n I know. But I just tell him we're all right 'cause God's got his hand on us. I know it's true."

"Frank, just the same—I think I ought to talk to Mr. Wortham and maybe your father too. It's not a time for him to be separating himself with a bottle. He's got three sons in the service. Your younger brothers and sisters are bound to miss them and be very worried for them. They'll need stability from him at home all the more."

I just nodded my head. I didn't know what else I could say. Pa's ire would be stirred at me already once the pastor talked to him again. Not that that mattered so much. But I hated that Mr. Wortham might feel some kind of obligation to us in this. He'd been doing for us for so long I figured it ought to be enough by now.

I had a lot of mixed feelings right then. I walked away from the pastor, thinkin' I oughta be able to take care a' things at home and with the woodworkin' too. Even without William. Even if Pa kept himself drunk and unavailable. Me an' Harry an' Bert, Rorey an' Emma Grace could handle most anything, an' there was always Lizbeth and Ben we could fetch, or Sam and Thelma, if we needed to. And Mr. and Mrs. Wortham, though they didn't need to do anythin' else for us.

But at the same time that I was thinkin' all that, I was also wishin' I could just get away. Go far across the ocean my own self and fight like a man oughta fight to defend the country he believes in. I'd wanted to be goin' away tomorrow along with William and Robert. I didn't care what Mrs. Wortham said, that we could see it a blessing for me to be turned away 'cause I was needed so bad right here at home. When I looked at it straight I knew she was probably right, but I still hated it to be this way. I hated that they were goin' without me. I knew I should be grateful for stayin', 'cause war's a terrible thing. But I wasn't grateful, even though I wasn't sure why I wanted so bad to leave.

Crossing the community hall toward my sister an' her family, I hated the limp that everybody could see even when I was tryin' my hardest to hide it. I hated that I couldn't read the forms an' papers the recruiter'd had on his desk. I hated whatever reasons there was that made me like I am.

*"You're 4F, son."* That's what the man had said. *"You might as well go home and work hard at what you can."*

I couldn't remember questioning God like this before, not through any of the things that had happened in my life. I don't know why that soldier's words was so hard for me to take. I just wanted to bust back in there an' tell him he was wrong. That I could work hard anywhere, just as hard as anybody else. That I was just as good as my brothers or anybody that ever walked through those doors.

It scared me how I'd felt on the way home that day—like yellin' at God for makin' me the way I was. I'd never been bothered like that before. I'd never blamed God for nothin' before. And I still felt kinda angry and ashamed at the same time. Because I couldn't shake the feelings, but I well knew the Scripture. So I figured I didn't have no excuse. "O man, who art thou that repliest against God? Shall the thing formed say to him that formed it, why hast thou made me thus?"

Lizbeth was lookin' my way. I did my best to smile at her and Ben, and at little Mary Jane, who came runnin' up to grab at my legs like she always does. I picked up the teeny little girl and twirled her, trying to choke down my bitter thoughts so she wouldn't see her Uncle Franky frownin'. Mary Jane wasn't but two and a half. And when you're that age, life oughta be light.

"Everything okay, Franky?" Lizbeth asked me right away. Lizbeth was like that. She could sniff out problems faster'n a coon dog. But I didn't want to talk no more tonight. I'd done talked enough.

"Yeah," I said 'cause I had to answer. "I'm all right. It's just differ'nt for everybody, thinkin' about Willy and Robert leavin'."

"I know. I haven't thought much on anythin' else all day."

She gave me a hug. An' I hugged her back. In that, she was like Mrs. Wortham. There wasn't nobody else in our family quite so much on huggin'.

"Rorey's with that Turrey boy again," Lizbeth said with a shake of her head. "I thought she learned her lesson a long time ago on that. What's she see in him anyway?"

"I couldn't say."

"He doesn't still give you a hard time, does he?"

"I don't reckon there's time most days. Don't see much of him."

Mary Jane was tuggin' at my hand now. Her smile was big as sunshine. "Ride Unca Fwanky?" she asked. "Up? Up?"

But Lizbeth shook her head right away. "We're not out to the farm, Mary Jane. And I'm sure your Uncle Frank's had a full day. It's not the time to be gettin' shoulder rides right now."

I looked out at the dance floor. Rorey and Lester were doin' some kinda steps I didn't know the name of. Willy was with the Mueller girl again. Charlie and Millie were dancin'. And several other folks I knew. Pastor'd asked if I was gonna dance with anybody. I could almost laugh on that. Unless Emma Grace got the hankerin', I didn't expect nobody'd wanna dance with me.

"Don't know why I couldn't dance her around a little," I said. "I ain't doin' nothin' else."

I lifted Mary Jane right on up like she wanted. Lizbeth give me a look that said, *Are you sure?* But I just smiled at her. Wouldn't be nothin' wrong with makin' Mary Jane happy. I'd probably look like a fool dancin' around, but when there's a two-year-old on your shoulders, that's all right.

Robert found his girl, Rachel Gray. They were talkin' over against the wall. Oliver Mueller come in with his new wife, Elizabeth. They'd be havin' a little one before long, that was plain to tell. Richard Pratt an' his wife already had twins.

Mary Jane was hoppin' on my shoulders. Squealin' and lovin' every minute of my silly bouncin' that she could get. But I was hurting inside, and it was more than I could understand. *"A lot of young men save for their futures,"* Pastor had said. *"To start a family of their own."*

Lookin' around, I could plainly see that most of the

young fellas I knew were workin' on that very thing. Even Willy and Robert, I guessed, in their own way. I wasn't but eighteen. Nineteen in another month. But a lot of boys I'd known all my life were married already, or making plans to be. Or going to the war. Or already gone. It felt like they had something I didn't have. Like life was leavin' me behind.

*That's stupid,* I told myself. *You ain't supposed to have your whole life planned when you're eighteen. You don't need a girl yet. You don't need nothin' but to be the kinda brother you're supposed to be.*

"Dancey! Dancey!" Mary Jane squealed.

So I danced till my shoulders an' legs were tired an' Mary Jane's daddy came over to get her. Then I twirled her down and around and right into Ben's waitin' hands. She laughed and laughed.

"Fun, Unca Fwanky!"

"How 'bout some punch?" Ben asked me.

"Guess I could use some by now."

We went to the table together, Mary Jane reachin' over to pat at my shoulder most of the way. Seemed like makin' her happy had worn me out more'n usual. My leg was botherin' me some. But I wasn't gonna limp no worse. Lookin' a fool for Mary Jane was all right. But lookin' like a lame fool was not.

# 4

## Sarah

I'd never seen all the Turrey boys behave themselves
before. Usually it didn't take them long to find a way to
start trouble. Maybe somebody'd told them that they'd
better have respect for the Porters and for the occasion.
Eugene tried several times to catch my eye, but I made
sure to look away and act like I didn't notice him. I sat
down to talk to Katie, hoping he would just turn his
mind to something else. But finally he came right up
and asked me to dance.

"No, thank you." I tried to sound polite.

"How come? You was dancin' with your pa a while
ago."

"Well, he's family. That's different."

Katie gave me a tiny smile.

"What about Wilbur Rush?" Eugene persisted. "You
mean to tell me that you wouldn't dance with him if he
asked ya? He ain't kin neither."

It had never occurred to me that Wilbur would ever ask,
but my answer was just the same. "No, I wouldn't."

"What about Tom Porter then?" he said, making a face.

"All the girls wanna dance with Tom Porter." He looked at Katie, as if he were expecting her agreement.

But she just shook her head.

"If Tom asked me," I said with a sigh, "I might do it just once. But only to be nice because he's leaving tomorrow for the service."

Eugene folded his arms across his chest. "Then you'd dance with Lester, but not me."

"No. I wouldn't dance with Lester. Rorcy might get mad."

He shook his head. "You're hard to figure, Sarah Wortham. You gonna sit an' turn the boys away all night?"

"I don't see anybody lining up."

Katie smiled again, bigger this time.

"Can I at least get you some punch?"

I almost felt sorry for him, but not enough to accept. "I already had some, but thank you anyway."

He was looking at me pretty impatiently. "You're sixteen. How would it hurt for you to let a boy give you a little attention?"

"I don't know," I told him honestly. "But I don't feel a need to find out just yet."

He stared at me with a frown. "You prob'ly just think I ain't good enough," he said before turning his attention to Katie for a moment. "What about you, Kate? You think that too? You waitin' for Tom Porter or some other rich boy to run after you?"

Just then I noticed Frank clear across the open dance floor. He was sitting down watching us. Probably because he didn't trust the Turrey boys any more than I did, and he'd want to make sure Eugene wasn't bothering us.

"No," Katie was answering Eugene sweetly. "We're not interested in being run after at the moment."

But Eugene turned his eyes to where I was looking. And I sure wished he hadn't. Because his reaction was loud enough to attract attention. "You gotta be kiddin'!

Franky Hammond? Sarah Wortham's sittin' here lookin' at Franky Hammond! You're crazy, that's what you are. Franky ain't gonna dance with you. He'd prob'ly trip over his tongue if he tried to ask. Anyhow, he's half lame. And you're the purtiest girl 'round Dearing, Sarah. You don't wanna think on him. He ain't nothing! The army don't even want him. Did he tell you that?"

I knew Frank wouldn't tell Eugene any such thing, and anyway it was the marines and not the army he'd talked to, but I wondered how it had gotten talked around.

"He can't help his limp," Katie defended. "And you're being very mean. He's a friend of ours."

"Well, yeah. I guess he'd have to be, seein's your pa's took him in like a stray dog. Guess he's too much bother for his own pa to keep around. Rorey's told us plenty how odd he is."

Rorey! I could imagine her talking to Lester and things spreading from there. And I was suddenly so mad I couldn't sit still. I was on my feet before I knew it, facing Eugene straight on. He backed up.

"Rorey doesn't have the sense God gave a goose anymore!" I raged, trying not to be too awfully loud. "Maybe her pa doesn't either, if he thinks Frank's a bother. Because he's no such thing! And my father didn't just take him in. They're partners in a business that puts food on the table for both our families. Rorey oughta well be thankful. Frank's very talented, and good-hearted too. He's a blessing."

Katie stood up beside me. "I don't like mean talk. What do you think, Sarah? Maybe we should go across the room and sit and talk to Franky a while. He knows how to be nice."

I could've hugged her. That was just like Katie. She didn't think like me all the time, but we sure had an understanding on the important things. "Sure," I told her. "That'd be great. Come on."

We left Eugene standing there looking after us and went over to sit with Frank, one on each side of him. He probably didn't know why we'd come, except to get away from Eugene. None of us said very much, but I was glad we'd moved anyway. There was no reason to tolerate somebody talking so unfair.

I wondered at Rorey. Things had been a little strained between her and Frank for a long time, and it was all her fault so far as I could tell. It'd been stupid of her to blame him for his mother getting sick in childbearing, or for her getting sick when they were just little kids. And it had been cruel to go along with Lester and try to blame Frank for the barn fire. But I hadn't heard her say anything against him in so long that I'd thought maybe she'd finally let that stuff go and decided to see Frank for who he was.

Now I wasn't so sure. Maybe she didn't tell me anything about Frank anymore because she knew I wouldn't hear it. Maybe she did all her bellyaching to the Turreys now. And they probably enjoyed it. They seemed to like giving Frank a hard time.

In a little while, when Frank went to get himself a piece of cake, I saw Lester and Eugene head over to the table at the same time. I hoped to goodness they wouldn't start causing trouble. They acted like they were just there for the refreshments too, but when Frank started leaving the table, Lester leaned over and dumped his cake right on Frank's shoe. Eugene moved around behind Frank real quick, and I knew he'd have grabbed him if Frank said one word. And then they'd have been fighting, two on one. But there wasn't any trouble, because my mother and Mrs. Porter were there at the table, and they both rushed around with napkins and started cleaning up the mess. Frank was polite enough to hand Lester his own untouched piece of cake and get himself another piece. That made me smile, and nobody bothered Frank after that.

The party lasted for several hours. Dad and Robert disappeared for a while and came back with the carved bookshelves. Mrs. Porter and Thomas were both pleased.

I was getting tired after that, but people lingered like they thought we could hold off tomorrow by hanging on to tonight. There were four tables of checkers and three jigsaw puzzles over on one side of the hall. And of course, all the people talking, enjoying the music, and dancing. I peeked outside a time or two, just to see if it was still snowing, but it had stopped again.

Katie and I both danced with Robert. And with Tom Porter and a couple of other guys that were leaving. But Willy didn't ask us. Neither did Lester. I noticed that Frank didn't dance with anybody. Except little Mary Jane. But I was sure he could have if he'd wanted to ask, despite what Eugene had said.

When it came time for the last dance, Robert finally walked out to the middle of the room with Rachel Gray. They hadn't danced yet, and I'd been wondering most of the evening if he was going to have the nerve. They were something to watch. It seemed like everybody got quiet. The music was slow, and they held each other so close.

I'd never seen Robert look at anybody the way he looked at Rachel then. And she was the same way. Maybe worse. I knew he'd be writing her all the time. He'd do just what he said and propose to her the very day he got home. And she'd be jumping at the chance to accept.

Mom could see it too. For just a minute, I thought I saw tears welling in her eyes, but Daddy came and put his arms around her, and pretty soon they were dancing too.

# 5

## Julia

I knew I'd never forget that dance. And I'd never again think of Robert as a little boy. He was grown. I saw it in the way he moved, and so plainly in his face as he looked at Rachel. He was grown and beginning his own life. I was proud, but heartbroken at the same time. I'd never dreamed when I was holding him as a baby in my arms that I'd feel this way seeing him become a man. Life had passed by in a whirl, and I hoped I'd given Robert all the lessons he would need.

Samuel held me so close, and his arms were warm and comforting, but I wished I knew what he was thinking. Had he seen the same thing I had? Rachel had won our son. He wasn't ours anymore.

The dance was far too short. I didn't want it to end and have to hear the band leader tell everybody good night. I didn't want to leave yet, because it would mean today was over. And I wasn't ready for tomorrow.

I stayed in Samuel's arms even after the music stopped. Looking up into his eyes, I saw their moistness and knew he was touched the same way I was. It made me love him all the more. "What are we going to do, Samuel?"

"What do you mean?"

"Sarah and Katie will be next. They're already sixteen."

"Katie won't be sixteen for a few days yet," he said. "And I don't guess we'll ever have to worry about being left alone. When they're not bringing us grandkids, the Hammonds'll be dropping in." He grinned at me.

"Oh, Samuel."

"I think it's exactly what Emma Graham wanted. For us to fill her farm with children and grandchildren, Hammonds as well as ours."

I had to nod about that. "Children and flowers. That's what she liked, all right." I looked around at the crowd, so many of them already gathering coats to leave. And for the first time I noticed what should have been a conspicuous absence. "Honey, where's George?"

Samuel looked one way and then turned his head and surveyed the entire hall. "I didn't figure I had to keep watch on a grown man. Where could he take himself to?"

"Someone must have seen. Maybe he just stepped outside for some air."

"I heard it's ten below."

For some reason I remembered the bitter December night when Mrs. Hammond died. George had been unable to accept it. He ran off in a snowstorm, and we didn't find him till morning. The sudden thought chilled me. Grief had nearly made him crazy then, and could have cost him his life. Nothing had happened now, but three of his sons would be in harm's way, and he was already acting strangely. "Samuel, do you think he's really all right? Maybe I should have talked to him earlier. I think it's really bothering him about tomorrow."

"He wouldn't have talked to you, honey. He'll barely

talk to me. But I don't think tomorrow's the only problem. He hasn't been really all right for quite a while now."

I was just thinking we ought to check the front steps when Ruby Lawson came bustling up the basement stairs into the main part of the hall. Her husband was right behind her. "Anyone else down there?" I called to her.

"Two or three men," Ruby said with a frown. "You'd think they could get through one public gathering without doing somethin' disrespectful."

Samuel and I glanced at each other.

"Just an innocent game a' cards," Ruby's husband said weakly.

"If that was all, you'd a' had a table up here with ever'body else," Ruby declared. "Shameful, that's what it is. The Porters is decent people. They wouldn't cotton to no liquor being brought to their party."

Samuel's face turned stony, and he started for the stairs. I almost followed him, but I knew he wouldn't want me to. George couldn't handle liquor. But he turned back to it sometimes in times of weakness. I knew Samuel would find George in the basement. I could only pray he hadn't broken his promise to us again, to leave the liquor alone for the sake of his children.

Two men left the basement in a hurry and looking pretty sheepish, but Samuel didn't come back up. That was enough to tell me that things were not good with George, and Samuel was upset enough about it that those men had not wanted to stick around.

I let the kids linger a while, talking to friends. I wasn't sure what else to do. The only one who suspected anything was wrong was Franky. It wasn't long before he put things together and started downstairs on his own. Maybe I should have stopped him, but Franky was as much a man in my mind as Robert. He had a right to know if his father had a problem.

They were a very long time coming back up the stairs.

Mrs. Porter walked over from the refreshment table to tell me that Pastor and Juanita Jones had left during the last dance to walk the widow Putnam home, and they'd have their house warm and waiting for us when we got there.

"Thank you so much for the cake, Julia," she went on. "Lemon is my absolute favorite." She just stood for a minute, as if she was waiting for something important.

"It was a wonderful party," I told her. "And so good of you to include everyone."

She looked like she would burst into tears. "Oh, Julia! I've been wondering the whole night how you can be so calm! I feel like I'm about to fall apart." Her hand fumbled with a lace-lined pocket until she'd withdrawn her kerchief, but all she did was squeeze it in her hands. "You and Mr. Wortham looked so lovely on the dance floor. I wish to God you'd pray for me to have your kind of faith. I wish I could be half so peaceful."

I just stared for a moment, not sure what to say. If she only knew what was going on inside me she'd have gone asking prayer of someone else. Across the room Rachel Gray had her hand in Robert's hand and tears in her eyes. And downstairs, I didn't know what Samuel was dealing with, but it couldn't be good.

*Lord,* I prayed in my heart, *grant Mrs. Porter the peace she needs. Not my kind of faith, but yours.*

I gave her a hug. I wasn't sure there was anything else I could do or say. And right then I heard George Hammond's voice coming from the bottom of the stairwell, and I was glad most of the crowd had dwindled away.

"I don't need you an' this boy comin' an' lookin' about me, you hear!"

"You could have told him no, George," my husband's voice answered. "Just a simple, polite no."

"We was jus' toastin' our boys and the U.S. of A," George shot back. "Wha's the hurt in that?"

48

"Oh, dear," Mrs. Porter said.

"I'm sorry—" I started quickly.

"Julia. You've nothing to be sorry for. I should've thought to have Oliver check about such things. There's always somebody in every crowd looking for occasion for drinking, doesn't it seem like? I wish they'd never repealed the Prohibition. That's George Hammond, isn't it?"

"Yes. It is."

She shook her head. "I declare, Julia. You're truly a saint, half raising that man's children and putting up with his ways."

I sighed. "Samuel's the saint dealing with him right now."

"I hope he doesn't cause you nor the pastor too much trouble tonight. Can you imagine? He can't have been thinking on how William's going to feel! And with all of you staying at the pastor's house . . ."

I didn't answer her. Samuel and George were coming up the stairs. And Franky, surely.

"You know how liquor does you, George," Samuel was saying. "You've got your kids and William to think about—"

"They ain't gotta know."

"C'mon, Pa," Franky answered him. "You know better'n this! Did you think nobody'd notice?"

"You jus' keep your mouth plum outta this—" Mr. Hammond kept up his arguing as they came into view. But then he stumbled, and Samuel grabbed him and helped him the rest of the way up the stairs. Samuel was still upset, I could tell.

"God help you, George," he was saying. "There's no mistaking the smell. We're going back to the pastor's house. You could've had a little respect."

"Was toastin' our boys," Mr. Hammond repeated. "Wha's wrong with that?" He pulled away from Samuel and Franky and made his way to the coats. Lizbeth met him there, and she didn't look happy, but I couldn't hear what was said between them.

Emmie Grace, Harry, and Bert went with William to the coats. Robert was still with Rachel but looking our way, aware now of what was going on. Katie and Sarah were closer to me. "Can you get Rorey's attention?" I asked of Sarah. "It's time to go."

"God bless you, Julia," Mrs. Porter said to me quietly. "Please remember me and especially Thomas in your prayers."

"I will," I promised. "Pray for us too. And the Hammonds."

She nodded and turned away toward her husband. Sarah went straight over to Rorey but obviously had no easy time of it getting her to leave Lester's side to come with us. But finally Rorey turned loose of Lester to get her coat.

Mr. Porter graciously thanked us for coming. I thanked him again for having the party.

George was pulling on his old coat. I was glad we had the truck outside, even though it was only three blocks to the pastor's house. Driving would be easier than walking George that distance.

But he insisted on walking. Maybe because he was mad at Samuel for disturbing him, and it was our truck. Samuel was pretty disgusted at this turn of events. He told George he was walking too, then, just to keep an eye on him. One of the boys could drive the truck on over to Pastor's.

I guess that was enough to make George give up because when we went outside, he climbed into the back of the pickup and sprawled out on the flooring.

"You mind if I walk?" Robert asked his father. "I've got some thinking to do."

"I'll come with you," Willy said before Samuel could answer. I hoped Willy wasn't upset about his father.

50

It was Frank who first climbed up with their father in the back of the truck, though George protested at him about it. Then Bert climbed up too. And Emma came around to the front seat with me. Everybody else wanted to walk. And I could understand that, under the circumstances. The snow had stopped again, and the sky had gotten beautifully clear. It was cold, but they didn't have far to go. And George Hammond was a less than pleasant riding companion tonight, to be sure.

So on this night that was supposed to be about us being together, we left most of the kids walking behind us. And I had the strange feeling that this was just the beginning, and we would never be together in quite the same way again.

# 6

## Sarah

We'd only gotten about a half inch more snow. The weather was crystal clear and colder. I didn't know what to think of Mr. Hammond. I guess nobody else did either, because we were all pretty quiet walking away from the community hall. The moon was bright. We didn't have far to walk. Robert and Willy started out ahead, with Harry not far behind them.

Rorey was pouting, I could tell. She started lagging behind, and I knew she wanted to speak to me. But I was sure she'd been bad-talking her own brother to the Turreys. I was mad, so I didn't slow up for her until she called at me.

"Sarah?"

Katie turned her head just a little but didn't say anything. She was walking right behind Harry and didn't slow down. Robert and Willy were talking about something and not paying any attention.

"Sarah?" Rorey called me again.

I kicked at the snow a little. "What?"

"I want to talk to you."

I turned around and started walking backwards so I wouldn't have to stop in the cold. "What about?"

"Come here. I wanna talk."

So I slowed down, matched her pace, and ended up six or eight steps behind everybody else. I wondered if she was thinking about the way her pa had acted and him stumbling the way he did on the way to the truck. But evidently not.

"Lester said a lot a' sweet things, Sarah," she started in. "He must a' tol' me half a dozen times he loves me. But he didn't say nothin' 'bout marryin'. Maybe if I coulda just stayed a little while longer."

"Oh, Rorey. If he was minded to propose tonight he'd have found a way, even if he had to follow us down the sidewalk."

She took a quick glance behind us, and I sighed.

"Don't you think you have plenty of time yet?" I asked her. "You're not even eighteen till next December."

"But he don't have much time 'fore the train tomorrow." She kept up her pout.

"Maybe he's not ready. Maybe he's not even sure he wants to marry. And that's okay. There's no reason you have to be engaged before he leaves."

"I just wanted it so bad." She looked like she could take to blubbering any minute, and I shook my head at her.

"Robert didn't get engaged," I told her. "Or William. Or Thomas Porter. Maybe Lester just didn't feel like being different."

"But we *are* different, Sarah. You know that."

I didn't. I didn't know what she meant by that at all. But I didn't ask. "Eugene was talking awfully mean about Frank tonight."

She made a face. "That's just Eugene. You gotta take him with a grain a' salt."

"Did you tell him Frank got turned down for the service?"

"He asked me about it. Why shouldn't I answer?"

"Because it's nobody's business, that's why!"

"Why are you always stickin' up for Franky, Sarah? Huh?" she suddenly demanded. "You act like you're his mama or something."

"I'm about the same as a sister. You know that. So I don't understand why *you* don't stick up for him. Lizbeth would if she knew the way Eugene was talking. So would Emma Grace."

"Then he don't need no more. Everybody feels sorry for him anyway. Everybody babies him—"

"That's not it at all, and you know it."

"Well, then, what is it? Huh, Sarah?"

"It's just not fair how you talk about him."

"All I been is honest," she snipped at me. "It's not my fault your Uncle Edward run over his leg when he was little. And it sure ain't my fault he's so bleary-headed he can't read."

"Shush, Rorey. Everybody'll hear you."

"So what? Everybody knows Franky has problems."

"He works hard. And he's sensible. Seems to me he doesn't have near the problems you do."

She stopped. "Just what do you mean by that?"

"Nothing," I told her, knowing I could never explain without causing a big argument. I pulled my scarf tighter. "I'm cold. I wanna walk faster. And besides, I ought to be up there with my brother now. Hard to believe he's leaving tomorrow."

She didn't say another word. I hurried ahead to Robert's side, but Rorey just stayed lagging back like a dunce. Maybe she'd give William a hug or something tomorrow. I hoped so. Because she sure hadn't given him the time of day tonight.

By the time we got to Pastor Jones's house, Mr. Hammond was already in the back bedroom getting in bed.

54

And Mrs. Jones was starting to get everybody else situated too. It felt strange to be staying over. I didn't think I'd sleep very well. Katie, Rorey, Emma Grace, and I were all to share the larger guest room. It wasn't long before the whole house was quiet.

I lay awake a very long time thinking about the party and tomorrow. Rachel Gray had tried to hide her tears when her folks told her it was time to leave. I felt sorry for her a little, knowing how she'd miss Robert. I tried to picture her in a lacy white dress, and my brother standing at the front of the church in a suit ready to claim his bride. And those thoughts made me smile and feel a little sad inside all at the same time. If it wasn't for Hitler and the horrible Japanese attackers, they might be getting married a lot sooner.

*God, why do you let war happen?* I lay there and prayed. *Good men have to interrupt their lives. Some of them lose their lives. And their families and the girls who love them are left behind with nothing but the memories and their tears. It hadn't ought to be this way!*

I had to quit praying then because I was afraid I'd cry and wake up Emmie Grace, who had snuggled beside me. I lay staring up at the dark ceiling and turned my thinking to Rorey, knowing I wouldn't cry on that. I might get mad, but that was better than crying.

Rorey had no right to be such a baby about Lester. Just four months ago, she'd been interested in a fellow named Jude Jenkins who was in town visiting his cousin. And last year she, along with a couple of other girls I knew, had been sweet on Thomas Porter, and there was no way that was going to work out. But she'd started liking Lester almost four years ago, young as she was, and she'd come back around to liking him over and over since then. Lester liked the attention. He was always glad to have Rorey around, but I didn't know if he'd ever propose. I figured it'd be the best thing for her if he didn't.

I don't know how long I lay there, letting my mind drift one way or another. Finally I dropped off to sleep. But I couldn't have slept very long.

Before the sun in the morning, I heard someone stirring in the next room. Soon my parents were talking in quiet voices, and I decided I might as well get up and dress for the day. If we'd been at home, there would be chores to do to take my mind off what was coming, but here at the Jones's house I wasn't sure how I'd manage. But I remembered the Jones's chickens and decided that I might as well go and check for eggs, even if someone else had gotten there before me.

Buttoning up my sweater, I thought about Katie's birthday in another week and wondered if she'd feel any different about it with Robert not around. She rolled over just a little, and I stood real quiet so I wouldn't disturb her.

We'd have breakfast here this morning, and then it wouldn't be long before it was time to go to the train depot. For a moment, I wished for more snow again, but then I thought that was selfish of me, and I prayed that God would be with my brother wherever he went.

Walking across the room I thought about what it had been like to dance with Robert last night. A few years ago, he never would have been willing to dance with his sister. And I wouldn't have been willing either. I guess growing up was changing us. That was a little scary.

I knew I'd miss him. A lot. Like any brother, he'd been a pain sometimes. Not as bad as Willy or even Harry could be, but he'd had plenty of ornery moments, especially toward me. But he'd outgrown most of that. Now he was nice. And shy. Rachel had liked him for years now, but it wasn't till just a few months ago that he'd gotten the nerve to admit that he'd liked her too, all along.

Behind me, Katie got up real quiet and started getting dressed. I didn't know why she didn't talk to me. I

56

don't know why I didn't talk to her. Maybe we were both thinking too much to say anything out loud. I wondered what life as a grown-up was going to be like. Would the war be over in a year, like some people said? Would Robert and Rachel live close around here when they got married? And then start having a family? Would I meet somebody as nice as Dad, fall in love, and have kids of my own?

Maybe I'd live right next door to Robert and Rachel. And next to Katie too, with her family on the other side. But I couldn't picture Rorey with Lester in my imaginings. Not at all. I couldn't even picture Rorey wanting to stay anywhere nearby. Sometimes she talked about Chicago or St. Louis. Neither of us had been to either place, but Rorey wanted to go some day. She said it would be exciting.

I wondered how different Robert would be when he got back. He'd be a man, that was for sure, with stories to tell. Hopefully not all bad. Hopefully the war would be over in even less than a year and there'd be nothing more for our boys in the service to do but come home happy.

I heard a rooster crowing outside. Mom was folding their bedding in the sitting room. I just walked past without saying anything. I'm not sure where Dad had gone. In the kitchen, Mrs. Jones was stirring batter in a big bowl, and I told her I'd be happy to get her eggs if she didn't mind.

"Thank you, Sarah. But Paxton's already taken care of that."

Paxton was the pastor, but nobody else called him by his first name that I ever heard, except my dad, and then only rarely.

I guessed I could have asked Mrs. Jones if she needed help making breakfast for all of us, but I really wanted to be alone. I wished it was summer so I could volunteer to go outside and pull weeds in the garden, or maybe just sit under a tree and think.

"Are you all right this morning, Sarah?" Mrs. Jones asked me.

"Yeah. I guess."

Right then, Frank came into the kitchen from the next room, and the first thing he did was look out the window. "Mrs. Jones, I seen it snowed a little more in the night. Would you like me to shovel the walks?"

Mrs. Jones smiled over at him. "I hardly think it snowed enough to make that necessary, Franky, but if you want to, I surely wouldn't mind. Thank you."

I watched him nod and go to get his coat. Strange how he almost seemed to be thinking like me, looking for something to do to take his mind off the day. It made me wonder where my dad had gone. But it wasn't long before I heard him coming up to the back door with the pastor. They'd both been to the chicken coop. They came in together and sat down at the kitchen table for a cup of Mrs. Jones's fresh-brewed coffee.

"Maybe I'll help Frank with the sidewalks," I offered.

Pastor looked up at me with a strange expression. "You don't have to do that. Either of you."

"I know it. But we don't mind, really." I went for my coat before he could say another word about it. Mom and Katie were just coming into the kitchen, and before long there would be others up, and I just wanted to get outside away from everybody for a little while, cold or not. Maybe Frank felt the same way. If the pastor had two shovels, one of us could do one side of the house and one of us the other.

But there was only one shovel. And Frank insisted he should use it because I was a girl. "Fine," I told him, and went around to the backyard to brush the snow away from all the chicken coop windows even though I knew nobody'd be opening them. Then I pushed the snow off

58

the Jones's cellar door with my feet, even though they probably wouldn't need to open that either since they had another door inside the house. Finally I just sat down on the cleared-off cellar door and looked out over the frozen yard. At ten o'clock the train was coming. And I figured that I wouldn't feel like a kid anymore after it left. If Robert had to be grown-up, then I ought to be too.

After a while, Frank came around the side of the house. There wasn't enough snow to keep him busy very long. He looked at me and suggested I go inside and warm up. But I didn't move. I just watched him finish the shoveling and then knock the snow off the fence in the side yard though there was no need for that at all. Pretty soon, he walked over and sat beside me.

I didn't say anything. Neither did he. I didn't know why he was sitting there, except to rest a minute and maybe avoid going inside just yet. But he didn't sit for long. He went and scooped the snow from in front and behind the wheels of the pastor's car and our truck even though it wasn't deep enough for either of them to have any trouble moving. I knew he'd put the shovel away and go on in after that, so I went in first. I was plenty cold by then too.

Mrs. Pastor set me right down with a cup of hot cocoa and a plate of buttermilk pancakes. "Goodness, girl," she said. "Are you always so raring to go in the morning?"

I sipped my cocoa and looked across the room to my mom, who was scrambling eggs. "No, ma'am. Not always."

Katie sat beside me. She had a different kind of look on her face. I wondered if she felt the same way about Robert as I did. Of course, she hadn't known him as long, but she was bound to look on him as a brother anyway. I was glad my birthday wasn't till August. Maybe by then things would seem right again.

Frank came inside, and Mrs. Pastor made him sit down

59

with hot cocoa too. He hardly touched his pancakes. Maybe he wished he was going away today with the others. But I was glad he wasn't. It would be strange enough without Robert around. Frank being gone too would make things extra odd, because we were all so used to him working with my dad every day and staying with us or in the wood shop. And before that, he'd been over all the time when Mom was teaching him. He ate with us a lot. He worked in our fields like they were just as much his.

"God be merciful to us, and bless us, and cause his face to shine upon us," Frank was suddenly saying almost under his breath.

My father smiled.

"That thy way may be known upon earth," the pastor continued. "Thy saving health among all nations. Psalm 67. An excellent choice for today, Frank."

But Frank didn't even look up.

Breakfast was kind of stretched out, with the first of us eating, and then the next ones up, and finally Willy and Harry last of all. Katie and I helped Mrs. Jones clean the kitchen. Mom didn't this time. She disappeared. But Robert was out of sight too, so I figured they were together. Mom had disappeared for a little while yesterday too, before we came to town. I knew she'd been in Robert's room, helping him pack his bag and just being with him while she could. I thought of Mom hugging us in the summer sunshine or snuggling with us on the old davenport in our sitting room. "Just enjoying my babies," she'd said once, and I of course responded that we weren't babies anymore.

"You'll always be my babies," Mom had answered. Her kisses made me smile. And even though Robert had tried to wriggle out of them since he was about ten, I knew he liked her attention too. He was probably soaking up all he could right now.

60

That made me sorry for Willy, who didn't have a mother to hug him good-bye. His father sat in the pastor's chair and didn't say a word to him or anyone else. But Willy didn't act like he needed it. He was talking a mile a minute about "givin' the Japs what for" and seeing some of the world besides. It kind of made me feel raw inside. Japan was a hard enemy. They'd already proved that.

Pretty soon after everybody'd eaten, Lizbeth and Ben drove up with Mary Jane wrapped in a quilt and tucked between them on the front seat of their Ford. They came inside and unbundled, and Lizbeth and Mary Jane looked so nice again in dresses made from matching print. Lizbeth sure did sew a lot, now that she wasn't teaching school. She was always making something. And she was an awfully good cook too. She brought the pastor and his wife a pan of succotash and a big basket of hot rolls for dinner later. Those rolls smelled fantastic, right through the towel over top.

It wasn't long before Sam and Thelma came too, because we'd all agreed to meet here and go to the train together. Their entrance was always something of a big event, much different than Lizbeth's, because their kids let everybody know right away that they were getting close. We heard them outside before they even parked the car. It sounded like Georgie and Rosemary were singing at the top of their lungs again. And little Dorothy was crying like babies do.

Didn't seem possible that Georgie could be almost six already. And precocious as anything. Smart as a whip and loud as firecrackers. Rosemary was a real pretty three-year-old and nearly as loud as her brother. Lizbeth's Mary Jane kept her distance from them sometimes, when they got to be a little much.

Little Albert was the quiet one of Sam and Thelma's bunch, and you wouldn't expect it because he was barely two. But he'd sit quiet on his father's knee for a long time, just watching everything going on around him. He liked to sit quiet with Frank too. Once in the fall I saw him with Frank, just looking up at the clouds in the backyard. After a while, he gave a nod like he was satisfied with something. Frank nodded right back, and the little tike hugged at him like they'd just shared something special. I didn't know what, but Thelma said Franky probably did.

Dorothy was still a tiny thing. Only three months old, and Sam and Thelma were already talking about the names they'd use when they had another baby. It wasn't strange for Sam to think about more children, coming from a family with ten. Or Thelma either—she had eleven brothers and sisters. But it worried Mom and Lizbeth a little, I think, about them having to stretch what little they had so far.

Mom came back to the kitchen and helped Lizbeth pack sandwiches to send with the boys on the train. Mrs. Jones put a cake in the oven for dinner later. She wanted us to come back here for that, so we wouldn't have to drive all the way home and think about dinner right away. I knew she was trying to make things easier for Mom, but I wondered if anybody would care about dinner after the train left.

The kitchen started smelling really good, with the cake in the oven and the spices Mrs. Jones got out to mix with the meatloaf she was making ahead. Mom opened the bag of gingersnaps we'd baked at home and repacked them along with the sandwiches. They were Robert's favorite. I was glad we'd made them.

Dad and Mr. Hammond sat in the sitting room with the pastor. Willy and Frank and Sam went walking outside, which I was glad to see because Willy didn't pay much attention to Frank a lot of times. I figured they had things to talk over about their pa, and how things should be at home while Willy was gone.

Mr. Hammond acted a whole lot better this morning than he had last night, but I guess everybody still knew there'd be a lot on Frank's shoulders, and on Rorey and Harry too. Mr. Hammond had trouble keeping up with things on their farm. And if something was bothering him badly enough, he didn't even try.

Georgie and Rosemary tried to insist on playing with their grandpa, but he wasn't in the mood to be climbed on or hear their racket. So Dad sent them upstairs with Emma Grace and Bert to play until it was time to go. Lizbeth's husband, Ben, was pretty serious-faced, and he sat with Pastor and Dad and Mr. Hammond for a while, but everybody else left them alone.

Way too soon, it was time to get everybody's coats and go meet the train. Sam and Ben carried Robert and William's bags, though they wouldn't have had to. William seemed even more excited than he had earlier. But Robert had gotten really quiet. We all went out of the house together to walk up the street past Charlie Hunter's station to the train depot. Only Mrs. Jones and Thelma, with little Albert and the baby, stayed home. Mr. Hammond didn't want to come. But I heard Sam remind him that he'd promised, so he dragged along with us, trying to act like he was at least doing better than last night.

Rorey was extra anxious again. She had her scarf over her head this time like a sensible person, but she was walking fast, hoping for the chance to linger with Lester for a while, still hoping he'd use his last minutes before the train left to propose to her.

There were more people than I expected waiting at the depot. Of course I knew the families of the boys that were leaving would all be there, but there were other folks too, friends and relations from church and from town. Rorey got all silly, running into Lester's arms. Robert and Rachel were different, like they both wanted to savor the other one's looks before they even got close. And when they did, they kissed. I hadn't expected that.

Dad was holding Mom's hand. I knew this had to be hard for them. It was hard for me, and just as hard for Katie. I saw tears in her eyes, so I took her hand.

"We've gotta pray for them every day," she whispered.

"Okay," I told her. "We will."

There was so much hugging then. Mrs. Porter just about wouldn't let Thomas go. Mom hugged William first. And then she held Robert a really long time. Lizbeth and Emmie and all the rest took their turns hugging William. Their father hung back. I don't know why. He was just like that. And Rorey was busy with Lester.

Katie and I hugged William too. That was strange, because he was still our neighbor, and Rorey's brother, even though they were all so close they were the same as family.

Emma Grace got teary. "I'm sure glad Franky's not going too," she told me. "I'm sure glad Harry and Bert is too young."

I put my arm around her, and so did Lizbeth. Then Robert was hugging the rest of us. When he got to me, I just held on.

"It'll be all right," he told me. "You'll see." He gave me a big squeeze and told me not to let Mom listen to too much news.

Then he was hugging Dad and Mom again and it was time for all of them to get on the train. I saw him reach for Rachel's hand one more time and leave a folded-up piece of paper in it. I wished I knew what that said.

Lester's sister Rose seemed to be crying worse than anybody, and I didn't quite understand that, because I'd seen Lester being awfully mean to her more than once. I didn't figure there was much about him to miss. But I went over and gave Rose a hug. She was a nice girl. She couldn't help what some of her family was like.

64

Katie went with me and hugged Lester's mother, which was a gracious thing to do since a lot of people considered her an embarrassment to the community. Edna Turrey'd been arrested four times for stealing. The only reason she wasn't in the women's prison was because she had so many kids the judge figured the stealing was for their sakes. He'd ordered her to go to church and have her husband bring her to see an officer every week. But her husband wouldn't bring her. Not to the church either. So the officer went to them. And the pastor did too, sometimes.

"We heard Earl Wilkins got killed," Rose suddenly whispered to me.

It was hard to understand the words because of her crying. But they shook me. We knew Earl Wilkins's family a little bit. He was a cousin of some people from church, and he'd gone in the army at the same time as William's brother Kirk.

This was a bad time to hear news like that. I hated to let the train carry Robert away. But he was already up on the platform waving to us. William was right behind him. Thomas and Lester were just a little farther in, waving out a window. Rorey ran up and reached to touch Lester's hand one last time. I shook my head at her, hoping William didn't feel bad over not getting any of her attention. He didn't seem to. He had the biggest smile on his face I'd ever seen.

The whistle blew. And it was a hard thing, watching the train pull away. I went over and reached for Mom's hand, thinking maybe she'd be quiet the whole rest of the day. Maybe all of us would be. Everybody just stood there for a while, waving.

"Well," Mom finally said when the train was out of sight. She might've meant to say something more than that. About going back to the pastor's house. Or something. But not another word came out. She just stood

65

there looking at the track. And then the sky started to sprinkle snow on us, teeny flakes floating down real slow.

"We'd better go, Juli," Dad told my mom. But instead of going anywhere he gathered her in his arms and held her for a long, long time.

I didn't care. I didn't want to move anyway, even if I was getting cold. Watching the people around us, some of them leaving, some standing like they didn't know what they were supposed to do, I felt like the whole world had changed. The things we heard on the radio had been thousands of miles away not so long ago. We'd cared a lot all along. We'd prayed about the war over and over again. But now it would fill our minds and squeeze on our hearts. Now it might as well be in our own backyard.

I looked down at my overshoes, feeling the tears well up in my eyes and not wanting anyone to see. Lizbeth came and put her arm around me, and Emmie took hold of Katie's hand on the other side of me, and they stood together just as quiet as could be.

"They'll be okay," Lizbeth whispered to me. "God will go with them."

I didn't say anything. God had been with Earl Wilkins. Earl had wanted to be a preacher some day. But now he was dead. The first casualty we personally knew from a war that had just snatched Robert into its grasp.

I couldn't reconcile that kind of thing in my mind. And if there was anybody who could, I figured it'd be Frank. It was so like him to quote Scripture at challenging moments that I could almost expect him to start any minute now. But he didn't. I looked up and realized that he wasn't there to tell us anything. Where could he have gone?

I turned from Lizbeth to look around a little more. Finally I spotted him up against the depot, looking terrible thin and pale in his overcoat and far more upset than I expected. His pa was right next to him, saying something I was too far away to hear. It didn't look like Frank answered him. It didn't look like he wanted to hear whatever it was.

"Pa?" Lizbeth called. "Are you ready to go?"

"Guess we better," Mr. Hammond answered. "Ain't nothin' else to do here."

But he didn't move right away, and Lizbeth turned to my parents for a second. "I know Pa says he's fine. But I'm not blind. I know he did some drinkin' at the party last night. Has there been more of that?"

"I don't know," Dad told her. "Let's hope that's the end of it."

"Tell me if he gets any worse. I'll come out. I'll stay with them a while if I have to."

Daddy nodded. "Thank you, Lizbeth. We'll keep an eye on things."

She nodded and took Mary Jane in her arms. They were the first of us to start off, and Mr. Hammond went with them.

Frank just stood against the depot. He closed his eyes for a second, and I almost went over to him to ask what in the world could be troubling him so much, even with Willy leaving. Was it something his pa had said? I knew Frank'd been quiet last night and this morning, but he'd endured an awful lot in his life, and he usually took things pretty much in stride. It'd been a long time since I'd seen him looking this upset.

Rorey grabbed my arm. "Look, Sarah! Lester gave me a locket. Ain't it pretty?"

I looked, but I scarcely even saw the thing. "Where'd he get it?"

"How would I know? What difference does it make? He gave it to me. And he told me to write."

"You were planning on that, anyway," I said, starting to move away from her.

"Well, I know! But it's different now that he's practically begged me to! Don't you see? That's like being promised! Ain't it?"

I sighed. "At least you know he's wanting to get mail."

"Oh, Sarah! Why do you have to be such a killjoy all the time?"

I didn't answer. Mom and Dad were starting to walk away, so I went too. By then Frank had pushed himself away from the side of the depot and was up ahead with Sam and his kids, lifting little Rosemary onto his shoulders. He must have been okay because he started quoting the Bible then, just like I'd expected him to do before.

"The salvation of the righteous is of the Lord. He is their strength in the time of trouble."

Everybody was quiet for a minute. And then my mother added her quiet amen.

Another dinner at the pastor's house was even stranger than before. I wished we would just go home and get back to normal, but we wouldn't have felt normal today anyway. It was a big job for the Joneses to feed us all again, especially since they'd invited Sam's family and Lizbeth's family to join us. The house was pretty full, but we had plenty of food. Mrs. Jones's meatloaf was almost as good as Mom's, and Lizbeth's rolls were wonderful. Having so many people at the pastor's house felt kind of like a holiday. But it wasn't the same without Robert there.

Looking down at my green beans and onions, I wondered why God had chosen to make time pass. I could still remember when Katie first came to us and all the fun we'd had then. She hadn't been used to the country. Most everything was new to her, even picking green beans. So many happy things happened when we were kids. Maybe nobody else in the world wondered the kind of things I did, but I wished I could know why we're born little and then grow and everything has to change. Why couldn't God have just picked a special moment, like when we were wading in the creek, and let us stay there as long as we wanted to? And be whatever age we wanted our whole lives? But maybe that's heaven. And maybe I was just being silly.

Pastor and Mrs. Jones were being very nice to us. They got out some sheet music, and we sang along with Mrs. Jones playing piano for a little while. But then it was time to go home, and despite what I'd thought earlier, I didn't really want to. But Mr. Hammond did. I could tell that. I think he was extra bothered about another of his boys going away. He let little Georgie climb on him some and Rosemary muss up his hair. He acted all right to them. He even talked all right, but he didn't look too happy in his eyes. And I knew that Frank and Lizbeth saw it too.

We waved good-bye to Sam and Lizbeth and their families, and Mom hugged Juanita Jones. The weather had gotten clear again with just another dusting of snow over top the roads. Dad said that was a good thing or we might have been stuck in town. Mom and Mr. Hammond climbed in the front of the truck with him. Katie climbed in the back of the truck with me, and we shared a quilt to wrap up in. Rorey and Emmie wrapped up in another one. Frank and Harry and Bert acted like they didn't need one, but Mom had stuck in extra for them, and I knew if the wind got cold enough on the way home, they'd use them.

Bert was busy talking about the things he'd been reading about the Revolutionary War. It wasn't hard to let those kind of words sail on past my ears without much notice. He liked to read, and he always seemed to remember everything. That was fine, except that I didn't always want to hear about the kind of things he liked. Neither did Rorey, and she wasn't so quiet about it.

"Why don't you hush?" she asked him. "What makes you think we wanna hear 'bout Lexington?"

"Well, history's important," Bert told her with a frown. "You ain't in school today."

"Learnin' ain't only for school," Bert defended himself. "Right, Franky?"

Frank had been staring off somewhere, thinking deep, as he usually did when we were driving down the road. But he must have been listening too. "Education's the apprenticeship of life," he said suddenly.

Rorey shook her head. "Did you make that up?"

"Nope. Mrs. Wortham read it to me once from a book Mrs. Post loaned us. Robert Willmott said it."

"Mrs. Wortham ain't read nothin' for a while! Who's Robert Willmott?"

"A English author. I know it's been a while."

I smiled a little. Frank's memory was even more amazing than Bert's, because it seemed to last forever even though he'd never been able to read much of anything for himself. None of us knew why he couldn't. He was sure smart enough.

But his words seemed to bother Rorey. "I got two a' the craziest brothers!" she lamented. "A couple a' smarty pants! If you was to get a regular job, either of ya, nobody'd wanna hear it."

"I'm not gonna get a regular job," Bert announced. "I'm plannin' on bein' a doctor or a newspaper reporter."

"Says you," Rorey answered with a frown. She didn't say anything else the whole rest of the way. But Emma Grace reacted completely differently.

"I think that's swell, Bert," she said. "You could write all about the war or fix up the soldiers if they get hurt."

"Goodness," I told her. "Bert's not even fourteen,

70

Emmie. By the time he's a doctor or a reporter the war'll be long over."

"Good. Then he can help deliver babies or write about that."

"Not much writing to do about the birth a' babies," Bert protested. "I'd wanna do real news. Or investigation. You know, like about the mysteries of the past."

"What mysteries?" Emmie asked innocently.

"Oh, maybe the Roanoke colony, or the underground railroad, or the hidden gold of the James gang."

"You mean you wanna find the gold, if there is any," Harry put in.

"That'd be all right. But the best thing'd be findin' out everythin' I could an' writin' it up in a series of installments—like the way they used to do a Horatio Alger story in the local paper."

Harry shook his head. "I could never be a doctor or a reporter. Nothin' that'd take a lot a' extra education. I been thinkin' 'bout come summer maybe prunin' an' cuttin' trees for folks. Could have a firewood business on the side an' keep Franky an' Mr. Wortham in some wood too."

Katie nodded her head at that idea. "I think we'll all have to do our part. That's what the president says. To help our families and our country."

Everyone was quiet for a moment at that somber thought.

"I wanna have a café someday," Emmie told us in a while. "Till then, I can help with the cookin' at home and maybe even sell pies and such at the open market in Dearing when the weather turns nice. What do you think, Sarah?"

"Sounds nice," I told her.

"What do you want to do?"

I didn't know if she meant in the next few months

or with my life. But it didn't make much difference. "I don't know."

"The best preparation for the future is the present well seen to," Franky said soberly.

I didn't think those were Bible words, so I wanted to ask him who he was quoting this time. But I didn't. And his eyes turned again to the snow-sprinkled fields.

# 7

## Frank

Mr. and Mrs. Wortham took us Hammonds home first.
I don't think Pa expected me to stay at our place since I
was so much over t' the wood shop at the Worthams. But
I planned to stay overnight at home for a while 'cause
I figured Harry and Bert and Emmie would be missin'
Willy, and I wanted to be there for 'em, just in case. Me
an' Willy had talked about that. And Lizbeth too, 'bout
me stayin' to home more now. And it was a good thing
I did. After the Worthams left, Pa was in a foul mood
worse than usual.

He didn't say much while we checked the stock. Mr.
Mueller had set out plenty a' feed that morning, but the
water troughs was froze, so me an' Harry pumped fresh
for all the animals while Bert helped Rorey get more
wood in and light the stove in the house to get the chill
off. The sky was gettin' gray early. We were in for more
snow.

While we were working, I prayed for my brothers and
for Pa too, turning over in my mind the things he'd told

me at the depot, trying to figure if he had some reason for saying 'em besides just to be hurtful.

I'd a' been the one on that train if I had more smarts about me, that's what he said. That I was old enough to be on my own, but I couldn't do nothin' right without Mr. Wortham's help. An' they were stuck with me and it'd prob'ly always be that way.

I gave our best milk cow a pat, remembering the calf we'd butchered in the fall. He'd looked just like her, 'cept he'd gone lame after steppin' in a hole. We would've butchered him anyway for the winter's meat, I knew that. But for some reason it bothered me right then, and I had to shove those thoughts out of my mind.

"I have learned, in whatsoever state I am, therewith to be content." Paul had said that. In the book of the Philippians. After being shipwrecked and stoned and all that, he had a lot more to deal with than I did, but I was having some trouble nonetheless. And it didn't help to see the state Pa was in.

When the sun got low, Rorey and Emmie put together some supper while Bert and Harry and me did the milking. Pa did nothin' but complain 'bout all of it. He didn't eat more'n six bites 'fore he put on his coat an' hat and disappeared. I knew he'd took a horse, foolhardy as that was on a cold night when we were fixing to get some weather. But I knew he didn't care. He'd be gone for hours, maybe all night.

I didn't tell my brothers and sisters that. I just prayed in my head for Pa, not understanding why Willy leavin' seemed to be upsettin' him so much more than it ought to. It hadn't been this bad when Joe left. Nor even Kirk, and we knew by then he could be facin' war. Maybe it was the three of 'em all put together weighin' on him kind of hard.

I hoped it wasn't me he was bothered about. It'd almost seemed that way at the depot, but sometimes folks lash out at what's handy, rather than bringin' up what's really eatin' at 'em. I'd seen Pa that way plenty a' times. So I tried not to take the words he'd said too personal.

I knew he hadn't thought I needed to stay at home that night. But I was glad I did. Harry and Bert'd seemed kind a' solemn and distracted. I was glad I was there to give 'em a hand with chores and be with 'em a while.

As soon as supper was done, Rorey went up in the loft room by herself to write a letter and told the rest of us to leave her alone. Emmie got kind of weepy. I wished we'd thought to send her home with the Worthams tonight. That would a' been easier for her than seein' Pa so down in the mulligrubs and then takin' off the way he done.

Not knowin' what else to do, I got her singing. She didn't really want to, but I told her Willy wouldn't want us actin' all funny when he seemed set to enjoy himself along with doing his duty. And besides, she was supposed to sing with the choir in church tomorrow. I told her I wanted to hear her part all by itself so's I'd know what to listen for when the whole group sung together.

Bert asked me twice where Pa went, but I didn't give no real answer. "Ridin'," I said once. "Off to be alone a while," I told him the other time.

"In the cold?" he questioned.

But I just tried to assure him that Pa'd get back all right, even though I knew he'd be riding to Fraley's or some other place he knew to drain a bottle before he come home. We might not see him till morning. An' it might be better not too. Maybe he'd sleep off the drunk in Fraley's back room and be ready to come to himself in the morning.

"Are you sure we're goin' to church tomorrow?" Bert asked me then.

"Yep. Lord willin'."

"Is Pa goin'?"

"Can't say. But we're goin' either way, long as the roads are clear enough."

"We can't take the wagon if Pa ain't back with Star," Harry protested. "It's too much weight for Tulip to pull alone."

"Then if Pa ain't here we'll get over to Worthams' early enough to climb in the back a' their truck again," I said, thinkin' they oughta know that. We'd done it before plenty of times, even with Pa along.

"If Pa ain't here, maybe we shouldn't leave," Bert said with a worried expression, and I wished Harry hadn't brung up that possibility.

"He'll know right where we are," I assured him. "He'll expect us to go."

None of 'em asked why Pa might be gone so long, nor any more on why he left in the first place. Maybe he'd took off a lot when I stayed over in the wood shop. Willy hadn't told me that, though.

"Pa likes to be off alone," Emmie Grace said. "Willy said that's just the way he is sometimes."

"Ain't nothin' we can do about it then," I told them. "Maybe we oughta get some Bible readin' in. That'd be a proper thing to do after the sun's down when tomorrow's a Sunday."

"What are *you* gonna do?" Harry was quick to ask. "You ain't gonna be readin'."

"I was hopin' one a' you'd offer to read aloud for everybody."

Harry made a face, 'bout like I'd expected. So I was glad when Bert volunteered, because I knew readin' would be hard for Emmie. She didn't have quite the struggle I did, but she had more trouble than the rest when it come to letters.

Bert was good-hearted about it. He asked me where I wanted him to read, and I told him Psalms. So he just opened to the beginning of the book and started readin'.

76

It was familiar comfort to me, the words I could speak in my head right as he was readin' 'em. I'd heard 'em read by Mrs. Wortham when she was home-teachin' me, and quoted by the pastor too. He loved the Psalms as much as I did.

Pa showed up at about three in the mornin'. I always sleep light, so I woke when I heard Star comin' back through the snowy yard. I hoped Pa hadn't let himself get too cold. I got up to throw wood on the fire, and then I went out to the barn in case Pa needed help puttin' the horse up. He didn't. Or at least he didn't want help. But he was stumblin', mutterin' somethin' about some drunk arguin' and makin' fun of him in town. I made the mistake a' saying I wasn't surprised because wine was a mocker and strong drink was ragin'. And even though those were Bible words out of Proverbs, Pa yelled at me. I helped him to the house, almost surprised he'd let me, and he passed out as soon as he hit the bed. I was glad everybody else was asleep.

In the morning I roused the kids early. Me and Bert and Harry did the chores again while the girls stirred up breakfast. Pa didn't get up. I didn't expect him to, but I went to check on him before we left. He looked true horrible, with his eyes all red and uptight lookin', his hair a crazy stick-up mess, and a scratch on his hand he didn't know how he got. I couldn't help thinkin' of some other words in Proverbs: "Who hath contentions? Who hath babbling? Who hath wounds without cause? Who hath redness of eyes? They that tarry long at the wine; they that go to seek mixed wine."

I didn't say it out loud, 'cause I knew he wouldn't hear it. But I prayed. *Lord, help my pa. And help me an' all my family learn this lesson by example and not by experiencin' it our ownselves.*

"Pa, we're going to church," I said. "You wanna come?"

"Not this time, boy. I gotta sleep."

"All right," I told him. "We'll see you about dinnertime."

I didn't ask him about takin' the wagon 'cause I didn't want him to tell me no. And I didn't want to leave him a horse lest he get to feelin' stronger an' think he had plenty a' time to go after another bottle. So without no more words I went an' hitched both horses to the wagon, got everybody bundled and loaded the best I could, and headed out for the Dearing church.

"Is Pa sick?" Emmie asked on the way.

"Yep," I told her without any explaining. "I reckon he is."

# 8

## *Julia*

My world had a hole in it without Robert home. We listened to the radio the next few days to hear news of the war, but none of it was good. And then the radio quit on us the way it was prone to do sometimes, and Samuel couldn't get it going again.

The girls and I sat down for a few minutes every evening to write a letter to Robert or to Willy, Joe or Kirk. Samuel didn't do much writing, but he would tell me some things to say. We were all worried about George after the kids came to church Sunday without him, and Emmie told us he'd been gone almost all night. Samuel went to talk to him twice, and he seemed better then. Franky told us his father had quit most of his grumbling at them and didn't disappear like that again.

"He's prone to weakness," Franky explained when he came through the snowy timber to finish Pearl Daugherty's hope chest. "He says he's doin' better. He says he don't need the drinkin' so much now, if things is goin' all right."

Those words bothered me more than I let on. What

if things didn't go right? What then? But I didn't want to voice such doubts to Franky, who seemed to have enough of his own.

"It scares me, Mrs. Wortham," he said with an earnest frown. "It's like he's givin' himself permission to act any kind a' way if we come on hard times or somethin' don't suit him. Emmie an' Berty ain't said much about it, but they're bein' careful around him, not wantin' to give him no excuse. An' I don't wanna be the cause a' him runnin' to the bottle again neither. But sooner or later he'll find somethin' wrong around me. He always does."

There were times over the years when George Hammond made me just plain mad. And this was one of them. "Oh, Franky. It sounds like he's trying to find a way to blame someone else for his own behavior. But we all deal with difficult things, and we can well choose to be sensible about it."

"I know. But at least he's doin' better'n he was. I just hope he listened good to Mr. Wortham, an' it sticks with him longer'n the last time."

"I hope so too," I agreed.

Franky shook his head. "He can be so awful hard-headed. Like he's got a wall up against what God would do if he let him. I ain't for sure if he's really saved, an' it's botherin' me."

I nodded, not sure how to answer those concerns. Franky'd always been one to wonder about a person's eternal well-being, but his father found such talk simply annoying more often than not. "I'm not sure what we can do except pray for him. I know he's heard the Word. I know he's prayed both with Samuel and the pastor."

"Yeah, but I'm not so sure if he done that of his own true heart, Mrs. Wortham, or 'cause they expected it."

His strange, almost silvery eyes looked hurt. It was easy to picture him again the way we met him, as a scrawny, sad-faced eight-year-old, lonely in the middle of a big family, with deep questions nobody tried to address.

"Frank, only God knows for sure. All we can do is pray that your father long to walk close to God now and do right by his family."

He looked down at the floor. "I know. I need to let it go from my mind and get on with the business a' the day. I guess Pa's right sometimes that I let my thinkin' get in the way a' my doin', but most the time I manage to do both at the same time all right. I guess I'm just in a test when it comes to trustin' right now."

"I know exactly what you mean."

He looked at me with question. "You do?"

"Very much so. Samuel and I agreed we would trust Robert in God's hands. But it's not been one bit easy for me the last few days."

"That's just natural."

"And it's the same way with you."

He smiled, just a little, and I was glad if I'd managed to set his mind to ease some. I thought it good that he'd come over. We hadn't seen as much of him this week as we usually did. He was taking responsibility for his younger brothers and sisters very seriously, and it seemed a little strange not to see him every day. Franky had been a welcome feature at our house for a long time.

Before he left, Franky dictated to me a letter for Joe, who wrote to him fairly regularly. Joe's last letter had come from the Philippines. He'd been sick, and though he gave us no details, he sounded less than pleased about being there. Franky encouraged him that all things were for a purpose and would work out for good in the end. I couldn't have managed a better letter myself.

Then he asked me to add a line in my next letters for Kirk and William. He never had quite as much to say to them. They'd never been close. But he wanted to be faithful to communicate with them regularly anyway.

"Can you stay to dinner?" I asked.

"No, ma'am. I promised myself I'd pretty much stay t' home this week 'case I'm needed, then next week we'll see. I won't let the work go, though, I promise you. I'm takin' the back of a chair with me to carve on after supper."

"All right, Franky."

I watched him scrunch his hat down over his ears and head out across the timber with a chunk of wood under his arm. His limp seemed very pronounced as he stepped over snowdrifts on the unshoveled path, and I sighed, feeling heavy for him and not sure why. Franky always handled himself so well. He didn't see himself as handicapped at all. He didn't let anything slow him down.

I was glad Franky had chosen to be home more. For one thing, he made his younger brothers and sisters get off to school whether they wanted to or not, which was something Willy and their father had never concerned themselves about. It hadn't been a problem with Emmie or Bert, but Harry and Rorey had always missed far more school than they should. But not a day this week so far, and that was Franky's doing.

Franky had always loved learning, despite his troubles with it. I decided to ask Sarah to borrow a few books from the teacher for me. I hadn't been teaching Franky regularly for almost two years, and it'd been far too long since I'd read him anything. I thought he'd appreciate the opportunity next time he was over.

The next day, Sarah came home with an atlas of the world, Shakespeare's *Hamlet*, and *In His Steps* by Charles Sheldon. I had to smile at those choices, especially when Sarah told me the teacher had decided on them herself. This new teacher certainly understood our needs better than the last one, who had insisted on sending me little stories at the primer level "to help the poor boy read."

After so many years of trying, I honestly didn't know if anyone could do that. None of the teachers since Mrs. Post had been willing to give Frank their time after hearing of our previous efforts. But the primer stories were ridiculous boredom to him.

Franky loved a story to make him think. He could soak up words and thoughts like a sponge, even when the rest of the family scarcely understood what was being read. It was a mystery to me, and something I'd taken to the Lord many times, that Franky could be so brilliant and yet hopelessly lost when faced with a written page.

But it was a greater mystery and a frustration that George Hammond still failed to appreciate his son. He'd chosen years ago to see only Franky's difficulties, and no amount of time or persuasion had been able to open his eyes to the gifts.

As often as not, Franky's presence seemed to trouble George, though he'd freely acknowledged that his son bore no real fault for it. He'd wanted Franky away from him, out of his house for a while, when the boy was only fifteen. And he'd never truly asked him back. I hoped that didn't cause friction between them now.

But George's willful loss had been our gain. Franky was quiet and considerate. He loved us, maybe because we understood him, at least most of the time. We wanted him around as much as he'd care to be. I'd dreamed more than once that he was my own son. And for most practical purposes, since his mother died, he might as well have been.

The rest of January got bitter cold. We were snowed in a couple of times, though never badly enough that we couldn't make our way through the timber to the Hammonds, or them to us if need be. The girls and I looked up the Philippines in the atlas once when Emmie was at our house. She was amazed to see just how far from

83

us Joe really was. But we weren't sure where Kirk was stationed. He'd said his unit was moving and his next letter would give an updated address, but the next letter hadn't come.

Samuel finally got the radio working again. We listened to the president's stirring speeches and the sobering war news. A local radio announcer signed off in the evening with a plea to buy war bonds. I wished we could. But we didn't have a dime to spare yet.

Samuel was confident there would be work enough when the weather warmed. He intended to find something extra, though I thought with the farm and the woodwork he'd have his hands full. But I think he expected to leave most of the business with Frank and get something else to pull in extra money. We heard that a couple of coal mines might reopen south of Marion. And in some areas, there were plenty of jobs as industries called for more workers to supply our troops, but I didn't want him to go far. I didn't really want him to leave the farm for work at all.

I could be happy just living off what the farm could provide. We'd managed to survive the worst of the thirties that way, though we'd come here with nothing but hope. I felt blessed here. But Samuel was ready for more. A way to get ahead, not just get by. I was a little nervous of what that might mean. I prayed that WH Hardwoods would prosper and Samuel and Franky would both have all the work they could handle with that and the field crops.

When we'd lived in Pennsylvania, Samuel'd had a good job at a manufacturing plant. Good pay. And I knew he could do that kind of work again. But it was the distance he'd have to go that bothered me. We'd either be without him or have to consider moving, and I couldn't imagine that. This was our life, where we were planted by God, for the Hammonds' sakes as well as our own. In my mind, there were still both families to consider.

But I didn't need to be worrying over such things. Maybe it was a test of trusting, like Franky had said, and I needed to trust the Lord and my husband to know and choose what was best for all of us.

February started off just as cold as January had been. We let Whiskers in the house at night because he still didn't seem like himself. The poor old dog would curl up on my feet or go and push his nose under Sarah's hand and then go back and lay in front of the fire again.

"He's just not feeling well," Sarah told me again.

And then one morning, Samuel rose to find the dog dead, still lying there at his place by the fire. He had Whiskers up and out of the house before I could encounter the body, but I was sad over it just the same. Whiskers had been a friend. A good dog, never any trouble. Sarah was crushed. A little to my surprise, she got into a pair of her brother's overalls, rolled the pant legs so they wouldn't drag, and went to help her father bury Whiskers.

When they got back inside, she sat down with paper to tell Robert about it.

I wondered what he'd think of so many letters from us. In the winter evenings, we had time to write them. But the arrival of a letter from him could stop me in the middle of whatever I was doing. I couldn't wait two seconds to open those envelopes and see what he had to say. He always gave us some idea of how his training was going and what Willy, who had carried his mischievous streak right along into the service with him, was up to. We savored every letter, passing it around and sometimes reading them out loud. And then I stored them all in a box on our chest of drawers. I'm not sure why. I guess I just needed them handy in case I wanted to read them

85

again. Sometimes, late at night, I would take a letter out
of the box and walk about the house, praying for Robert
with his letter in my hands. I felt close to him then. Like
he was just upstairs, asleep in his own bed.

Whenever Franky came over, I would read for a few
minutes from one of the books the teacher had sent. I
usually saved the atlas for when Bert or Emmie were
there too, because they liked seeing different places of the
world, though Bert had read enough of the school's books
to be familiar with most of the places I looked up.

When it was Franky and our family alone, I read
*Hamlet* or *In His Steps*, and Franky liked them both.
He listened to *Hamlet* as though he were sifting for any
insight he could hold and put to use, and to *In His Steps*
as though he were taking in manna from heaven. One day
he would ask for one book, and the next day the other.
I wondered how he could keep either story straight in
his head that way.

Samuel told me that although George was in no way
cheerful, at least he was causing no real problems. Things
were as normal as they could be for the times we were
in. Along with everyone else in the country, we set the
clocks an hour ahead for the duration of the war to save
evening daylight.

Sarah didn't like me listening to the news. She said
Robert thought it would make me worry. But I wanted to
know what was happening. I'd turn the radio on myself
if no one else did. And I thanked God repeatedly that it
stayed working the rest of that winter.

When the weather warmed, we planted the garden as
early as we could. Emmie was pleased to call our gar-
dens "victories" and promised to tend them faithfully,
glad for the knowledge that everything we produced
could mean more "store food" could be shipped to her
brothers overseas. The radio quit working again in the

first week of April, and by that time letters from Joe had stopped. Kirk's had never started up again, and Robert and William had begun specific preparations for their roles overseas. As the sun continued to chase away the last chill of winter, something cold settled over my heart. I tried to fight it. Most of the time I denied it. But dread closed over me like a cloud. And I feared we'd never go back to the way we were.

# 9

# Frank

I'd never heard anything quite like that Charles Sheldon book Mrs. Wortham read to me. I liked it better than Hamlet because to my mind there was no denying it had more purpose. Shakespeare maybe liked to make people think about life and human nature, but Sheldon had the most practical, simple lesson on how to live godly that I ever heard. I went and told the pastor he oughta recommend that book to the whole congregation. It sure got me thinking. Was I doing what Jesus would do? What ought I be doing different?

About the first of April, Pa asked me if Harry was gettin' old enough to take care of things on the farm. The question made me shake my head. There didn't seem to be no reason for it.

"Not by his own self," I said. "But there ain't no need a' that anyway. You an' me an' Bert an' Rorey'll all take a hand."

"You got the wood shop," he argued. "An' you ain't no good in my fields."

I knew I wasn't the fastest worker in the world. But I did what I could the best I knew how, so I didn't figure he oughta have a real problem with that. But I didn't answer him back about it. "Pa, I plan on helpin' in the fields an' keepin' up the orders too. There ain't been all that many orders to worry about."

But Pa seemed to think I had my head so full that I wasn't gonna be much help. I'd been bringin' some of the wood projects home to work on at night and spendin' less time gone, hoping Pa would see I was serious about being available while Joe and Kirk and Willy were gone. Wasn't that what was needed? But Pa wasn't comforted on that at all, even when I tol' him I was using my Hardwoods money to pay the Farm Service for our order of spring seed.

Maybe to my pa it just seemed out of the ordinary to have me around so much more. He hadn't been happy over the winter, that was sure, but he'd seemed to get better, and I could thank the Lord for no more ugly bouts of drinkin' like that first night.

Two of our sows'd had big litters, and Marabelle the cow had a fine-lookin' calf. Pa seemed to cheer up at those things, like he did every spring. So I started thinkin' maybe his winter mulligrubs wasn't so much more than usual. His complainin' hadn't been too awful bad, an' he was a lot better in the sunshine.

It didn't seem to worry him much about not hearin' from Kirk or Joe in a while. He said Kirk didn't like writin' anyway, and Joe'd be awful busy off in the Pacific with men under him needin' his attention for a few more months. Besides, the pastor said mail could be awful slow over such a distance, and maybe they couldn't even send mail out for a while, just to keep their positions a secret if a move against the enemy was comin'. Pa didn't let it bother him. One of Joe's letters had said he should be comin' home in July, and we were all glad about that.

I decided to stop and think about things a little differently. Harry and Bert were both near as big as me anymore. And strong too. They could do what the farm needed with

Pa's help until Joe got home. I didn't much question that. It was getting warmer. Mr. Wortham and I had already talked on what we'd plant in which field in which order an' how soon. If I could just help him an' Pa get the seed in the ground, they wouldn't need me so much after that.

The feelings I'd put down in January came back at me again, and I thought that if Jesus was in my shoes, maybe he'd want to go a world away and help our soldiers too.

I told myself that, but I still felt a little funny to borrow Mr. Wortham's truck to go and visit the recruiters when they come to town again. I didn't tell Mrs. Wortham nor Pa and the kids what I was doing, figurin' there was no use gettin' them excited ahead if I couldn't go.

It was the marines I'd talked to with Robert and Willy before, because Willy'd seen a poster of the marines and decided that was for him. This time I searched out the army recruiter. I knew they wouldn't call on me for a draft like they had Kirk and some others I knew, but I figured that if I volunteered myself maybe they'd consider what I had to say an' let me sign up. I still wanted to go. Seemed like Harry an' Bert were old enough to manage fine. Rorey too. And before long, Joe might be home. They'd be all right if I was gone. Pa seemed like he might already be all right. They didn't need me as much as I'd thought. What good was I doing anybody, makin' wood things? I oughta serve, if I could get the chance.

But there was nobody who'd listen to what I had to say. I left Dearing feeling awful discouraged and kind of stupid for tryin' again. I shoulda saved myself the trouble. The army man turned me away.

"I can drive," I told him. "I can operate a radio or somethin'."

But he just shook his head. So I went to the navy recruiter, and he said he was sorry but I oughta just do whatever I could to help the war effort at home.

90

It was a bother being rejected again. But worse than that was wondering why I'd felt so strongly that I oughta try. How could I be so wrong? Was I just deceiving myself to get out of shoulderin' things at home? Sometimes I thought that if I could be in the service and do as well as Joe had, maybe Pa would think more of me. Maybe even the Turreys would find a little respect. But I knew enough to understand that that kind of thinkin' was vain. It didn't matter what any man thought of me. Only what God thought.

So I must have had it wrong. If Jesus was in my shoes, maybe he'd want to stay right here and do what he could for my family. That thinkin' made me feel bad that I'd come into town at all. With three brothers gone, I shouldn't want to be leavin'. I should have the right kind of heart for my brothers and sisters. Why was I tryin' to get away from things?

I didn't like my mind going two ways like this. A preacher named Cuyler wrote that God always has a helping angel for those who are willing to do their duty. I remembered Pastor tellin' me that once. An' I was always willing to take on whatever duty I could. To my country now especially. But maybe I was just kiddin' myself and lettin' my pride get in the way of the practical.

Pastor also said once to do the duty that lies nearest thee. An' that had to be farm an' family. I'd be blind not to see that. Harry and Bert were still young, and they had school this spring to think about. An' Joe'd need a break come summer, not a ton a' hard work waitin' for him when he got home.

I didn't want to despise God nor his helpin' angel by scornin' the obvious. So I prayed for peace about it all. I prayed to be happy at home. But my feelings stayed as mixed up as before. I was glad Pa seemed to be doin' all right. I just couldn't figure out why I was such a mess.

# 10

## Sarah

Dear Robert,

Mr. Thomas from the school board came to talk to Mom and Dad last evening. Katie and I were nervous when we saw him coming, but he didn't have any complaint against us. I could hardly believe it, but he said they're wanting to graduate Katie, Rorey, and me, along with Eugene Turrey and Joshua Mueller, this year instead of next. I didn't know what to say.

They can't afford to add on to the school, so it'll still be one room, and they can't afford to bus any of us into the Dearing school either. So with us graduated, Miss Aimsley won't have the top graders to think about, and the school will be less crowded. That was the school board decision. Mr. Thomas said they figured we were ready anyway, and with the war on we'd probably be needed somewhere else.

I'd like to feel ready to be an adult at sixteen, but I don't,

*Robby. And imagine how Katie feels! She's five months younger and started school a year later than I did. We both thought we'd have another year. Katie thought she might have two.*

*Rorey didn't go to school today. Neither did Eugene Turrey. Emmie says Rorey doesn't want to bother with school now since we know they're going to graduate us anyway. She's going to start looking for work right away. But Mom and Dad want Katie and I to go as long as we can, and I'm glad. I don't want to look for outside work yet. I want to be home to help get the rest of the crops planted, and you know there's plenty of work right here for the summer too, plus harvest in the fall. I figure the more I can do, the less left on Dad, and he'll have more time for the wood shop. They just finished a rocking chair, and I think it's the nicest one yet. Frank made a couple of wall plaques that are so pretty I wish I had the money to buy them myself. Eagles, carved so nice the feathers look almost real. I wish you could see.*

The cuckoo clock sung out all of a sudden, and I set the paper and pencil back in my stationery box. I was just writing Robert a quick note after getting the laundry in off the line, and could finish the letter later. Mom would appreciate it if I took a bowl and gathered in some greens for supper.

Harry had come over after school to help Dad and Frank seed the field north of our house. I could see them from where I got started picking lamb's-quarter. I wondered about my brother and what he'd be eating tonight. I hoped they fed him good at his training camp.

Filling my bowl with lamb's-quarter, dock, dandelion, and a little winter cress took longer than I expected. I rinsed my pickings at the well, glad there were things growing in our yard to forage while we were waiting for the garden vegetables.

Once the greens were ready to cook, I mixed up some muffins while Mom fried potatoes and opened a home-canned jar of pork tenderloin. Katie set the table and got some jam from the cellar. Pretty soon the muffins were in the oven, and Mom asked me to go out and get some winter onions to set on the table. They hadn't seeded yet, so they were so good right now.

Dad and Frank and Harry came up from the field while I was still by the garden. Harry was kidding Frank about not being able to hear them call while he was working. Mom had said once that Frank thinks so deep sometimes, especially when he's working, that he doesn't hear anything outside his own head. She said it was a gift. But Harry didn't seem to think so. He said they should have just left him in the field all night to see if he ever noticed that he hadn't had his supper.

Frank was pretty good-natured about the ribbing. "It's better not hearing when you work than not working when you hear," he teased right back. "Good thing the birds quit singin', Harry, or you'd a' never got the job done."

Harry smiled. I joined them with the onions in my hand as they went walking to the house. Harry seemed happy for Frank to return his teasing. Harry loved to joke around, and he was always glad whenever anyone in his family joined in, which didn't happen very often.

But Frank wasn't joking for long. "I was thinkin' about that fella named Beethoven," he said suddenly. "He could write music when he was deaf as a post. And if he could do that, seems like anybody else could do most anythin' they set their mind on, you know?"

Harry looked at him sideways. "You're the strangest fella I know. Who said anythin' about a deaf man writin' music?"

94

"Mrs. Post did, after Emmie's choir practice last Sunday. She said it should be an inspiration to persevere daily, and I think it is."

"How come?" Harry asked, giving him a funny look. "You don't write music. You're not even deaf. At least not all the time."

"Everybody's somethin'," Frank said with a sigh. "I guess I'm a couple a' things, maybe. Whatever anybody'd wish to call it."

"Half lame and illiterate. That's what you call it," Harry said immediately, though he didn't sound mean. "You think you could do most anythin', huh? You want to race me to the porch?"

Frank smiled. "I'll race you tomorrow to see who can get the most work done."

Dad laughed a little. I could tell he was glad they were getting along. It hadn't always been that way. There'd been times when Frank didn't get much consideration out of his brothers, except maybe Sam or Joe.

The sky was getting gray, and a stiff breeze started blowing. But it'd been so warm today that it felt good. I figured it'd rain overnight, and we sure needed it. Harry said something about looking forward to my Mom's cooking tonight instead of Rorey's. And then I heard something off a ways. Somebody was running through the timber. But there was no way we could have expected what we heard then.

Screaming. Emma Grace was somewhere in the trees, screaming and yelling for Frank and Mom and Dad and Harry. We all started running. I couldn't imagine what in the world could be wrong. She ran out of the timber straight toward our garden. She was yelling so loud Mom came running out of the house right away.

"Emmie!" Dad was the first one to get hold of her. "Emmie, what's wrong?"

"I don't know! Just come! Will you come? Pa's actin' all crazy, throwin' stuff and knockin' things around—"

"He can't be drinkin'," Franky said, suddenly looking pale. "Not now." He started away from us before she even answered him.

"I don't know. I don't know!" She took a deep breath, trying to calm down. "I was weedin' by the strawberry patch, and Berty went inside with the mail to read to Pa, an' I don't know what happened! I heard the awfulest commotion. I went to see what all the noise was, but Rorey yelled at me to run and get you! I could tell she was scared—"

"Dear Lord," my mother said so softly I almost didn't hear her.

"Stay here with Katie and Sarah, Emmie," Daddy told her with a terrible solemn look. "Help yourself to the supper. We'll go see what this is about. You stay too, Harry."

Dad didn't say anything to Frank. But it wouldn't have done any good because Frank was already gone.

# 11

# Frank

At first I thought it must be the drinkin', an' I was ready to be mad at Pa over doin' that in the daylight in front a' Emmie and Bert. But then when Emmie said Bert had brung the mail, somethin' worse crept over me all the way to my feet, makin' it hard to walk because I was feelin' so stiff and cold. What if Pa went all crazy because of a letter? He never could take no kind of bad news.

Something raw started burnin' at the pit of my stomach, and I was scared and feeling heavy like no weight I ever did know before. What kind of news could be so awful as to make him go half crazy? I knew, but I didn't want to give it no place in my mind.

I tried my best to run through that timber. Mr. and Mrs. Wortham caught up to me pretty quick. Mrs. Wortham put her arm in mine and stayed with me. But Mr. Wortham run ahead. He could get there faster'n me. But I wouldn't stop. I couldn't. He disappeared in the trees ahead, and I kept right on going, tryin' to catch up.

"Frank?" Mrs. Wortham said.

But I didn't answer. An' she kept comin' beside me but didn't say nothin' else.

By the time we got to the house, Mr. Wortham was already inside. I didn't hear a thing. But I'd seen the barn door hangin' open, and I knew Rorey and Berty hadn't been able to hold Pa here. He was gone again.

Bert was sittin' on the floor looking white. Rorey had her apron on, but she'd left the stove unattended and was just sitting in a chair. Mr. Wortham was holdin' a letter one of 'em must have handed him. I knew it said something awful from the look on his face.

"It's Joe," Berty said in a choked little voice, and I wished I was able to snatch the letter and read it for myself.

"What?" I demanded, feelin' like I was choking too. "What happened?"

Mr. Wortham took a deep breath. "It says he's missing, son. On an island of the Philippines. He's unaccounted for after a troop movement there."

I just stood. I couldn't think straight. I couldn't answer. Missing? *No, God. That can't be right. He's in your hands. How could he be missing?*

I knew I ought to say somethin' hopeful for Bert and Rorey. I ought to tell them that all kinds of things can happen in a strange place and God's in charge of them all. Maybe Joe was lost, but he could be found, safe as you or me, maybe even before the day was out. Maybe he already had been found and we'd soon get word. We could believe that. I wanted to tell them so. But I didn't.

I just sunk, right there on the floor. I didn't want to. I knew it wasn't the right thing to do in front of my brother and sister, but some things come on you without leavin' you any choice, and I felt like I'd been yanked sideways and turned upside down.

This weren't right! Joe had a heart of gold and a load

of faith! Everybody was lookin' forward to him comin' home. How could anything happen to him? I should be over there with him. It wouldn't be so bad if I was the one, if somethin' was to happen to me.

I told Bert and Rorey they'd better go back with the Worthams to their place. I knew that'd be more comfort than stayin' here waiting for Pa to get back home. It'd be better if they weren't even here when he got back. Who knew what shape he'd be in? He prob'ly felt like he'd been slammed down a hole.

"Maybe you should come too," Mr. Wortham told me. "Stay with the rest at our place and let Emmie and Harry know what's happened. They'll need you. And it's not going to do any good to wait here. I can take the truck and see if I can find your father."

"I wasn't gonna wait," I answered him. "I was gonna head straight to Fraley's with the other horse an' get Pa home 'fore he's clear out of his mind."

Mr. Wortham nodded. "All right. If you think that's where he went, I'll take you in the truck."

I don't know why I didn't let it go like before and let Pa drink if that's what he was going to do. I guess this was just too different. I wanted him home. I was scared for him not to be home. Or maybe just plain scared, period. I kept thinkin' of when Mama died, and it seemed like our whole world fell into a thousand pieces and wouldn't never come right again. I'd carried such a bitter ache for such an awful long time. And Pa had too. He'd almost died over it. I don't know if the rest of my family understood all that, but I sure did.

"What if Pa comes back 'fore you find him an' there ain't nobody here?" Bert asked. He was worried. And he knew we couldn't leave no note. Pa didn't read no better'n me. But I told Bert Pa'd know where to find everybody. If we wasn't at home we'd be at the Worthams. That was just the way things had been with us since Emmie was a baby. Mrs. Wortham pretty much agreed that was right. So Mr. Wortham folded up the army letter and put it in his pocket.

Everybody was quiet walkin' back through the timber. Bert seemed to have a hard time keeping his feet going. Maybe he was thinkin' the same kind of things I was. When we got close to the place where Mama was buried, he choked up again, and I put my arm around him. "It'll be all right," I told him. But I wasn't sure I believed it, or if he did either.

*God, why?* I started praying. *Why Joe? Is he dead? Why would you let this happen?*

I swallowed hard, feeling shamed to be questionin' God again. Things had always been so clear to me before. God was the God of everythin'. Sun and moon. Seed and harvest. The earth and the fullness thereof. What was happenin' to me, that I would start doubtin' him and thinkin' so uncertain? My mind was full of questions I didn't know how to stop.

*Are you here, God? Are you takin' a hand in this at all?*

The tears I had to fight off then were for Joe. But they were also because now when I really needed to be strong, to hold on to faith and give my brothers and sisters and maybe even my pa some kind of hope, it was slippin' away from me. I just wanted to keep crying "Why?" over and over. And I hated it. I hated to admit to myself and especially to God that I was pitiful weak in the faith I wanted to be so strong in. I felt like I was failin' everybody. God and my pa and all my family. But especially Joe. I oughta believe for him. I oughta stand in faith, insistin' everything was all right. But in my heart, I couldn't shake the awful feelin' that Joe was already gone.

# 12

# Sarah

Dear Robert,

We got terrible news today. I didn't want to tell you, except I knew you'd want to know. Joe is missing in action. Mom says there's always hope, even though the official letter didn't sound very hopeful. I'm not sure if you should tell William. The rest of his family is taking this awfully hard. And there you are still starting out. I hate to burden you with something so awful, but I knew you'd be upset if nobody told you. Maybe William would be too.

I know Mom will write you a letter, and probably Katie again too, but I had already started one and thought I'd best sit down and try to finish. I pray for both of you there. And for Joe, wherever he is. And Kirk. Do you think the army will tell Kirk about this? We're not sure if he's been getting our most recent letters because he said there would be a new address and he still hasn't sent it. At least our *letters haven't been returned. But not hearing from him is worrying everybody too.*

*Robert, pray for Willy's father. And the kids. They're so scared right now. I wish I could send you only the letter I started before and just tell you about school and planting and things around home. But now it's different. Mr. Hammond's in a bad way. He ran off and started drinking, and when Dad and Frank brought him home he was carrying on crazy.*

*I just don't understand things. Why does stuff like this have to happen? Why does the world have to be so hard? Maybe you're asking yourself the same things and I'm being no help at all. I'm so sorry. But I love you, Robert. You're a good big brother. I feel like I could tell you anything. Even when you're far away. I miss you so much.*

*Your sister,*

*Sarah*

I folded the letter and put it in an envelope to mail. I felt like we were all carrying six tons of extra weight that we couldn't shake loose.

For the next few days, Mr. Hammond didn't talk to anybody. Rorey got a job at the five-and-dime in Dearing and rode back and forth every day without saying much to anybody either.

She kept writing to Lester, and I kept writing to Robert and Willy. But for a while we didn't get an answer from them. That was hard. Rorey told me she dreamed that everybody that went away on that train was coming home in boxes. I told her she better not tell Emma Grace that. Or anybody else.

Finally, about three weeks later, the mail brought let-

ters from Robert. One for Mom and Dad. One for Katie.
And one for me.

*May 18, 1942*

*Dear Sarah,*

*Willy and I thank you for the letters. Sorry you had to wait
to get an answer. We got a new commanding officer, and
he says there's no question that we'll be sent overseas. He
said he wants us to get used to feeling far from home. So he
made us wait a week before getting any mail, and another
week before sending any out. He says that's "sweet potatoes"
compared to how long mail's going to take later.*

*Awful hard news about Joe. I couldn't sleep the first night
after I read your letter, but I showed it to Willy right away
because I knew he'd be mad if I didn't. He's still glad he's
here. Maybe even more so now. Like this war just got personal for him. That scares me a little, Sis, but I sure understand him. If we could do anything to help Joe or anybody
like him we would. Gladly. There's evil at work in this
world, and God has raised up the United States military
to fight it. I'm proud of that, and I want you to be too. So
keep praying for Joe, but don't worry about me. Okay?*

*I got a letter from Rachel too. She said she's praying that
God will give us peace in this time of being apart, make us
stronger, and give us a greater understanding of himself.
Of course I agree with all that. Except I'd have to admit, at
least to you, that the last part makes me nervous. Did you
ever feel like God's got things all planned? I don't mean that
he did anything to Joe, just that he knows all about it. He
always knows what's down the road for us. And I've had
a feeling for a while that he's waiting on me. I don't know
why. To do something maybe, but I don't know what.*

103

*I used to think that because Rachel's so religious, she couldn't be the one for me. Cause I'm not like that. You know me. I like a good baseball game better than church, and I'm not even holy enough to be afraid to admit it.*

*I used to think Rachel would be a good girlfriend for Franky because they were always the quietest kids in church, remember? More than anybody else our age they'd listen and take it all in, like Mom and Dad do. And I wasn't ready for that. That's why I waited so long to talk to Rachel, in spite of my feelings for her. I figured Franky'd notice her, and they'd end up pastoring a church somewhere together someday. Do you think that was silly? I even asked Franky once if he liked her. And he said he loved his church family and she's a real sincere girl, but he had nothing specially personal her direction. Don't that sound like him?*

*You're probably wondering why I'm telling you all this, and I'm not sure I even know. But, Sarah, I've got a feeling there's a lot on Franky's shoulders right now, and it's bound to stay that way a while. I know how bad he wanted to serve, but I expect God has him home because that's where we need him most. I hope he's not taking it too hard about Joe. Help him if you get a chance, okay, Sis? You know how things have been with him and his pa, and it sounds like it's even harder now. I've been praying for all of them like you said.*

*I miss all of you, more than I thought I would. I think about you all the time. Especially at night when I'm trying to sleep. So I've been repeating Rachel's prayer for all of us. I love you always,*

*Robert*

# 13

*Julia*

Having mail from Robert was a blessed relief. Samuel took our letter over to share with George as soon as we were finished. Willy didn't like writing letters, so Robert had included several paragraphs from Willy to his father, as he'd done so many times before.

They were shaken up about Joe. Perhaps angry more than anything else. And training for conflict in the Pacific. Of course that made me nervous. Picking a mess of peas in the spring sunshine, I thought about the reports we'd heard on the radio, the tragic losses. And I guess I got mad too. Our young men were at risk, and nothing should stop us from doing everything we could to help. I decided that the sugar bowl where we tried to collect change would now be drawing savings to go to war bonds if we could manage it. There should be no buying anything else, unless it was absolutely necessary.

That was the first time I considered that Samuel going away to work might be better for the war effort even if it wasn't better for me. He'd had the kind of factory experience that would be valuable in a defense plant. He wouldn't need much training. But working the farms was important too, and I wasn't sure whether George and his sons could handle both farms without Samuel. Especially now.

"I'm sure George was relieved to hear from William," Samuel told me when he got back from the Hammond farm. "But he's not saying much. He told me he's fine, but I know better just looking in his eyes."

I wondered about George as I finished picking the peas. He always did his best to act all right in front of Samuel. Even when he'd been walking stiffer through part of the winter, he'd done his best not to show it to Samuel. I was glad the stiffness had seemed to disappear. But George'd been so wild-eyed and unreasonable after that official letter came that I knew he wasn't really all right. It was normal to worry. Or to be in a state of shock, anger, or despair. But there was something different about George somehow. Something that made me wonder if he had the wherewithal to continue with the farmwork, or even get through this at all.

I prayed for him, right there in the garden. And I prayed for Emmie and Bert and the rest. It had to be hard for them about Joe, but their father's reaction made things even harder. Samuel said George had been in bed when he took Robert's letter over. And we had a lot of sun left to the day. He didn't claim to be sick. He didn't claim anything at all.

With a sigh, I looked around me at our yard of May flowers. Emma Graham had loved the flowers. When she gave us this farm, just over ten years ago, she'd asked us to keep up the flowers, and plant more, clear to the road. She'd had a lot of ideas how we could take care of the place. But she'd also expected us to take care of the Hammonds, though that hadn't been clear to us at first. She'd known all along that they would need our

106

help, and that we should end up being about the same as one family.

We'd managed with the kids all right, at least the best we knew how. But it wasn't so easy with George. There were times when I thought he shouldn't have needed so much of our help, at least not for so many years. And yet, when he needed help the most was when he wanted it the least.

I sat by the side of the well, by the bluebells and the dayflowers, and shelled out the peas in the sunshine. What might Robert be doing at this very minute? And what about Joe? I tried to imagine a positive explanation for his disappearance but couldn't come up with anything that made real sense. And the negative possibilities were painful to think about. Yet it didn't seem right *not* to think about him. We couldn't just go about our days as though nothing had happened. Maybe George's extreme reaction was the only way he knew to honor his son.

We had to carry on with things, of course. There was so much work to do around us. But shutting down, at least for a while, drawing back from things and going to bed in the middle of the day might be George's way of keeping Joe in his thoughts through this trial. It wasn't good for the rest of his family, but we could certainly understand and be patient with him while we waited for more word.

I decided to make cookies again once supper was out of the way. I'd saved back several small boxes just for mailing packages, and I could send the biggest of those full of cookies for Robert and Willy to share. And Joe loved cookies, especially snickerdoodles, which I hadn't made since Christmas time. I'd package a box for him and mail it to the address we had. And then pray that he'd have a chance to enjoy his cookies too.

Surely we'd be getting word before long of him getting back to his unit or his base. Maybe he'd been hurt and lost, or had to hide in that strange place. Maybe he was in a hospital hankering to write us a letter to relieve our worrying. He was a brave, sensible young man.

My thoughts turned to Kirk as well. Unlike Joe, he hadn't planned his military service. He'd been called in the peacetime draft and was less than happy about it at first. But he'd accepted duty well enough and even decided before he left that he'd probably like the army and would gain all he could from the training.

George Hammond had good boys. There'd been some trials, sure. The kind of antics you might expect from boys, especially from Willy and Harry. But over all, they'd been growing to fine young men. There were people at church who said that was because of Samuel and me. But George was still their father, and most of them remembered their mother. I thought it at least partly true that the apple didn't fall far from the tree, despite George's problems.

Katie had been across the field picking red clover for tea. I could see her on her way back with her basket full. I'd only made clover blossom tea occasionally until she took a liking to it a couple of summers back. Now she'd gather it herself and set a jar out in the sun to steep for the family. Sweetened with sugar and cooled in the cellar or down the well, it was a nice treat, though Samuel said it tasted a little too much like hay for his liking.

Sarah was inside helping Emmie with her homework. The younger girl needed a lot of help, and Sarah was always glad to do it. I wondered about the school board's decision to graduate most of the high schoolers early. It didn't seem to me that any of them were ready. Especially not Rorey, though she fancied herself the most grown-up of them all and was the only one to have gotten a job.

Rorey was a worry sometimes, more than her brothers. Headstrong and willful, she didn't always make the wisest of choices. Samuel and I had tried to guide her, but George scarcely thought she needed guidance.

"Let her pick a boy an' get married soon as she's a mind to," he'd said. And in his opinion, that was all the thought for her future that was necessary.

I dumped empty pods from my apron into a bucket for Frank to take over to the pigs later. Then I took my bowl of peas toward the house to start supper. The sky was clouding over. It looked like we were in for some rain.

*Heavenly Father, let the natural rain water our fields, and at the same time rain peace down on our hearts about Joe. Rain your faith and courage upon George, and Joe too. And Kirk, Robert, and William. Bring us all together again.*

With another sigh and a glance at the clouds above me, I went in the house. Sarah and Emmie were just closing their books at the kitchen table.

"I can help you make supper," Emmie was quick to offer.

Sarah moved the books and started setting the table without saying a word. I asked Emmie to get me the butter from the cellar, and she ran to obey as quickly as she could.

For some reason, my eyes filled with tears. I couldn't imagine loving any of these kids more. I couldn't imagine any other kind of life. But I felt like we were at the junction of changes that I didn't want. I couldn't have explained anything to the girls about it. I just leaned to the cupboard to get a pan for the peas, dipped in a little water from the pail, and turned to the stove.

Life was never easy. It was like a bendy road, first this way, and then that. Up and down and around corners, till you didn't know what direction you were going or what you'd meet up with next. But God works all things for good. I remembered reading that. He works all things for good for those that love him.

*And we love you, Lord,* I prayed in my heart. *Joe loves you. Even George loves you, at least I think he does, in his own way. Let good come. Like the rain, let it pour down on our lives. Let the war end swiftly, and then the sun come out. Let the clouds of uncertainty be swept away.*

For some reason I thought of the book that Frank had liked so well, *In His Steps.* No wonder he'd liked it. I'd found it pretty inspiring too. Adding a chunk of wood to the stove, I thought about the pledge all those characters had made and what it had done in their lives. What would Jesus do in this situation, right here and right now? I dropped a piece of wood, and it went rolling a few feet.

Sarah looked up. "Mom? Are you all right?"

"Sure, honey. Just dropping things." I picked up the wood, gave it a sling into the stove, and shut the iron door with a clank. There was a war going on. A terrible war with enemies who committed terrible things. My only son was about to be in the very midst of it. Along with three young Hammonds that I'd fed, guided, and loved all these years. And one of them was missing. What would Jesus do in my place?

It was a good thing I'd set the pot down and wasn't holding anything else. It was a good thing Sarah had turned around getting plates out of the cupboard and Emmie was out of the room. I started shaking. Standing there at the stove, my hands were shaking. And churning in my heart was the knowledge of exactly what Jesus would be doing.

*"Love your enemies, bless them that curse you, do good to them that hate you, and pray for them which despitefully use you, and persecute you."*

I didn't know of a single thing I could do good for someone so far away as Germany or Japan. But I knew I could pray. The knowledge of it nearly choked me somehow, it came so fast. Pray for our enemies. *Oh, God, how?*

"Sarah, do you mind watching the peas and helping Emmie make everybody some egg salad?"

She looked at me with some surprise. "I don't mind."

I went straight for the bedroom.

"Are you all right, Mom?" Sarah asked again.

"Yes," I assured her from the bedroom doorway. I closed the door behind me and got down on my knees.

I didn't know how to pray the kind of words a situation like this warranted, but I expected there were plenty of Germans who prayed, plenty of Japanese who wouldn't harm a fly. I prayed for them. I prayed for their soldiers. And then, hardest of all, I prayed for their leaders, selfish, power hungry, or mad; I prayed for them all. And then my strength spent, I lay on the bed for a moment. My eyes filled with tears, but only a single one dripped down. I wiped at it and then at my whole face before I could present myself to the girls again. By that time they had supper on the table and didn't ask what I'd been doing. I was glad, because I didn't think I could find the words to tell them.

# 14

## Frank

I tried to pour myself into workin' just as much as I could in the days and weeks after we got that letter. When I wasn't in the field I was fixing tools or in the garden, tending stock, or mending fence. Seemed like there were a hundred things waitin' on a pair of willing hands, just like every spring. For a while, I didn't get much wood work done, but that was all right with me.

Pa stayed in bed a lot, but at least he wasn't takin' off again. I guess Mr. Wortham had pretty much talked him out of that. Rorey wouldn't hear any more about school now that she had a job, but I made Emmie and Harry and Bert keep goin' to the end of the school year, even though there were days they didn't feel like it. Harry especially thought he oughta stay home and work. And there was plenty to do, so he was glad when they let out for the summer.

It wasn't hard to keep everybody busy, but I didn't push Pa 'cause I didn't figure it'd do any real good. He would get up a little while, 'specially if Mr. Wortham was around, and act like he was gonna be busy at somethin' or other around our place. But he didn't get much of anythin' done, he didn't join us in the fields, an' he was always back in bed 'fore I got back to the house.

Mr. Wortham talked to him some more. Pastor come out and talked to him too. But I wasn't sure if it was really doin' any good. He got so he'd cuss me when I come to check on him, and then he'd hardly get up at all. After another week or so of that, I told Mr. Wortham that Pa was taking things too hard about Joe, that thinkin' about him and waitin' to hear some kind of word was making him sick. I understood him in it, at least a little, but it wasn't doin' him nor anybody else any good.

"I understand it too," Mr. Wortham told me. "But life is going on around him, especially with the rest of his kids. He'll have to open his eyes and see that."

I told Pa about my talk with Mr. Wortham when I got home from the field that day. I was hopin' that and the farm work waitin'd be enough motivation to stir him back to himself at least a little, but he didn't pay no attention. He didn't eat supper that night, didn't even answer when Rorey came home an' tol' him she'd make a cake just for him.

I knew there was somethin' wrong about Pa different than the way the rest of us was handling being worried over Joe. But I didn't know what to do about it. I was glad when Rorey said she'd stopped to see Lizbeth in town an' told her how Pa was acting. The next day was Saturday and Lizbeth'd be out to see us. I knew that. And she was always good at reasonin' with Pa. She'd know what to do.

I prayed for him that night. I prayed a lot, that we'd get answers and everything'd be all right again. But in the morning, Pa was worse. I didn't so much mind him cussin' at me. That wasn't far off normal 'cause he'd always had a short fuse with me anyhow. But Bert checked on Pa first, an' he tore into him jus' for knockin' on the door. And then Emmie tried bringin' him breakfast right to his bed, and he yelled at her so hard it made her cry. I sent 'em both to the Worthams again. There wasn't no use them stickin' around bein' treated like that. They'd seen too much a' Pa bein' ugly already.

We ate without him since he didn't want nothin' anyway. Then after Bert and Emmie left and Rorey took off to her job, Harry and me worked a while in the barn. Harry was pretty solemn, the quietest I ever seen him, and it bothered me, knowin' he was concerned over Pa right now maybe as much as he was about Joe. Finally, I left him alone a while and decided to try talkin' to Pa myself 'fore Lizbeth got there.

I prayed on the way in the house. *Lord, help me handle this the way you would. Help me to be wise and kind and patient, and strong enough not to be upset if he don't respond.*

I went in the house with my breath feelin' heavy, like somethin' about the air around our place was getting harder to breathe. I knew it was just the gloom. Just sadness hangin' over the place like a fog. I wished I could take Mama's old broom and sweep it away.

"You oughta get up," I told Pa as gentle as I could when I got to his room. "You wanna put a comb through your hair? Lizbeth's comin' over."

"Lizbeth knows her way 'round this place," he grouched at me without even moving. "She don't need me for nothin'."

"She'll think you oughta put your hands to somethin', Pa. You're makin' things worse for Emmie and Bert, and Harry too, carryin' on like this. It's got 'em upset. More'n they oughta be."

Pa rolled over on his bed and glared at me. "Jus' keep 'em all outta here! I never asked for nobody to bring me no breakfast nor nothin' else! An' I never asked for you nor Lizbeth to be mindin' what's my business. Get!"

114

"Pa, we'd leave you alone real easy if you was seein' to your own business—"

"I said get!"

I just stood for a minute, staring at him. I didn't remember him gettin' down this bad since his trouble when Mama died. He was probably thinkin' like I was about Joe, but neither of us would dare speak somethin' so bad as that. It would just make things worse to talk about him maybe bein' dead. I wasn't even sure how I'd act, let alone Pa. I was scared he'd go plumb crazy.

"Pa," I tried to reason a little. "You know Joe. He wouldn't want none a' us to fall apart on his account. He'd want you to get up and take care a' yourself."

"Shut up."

"But, Pa—"

"Tarnation, boy! Get out a' here 'fore I hurt you."

I stood still for a minute. I didn't know what he'd do. But he'd lit into me plenty a' times with his belt or a stick over the years, and I figured lettin' that happen again might be worth it today just to get him stirred out of bed. But then I thought I heard a car outside. If it was Ben and Lizbeth and they had Mary Jane with 'em, I'd better just go and greet them. Better to shut the door and not let Mary Jane see her grandpa this-a-way. She was too little to understand. She'd prob'ly climb right up on the bed with him and end up gettin' growled at.

I shut the door to Pa's room with another prayer stirrin' 'round inside me.

*Lord, you've searched me and known me. You know all the inner ways of my heart. You know I'm more like my pa than I let on. Maybe I would just lay down too, if it weren't for Emmie and Mary Jane and the rest. Help me. Help all of us. 'Cause we're walkin' around under a cloud. Not knowin' about Joe is sappin' everybody's strength dead away.*

I went on outside, smoothin' my hair a little and tryin'

115

to look like I was doin' all right. It was Lizbeth, just like I'd thought. Harry came from the barn as she and Ben were getting out of the car.

"Is Pa doin' any better?" Lizbeth asked right away.

"No," I said. "An' I'm glad you come. If anybody can get him perked up, maybe it'll be you."

"I think the only one'd be Joe," Harry said under his breath. And I heard him, but I didn't look his way or say nothin' in response.

"Where's Mary Jane?" I asked.

"We stopped at the Worthams first," Lizbeth explained. "We figured she'd have a nicer visit over there if I have trouble with Pa. Mrs. Wortham's going to make cookies. I'm glad you sent Emmie."

I wasn't sure what Lizbeth meant to do, or if Pa'd respond to her any better than he did me. But she sure meant business. She headed in the house right away and started callin' for Pa before she ever got to his door.

Lizbeth's husband Ben hung back a little. "What Rorey said yesterday got us pretty concerned. I hope Lizbeth can talk some sense with your pa."

"I hope so too," I told him. "But the pastor already tried. Mr. Wortham too."

"I know. But maybe you're right that Lizbeth could perk him up. She'll stay if you need her to, to make it easier for the rest of you. Maybe he'd do better with her here."

"I don't understand it," Harry admitted. "He don't have no thought for us."

"He was the same way when Mama died," I said solemnly, my head almost reeling just thinkin' about those horrible days.

"But Joe ain't dead!" Harry protested. "They never said that!"

"I guess Pa don't know how to expect the positive," I said quietly, feelin' like a hypocrite. I was so much like

116

Pa in my own way. I wanted to believe as much as anybody that Joe was okay, hiding some place, or maybe in a hospital. I sure hoped he wasn't a prisoner. But I couldn't shake the feeling that he was lookin' down on us all the time now, watchin' and knowin' every move we made. And I didn't know how to explain somethin' like that except that he must be with Jesus.

I couldn't give any words to that kind of thinking, and it was botherin' me to have it occupying my brain, even after I tried shovin' it away.

"We can believe he'll come home," Harry maintained. "That's what the pastor said. We can keep on prayin' for him."

It was really good to hear words of faith from Harry. Especially since he'd never taken any interest in godly things before this. It used to be he'd sooner mock me over Bible words than ever repeat any for himself. And now here he stood, stronger than I was. So I agreed with him. What else could I do?

"We've got to keep prayin'," I said. "You're right. Can't listen to worryin' an' sad feelin's." I took a deep breath and followed Lizbeth inside. Harry and Ben didn't come. Maybe they didn't want any part of Pa's raging, and that was sensible enough. But I figured somebody oughta be close by, just in case Lizbeth needed a hand.

In the sitting room she called for Pa again, but he didn't bother to answer. So she walked right into the bedroom and plunked herself down on the edge of his bed.

"Good morning, Pa. Did you know it's almost ten o'clock?"

He turned his head a little and looked at her with a scowl. "What's it matter? There ain't no special doin's nowhere today."

"Would you go if there were?"

He started turnin' around from her again. "No."

117

"You've got company, Pa. You oughta get up."

"You ain't comp'ny. You're flesh and blood."

She sighed. "Fine. But Pa, layin' around isn't gonna help anything. Emmie and Bert and Harry need to see you up tryin' to take care of things, no matter how worried you are for Joe. They're pretty worried too."

"Then they can leave me alone," he grumped.

"Pa, you're not listenin' to me. They need your help."

"They don't need nothin'. Ain't none of you need nothin' from me! Get outta here."

Lizbeth looked up at me for just a minute. An' I remembered a time when I was a little kid and Mama got so mad that she threw a sack a' somethin' right at Pa's chest an' then shoved him clear outta the house. Right now Lizbeth was lookin' almost like Mama did then. She stood to her feet, took hold of the bedcovers with both her hands, and yanked them clear off the bed. Pa sat right up in his dirty old clothes, sputtering angry.

"What the blazes is got into you, girl!"

"It's almost ten o'clock," she answered him with a lot more calm than I expected. "I remember the times you got up with the chickens. Especially on good days. There's work to be done, that's what you told us. Rise and shine! Well, it's a good day, Pa, whether you want to see it or not. The sun is shinin'. The fields are waitin'. There's no sense at all you leavin' this whole farm on the boys."

"They ain't no little boys," he said. "And you don't live here no more. Go home."

"You can't chase me out," she told him. "I aim to see you shake off whatever it is that's got hold of you."

"Shut up."

She sat beside him again. "Things happen, Pa. And they don't just happen to you. Don't you think Rorey and Frank and Emmie and all the rest are hurtin' just as much as you are? Is it fair for you to lay here and make them face up to everythin' when you won't? Everybody's trying to do their part except you. Is it gonna help Joe any for you to lay here like you're half dead? Will it get him found any quicker?"

He looked miserable, and his voice was softer. "There ain't nothin' I can do, Lizbeth."

"There's plenty you can do. Right around you. You got your other kids. And the crops. 'Leven piglets and a calf too, I understand."

He shook his head. "Just go home."

She sighed again, looking awful sad. "I'm not leavin', Pa. I've seen you do so well in times that were hard. I know you were heartbroke when Mama died, but you came out of it. You've done so much, and this place is producin' more now, lookin' better than ever. You're a good man, Pa. You've managed all these years. I know it hurts." She took his hand. "Thinkin' 'bout Joe and what he might be going through makes me kind of sick inside too. But we've got to go on with things. Do you think he'd want you givin' up, when we don't even know what happened?"

Pa turned his eyes in my direction. "You asked her to come out here an' get after me, didn't you?"

"No, sir," I told him. "But she's right what she's sayin'. Every bit."

He looked at her and then at me and shook his head again. "There's somethin' neither one a' you unnerstands," he said real slow. "Things wasn't s'posed to be like this. I had it worked out. But ever'thin's fallin' apart, and it's gonna get worse, that's all I can figure."

"You had what worked out?" Lizbeth asked.

"What come next. I had it all figured when Joe went in the service. By the time he come home, I'd have more'n half my kids growed an' on their own. But he stayed longer, an' Kirk and Willy's gone too, an' I never planned on that." He stopped and took a deep breath, looking over to the wall with something strange in his eyes. "War's come up, an' now Joe ain't comin'. It ain't gonna be like I thought. An' I still got half at home."

"What are you sayin', Pa?" Lizbeth asked.

I was glad it was her asking the questions. I couldn't have managed to. I was feelin' bitter hurt inside for some reason, knowin' that whatever Pa said next was gonna hit at us.

"Pa?" Lizbeth prompted when he didn't answer right away. "What are you tellin' us?"

"I wanted to be done by now," he said. "I was thinkin' Kirk an' Willy'd marry like you an' Sam. Rorey too, way before now. And Frank'd stay over there with Mr. Wortham. Only thing that makes sense for him. But now all I got's him here with the kids, when I was lookin' for Joe to come back an' take over the farm . . ."

He just stopped, like he couldn't go on.

"You got no call to doubt Frank," Lizbeth maintained. "But all of the rest of that can still happen."

I had an awful feelin' in the pit of my stomach. There was more to what he was saying. "What do you mean?" I dared ask him. "About wantin' to be done?"

He looked at me. He swallowed kind of hard and seemed almost scared all of a sudden. "I kinda made a deal," he said with his voice soundin' shaky. "'Least I thought I did. I kinda made a deal with God after your mama died and Mr. Wortham tol' me I had to consider you young'uns. I had to be here for you."

"What kind of deal?" I pressed him further.

"I tol' the good Lord I'd stick 'round long enough to see over half a' you big 'nough to get your own life, you know. Then you'd be so used to standin' on your own you could see to the rest an' you wouldn't need me no more. I figured one of the boys'd take on the farm for me. I figured it'd be Joe. But some of you been slow to move on. An' the army, that jus' changes ever'thin'. It weren't no part of the deal to be buryin' none of you."

"Pa?" Lizbeth looked shaken. "All these years you've been plannin' on leavin'?"

"Oh, girl," he moaned. "What diff'rence does it make? You got one brother gone already. Kirk and Willy, they're next. They ain't comin' home. I been hearin' it in my head for days. They ain't comin' home."

"Pa!" Lizbeth exclaimed. "That's the devil talking! That's fears takin' hold of you. There's no reason to think—"

"God's got all mad at me 'bout it, that's what it is," he said, staring down at the torn sheet underneath him. "God's maybe done decided you're all better off with your mama."

"That's crazy talk." I didn't mean to say it out loud. It just come out before I could stop it. Lizbeth looked up at me and didn't answer my words, but I could see in her eyes that she was thinkin' the same thing. It wasn't just Pa drinkin' or feelin' lazy sometimes that was the problem now. Nor even bein' fretful over Joe. There was something bad wrong with his thinkin'. Maybe there had been for a long time and we just didn't know. But it was scary to see it lookin' at me out his eyes. He weren't right, and it went past the worry. Lizbeth knew it too.

"Pa, there's no sense at all talking like this," she said. "Nobody's died, and there's no use expectin' that anybody will. God is with Joe, wherever he is. And with Kirk and Willy too. They're gonna make you proud. They're heroes already, and they'll come home and get married and give you loads of grandchildren."

Pa didn't even seem to hear her. "I still got five home. Half. Unless I figure Frank to be on his own, but I don't know what he is. If I go now, what's gonna happen? Are you an' Ben gonna move out here? Or Sam? You got your own places already. Frank ain't gonna take this place on.

He can't. He does all right with the wood, but he's got his head in the clouds."

"Pa," Lizbeth kept trying to reason. "We don't have to decide the future—"

"I ain't talkin' 'bout the future, girl! Are you gonna be the one seein' 'bout Emmie and Harry and Bert, till they're outta school an' workin' or somethin'? An' Rorey, till she's married? Sam's got five in his own family to think about now. You gonna be the one to take on this farm an' the kids? Are you? I promised God I wouldn't leave it all on the Worthams! I swore I wouldn't! But tarnation! It ain't nothin' to be left on Franky an' Rorey! Who else I got?"

"Pa!" Lizbeth looked scared. "You're not goin' anywhere! You got no reason to talk like this—"

Before we could realize what he was doing, he shoved her away. Not hard, but it was a shock just the same. And I reached to help her steady herself.

"Franky," she said stiffly. "Go tell Harry to fetch Mr. Wortham. He's got the best sense of anybody I know talking to Pa. He'll know what to do."

More than anything else, *her* not knowing what to do shook me terrible. I'd always had faith in my big sister. Lizbeth held us together in rough times. Lizbeth had always known what to do.

I hurried outside, feeling as miserable as Pa looked. "Harry," I called. "Lizbeth wants you to go ask Mr. Wortham to come an' talk to Pa."

"How come?" he asked immediately. "What's wrong?"

He must have thought like me that Lizbeth could surely handle this. I shook my head. "Pa's thinkin' muddle-headed, I don't know. Just go on, okay? Don't tell Emmie or Bert much a' nothin'."

"I don't need Sam Wortham over here!" we heard Pa screamin' at Lizbeth inside the house. "I'm doin' just fine!"

122

Harry looked at me questioningly.

"Go on," I told him. "Lizbeth says go."

He went. And I stood, feeling a little shaky. It was bad enough that Pa was expectin' trouble for Willy and Kirk as much as Joe. But besides that, he had talked like he didn't expect to be here much longer, or maybe was choosing not to be. Was he thinkin' on running off? Or dying?

Lizbeth came out and told Ben and me that Pa was getting dressed. She looked kind of pale. She knew as well as I did that he'd confessed something to us that he hadn't really meant to share, and never would have if he weren't feelin' so low. But now what? Here he was gettin' up, just like we'd wanted. Maybe he'd eat and go about his farm work as though everything was all right. But was he really different? What was he thinking to do?

It scared me, even though I was tryin' to strengthen myself with the Scripture that says "God has not given us a spirit of fear, but of power, and of love, and of a sound mind." That could apply to my pa as much as anyone, if he believed it. But I didn't know where he stood. And I knew if he wanted to bad enough, he could hide. His drinking. His thinking. Maybe even some careless plans.

"Lizbeth," I said, "I'm glad he's up, but I don't think it's settled."

"I know." She reached for Ben's hand. "Honey, I'll have to stay a while. Even with you working Monday, I need to be here to make sure Pa don't take off and do somethin' stupid."

He nodded and then put his arms around her. Ben was a good fellow. And it was a good relief to have them stay. I could hear Pa in the sitting room of the house now, muttering somethin'.

*God Almighty,* I prayed. *What kind of things have we got in store?*

# 15

## Sarah

I was kneading bread dough when Harry came to get Daddy. Nobody was sure what was going to happen. Daddy went and talked to Mr. Hammond, but he didn't come back for hours. The regular baking got done and then dinner too. Katie and I went outside to weed the garden while Mom finished up the cookies with Emmie and Mary Jane. After a while Emmie came to help us. She told us she knew her pa was sick because he'd yelled at her that morning just for bringing him breakfast and well people don't do that. Bert looked over at us from where he'd been splitting kindling by the back door, and stopped to join us for a while.

"Frances Mueller says bad things happen in threes," he said.

"That's just superstition," Katie answered.

"But what if it's true? What if the news about Joe is jus' the beginnin'?"

Looking at him, I knew he was already scared. I tried to think what the preacher might tell him. "Numbers don't matter," I said. "The devil brings whatever bad he can, and we just make his job easier if we expect it. We're supposed to look on the bright side of things and expect good because God sends his angels around those who believe."

Katie nodded her approval as she pulled a handful of henbit and threw it in the pile behind her. Of course I knew that my parents would approve of such words too. But I felt a little funny inside when I said them. I guess because there was a tiny seed of doubt taking root in me. Earl Wilkins had believed. I knew that very well. And Earl Wilkins was dead.

I didn't like such thoughts. I even felt guilty, but I wasn't sure what I could do about it. I still believed in God, but it seemed to me that faith would be much easier if godly people were blessed all the time and ungodly people had trouble till they decided to mend their ways. But life wasn't like that. Good people still went through plenty of trouble.

I sighed and yanked at a dandelion. It snapped off, leaving the root in the ground. And it was almost like a message. *That's just like me,* I thought. *I know how to seem all right on the surface. But down underneath I've still got questions that won't go away.*

I heard the back door, and little Mary Jane ran out to us all excited. She was having the time of her life staying with us today. She didn't have an inkling that everybody was feeling sad and worried for her Uncle Joe and bothered for her grandfather's sake. She was full of cookies and fun and didn't have a care in this world.

Mary Jane went bouncing around the garden and then stopped to stare in wonder at a bug crawling on a little spinach leaf. I remembered that I'd liked critters too when I was little. And I usually liked little kids and their boundless curiosity. But right then, I didn't feel like watching her. I don't know why, but her joyful ignorance of our problems made me uncomfortable. "Maybe I'd

125

better go help Mom with something," I said, looking over at Katie. "Do you know what she's planning for supper?"

"No. Do you suppose Lizbeth and Ben'll be over by then?"

"Maybe not to eat. But they'll be back for Mary Jane before it gets late."

Evening came, and Ben and Lizbeth weren't there for supper. Dad wasn't back, either. But he and Ben came through the timber together a little while after our supper, and neither of them said there was anything wrong. Mary Jane went running for Ben like she hadn't seen him in a month.

"Daddy! Daddy!"

Ben laughed and picked her up.

"I was just coming to find out if you wanted to go over to your mama and Uncle Frank," Ben told her. "And Grandpa too."

"Yeah!" Mary Jane squealed.

"Bert and Emmie," Ben called. "Lizbeth said you might as well come too, so you can get settled in and ready for church in the morning."

Bert looked skeptical. "Did Pa say to come back?"

Ben shook his head. "He didn't really say. But you're used to listening to Lizbeth, aren't you? She said you might as well be home. Come on."

They all went down the path through the timber toward the Hammond farm. I watched them for a while. Mary Jane was bouncing on her daddy's shoulders and waving her arms like she was directing the trees in glorious song. I wished I could be more like her. I suppose I was odd in that way, when so many people my age were glad to be nearly grown, and wishing they were even older. But I was in no hurry. Better to be a kid as long as possible, I thought. When you're little, people

126

don't wonder at you if you cry. And the world is still your great big plaything.

I sighed, and turned my attention to the Saturday night bathing. At almost seventeen, I was too old to act like a child. There was a war going on. The world wasn't playing anymore.

It was hard for me to sleep that night. I guess I was thinking too much. I wondered how Mom and Dad would react if it were Robert that was missing. And how I'd react. And then, after those notions drove me near to tears, I wondered how Mr. Hammond would react if they never did find Joe. Or if he died. My stomach got to feeling sour, but I didn't get up or tell anybody about it. I just tried to pray, the best that I could. But I couldn't put words together the way the pastor did. Or Frank. Or Rachel. Finally I went to sleep with Rachel's prayer still on my mind. *God give us peace in this time of being apart, make us stronger . . .*

In the morning we got around for church a little earlier than usual. Oftentimes, Hammonds got to church on their own, so we usually drove straight to town without them if they didn't come by early for a ride. But that day, Dad drove over to the Hammond farm and told us all to wait. The kids were ready. Lizbeth and Mary Jane were ready. But Dad wouldn't leave until Mr. Hammond came out to go to church too. We waited quite a while.

"He promised me, Julia," Dad told Mom. And then he jumped out of the truck to go inside. Frank and Ben must have been in the house too. I didn't know what to expect. So I guess everybody was relieved when Mr. Hammond finally came out in Sunday clothes, looking cleaner than I'd seen him in a long time. That must have been Lizbeth's doing. None of the rest of the kids had been able to persuade him in much of anything.

Dad wanted him up front in our truck, to talk to him

127

a little. Rorey and Emma Grace climbed in the car with Lizbeth, Ben, and Mary Jane. The rest of us were in the back of our truck, even Mom. She looked so pretty in her calico dress with her hair all pinned up. I wished I could tell what she was thinking.

Mr. Hammond seemed mostly normal at church, and everybody else was trying to act like normal too. I kept thinking about Robert's letter to me, and especially Rachel's prayer again: "... *that God give us peace in this time of being apart, make us stronger, and give us a greater understanding of himself."*

Rachel was pretty wise. I wasn't surprised that Robert would think she might relate well to Frank. I'd thought him wise too, ever since the day of the accident so long ago when his leg got broken. He'd been just a little boy trying to tell my Uncle Edward about the love of Jesus. And then the accident happened. Uncle Edward didn't listen real well back then, but he respected Franky's bravery and he remembered. He'd come to God since then, partly because of the things Frank had said.

I looked at the next pew, where Frank and his brothers were sitting across the aisle from us. All of their hair looked a little too long, and Frank especially looked so tired. I could tell it in his eyes. Dad asked the church again to pray for Joe, and when he did, Frank bowed his head and started to cry. My stomach got sour like last night, and I almost couldn't stand to just sit there. Frank hadn't cried on the day they got the letter, or in all the time since then, so far as I knew. Seeing him do it now made me want to cry too. I remembered Robert telling me that I should help Frank if I got the chance, but I didn't know how.

The whole church prayed for Joe. And that felt good in a way, but I could tell it didn't take away Frank's hurt. I looked at Mr. Hammond, and he was staring down at his lap. He didn't even lift his head when the prayer was done. Lizbeth put her hand in his, but he didn't look up at her or move at all.

I wondered what could cause a soldier to go missing. Dad said some men had died on the last day that Joe was accounted for. There was probably a lot of shooting, but I couldn't picture Joe running from it. Especially not since he had men under him.

*Where is he, God? What's happened to him?*

For some reason I kept thinking of Rachel's prayer again. *"God, give us peace in this time of being apart."*

We needed the peace, all right. I needed peace not to worry about Robert. But much more than that, the Hammonds needed peace about Joe. And Joe, wherever he was, however he was, needed peace too. But I knew only God could give us that kind of peace in uncertainty. I took a deep breath and turned my eyes to Pastor Jones at the front of the church. He was just starting to read from the Gospel of Matthew:

"Come unto me, all ye that labor and are heavy laden, and I will give you rest."

I didn't remember very much of what else he said, because thoughts of my own kept crowding my mind. *"Make us stronger,"* Rachel had written. And that part of her prayer was almost a surprise. Robert was so strong already. A sturdy young man who could do hours of hard work without complaint. And while Rachel herself was much daintier, she was strong in what my mother would call womanly ways. She could cook and can, sew, crochet, and make her own soap and candles. I once saw a quilt she'd made, and I was impressed that somebody younger than my mother could do such nice work. My quilting left much to be desired. But more than all that, Rachel was strong in godly things. She believed in prayer. But she'd prayed to be even stronger.

She'd prayed for God to give us a greater understanding of himself. Sitting there in church with a Bible on my lap and the preacher's words as a soft backdrop to my thinking, I had to admit that I wasn't sure whether what she'd written was even possible. Could we understand God better? He was almost incomprehensible. And invisible. Good thing he'd given us the Bible. And church. And people like my parents.

I remembered professing my belief when I was twelve and being baptized by the pastor in our farm pond. But things hadn't really changed since then. I had the same feelings about God, the same understanding, as I'd had then. I didn't have a greater understanding. Was I supposed to?

I'd always thought that with God it was just a matter of believing or not believing. And I definitely believed. So everything was settled. I'd keep coming to church and go to heaven when I died. But I'd never thought it through like this before, that maybe there was more to learn, more to think about and hold on to, about God. I talked about God, I mentioned him in letters, and I said my prayers before bed like everybody else. But was I missing something that Rachel knew about? And that Robert figured Frank must know about too?

I tried to turn my mind to what the preacher was saying then. Maybe that was part of the trouble—that I let my thoughts roam around so much when I was supposed to be listening. I didn't think I could ask the preacher about this. Maybe I could ask Mom or Dad. I glanced over at Frank again, and he still looked a little teary-eyed. But there was no question that his attention was on the pastor. Just like always, he was taking in every word. I tried to. But after a while, without really meaning to, I started thinking of something else again, about what I might put in my next letter to my brother:

*Do you think God uses bad times to make us think more about him? It's hard not to worry about Joe, and*

130

*even about you and Kirk and Willy just because you're not
here with us. But at the same time, I can't stop thinking
about the prayer Rachel wrote, for us to become stronger
and understand God better. I wish I knew how that was
possible. Do you think I should ask her? Or maybe ask
Frank?*

At the end of the service, Frank went up to the altar
even though there hadn't been a call. He knelt down alone
and stayed there a very long time. Nobody seemed to
know quite what to do. Pastor Jones went over to him
for a little while, but not for long. I heard the pastor
tell my father that Frank had some things he wanted to
set before God on his own. Dad nodded like that was
something he understood well enough. But it made me
wonder all the more.

Before we left the church that day, Rachel Gray came
up to hug every one of us Worthams and Hammonds.
She wasn't the only one, but it seemed extra important
to me that she would do it.

"Thanks for writing to Robert," I told her.

"I'm glad to," she answered me. "I'm glad you don't
mind."

I almost told her there was no way I could really mind.
But instead of saying the words, I looked into her pretty
face for a minute and remembered my brother's eyes
when he danced with her. "You really like him, don't
you?"

"I really do."

"I'm glad," I told her. "Because I think he loves you."

She smiled, just a soft little smile. "He told me he
did."

"I'm glad," I said again, feeling kind of foolish and
unable to ask her if she loved him too. But there really
was no need to ask.

She hugged me again, and I told her he'd written to

131

me about her prayer and that I was grateful for it. She looked like she might cry.

"Oh, Sarah. I've been praying that we could be close! I've been thinking the way we both love Robert, it makes us like family already."

From that moment, I thought of Rachel the same as a sister. And I felt honored that she would want it so because she seemed something like Frank—an ordinary person full of human foibles but at the same time somehow special. Because of God. Or maybe more precisely, because of how important they made God in their lives.

Lizbeth stayed that next week with her father, and Ben came out every night after work. We had Mary Jane with us the first day because Mr. Hammond was so grouchy that Lizbeth didn't want her with him. But after that they said he did better.

I helped Mom plant beans and move the volunteer tomatoes into a row. The whole time I kept thinking of Joe and then of Robert, Willy, and Kirk. I wished the war had never started. I wished the Germans and the Japanese would leave the rest of the world alone. If there'd been no foreign threat, maybe Joe wouldn't have chosen to stay in the service so long. Maybe Kirk wouldn't have been drafted. And surely Robert and Willy wouldn't have gone. It wasn't fair for evil men half a world away to step into our lives and rearrange our futures.

Such thinking almost made me mad, but then I thought of Franky, alone at the altar on Sunday.

*"Help him if you can, Sis,"* Robert had written.

I decided I didn't have near as much right to be angry as Frank did. With three brothers away and one of them missing, plus his father not doing so well, it was a lot for him to carry. Seemed like I hardly saw him anymore when he wasn't working, too hard maybe, at somebody's order or the business of the farm. He didn't eat with us like he used to. He either went home to check on his father and eat over there, or he skipped eating altogether to keep right on working. Dad said Frank was going at it a little too hard and getting even thinner than he was before. He tried to get him to take a day off or to take it a little easy, but Frank said that keeping going was all he knew to do.

I wished I knew whether Frank had really wanted to go into the service or if he had only been willing because of the sense of duty that always kept him doing right. I wished I knew if he was really angry, as I could imagine myself being in his place.

I got really bothered at Frank's father when Bert told me he'd scolded Frank up one side and down the other the night before. And only for spending extra time checking the calf's legs when he hadn't fed the pigs yet. What difference did it make? Their pa was leaving so much on Frank's shoulders, and giving him grief to boot! No wonder Robert had been concerned. He knew what Mr. Hammond was like. Mr. Hammond never gave Frank the benefit of the doubt about anything. It wasn't fair when Frank always tried so hard.

Once, a couple of years ago, Robert had told me he wouldn't be surprised if one of these days Frank hauled off and busted his pa in the mouth over all the bad talk he gave him. But I knew it would never happen. I could see something churning in Frank's eyes every once in a while, but whatever it was never broke the surface. He was meek, which was a good thing according to our pastor, but it left him enduring too much, I thought. There'd been times when I wished Frank would go ahead and bust somebody good, maybe one of his brothers or one of the Turrey boys, just to get them to leave him alone.

But nobody really gave Frank a hard time now except his pa. Mostly because we didn't see other folks much except at church on Sunday. And also because everybody around knew about Joe, so the whole Hammond family was gaining more prayers and consideration than usual.

I wished I knew what Robert thought I could do to help Frank. I sure didn't know a way except praying for him. But that seemed almost out of place. Frank was the one who knew how to pray, and knew when he belonged at the altar even when nobody else was stepping forward. He knew more Scriptures in his head than anybody else around, at least it seemed that way.

It was strange that Robert would ask *me* to help Frank. My mom and dad were the ones who had been closest to Frank ever since we were little. I guess they understood him. It seemed like he'd been talking to them like he was another grown-up all the time we'd known him. But I knew he didn't talk about everything. Not much about his pa. Even less about himself.

Patting the dirt close around a little tomato plant, I sighed. *Lord, what Frank needs now is the same as everybody else. Some word from Joe. And Kirk, now, too. It's been so long since we heard from him.*

"Sarah," Mom suddenly called to me from across the garden. "I'm going to cut the rest of that coffee cake and pour everybody some tea. Why don't you go ask Frank if he'll join us?"

Her request almost made me tremble inside. I didn't know how to talk to Frank right now. I didn't know what in the world I would say.

"Tell him I said he needs to come and sit a while," she continued, as if she'd heard my thoughts.

"Where is he?"

"He was going to cut posts. By the east field. If any of the rest are over there, tell them to come too."

I think she knew they weren't, or she wouldn't have put it quite that way. If my father weren't working on the

134

tractor, he might have been over there with Frank, or at least checking on him. Harry was doing some work for the Posts, so he wouldn't be back till almost sundown. I didn't know what Bert was doing today. Or their pa, either, but I wouldn't have been surprised if it wasn't much. Not even Lizbeth could motivate Mr. Hammond to do much more than get out of bed.

I walked across the yard, wondering what it would have been like to have been born a Hammond. Would I be like Rorey, tempestuous and full of herself? Or more like Lizbeth, who kind of acted like everybody's mother? Or maybe like Emmie, who was quiet and insecure but at the same time full of questions and determination.

Even stranger considerations filled my head then. What would the Hammonds be like if we'd never moved here, if we'd never left Pennsylvania, or if Mrs. Graham had refused to let us stay? I didn't think Mr. Hammond could have raised the kids without his wife. Robert told me once that Mr. Hammond had come real close to killing himself after she died. I didn't know how he knew that, or even if it was true, but I could imagine him gone away, and all the kids split up to whoever would take them. That was an awful picture. Emmie hardly knowing her family, Harry and Bert raised up apart from each other and the farm, and us not knowing any of them.

And then my thoughts settled on Frank again. He'd been a scrawny kid when we met him, not any bigger than I was, even though he was older. Dirty and lost-looking, with those odd silvery eyes that made some people stare and other people look away. I couldn't picture what the world would be like for Frank without my parents. It made me a little mad to find my thoughts so similar to the kind of things Mr. Hammond said sometimes. But I didn't mean it the same way. Not that Frank would be nothing without my folks' help. Just that things would've been so much harder for him. So much lonelier.

I started praying as I walked along the edge of the timber. *Lord, if there's a way I can do what Robert asked and help Frank somehow, show me.*

I thought of the time I'd followed him into the timber after the barn fire. The Hammonds had lost so much, and Frank's pa came down on him hard, blaming him for the fire when it hadn't been his fault at all. I'd never talked to Frank alone before that. I'd never seen him the way he'd looked then. I guessed it was the only time I'd ever seen him angry. But more than that, hurt. He'd seemed broken apart because he couldn't gain something I'd always had without trying. A father's trust. A sense of belonging in your own family. A future, even, unhampered by people's doubts.

Rorey said everybody felt sorry for Franky. Everybody babied him. But I didn't know how she could be so blind. I didn't remember anybody ever babying Franky, and he wouldn't have let them if they tried. All he wanted was to be accepted just like everybody else, not shoved aside or put down for being himself.

It occurred to me that I'd thought of him as "Franky" again. Maybe because I was thinking about the past. But I hadn't called him Franky since that brief talk in the timber when I'd told him I believed him and decided he was one of the bravest people I knew. Everybody else usually called him Franky. Even my mother. But not me. To my mind, he was already acting grown more than three years ago. He was even more grown now. And acting like more of a father to his younger brothers and sisters than their own father did, whether Rorey liked it or not.

I could hear the ax hitting against wood before I got close. I tried calling out, but he didn't answer. I wondered if he was thinking about Beethoven again, or somebody else that inspired him. Pretty soon I could see him through the trees. He was cutting posts out of hedge

136

wood. He'd downed a tree and was whacking off the side branches. Bright yellow wood chips went flying.

"Frank?"

He didn't turn his head, and I thought of the way Harry might try to get Frank's attention. He'd probably throw an acorn or something, hit him with it on purpose. I didn't want to do that, but I did want him to stop. He was glistening wet with sweat, with his shirt off and tossed aside and his hair stuck to his forehead. He looked tuckered out, but he was still swinging the ax, whacking on that tree for all he was worth. Behind him, against a bigger tree, were three stacks of wood sorted by size. One for fence posts. And he probably had something in mind for the other two besides firewood, but I wasn't sure.

"Frank!"

Another whack.

"Frank!"

I hollered two or three more times while he kept on working away. Then maybe I was finally loud enough, or whatever train of thought he'd had was broken. He spun around, his ax still in hand, and looked at me with his silvery eyes full of worries.

"Sarah Jean? What's wrong?"

"Nothing's wrong," I said, suddenly needing to take a breath. "Mom just sent me to tell you to come sit a while. She thinks you need a break. She's cutting coffee cake and pouring you a glass of tea."

He smiled, just a little, quick as light. "Tell her thanks, but I'm fine. I wanna finish this so I can put new posts on the west side of our pasture. They's too far apart, and some of 'em's weak. We've had cows out twice, an' I don't want it happenin' again."

Frank was the only one besides my mother that ever called me Sarah Jean. He'd been doing that for a long time, and it didn't even bother me. "You know my mom," I told him. "If you don't come when she thinks you should, she might walk out here herself to persuade you. Besides, you look hot."

"Guess I worked up a sweat." He took two steps and picked up his shirt.

Frank was really slim. But he wasn't scrawny anymore. He had muscles like my dad's. Like Robert's. It was from all the farm work. I turned my eyes to his stack of fence posts.

"Do you have enough?" I asked him.

"Not quite."

"Maybe after some tea, I can help."

"This ain't a job for a lady."

I looked up. He was putting on his shirt.

"Why not?" I asked him. "I could bring a saw of Dad's from the wood shop and saw off the little branches from the pieces you want. Work goes faster with two sets of hands."

He looked at me like he was studying on it for a minute. His hair was so damp it looked black, and he ran his fingers through it without thinking and got it standing up a little in front with pieces of wood chip here and there. "Why would you want to cut wood out here in the timber?"

"Just to help. Doesn't everybody try to do whatever needs to be done?"

He was staring at me kind of funny. "Well, no. I don't guess everybody does. Not all the time, at least."

"You know what I mean. It looks like you could use a hand."

"I coulda went an' got Bert."

"But you didn't."

"Sometimes I like workin' alone. Good for thinkin', you know?"

"Are you going to come and take a break?"

He didn't answer me. I saw his eyes wander out across

the field. "Do you ever need time just to think, Sarah Jean?"

"I guess everybody does. What are you thinking about?"

"Something Joe told me once. That the day'd come when we'd be without our pa, an' it'd be easy for all of us to go our own ways. He said me an' him oughta make sure everybody keeps gettin' together."

His eyes were suddenly moist, and it made my heart hurt for him. "Oh, Frank. That's a lot of years away."

"Is it?"

I couldn't answer him. I wasn't sure what he was afraid of. I wasn't sure I could handle it if I did know. "Maybe we should go to the house."

"Will you promise me somethin', Sarah Jean?"

My shoulders were suddenly tense. I hardly knew what to expect. "If I can. What do you mean?"

"No matter what happens, even years from now when we don't know where life's gonna end up puttin' us, I want you to still be my friend just as much as you was three years ago when I needed somebody to believe me. Do you remember that? When you said you believed me about the fire?"

"I—I wasn't the only one. My parents believed you too."

"They always think good of me. Everybody thinks I wouldn't amount to nothin' without them."

My heart was pounding, trying to comprehend why he was talking this way. "That's stupid. You know that. Your talent didn't come from my parents."

He sighed. "We're gonna have hard times, Sarah. I couldn't say that to nobody else. I don't like talkin' negative. I don't like thinkin' it. But I thought maybe you'd understand if I feel like I gotta put it in words. You was always my friend before. If you don't mind, I think I'm gonna need that again."

He turned away, and I knew it was because it was hard for him to let me see the hurt in his eyes. I stood for a minute, just looking at his back, wondering what in the world he was trying to tell me. "I'll always be your friend, Frank. I promise."

"Do you think much on Joe?"

"Sure. I can't help it."

He turned and looked at me but then lowered his eyes. "I think he's gone. I feel like he's standin' in the clouds, hopin' I understand what a lot I got to do to hold things together."

I swallowed hard but couldn't answer. For Frank to admit something like that to me was a complete surprise.

"I'm afraid Pa's gonna come apart, do you know what I mean?"

"I—I think so."

"I'm scared, Sarah. I don't know when I ever been so scared."

He stood looking almost trembly. I wasn't sure what to do or what to say. He was baring his heart to me, his worries, in a way I never would have expected. Suddenly I couldn't help it. My eyes filled with tears. "I'm scared too."

His whole face changed. "What about?"

"I'm scared you might be right. About Joe. And your pa too, and what that might mean for everybody. I'm scared something's going to happen to Robert . . ."

I couldn't go on. The tears got in the way, and I was feeling awfully ashamed. There was no reason for this. That I should come out here and let myself get all weepy over things that might not even happen.

Frank surprised me then. "Robert's going to be all right. Let's go back to the house, okay?"

I just stared. "I don't understand you. How can you

140

be so sure, when just a minute ago you were all upset about Joe and your pa?"

"I don't know. I guess I got faith when it comes to Robert."

"But not your family?"

"Pa's got some problems. I don't know what kinda sick he is. But he's not gonna get better without wantin' to, an' I don't see much a' that in him. I hope I'm real wrong about Joe. But when I pray on it, it seems like the only peace I feel is when I picture him with Mama. I think he's gone. And I think Pa's gonna let the next piece a' bad news tear him away."

I wanted to tell him we shouldn't worry like this, that maybe it was a mistake to give voice to our fears. But I knew Frank had been carrying this burden, probably trying to rid his mind of it. Maybe talking it out was the only way to do that. But what surprised me most was that he was telling me, not my mother or father.

"I don't know what's gonna happen," he confessed. "I don't know how it'll be with Bert and Emmie . . ."

"We'll help," I told him. "No matter what happens, we'll help."

He started walking toward the house, and I stayed beside him.

"I think it'll be all right," I said. "Maybe Joe'll get home okay. And your pa'll decide to pick himself up and go on all right, like he did after your mother died."

He was quiet for a minute, but then he sighed. "Pa didn't decide to be all right back then, Sarah Jean. He just decided to bide his time."

We kept on walking to the house. His words were a heavy load for my mind to carry, and despite wishing I had something cheerful to say, I couldn't answer him a word.

# 16

## *Julia*

I almost went looking for Sarah and Frank, they were such a long time getting back to the house. Maybe Frank had decided to cut hedge trees a little farther out than what I'd told Sarah.

They were very quiet when they came in for tea. Frank drank his practically in one gulp and finished the coffee cake just as fast. I refilled his glass and would have given him another piece of cake too, but he turned it down.

"I'll get the saw," Sarah suddenly said. "And a pair of work gloves."

Frank saw my surprise at her words and shook his head. "You oughta stay here. Help your mama with things. I'm doin' fine at it."

But Sarah didn't give up easily. "Mom, I was planning to help Frank with the rest of the posts. Is that all right?"

It was certainly unexpected. With boys around much of the time, Sarah had never had to do much wood cutting of any kind, nor cared to. I looked at them both, wondering what might have transpired between them. "I've got Katie here, honey," I said after a moment's thought. "If you want to help Frank, it's all right."

"Good." She nodded. "He'll get done faster that way."

Frank didn't say anything one way or the other. But when he got up from the table he surprised me too, by giving me a hug. "Thanks, Mrs. Wortham."

Suddenly I wasn't sure if he meant for the tea and cake, or for Sarah. He headed over to get his father's wagon to haul the posts. Sarah went with him. And I stood for a minute, watching them go, still not sure what to think.

Mail usually came in the late afternoon, so after a while I was going to send Katie to check the box down the lane. But before I did, I heard an automobile coming and looked out to see the postman driving right up to our house. He honked the horn, and I ran outside.

"Thought you wouldn't want to wait to see this," he said as soon as I got close enough. "You haven't had one of these for a while."

I was tense, just hearing his words. *Oh, precious Lord,* I prayed. *Let it be a letter from Joe telling us he's all right.* Mr. Tanner handed me the envelope, and I looked down at the return address before I could tell him a word.

It was from Kirk. I took a long, deep breath. "Thank you. Thank you so much. We've been waiting to hear from him."

"I thought you surely were. God bless you, now." With another toot of his horn, he wheeled his mail car around and headed away again down our lane.

"Thank you, Lord," I whispered with my heart pounding. "At least Kirk's all right."

I opened the envelope before I even took a step. Kirk's letter was long, rambling, and included an apology for not writing sooner. He'd not seen any combat, but he said he knew he would before the summer was out. He sounded terribly lonely, but he was all right. And there was no indication in his letter that he knew anything at all about Joe.

I let the rest of my plans for the afternoon go and sat down and wrote to Kirk everything we knew, everything about how his family was doing, and what a relief it was to hear from him again. I tried to sound as positive as possible, closing the letter with a Scripture verse. When I was finished with that, I packaged another box of cookies to send with the letter and prayed that the gesture would cheer him up.

Before I started supper I heard another car on our lane. We weren't expecting anyone. Katie called to me that it was Sam Hammond and his family, but I would have known that before long anyway. Before they were stopped, I could hear Georgie yelling for me, even though I was still inside.

"Missus! Missus!"

I went out to meet them, wondering what had brought them out here on a week night. They used to come once in a while, close to supper when they knew I'd feed them. But they were getting along a little better now than they were, and they generally tried to let me know in advance when they were coming.

Right away, Thelma asked Katie if she wouldn't mind playing with the kids outside for a few minutes. Sam came along with Thelma and me to the house. He was holding seven-month-old Dorothy, and he was all smiles. I knew they had something to tell me. I even thought I knew what it was. Sam was obviously pleased as punch, but I felt a little uneasy.

"Mrs. Wortham," Thelma began. "After my mother, we wanted you to be the first to know that we's expectin' another baby."

"Oh." I tried to smile and wasn't quite sure I'd succeeded. "My! Congratulations. Do you know when?"

"Maybe around Thanksgiving. We're not altogether sure."

"Ain't it great?" Sam asked me. "Number five already."

Suddenly I wondered if George Hammond had ever been as enthusiastic as a young father. I'd never seen much of it from him. Even when his wife was alive. But then he hadn't really seemed young like Sam any of the time I'd known him. "I suppose you have names all picked out?" I asked.

"Henry, if it's a boy," Sam answered immediately. "Irma Lee if it's a girl."

"You haven't told your father yet?"

"No, we're going there next."

I suppose it was natural, to a certain extent, that they would bring the news here first. I'd been the one to deliver Rosemary, and I'd helped with both Albert and Dorothy. But not because I especially liked that kind of thing.

"Mrs. Wortham, I don't suppose it'll be no surprise that we want to have this one at home like the last ones," Thelma told me. "And my mama would be more'n happy to have your help again too."

"I've heard that Dr. Clyne in Mcleansboro is very knowledgeable with this sort of thing," I offered.

But Thelma shook her head. "Mama raised me with the understandin' that women you trust make the best midwives and a baby oughta be born in the comforts of home."

I didn't argue, but there was plenty I could have said. It certainly wasn't comfortable for me, home or not, to have a part in birthing babies. Thelma's mother loved it, but I didn't intend to put my hands to that business again unless necessity demanded it. I would let them know that soon enough. But this wasn't the right time. "Have you been feeling all right?"

145

"Oh, yes," Thelma answered cheerfully. "But then I usually do, this early on. Only one I was really sick with was Albert."

Sam's face changed suddenly. "I've been meaning to ask you about that, Mrs. Wortham."

"About what?"

"Albert. Do you remember my pa saying that Mama was real sick when she was carrying Franky?"

"I think it was Rorey who told us that, but what does it have to do with Albert?"

Sam looked down at baby Dorothy for a minute, and when he raised his eyes he looked nervous over the subject. "I been wonderin', Mrs. Wortham. Franky's a little different. Do you think Albert's gonna be different too? I mean, do you think he might have a little trouble—"

I interrupted him right there. "I was very sick early on with both Robert and Sarah. And they're fine. As far as I'm concerned, Franky's fine too. There's no reason at all for you to expect trouble for Albert."

"But he's already different," Sam persisted. "Surely you've noticed. He ain't never been one to cry. And he still don't say a solitary word."

"Robert was slow to talk too," I said quickly. "That doesn't mean anything at Albert's age."

"Georgie and Rosemary were talkin' up a storm by now," Thelma said with a worried sigh.

"Maybe he's having trouble getting a word in edgewise," I suggested.

Sam laughed a little. "Maybe so. It is a little noisy around our place."

I invited them to stay for supper, and even to fetch George and the rest for supper too. I had Kirk's letter to share, after all, and I thought we could all use a happy gathering. I was glad Lizbeth and Ben were still over at George's. That way, we could all be together. At least as nearly as possible.

146

But when we were all eating, I thought a little more on what Sam had been saying about Albert. I didn't believe for a minute that being sick in the first few months with child made any difference to the outcome. Or my own two would've had a hard time, indeed. But Sam was right that Albert was unusually quiet for a two-and-a-half-year-old. No doubt he was bright. He would point readily enough to what he wanted, and he loved to imitate his father or his uncles. He was a remarkably cooperative child. And he used to cry, but I hadn't heard that out of him in a long time. I guess I'd assumed he made more noise at home. Most children do. But now I wondered.

After a while, Albert was playing on the kitchen floor as Lizbeth, Thelma, and I were cleaning up from supper.

"Does he answer to his name?" I asked Thelma.

"I don't know. Not by sayin' anything. Sometimes he don't even look your way."

I squatted down a little bit. Albert was busily removing all my rubber canning rings from a box. "Albert?"

He ignored me completely.

"Albert," I called a little louder. Still no response. And I suddenly remembered that most of the time when Thelma was ready to go, she or Sam would just swoop up Dorothy and Albert. They usually only called for the other two, who were more likely to be farther away anyway. Sometimes Albert would see his mother getting up to get her purse or her sweater and just trot along behind her.

I called his name again, but he was intent now on stacking the rings on the floor beside his foot and didn't pay me a bit of attention. So I scooted around directly in front of him and called his name one more time, softly. He saw my movement and looked up. With a gigantic smile, he got up and toddled over into my arms.

"Maybe he thinks deep on what he's doin', like Franky," Thelma suggested.

"I'm not so sure about that," I told her. "Not at his age anyway." I looked up at the young mother standing over me with a handful of spoons and one of my dishrags in her hands. "I think you should get an appointment with Dr. Clyne to have his ears checked," I said quietly, hoping that the words wouldn't worry them unnecessarily. And yet I knew that this was something that shouldn't be ignored.

*Oh, Father in heaven, help,* I prayed in my heart. But I couldn't seem to pray anything more.

# 17

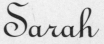

I wrote to Robert and told him all the things Frank had told me.

"Why does he talk to *me* this way?" I asked my brother. "What can I do?"

After a while I got an answer. "He can talk to you because he trusts you," Robert wrote back. "He must count you to be a special friend, so that's all you have to do. Just be his friend."

On the same day, Robert sent new pictures of himself and Willy in their uniforms to Mom and Dad and Mr. Hammond. They looked more handsome than anybody I'd ever seen. Like movie stars or something. And I was proud to know them.

That was toward the end of June, and folks around us started gearing up for the Hamilton County fair. Mom hadn't been sure that they would even have one, since the state fair had been canceled this year. But I was glad they were. It seemed like putting on something normal and happy would be good for everybody.

Then Dad had read in the *Times Leader* newspaper

that the Arnold's Store in Mcleansboro would be having an Independence Day window honoring the servicemen. They wanted pictures brought in of all the young men from around our area serving in the military.

"Robert sent his pictures just in time," I told my folks. "We can take them in to be in the window, can't we?"

"So long as we get them back," Mom said with a peculiar kind of lonely sound in her voice. She'd held Robert's picture a long time when we first got it. Then she'd put it on the mantel, where he seemed to be looking over everything that happened in the sitting room. All this time, Mom hadn't seemed to be very bothered over Robert being gone, but from the way she treasured that picture, I guessed that she was.

I walked over to the Hammonds' place that same evening to tell Rorey and her father about the Independence Day window and get pictures of Kirk and Joe, because the pictures we had of them weren't so close up and nice as a couple that Mr. Hammond had sitting on a shelf.

I was almost to the house when Rorey came running out practically screaming. At first I was scared to pieces that something terrible had happened. But Rorey was so excited to see me she was practically having conniptions right there on the porch.

"Oh, Sarah! Sarah! Wait'll you see! I got a letter today! I just got home! Oh, Sarah, how did you know I wanted to tell you! I was just gonna run over there, but Pa tol' me I oughta at least help Emmie put some vittles on the table!"

She grabbed my hand and pulled me in the house so hard I thought my arm would come off. Mr. Hammond wasn't anywhere in sight. Emma Grace was in the kitchen wearing an old apron that made her look far too little. She was stirring something in a big bowl. She looked over at me with a funny look on her face but didn't say a word.

"Oh, Sarah! Wait'll you hear! It's the most wonder-fullest thing—"

She plunked me in a chair and spun around to grab a letter that had been stuck under the Bible up on the shelf.

"What in the world—" I started to ask, but she didn't even hear me.

"Oh, Sarah! I'm gonna get married! Just looky at this! Did you ever see anything so fine! Lester wrote it his-self and put little hearts on the paper! Pa was so happy he went to tell it around, I guess. Didn't he go to your house?"

"No."

She thrust the letter in front of me but didn't let it loose from her hands. "You want I should read it for you, Sarah? He's done proposed! He really did!"

I just sat for a minute, wondering how in the world I was supposed to react. Rorey was beside herself, she was so happy about this. But to me, Lester was still a lout. Him marrying a friend that was practically like family was almost as distasteful a notion as I could have come up with. Maybe Emmie felt the same way. Maybe their pa did too. I wondered for a minute where he'd gone, but Rorey didn't give me half a second to think anymore about that.

"My dearest Rorey Jeanine," she started reading, and already I could hardly stomach the words. I couldn't picture Lester writing them. I couldn't picture him stand-ing in the church in front of everybody we knew, kiss-ing his bride. I wondered how long since he'd been in a church, and if he'd ever choose to go again once he got married.

"I can't stop thinkin' about you since your last letter," Rorey read on. "I put one a' your pictures in my pocket an' the other under my pillow so's you'll be near me all the time. Having nothin' of you to hold 'cept your pictures has made me think a awful lot, and I been missing you fierce. I decided, Rorey Jeanine, that you're the girl for me, and I hope you feel the same way. I know we've talked like that before, but this time I mean it. I want you to be my wife. Please write back as soon as you can and tell me yes 'cause I love you up and down and sideways."

Rorey stopped and took a deep breath. She looked like she was gonna swoon. "Oh, Sarah! Ain't that the greatest thing you ever heard? Lester's what they call a born romantic. He's so . . . he's so . . ."

"Lonely," I put it, without really thinking about it.

"Well, of course he's lonely! So am I! Wouldn't you be if the one you loved was far away? Honestly, Sarah, sometimes I wonder about you. Don't you understand nothin' 'bout romantic things?"

"Maybe not."

"Well, you're happy for me, ain't you? I wish I hadn't missed the mail going out today. It's a shame to have to wait till tomorrow to answer a letter like this! I'm gonna write 'yes' ten or twenty times real big and then put double hearts all around the page! Will you be my maid of honor, Sarah? I can't wait till he comes home! I'm gonna start makin' plans now, so we don't have to wait a minute longer than necessary. Do you think he wrote his mama? Should I go over there and show her this letter?"

"I'm sure he'll tell her, Rorey."

"How'd you know to come over? Did he tell Robert? Did you get a letter today too?"

"I came over to get a picture of Joe and Kirk for the special display they're putting in the Arnold's store window for Independence Day. We've got real nice pictures of Robert and Willy, but the ones your pa has of Kirk and Joe are better."

"They're putting up their pictures? Oh, I gotta find

152

one of Lester too! Do you think his mama knows about this?"

"If she takes the paper."

"Oh, Sarah. They wouldn't have no paper. You know that. They can't afford decent shoe leather. I better go an' tell Mrs. Turrey right after supper. She'll want to include Lester. Do you know she's really proud?"

I didn't know much of anything about Mrs. Turrey except for what had been talked around by folks who say they're giving you something to pray about. But I figured most of what was said was true, so maybe the whole Turrey family needed something to be proud of. "I think it's a fine idea to make sure they know," I told Rorey, but she looked at me a little when I stopped.

"Ain't you gonna say you're happy for me?"

"Oh, Rorey. You know how I've felt all along. I want you to be happy, but I'm just not so sure about Lester. At least he wrote a swell letter. And him saying that this time he means it leads me to think that at least he's been considering his ways and he probably means well by you."

"Well. I guess that's the happiest reaction I can expect outta you," she said sourly. "I should've known that."

"I'm sorry, Rorey. It's just hard for me to trust Lester. But I wish you well. I really do."

"You're gonna see, Sarah. He's gonna make me the happiest woman in the whole world!"

I hoped she was right. I hoped everything would work out wonderfully for her and Lester if they went ahead and got married. Maybe he'd use his military training to get a good job and they'd have plenty of money and beautiful kids. Maybe Lester would go to church, think some more on his ways, and end up being a fine brother-in-law to Frank and the rest. Maybe. I couldn't picture it. But then, none of that was up to me.

I went home with the photographs I came for, thinking plenty of thoughts about Rorey and all her silly ways since she'd become a teenager, fawning after one boy or another. Usually Lester. Her thinking always did come back to Lester, Lord only knows why. I couldn't imagine myself ever being so boy crazy as Rorey was, but then maybe her pa was partly to blame for that. I remembered her telling me he'd said she could get married as young as she wanted to, it was all right with him. I'd thought that an awfully dangerous thing to tell a girl that was already a little wild in her thinking. My father would never tell me something like that. He'd said he expected me to finish school before I ever went out on a date, not that I ever really cared to go anyway. But maybe Dad's attitude was part of the reason.

"You'll have plenty of time to be a grown-up once you're grown," he'd said once. "There's no reason to rush into tomorrow."

Dad was smart about that kind of thing. I was glad he'd passed along good sense. But then I wondered. School was out. And I wasn't going back. I guessed I could date now if I wanted to. But there wasn't anybody I could think of that I was anxious to be with in that kind of way.

Rorey would call me backward. And maybe I was, a little bit. Maybe I was a little like Frank, who never even tried to be with girls. He just concentrated on his work and his family and church, and that was good enough for him. I guessed he and I could just be friends and talk over things that bothered us, and not worry about dates with anyone until we felt good and ready. God didn't make us like Rorey. I could be thankful for that.

Maybe I should have thought a little more about Mr. Hammond that night. I told my parents all about Lester's letter, but I didn't mention a word about Rorey's pa going anywhere until Mom asked me how he was taking the news.

"Rorey said he was happy and went to tell people. But I don't know who, since he didn't come here."

He didn't get home in time for supper either, we found out. He wasn't home by bedtime, and Frank didn't find him at Fraley's or anywhere else he knew to look. He looked scared when he came to tell Dad about it. And I was ashamed that I hadn't known to wonder. Mr. Hammond was unpredictable anymore. Like grease in a hot pan. Liable to stay still or jump out in any direction. Maybe he wasn't so happy over the news after all.

# 18

## *Frank*

I didn't know how to let things rest. I couldn't sleep with Pa gone off again. I didn't even want to try. Lizbeth had gone home about a week and a half ago, thinkin' things were as back to normal as they were going to get. Pa had assured her that he wasn't thinkin' nothing crazy, and I guess she'd felt pretty settled about it since he'd been actin' all right.

But news of Lester Turrey proposing must have set him off again, though I wasn't sure why. He hadn't had any objection to Lester since things got back to normal and Lester helped do a little rebuilding after the fire. I would have thought Pa'd be happy about this.

Mr. Wortham was good enough to talk with me about some of the places Pa might've gone. Maybe even all the way to Dearing, to tell Sam and Thelma or Lizbeth and Ben the news. Mr. Wortham offered to drive in and see. I was grateful about that, and hopin' he'd find him, since he'd be using the gas of his truck for somethin' like this.

I was hoping to feel silly by morning over worryin'

'bout it. After all, Pa was a grown man who just got news that was far from sad. Maybe he was celebratin' with some friends I didn't even know he'd felt close towards. Maybe he had some kind of surprise in mind for Rorey, though I couldn't imagine what it might be.

*Oh, Lord, direct my path.*

I didn't feel like going into town with Mr. Wortham. I went twice by Mama's grave and once out to the machine shed where Pa spent some time alone sometimes. But he wasn't on our place, and I wasn't sure where to look. Bert's dog Boomer followed me and Tulip out toward the Curtis Creek bridge and beyond that to the one-room schoolhouse. There wasn't no reason in the world for Pa to come this way. But as we were going past, Boomer went running to the schoolhouse door. It was shut just like it was supposed to be, but Boomer was pawin' and scratchin' over something, so I got off our old horse and went walking up to the steps.

"Pa?"

Not a sound answered except Boomer's antics, but I knew he didn't act like that over nothin'.

"Is somebody here?" I yelled, but nobody answered me. I might have gone on, thinking Boomer was smellin' nothing but mice, except I saw that the window on the west was standin' open. School was let out for the year. There weren't no way the schoolteacher would leave the window open like that. Squirrels or coons'd tear up things mighty quick. But somebody'd opened it, sure as the morning sun.

"Pa?" I called again, even though I knew it wouldn't make a lick of sense for him to come here. The door was secured tight, so I went over to the window, wishing I had more of a way of seein' in the dark. The moonlight was plenty good enough tonight for seein' where I was going, but it was almost no help at all lookin' into the dark schoolhouse.

I wondered if the new schoolteacher still kept matches and candles in the same place that Mrs. Post had kept them years back when I was coming here. I wondered if they might have left any behind when they cleaned up things at the end of the school year. Thinkin' about sneakin' in to check was so strange to me that I started backing away, wondering what was wrong with my head. But then I heard a noise. Just a funny shufflin' noise coming from inside.

"Who's in there? Speak up right now or I'm comin' in to see."

I don't know why I didn't just figure the open window was an accident and some animal had gotten in. I don't know why I entertained the first notion that it could be my pa. But that was what I thought as I went up to the window again. Either that he didn't hear me callin' or he was too sloppy drunk to care.

"Pa? Why don't you come home? Rorey gettin' engaged ain't nothin' to worry over."

I heard the same shuffling noise and quick as anything I boosted myself up and started head-first through the window. For a second I wondered what folks'd say if they seen me. Mrs. Post and the teachers since then'd all be fiery upset over me or anybody else sneakin' into the schoolhouse this way. But there weren't anybody out here to know about it right now except for whoever else was already in there.

"Tarnation, boy! Can't you see clear to leave me alone a while?"

It was Pa, sure enough. Talking out of the dark. I shimmied one knee up to the windowsill and was half-way inside. "I can't see you at all," I called to him. "But what are you doin' here? This is 'bout the craziest thing you ever—"

"Ah, shut up. If I was wantin' to hear it, I'd a' come home."

158

I held my peace, wondering at him. He was talkin'
plain enough, but I knew he was drunk. Not so bad as
sometimes, but I could smell the liquor now, and I knew.
Quick as I could, I eased the rest of the way through the
window and landed on the floor. There wasn't much to
this schoolhouse. Just the one classroom and a coatroom
inside the door. I still couldn't see Pa, but I could hear
him a little bit, over by the woodstove in the middle of
the room. I felt my way real careful to the teacher's desk
and fumbled to find a drawer handle.

"Pa? I don't know why you're here, but I'm gonna try
to find a match so's I can take a look at you. Where'd
you tie up Star? I didn't see nor hear no sign of him
outside."

"Why'd you come here?" he questioned right back.
"How'd you know?"

"I don't know, Pa. It ain't nothin' I can explain."

"You always been different. You always been odd."

"I know." Just then my hand lit on to what I was sure
was a wax candle, maybe six inches long, and right next
to it was a little box of matches. I pulled a match out and
reached in the dark to find the chalkboard that'd be behind me. And then I lit that match against the underside
of the chalk tray, just like Mrs. Post used to do. I set the
candle in an empty inkwell in the front row and lit it.

Pa was over by the cold woodstove where I'd heard
him. Just leanin' against it, starin' off at nothing.

"Let's go home, Pa."

He turned and stared at me then, looking eerie in the
candle's light, like a specter with eyes as deep and black
as our old well.

"We's that much closer, boy."

"To what?" I couldn't help it. My skin got kind of
prickly. He was giving me the heebie-jeebies.

"Rorey's got herself engaged. I ain't got but Harry and
Bert and Emmie to look after now. And you."

He didn't sound drunk now. But I wasn't too sure. "Pa, you don't have to look after me, but Bert and 'specially Emmie's gonna need you for a long time to come. I ain't sure what you're gettin' at. Kids gets older. It's just natural. But we're always gonna need you."

"You never did need me."

"Yes, we did, Pa. We always have. We couldn't a'—"

"Ah, shut up. Go home."

I stepped a little closer. "I wanna go home. We oughta. We sure don't b'long in here. But I ain't gonna leave without you."

"What do you keep after me for?"

I swallowed hard, not sure I could speak the first words that came to mind when he asked me that. "Because I love you."

He turned around, took a couple of steps. Then he leaned hard against a middle grader's desk and slumped over kind of peculiar.

"Are you all right, Pa?"

"What do you think, boy? That I'm some kinda lost thing you gotta hunt up and save?"

"No. I just get bothered when you ain't home. And . . . and when you drink."

"You always had that kinda holier'n anybody attitude about you."

"I'm sorry," I said real quick. "I didn't mean it to seem like that. I just worry for you."

"Why ain't you ever took the time to worry over your own self?" he snapped back at me. But I stepped a little closer.

"Maybe you're right that I ain't got the sense for that," I said. "Come on. Let's go home."

"You wanna know why I came here?"

"We oughta get goin', but if you wanna tell me first, then yeah, I wanna know."

"I knowed you'd figure I been drinkin'. I knowed you

160

wouldn't like it, Franklin Drew, so I didn't wanna get home just yet."

Him usin' my formal name like that took me by surprise. I didn't think I'd ever heard it from him when he wasn't yellin'. "But why'd you come here?" I asked him, wishing he'd say what he wanted to say quick so we could get. Bein' snuck in the schoolhouse like this was uncommon strange.

"I didn't figure you'd look here, dadblame it," he answered impatiently. "I didn't figure you'd ever think to come out this-a-way to the schoolhouse. You don't even belong here. You never did."

I heaved a heavy breath. Even now, he seemed to pick his words to push me down. "I know. But there ain't neither one of us belongs here tonight. You're not makin' no sense to me. Why would you run off an' drink after Rorey was so excited about gettin' engaged? Now she thinks you're mad about it. We don't know what to do no more, Pa. We don't know what you want."

He answered with his voice real low, "Most of what I want, boy, is you to leave me alone. You more'n anybody. Why do you think I wanted you to stay over to the Worthams' before? I don't want you in m' hair. You always been weaselin' around, stickin' your nose in where it don't belong, an' I want shuck of it. Do you hear me? I want shuck a' you. That's why I come here. So's you'd leave me alone."

I didn't know what to say. I watched him slowly sink down and sit on the floor. And suddenly I didn't feel like I had much strength left to stand either. "Pa—"

"Ah, shut up. You ain't got nothin' to say worth hearin'."

I leaned my hand on a desk, feelin' almost like I'd been hit. There wasn't nothin' I could do with him. He wouldn't leave with me. I might as well just slip back out the window and go home to bed. But I couldn't.

161

His words was workin' on my insides too bad, and I felt like I had to know some things. Like maybe now in this strange place with him in this strange kind of mood, he'd tell me stuff he wouldn't never say otherwise.

"Pa?" I dared. "Why do you talk to me like that? Why do you think I'm some kinda worthless fool? Ain't I ever proved myself nothin' to you?"

He was quiet a minute. I thought maybe he'd yell, or maybe ignore me completely. But his voice came out steady and solemn, and calmer than I expected. "Is that what you think? That I reckon you're worthless?"

I swallowed hard. "Pretty much, Pa. An' I always did try—"

"Ah, shut up."

I did. What was the use doing anythin' else? Tears filled my eyes, and I got mad at myself over having them. This was ignorant. This whole thing, being here like this, and askin' him any questions. It was just ignorant.

"You pretty well figure I hate you, don't you, boy?"

"I—I don't know what to think sometimes, Pa."

"I reckon maybe I have hated the way you always been."

The tears tried to take over on me again, an' I had to fight 'em. "I'm sorry. I try—at pretty much everythin'. I don't know what else to say, 'cept I love you, Pa. No matter what you think a' me."

"You said that."

"I mean it."

He was quiet a long time. I sat down too. Despite my feelings, I knew I hadn't ought to leave without him.

He just sat. I just sat. I wanted to beg him to give up whatever this was he was doin' and just come home, but I didn't say a word. Finally he coughed a little. "Franklin Drew," he said finally, so low I almost couldn't hear, "I been afraid a' you since you was knee high. That's why I talk like I do."

"What do you mean, afraid a' me?"

"Ah, don't you understand? I ain't never understood the way you think, boy. You'd look up at the sky and ask me things 'bout God none of the rest ever thunk to ask me—stuff I couldn't answer. You always did remind me how ignorant I am. 'Cause maybe you take after me. I can't read a lick neither. But then you'd throw questions in my face an' crazy words 'bout things I don't know nothin' about, an' make me feel all the stupider. You always used to ask the kinda stuff you hadn't ought to think to wonder. I couldn't figure how your head worked, nor where it was half the time. I wondered for a while if you was even mine. You hadn't oughta have two kinda ways about you. It ain't natural."

"What do you mean?"

"You talk the Scriptures like the living Savior when you can't even read 'em. You act all high and holy and knowin' all kinds a' things when you's the same stupid cuss as ever, knockin' over stuff and failin' so bad at school they asked you not to come back. I never could figure you out, Franky. I got so I had to quit tryin'. It's plain easier to have you outta my hair most the time. I don't know if you can help it or not, but it ain't easy bein' around you."

"I—I'm sorry, Pa."

"Ah, shut up. I ain't tryin' to get no sorry outta you. I'm just tellin' you what it seemed like you wanted to know. I guess it's due you. I ain't liked it, the way you talk, like you know God's thinkin' or somethin'. The drinkin' ain't right. I ain't right. An' you's so holy you even know how to find me in the schoolhouse in the middle of the night."

"But I didn't know, Pa. Maybe the Lord just wanted me to—"

"You see? That's what I mean."

I kept quiet. I was so stunned I didn't know what to say.

"Go on home, will you?"

"But I wanna help, Pa. I just come to take you home. Just in case you need a hand—"

"Ah, boy, I know it. Your old pa's done got hisself in a mess again." He fumbled with a shirt pocket, and I realized for the first time that he had a little bottle with him.

"Don't drink no more. Please, Pa. Let's go home. Where'd you put Star?"

"Don't rightly remember. Ain't that jus' like me?"

"No. Not usually, it ain't. Did you tie him in the timber?"

"Don't think I tied him."

"Then he'll be headed home. An' Rorey'll wonder, if she sees him. We better go."

"Yeah, maybe you're right." Before I could say anything, he pulled the cap off the little bottle and took a swig. "Disobedient, ain't I? Hardheaded against the will of the Lord."

"I can't say that," I said with a sigh. "Just that it worries me. Where'd you get that stuff?"

"Bud Turrey. I got a lot to think on, Franky. I got decisions to make."

"So long as you realize that we do too, Pa. And we're gonna need your help."

He didn't answer that. He just struggled to his feet. I rose to help him because he seemed so unsteady. I blew out the candle and then shut the window once we'd gotten out it. He let me help him over to the hitching rail where Tulip was waitin'. And I let him ride, and I just walked alongside, holding the rein and making sure he stayed steady. I couldn't see Boomer around anywhere. Maybe he felt like he'd done his whole duty helpin' me find my pa and had gone on home without us.

164

# 19

## Sarah

I guess nobody ever knew what bothered Mr. Hammond about Rorey getting engaged. Frank said that their pa slept most of the next day, but after that he seemed to be better again.

"Do you think I'm too religious?" Frank asked me that afternoon. "Do you think I talk Bible words too much?"

"I don't know if there is such a thing as too much," I told him, pinning a pillowcase to the laundry line.

"But I don't want people to think I'm lookin' down on 'em."

"I don't know how they could, Frank, when all you're doing is speaking words of comfort. There've been times when my mother really appreciated it."

That seemed to satisfy him, at least a little. I was hanging wash, and he'd come out to talk to me and ended up helping. He held one end of a bedsheet off the ground for me while I started pushing clothespins in place. I always had trouble with bedsheets. I figured a person'd have to have arms like a gorilla to hang and fold them right.

"Do you ever wonder what people think a' you?" Frank asked me.

"Sometimes."

"Do you think it's a sin?"

I felt completely unqualified to answer that kind of question, but I knew he just wanted an opinion, so I did my best. "Maybe it's just human nature. I'm not sure we can help giving it a little thought."

"Well, I find human nature pretty sinful," he said with a sigh. "My own as much as anybody else's."

"That's reassuring," I told him. "Must mean you're as human as the next fellow."

He gave me an odd look. "I guess my pa's been wondering."

"If you're human?"

"I don't know just what. Do you think I look like him?"

"A little. But only when he's in a good mood."

"Pray for him, will you please, Sarah Jean? Last night was strange. It was good in a way, like I finally got a chance to see inside him. I hope it stays that way. I hope we can talk over the things that get to botherin' him."

I suddenly remembered Lester's letter to Rorey. He'd used her middle name. Nobody else used her middle name. And here was Frank, always using mine. "I'll pray for your pa," I promised, at the same time trying to remember Frank's middle name. Drew. Like that girl sleuth Nancy's surname. It was unusual. It kind of fit him. But I knew I wouldn't start using it.

"Are you going to the fair?" he asked me.

"I don't know. We're at least driving into Mcleansboro to see the Arnold's window display."

"I could take you, if you wanna see the fair," he offered. "I've got money from my last order to pay the ticket price."

Maybe I looked at him a little differently when he said that, I don't know. Maybe he'd had more in mind all along. But he hurried up and said the rest.

"I could take Pa's wagon, an' your pa wouldn't have to use his gas. I wouldn't mind bringin' whoever wanted to come."

"I'll ask Mom."

It had almost seemed like Frank was asking me special. Almost. I wasn't really sure.

And he did end up taking his father's wagon, and Harry and Bert wanted to go. And Emmie, Rorey, and Kate. But Mr. Hammond didn't want to go to the fair, and when Frank heard that, he almost didn't go either. But they talked a little bit, and I guess it was enough to put Frank's mind at ease. He went ahead and took us, and paid for all his brothers and sisters. He would have paid for me and Kate too, but Dad sent us money so that Frank wouldn't have to use all of his. For a while everybody stayed together. But then, Kate and Emmie and Bert were lingering in the livestock tent, and Rorey and Harry wanted to watch a wrestling contest.

"Did you ever ride a Ferris wheel?" Frank asked me.

"Once. When I was little. In Pennsylvania."

"I never did. But they got one this year. And I've got the dime. Mind comin' along?"

It was a funny way to be asked, but I agreed. And the ride attendant, assuming we were a couple, seated us together. But I didn't mind. I wouldn't have wanted to sit alone. Then just as we were edging upward, I saw Lester's brother Eugene in the crowd below. He stared at us like we'd been painted green.

"You've got to be kidding!" he yelled up at me.

"You just watch," I answered him back. "We're going all the way to the top."

Frank never asked what he meant. He never said anything about Eugene at all. He just sat back and breathed in deep, taking in the sights and sounds of the fair below us like it was all meaning something to him. I'd never thought riding a Ferris wheel could be something spiritual. I'm not sure why I thought it then. But I almost expected Frank to quote a Bible verse for the occasion. And he didn't disappoint.

"Ye shall go out with joy, and be led forth with peace: the mountains and the hills shall break forth before you into singing, and all the trees of the fields shall clap their hands."

I didn't think I'd ever heard that verse before. But I liked it, because it sounded happy. And that must have meant that Frank was happy.

The Arnold's store display window was the smartest I'd ever seen. And we were surprised when we learned that they were giving tickets to the Mclean Theater picture show and fifty cents in defense stamps to everybody that supplied a photograph. If Dad knew about that, he didn't tell us. But we'd brought four pictures, and they gave two tickets for each one, so that meant eight of us could go to the picture show. That was quite a treat, because we hardly ever spent any money on something like that.

Bert was quick to point out that Katie and me, him and Harry, plus Rorey, Emmie, and Frank were only seven. One more person could go. We drove back home and told our folks. Frank said he'd stay home so my folks could go, but they thought it'd be a better idea if we all took Mr. Hammond.

Frank didn't think his pa would go. At first, it didn't look like he would. But it was Rorey who persuaded him, telling him how much he'd like it and promising to get everybody popcorn from the money she earned at the five-and-dime. So we went back into Mcleansboro the next night and saw *To Be or Not to Be* with Carole

168

Lombard and Jack Benny. It made me sad because I knew Carole Lombard had been killed in a plane crash, but I liked the show anyway. I guess that and riding the Ferris wheel were the best times I'd had all summer.

# 20

## Julia

On the eighth of July, I was boxing up some old alumi-
num pans to go to the scrap metal drive when a storm
hit. I'd been knowing from the sky that we were in for
rain, but it turned nasty very quickly. Of course, Sarah
wasn't as terrified of thunderstorms as she used to be
when she was a little girl, but still she came down from
upstairs and peered out the kitchen window.

"Mom, the sweet gum tree is whipping around like
crazy."

"It's good and green, honey. It'll be fine."

"Well, what about the apple tree? It's going dead on
the one side."

"The good Lord'll mind the apples. Just watch, and
if your father should come running for the house with
the milk pail, open the door for him."

"He's outside?"

"In the barn, surely."

I knew she didn't like that. But Samuel was perfectly
safe, and so were we. Katie joined us from the living
room, where she'd been replacing a button on one of her

blouses. "Aren't you glad we already picked the string beans?" she said with a smile.

I truly was. The first of the season. And it was enough for supper, but not near enough to be canning yet. Katie sat down to snap beans, and Sarah started peeling potatoes and keeping her eye on the screen door at the same time. I was glad the porch roof was set so we could keep the inside door open if we wanted to when it was raining. It took a crazy change in the wind to ever blow rain through that door. I headed to the cellar for some bacon out of the cool pit to put in the beans, and just as I was coming back up, Samuel rushed in with the milk. He was soaking wet just getting from the barn to the house.

"We've got a gully-washer out there," he said, pushing the screen door shut behind him. "Wind's got the corn leaning pretty bad."

"It's young enough." I tried to sound positive. "Even if it lays over on its side, it can straighten."

"Ought to," Samuel agreed. He glanced back out the doorway. "It's coming down pretty fierce."

I didn't say anything more about it. I knew George Hammond worried that we'd have crop damage every time a storm came up, but I didn't think it did a bit of good to dwell on things like that. "Let's turn the radio on," I suggested. "It's almost the news time."

But Samuel couldn't get the radio to work again, and right away that made me miss Robert, who'd often had success tinkering with the thing.

"I guess we don't need the radio tonight," Sarah commented. But she never liked us listening to the news much anymore anyway.

"I'll be glad when they bring the electric line in," Samuel said. "It probably won't be till after the war now, though."

"A radio can be just as much trouble if it's electric,

171

especially with a storm," I told him. "We don't really need the electric line. We manage fine."

"It would just make some things easier," Samuel continued.

For some reason, talk of that bothered me. "If people aren't careful, with their electric heaters and freezers and things, they'll forget how to do a day's work," I said. "People need to carry wood and can their food so they'll know how to take care of themselves in a crisis. If we get to relying on contraptions, we'll have all the more trouble in bad weather or difficult times. Esther Maynard's new refrigerator quit working, and they lost four pounds of meat before they realized it."

Samuel was looking at me a little strange like he wasn't sure what I might say to him next. "I believe I'll put on some dry clothes."

He went out of the kitchen, and I wondered why I'd talked against electric things so strongly. But in thinking about it, I realized why I didn't want Samuel to wish for electricity. I didn't want him to think life would be easier if we lived in town or if he had a different job somewhere else. I didn't want any change, foolish as that was. The world changes, and we change too, like it or not. At the very least, we get older. And our kids get older. But none of that was comfortable for me to consider right then.

I wished we'd gotten the radio going. The wind and thunder and pounding rain were loud now. I hoped all the Hammonds had been indoors when the storm broke loose.

As if she'd been thinking along the same lines, Sarah gave a groan. "Oh, Mom. Rorey headed home from the five-and-dime maybe twenty minutes ago. Do you suppose she's stuck in this?"

It was more than a twenty minute ride home on Tulip's back in good weather. At least an hour in bad weather. But I didn't say that. Sarah already knew it, and I wanted to be encouraging. "She probably saw the clouds and stayed in town."

"I don't think she'd do that, Mom. The five-and-dime closes pretty prompt."

"She might have gone to Lizbeth's. It's only four blocks."

"But Rorey's more stubborn than sensible sometimes. She's been hurrying home almost every day to see if she's got more mail."

"If she started home today," I said, "she'll have a lesson on watching the sky. But she's seen plenty of storms before, Sarah. She'll get good and wet, but I'm sure she'll be all right."

We ate supper to the sound of thunderclaps and torrents of rain. The wind started pushing spray through the back door, and we finally had to shut it. About the time we were clearing the table, we heard an awful crack outside. Sarah nearly jumped out of her skin, and Kate froze stock still.

"I think the tree at the corner of the pasture was hit by lightning," Samuel told us after looking out. "Thank God it's raining. There won't be any fire."

"And the cows are still in?" I asked a little anxiously, thinking of Mr. Post's heifer that was killed years ago when lightning hit the tree it was standing under in a storm.

"They're in," Samuel told me.

It wasn't twenty minutes before we heard a thud that sounded like it was right over the sitting room.

"Tree branch on the roof," Samuel explained.

My stomach knotted a little, thinking of the sweet gum tree Sarah had seen whipping around. It was the only one close enough to lose a limb on the house. I hoped there wasn't much damage.

"Let's play checkers," Katie suggested as soon as the dishes were done.

Usually, the checker set only got out when the Hammond boys were around, but the girls evidently needed a little distraction. I sat down with my darning needle and a pair of Samuel's socks. Samuel sat on the floor in front of the radio and took the whole back end off.

"There's a bad wire to the battery," he said after a while. "But I think I can cut out where it's frayed and splice it back together."

Before long, we were listening to *The Pepsodent Show*. We'd missed the news, and Sarah was glad about that.

I thought of the Hammonds, and was glad that over the years Samuel had placed considerable attention on the repair of their house. I wouldn't have wanted to sit out a storm in that house the way it had been when we first met them. But it was solid now.

Still, I thought it might have been good to at least have Emma Grace over here with us, because she was the littlest. And Rorey. *Lord, let her have had the good sense to stay in town and wait out the storm.*

At about nine o'clock everything got calm outside. I was thankful, because Sarah would have a hard time sleeping with a racket going on. She and Katie had gone to get into their bedclothes, and I was just about to do that myself when we heard a knock on the door. For a moment, my mind turned every which way. The dirt roads must be horrible right now, for all the mud. Was there a stranded traveler? Or was Frank coming over to get our help? Maybe Rorey hadn't gotten home. But no, I decided. Frank would conclude the same thing I had. That Rorey was grown and responsible enough to have sheltered someplace to wait. She'd likely be home in the morning.

I went to the door having no idea who I'd find. And when I opened it, she practically fell in on top of me.

Rorey. Dripping wet and bedraggled. She looked absolutely miserable. It took me a moment to realize she was in pain.

"Mrs. Wortham—"

"Rorey, come in and sit down. Gracious, girl, you should have waited somewhere."

She sat in a chair and leaned over, cradling her arm against her side.

"Honey, are you all right?"

"Tulip . . . she—she spooked." Rorey looked at me, rocking just a little in her seat. She was a muddy mess, and her face was scrunched with pain.

"Samuel!" I called. He'd gone to lie down already, but I wasn't sure what I was dealing with and I wanted him here. "Rorey, were you thrown? Did you fall? Tell me where you hurt."

"My arm, Mrs. Wortham. It's broke. I know it is." She bit her lip and leaned into me, and I just held her close until Samuel came in the room.

"There's no way the road would be passable yet, is there?" I asked him.

"Not for wheels. But a horse could go alongside it." He knelt down beside us. "What's happened?"

"She was coming home in the storm, and Tulip spooked," I did my best to explain. "She thinks her arm's broken."

Slowly, carefully, he eased Rorey's arm out away from her body and touched it gingerly in two or three spots. Rorey could hardly stand it.

"I think she's right."

"Oh, Lord."

"We can't get her to the doctor tonight, Julia," he told me. "I wouldn't want to hold her on a horse if I had one here, and there's no way we can get the truck out after the rain we had. Storm could cut loose again at any time anyway."

I guess his words were a little much for Rorey, who

burst into tears. But at least she'd made it this far. "Where were you, honey?" I asked her. "When Tulip spooked?"

"Toward the corner. Most a' the way home. But I knew this was closer."

She leaned into me again. "Oh, Mrs. Wortham. The pain was making me dizzy, and the storm was so bad I just curled up on the ground and prayed it would go away."

She was crying, and I just held her. The poor child. God love her, what a horrible experience. "Samuel, what can we do? Her arm's going to need some help."

I knew exactly the kind of help it needed, but we couldn't give it. It would have to be set and put in a plaster cast. Ice would help to keep it from swelling any worse through the night. But we had no freezer. We'd talked of getting an icebox but had never done it because I always thought we were managing so well with the occasional chunk of ice down Emma Graham's old cool pit. But the ice had gone out two days ago, and the iceman wasn't due until Friday.

"Is Tulip here?" Samuel asked.

"I don't know where she went," Rorey answered through her tears.

Katie and Sarah came rushing downstairs in their nightgowns, but I made Sarah go right back up for a gown that would fit Rorey.

"I can't change clothes," Rorey pleaded with me. "I can't get the blouse off of my arm."

"It's all torn up anyway," I told her. "We'll cut it so we can get you in some dry clothes."

Before Sarah was back, we heard footsteps on the porch. I knew their sound pretty well by now. It was Franky's unique gait. And tonight he had surprising timing. Samuel went to open the door before he could knock.

"Tulip got home," he said before we could ask. "I come

176

with Star to see if Rorey got here or if I'd need some help out lookin'."

"Oh, Franky! Franky, my arm's broke," Rorey wailed.

Frank looked at me like he could scarcely believe her. He knelt at her side and looked her over. "Lord help," he said. "The road's awash. You reckon I could get her to the hospital on a horse?"

"I wouldn't want to try it," Samuel told him. "Did you see any stars outside?"

"Not a one."

"I'm thinking the storm's not done. But even if it were clear as a bell out, she'd still have a hard time being held in the saddle tonight. It's a painful break, and she's pretty shook from being thrown."

As if the skies outside wanted to lend credence to Samuel's words, a low rumble of thunder began again in the distance.

Sarah brought a gown, and I thought of a way that we could help Rorey put it on without hurting her. "Get me my sewing basket. We'll take off the right sleeve at the seam and loose the side seam a ways so we can put the gown on her. We can pin the side for now, and that way we can put the sleeve back on later without doing the gown any damage."

"I'll do it," Katie volunteered, and ran to get my basket.

"Have you got ice left?" Frank asked, knowing full well when the ice delivery was due. Two days away.

"No."

"The Posts might. They get double order. I'm gonna go see."

"Oh, Franky," Rorey exclaimed through tears. "It's storming out."

I'd never seen such concern in her for Frank, and I was glad to see it now.

But Frank paid no attention, as if the situation we

were in was an everyday thing. "I'll be fine. You just sit tight."

I looked at Samuel, but he just nodded and let him go. "I'll be back in the house with a board or two," he told us. "We'll need a pillow or a couple of thick towels, and some torn bedsheet."

Sarah helped me get Rorey's wet clothes off. Rorey couldn't be much help at that, still crying and hurting so bad as she was. I checked her over the best I could to see if there were anywhere else she was hurt, but I only saw scratches and bruises. Nothing serious.

Once we got her dressed in the dry nightgown, I sent Sarah to make her some mullein and shepherd's purse tea. Katie was fetching a couple of towels and the old sheet I'd saved back. When Samuel came in, he helped me move Rorey to the davenport. She was still crying, all the way into the sitting room. By the time we got her there, I felt like crying too.

"I'm gonna splint your arm," Samuel told her. "It'll hurt, but do your best not to pull away from me, all right?"

She nodded, biting her lip again. "Do you think Pa's gonna be upset?" she asked us through her tears.

"Any man'd be bothered to see his little girl hurting," Samuel replied.

"I'm not so little," Rorey answered back, surprisingly.

"You are to a pa."

He adjusted one of the towels to make it longer one way than the other and folded it carefully around the broken arm. "Too bad the ice isn't here already, but we can keep this still, and it'll feel some better."

"Good of Franky to go get ice," Rorey said bravely, trying not to let on about the pain so much.

"Yes, it was," Samuel agreed. "And after that horse got home, if you hadn't been here, he'd be spending the

178

rest of the night out looking for you. You've got a fine brother there."

Rorey didn't say anything more. But she nodded, and then she closed her eyes for a minute, and silent tears streamed her cheeks.

A thousand things raced through my mind. If there were more people down our country lane, the county would have covered the whole road with rocks by now so it would be passable even in the wet weather. If we lived closer to the hard road, getting out would have been no problem at all. If we were in town, we might have an electric refrigerator with ice in the freezing section. We wouldn't have to worry about dirt roads. And it wouldn't be so far to the doctor, either.

There'd been several times since we came here that being closer to the doctor and having decent roads would have helped us considerably. Certainly, those times were few and far between, thank the Lord, but there'd been more than enough of them. The fire. The horrible night when Emma Graham and Mrs. Hammond both died. The day Franky's leg was broken. Thelma's baby being born in my bedroom. Samuel falling through the pond ice.

*Lord, you've brought us through so much. And this might be small compared to some of that. Broken arms heal. But, oh God, they hurt. Help us through this now.*

Samuel put a board against each side of the towel on Rorey's arm, and I helped him tie them in place with torn strips of bedsheet. That way her arm wouldn't be bending or moving much, even if she managed to sleep. I tried to get her to drink some of the tea Sarah had made because I thought it might help the pain. But she couldn't manage much. She said her stomach was feeling nervous, whatever that might mean.

By the time Frank got back, the rain had started again, so he was soaking wet like his sister had been. But he had ice, wrapped in three dishtowels and two layers of

179

burlap bag to try to keep it over the distance. I wasn't sure at first the best thing to do with the ice now that we had it, but I finally decided to untie the boards for now, put ice between two layers of towel, and tie that on loosely with another towel around it. It was awkward, bulky, and of course uncomfortable, but we had to do something for her.

I hoped she could sleep. The night would go faster. I worried about tomorrow. With all this rain, the roads would still be bad for hours, maybe more than a day. When could we get to the doctor? I knew people who claimed to never go to a doctor at all no matter what happened, but I wanted to be sure the arm was set right, and we couldn't be sure of that at home.

Samuel offered Frank dry clothes to stay the night, but he declined, saying he'd better go back home and let the rest of the family know what had happened.

It bothered me a little for him to go back through the timber when it was thundering again outside, but he went, and he was surely right that it wouldn't be proper to leave his father wondering.

After several hours, Rorey finally slept fitfully. By then I was exhausted, but I slept near her in a chair in case she waked. In the night we had secured her arm more completely with one of the boards again and wrapped it to her chest to stay completely still. Samuel put the rest of the ice in the cool pit for me until she woke, and then I would put some on her arm again.

Katie and Sarah were both awake very early in the morning, a Thursday. Maybe none of us could sleep very well. Samuel had already gone out to milk. Rorey woke in a while and lay very still and quiet.

"Mrs. Wortham, I'm supposed to work today. How will we get word to Mrs. Mendel? I don't want to lose my job."

180

"You won't be back to work this week at all," I pre-dicted. "But if we can't get a message to Mrs. Mendel, she'll just assume you had trouble getting back into town today because of the storm. I expect there'll be a number of branches and trees down in the area. I thank the Lord we didn't have a branch through our roof."

"What if I can't do things? I'm right-handed."

"People find ways to manage," I told her. "It's only temporary."

I was glad that she seemed to be feeling better. The arm still hurt but considerably less than it had last night. I decided not to move it at all, even to apply more ice or get Rorey a change of clothes. She was managing better with it secured as it was, and I thought we'd better leave it till we had her to the doctor. When Samuel brought the milk in, he told me he'd checked the road when he first went out. The rain had stopped hours ago, but the dirt road was still too soggy for our truck tires.

"Samuel, I'm sorry," I said. "If we lived by the hard road and had electricity, life would be easier sometimes, just like you said."

"It's not your fault. It's only us and Hammonds out this way, with just Posts and Muellers on the connecting road. There just hasn't been the money to service us."

"I'm the one who wanted this farm."

"And thank God you did," he answered me. "What do you think our lives would be like without it?"

"I don't know. Maybe better."

"We had nothing, Juli. And the Hammonds had nothing. God has blessed us here. You know that. Rorey will be just fine. Don't worry, all right?"

I nodded, but I could see the concern on his face, calm as he was. He would have taken Rorey into the Mcleansboro hospital last night if he'd thought there was any practical way to do it. And he was wanting to go as soon as possible now.

"We might try horses in the daylight, Juli. It'll be a little easier. And it's clear this morning. That's a good sign. The road'll dry, but it'll be hours in the low spots, and I don't want to wait that long."

I thought it'd be a while anyway because we had no horses of our own, which had never been much of a problem before, any more than Hammonds not having a truck. But this morning I expected that Samuel would have to go to the Hammond farm for the horses. Before he could leave, though, they came to us.

Frank and his father came riding through the timber side by side. I'd never seen that happen before on any occasion. George was on Star and Frank was on Tulip. They'd come to check on Rorey and see what it was that could be done. Samuel and I met them on the porch to talk things over.

"I think we can get her to town," Samuel said. "But we'll need both horses. I wouldn't want to send one person with her alone. We can have somebody holding her in the saddle, and another person along in case they need a hand."

"Wouldn't be as much weight on the horse for me to ride with her instead of you or Pa," Frank offered. "She might sit alone all right, but she's not used to riding with one arm. I can ride her double."

Samuel nodded. Frank's words made sense. He probably weighed less than Rorey did, but he was strong.

"Star's the one can better handle the weight a' two," George told them. "You take Tulip, Samuel. She's none the worse for wear."

But Samuel looked at him oddly. "I thought you'd want to go."

"Don't know the doctor," George maintained. "An' I ain't no good tellin' people nothin'. Shoot, I wouldn't know what to do."

182

"Just get her there, that's all you have to do," Samuel said with what sounded like frustration.

But George shook his head. "You're good with these kind a' times. You always know how to make things work. I'd trust you real good takin' my girl in there to see the doctor. I'd trust you at it better than I would me."

Samuel was quiet for a minute. I knew he didn't think it right that George, being the father, wasn't wanting to go. But I thought *I'd* trust Samuel at the task better than I'd trust George too. George hadn't wanted a doctor called for the birth of any of his children, which could have been serious when Emma Grace was born breech. And after we took Frank to the hospital with his broken leg, George took him out of that hospital far sooner than the doctor was willing for him to go. I still wondered if that might have made a difference with his limp.

Maybe Samuel was thinking the same things. "All right," he told George. "But you tell her."

George went straight to the sitting room to find his daughter. Rorey was leaning against the cushions with Sarah beside her.

"Your brother an' Mr. Wortham's takin' you into the hospital," George said. "You be still as you can, and don't fret for nothin'."

That was all. But Rorey must have been used to her father's manner by now. She nodded. "Wish I didn't have to go in Sarah's gown, purty as it is. But I don't wanna try pulling nothin' else on."

She didn't want to try eating either. I packed some biscuits for Frank and Samuel and a change of clothes for Rorey. They lifted her onto the horse and the movement hurt, but she managed all right. I knew she'd be fine. Just uncomfortable and inconvenienced for a while as the arm mended. I hoped she could keep her job, though it seemed rather doubtful. I wasn't sure it would be safe for her to take a horse into town for work the

183

way she'd been doing, now that she'd have only one arm to use for a while.

George stuck around for only a few minutes after they left, and then he started back through the timber toward home after uttering a barely audible, "Thank you, Mrs. Wortham."

Sarah and Kate were neither one hungry for breakfast, and I suggested that it might benefit us all to lie down again for a few minutes before getting on with the business of the day.

"Did you ever notice how much alike Dad and Franky are?" Katie suddenly asked. "They think things through kind of the same, and they work like a team."

"That's what makes them good business partners," I answered her. "And good as family."

Sarah didn't say a word. She just looked at us like we were offering her a new revelation. Then her eyes turned for a moment toward the door, and I wished I could know what she was thinking. Katie'd told me about Sarah and Frank taking a Ferris wheel ride, just the two of them, though Sarah hadn't mentioned it. And I'd noticed them talking alone both before and since then. I knew things were changing. And eventually Sarah would talk to me, I knew that too. She'd always confided in me about almost everything. But she liked to have her thoughts in order first. She liked to have a grasp on her feelings if she could. And I thought, just maybe, that might take a little while.

# 21

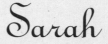

July 30, 1942

Dear Sarah,

*I felt sorry for Rorey when you told me what happened, but Willy said it served her right for riding Tulip in a storm. We prayed for her to mend quickly. Maybe by now she's lots better already.*

*We're moving tomorrow. I can't tell you yet where we're going, but Willy is pretty excited. He's been waiting quite a while "to get into the real war," and he's hoping they put us where we can be of use.*

*I want you to know that I'm not deeply afraid, even if I do feel a little scared sometimes on the outside. I wrote in Mom and Dad's letter all I can tell you of what we expect to do next, so I won't get into that here. But you asked me a while back about understanding God, and I thought I ought to reply to that subject, even though I avoided it before.*

*You might think I sound like a preacher, Sis. But I do be-lieve it's possible to understand God better than just what we know when we first say we believe. I think the more you talk to him and look for him in his Word, the more you can understand not just about what he's done but the way he is and the way he wants us to be. It's probably a good idea to talk to Frank about it. He'll probably have even better insight than mine, and you sure don't have to feel shy. You said he's talking to you more. So it's only natural that you should talk more to him too.*

*I'm happy for you in that, because I think everybody should have someone who's easy to talk to. I like writing to you, but I write to Rachel too, and I find it more and more of a blessing not just to get her letters but to share things with her. I still pray Rachel's prayer every night. And sometimes I think I feel God talking to me while I'm doing it, telling me that he's going to answer. Maybe not how we think, but some way better. I want us all to be strong, and have peace. But I think sometimes understanding God comes a little easier in the hard times, and maybe that's the reason for this war in the first place. I never would have thought like I do now if I weren't here. I never would have prayed like I do now. God is calling me, Sarah. It's frightening, because I don't know what he wants, but he's calling me. I feel more sure of it every time I pray.*

*Help Mom not to worry for me, all right? Tell her about Rachel's prayer. And tell her that Rachel and I both know God is calling us for something. Maybe he can use us together after the war is over. I don't know for what. But I aim to be obedient, whatever it is. I doubt I'll ever sit in church again and wish I was out playing baseball. Thank you for your letters, Sis, and keep things going on the home front for me.*

*May God give us peace in this time of being apart, make us stronger, and give us a greater understanding of himself. Now and always.*

*Yours for our victory,*

*Robert*

That was the last letter we got from Robert for quite a while, but we knew it would probably be like that because he was being deployed somewhere and it might be a while before things were settled for him. We prayed a lot. It was unnerving not to know where Robert was and where he was being stationed. I heard Mom up a lot at night, walking the floor and praying.

Rorey was doing better. But she couldn't do all the things Mrs. Mendel wanted done in the five-and-dime very well, particularly writing legibly with her left hand, so Mrs. Mendel said she would offer the job temporarily to someone else till Rorey's arm was better. Rorey suggested me, but I really didn't want to go. I wanted to stay and help with the farm. I was wearing work gloves and dungarees more and more, helping Dad and Frank in the fields as often as Mom would let me. So Katie got the job at the five-and-dime. And she loved it.

A lot of our area had wind and water damage from that awful storm. We had to repair a piece of our roof, but at least there wasn't a hole broken clear through. I figured it was God's protection that night, God's grace because he knew we already had enough to deal with. The corn crop was damaged, but Dad said we could just be thankful it wasn't worse. Mom was especially thankful that Mr. Hammond's fields fared better than ours. She was worried that another setback would be especially hard on him.

Months were going by with us still not knowing what

happened to Joe. Frank liked to talk about him every once in a while, but he didn't admit to anyone but me the way he really felt. I think he'd settled it in his heart that Joe was probably gone to be with the Lord. I couldn't agree, not till we knew for sure, but maybe it was more peaceful for Frank to picture Joe in heaven than suffering in the unknown. I didn't like to think about it much. It made me cry.

I turned seventeen in August, and it wasn't the happy day a birthday ought to be, because things didn't feel normal at all the way I'd hoped. Things were even more uncertain than they'd been when Robert went away.

A couple of weeks after that, Charlie Hunter at the Marathon station in Dearing asked Dad to come and work for him. He said he was friends with one of the foremen who was drilling for oil west of us and that fellow wanted him to come work with him a while. So Charlie needed somebody to run the station while he was gone. Business might be a little slower because of gasoline rationing, but he still wanted to keep the place open. And he liked that Dad was reliable and knew a thing or two about servicing cars. They'd been friends for years, and Charlie was sure he'd made the right choice.

But Dad didn't answer right away. I could tell he thought leaving the farm for that many hours would put a lot on Mom. And on Frank and Mr. Hammond too. Dad would hardly have time for the wood-working business at all. But I told him I'd keep on helping with the farmwork. It was making me stronger, I could tell. And Harry and Bert were a help too. They were strong young men.

Dad and Mom talked it over, and then talked it over some more. It took a week to finally make the decision. If we could keep the farm up too, there was more cash money in this than we'd had since Pennsylvania, because

Charlie was willing to pay a good wage. There were a lot of things we could do with extra money.

"Buy war bonds," Mom said.

"That's part of it," Dad answered her. "We wouldn't have to worry for winter anymore. And we could start one of the girls in nursing school or teacher college if they wanted to go."

Mom and I were cutting up buckets of tomatoes for canning. With her hands dripping juice, Mom turned with a sigh and looked up at Emma Graham's old cuckoo clock that just made clicking noises now on the hour instead of opening up. Dad and Frank had both said they could fix that thing, but neither of them had found the time.

"Samuel," Mom said with such a heavy sound in her voice that I stopped cutting for a minute. "Samuel, it's eight miles to town. Charlie only lives a block from the station. Won't you want to be closer too?"

"Eight miles isn't so far. And they've been talking again about spreading rock on our road. This time I think it's going to happen. I told Mr. Mueller what happened to Rorey, and he went and complained to the county people. He said there's going to be something done about it, that it's a matter of public safety to have decent roads."

"There's more involved than that."

"I know. He went to the electric company too, and they told him that if the farmers would pay an earnest on the cost, they'd be willing to start the work of bringing the line this way. We could have electric, Julia. Right here on the farm."

"But we can't pay. Neither can George."

"Maybe we could if I took this job. We could get a refrigerator just to make things easier. But you could keep canning. I love all your canning."

Mom smiled at him. "Do you really want to stay on the farm?"

189

"Where else would we fit in like this? God put us here, Juli. I wouldn't leave unless I knew it was his planning."

Mom got up and hugged Daddy, juicy hands and all, and got tomato splotches on his shirt. "Oh! Oh, Samuel, I'm sorry."

"No problem. I like tomatoes. Inside and out."

So it was settled. Dad started driving to work in Dearing early every morning, and Katie went with him on the days Mrs. Mendel needed her at the five-and-dime. On rainy days, they planned to borrow one of Mr. Hammond's horses, but they didn't need to do that but once the rest of that year. Before long, Dad and Katie both went to the office of the local war bond chairman and pledged to invest ten percent of their pay every week to war bonds. He gave them little target lapel buttons to wear that had a 10% on them. The bond chairman said that if enough people wore them, it would motivate everyone else, so he gave Katie one too, even though she was just sixteen and not working as many hours.

Rorey was anxious to get her job back, so Dad took her in sometimes, and Mrs. Mendel was willing to let her try. But she'd taken to Katie, and she really wanted Katie to stay. After a while she told Rorey that. And Rorey got really mad. It didn't matter what Katie said. Poor Katie even tried to quit so Mrs. Mendel would want Rorey again, but Rorey stayed mad, and Mrs. Mendel said she might not want Rorey anyway because Rorey talked to some customers too much and to others not near enough.

For a while I felt bad for not going to work in the five-and-dime myself when I'd had the chance. Maybe Mrs. Mendel would have been glad to have Rorey back if I'd been the one to replace her, and then Rorey wouldn't have been so mad at Katie.

But by the first of September, Rorey had found another position, at the soda fountain in the corner drug. And, oh, she liked that. She started investing in war bonds and got a lapel pin like Katie's, and she wore it every day. She carried around a picture of Lester and told everybody that she was engaged. She talked a lot, but her new boss liked that. Young people would come in and sit at the counter just to talk to Rorey, and they'd stay so long they just had to buy a fountain drink or a sundae or something, even if they hadn't come in the store for anything else.

It was strange having Dad and Kate and Rorey all going to town so often. I'd always spent so much time with all three of them that I hardly knew what to do with them gone. And Robert too. The farm just wasn't the same. It seemed half dead through the day sometimes, it was so empty. But there was still Mom. She and I kept busy with the garden and the regular things around the house, plus all the farm work we could handle. Dad said he didn't want us trying to do too much. After all, he was home in the evenings and weekends, and he'd hardly ever sit still. There was still a lot of farming to do, and he did what he could of what needed to be done, whether it was on our property or the Hammonds'.

Mr. Hammond had said he'd come over more and help since Dad would be gone more and we'd always been willing to help him. But it was Frank who came over every day. The Hammonds had more animals than we did, and Bert kept himself pretty well occupied with them. Harry was busy with his pa's fields and occasional work for the Posts. They both did their share with their farm, but without Frank we'd never have managed. A year ago, he'd had plenty of time for his wood carving, but this year, he seemed to be trying to fill Robert's shoes and William's both. I worked alongside him all I could, and it helped me not to miss so badly the way things had been.

"We used to run around in the creek all day in the summer," I reminded him one day. "We used to make silly little pots out of clay and bird's nest hats and things like that. Do you remember?"

"Idle time is the luxury of youth," Frank answered me without even looking up.

I didn't know if he'd made that up or heard it somewhere. "I know it," I told him. "And I know things have to change, and we have to grow up. But I kind of miss it, don't you? I mean lazy play, catching fireflies and all. Remember when your family taught my family 'twelve o'clock the ghosts come out'?"

"That's a pretty silly game, Sarah Jean," he said somberly, stopping only long enough to wipe his brow. I wondered if he wished I'd leave him alone and let him think. He was cutting hay with a hand sickle, and I was trying my best to rake it behind him, but I knew that when he finished his job, he'd be starting in to help me with mine.

"Frank? Do you believe everything that happens has a reason?"

It took him a minute to say anything. I thought at first that he'd gotten swept up in some quick thought and didn't even hear me. But then he answered. "Yes. I do."

I had no idea what I was starting him on when I asked the next question. "Then do you suppose everything, even a silly little game, has a purpose?"

"I guess so. But games is pretty unfocused. I mean, they don't fit with nothin' you're trying to accomplish to get you anywhere. So I figure the purpose of them kind of pleasures is distraction, to give the mind a break from the worries a' the mundane. Trouble is, it ain't but a step from distraction to temptation, where we's tempted off from responsibility. Excitement an' ease can be just as much curse as blessin'. Maybe more. That's the way I see it."

I stared at him. "You sound like a preacher . . . I think."

"You know what I'm talkin' 'bout, don't you?"

"Yeah. But I never would have thought it through like that."

"You didn't have to." He smiled. "I done it for you."

It was a rare moment. I'd seen Franky dripping with sweat plenty of times through this summer. But right then he seemed practically content, even pleased with himself, and I wasn't sure I'd ever seen him look that way before. "Frank, can I ask you something else? About the purpose of things?"

"That's deep kinda questions, an' I can do my best if that's what you want. But you might do a heap better goin' straight to the pastor or the Word of God."

I shook my head. "I don't always understand what I read, and the pastor's not here to talk to. I just want to know. Is the purpose of trials to make us want more of God? Do you think if things were easy, we wouldn't even think about needing him?"

"Lot of folks wouldn't," Frank acknowledged with a sigh. "Lot of folks don't. That's why Jesus said it's hard for a rich man to enter the kingdom of God. Too easy for a rich man to think he's already got what he needs."

"Well, then, did this war start so we'd pray to God more?"

"I reckon there's a lot more to it than that, Sarah Jean."

"I mean underneath everything else. God's reason. Men might have all kinds of reasons, but if everything has a purpose, I want to know about that. What's the purpose of war?"

"That ain't a question for me," Frank answered solemnly. "That's a question for God hisself."

"Well, I don't know how to ask him. At least not in a way I get an answer."

"It takes being patient," he said with a quiet sigh. "God don't always answer direct. Sometimes he wants to know if you think he's important enough to wait on."

I felt like I'd just tapped into something I needed. "Is that in the Bible?"

"Pretty much. But not in them words. You know verses like 'they that wait upon the Lord shall renew their strength,' and the story about Daniel waitin' twenty-one days for the answer to his prayer."

I leaned on my rake a little. Mom had read the whole Bible to Frank over the course of two school years. I wondered if there was any of it he didn't remember. "There's a lot I don't understand," I told him. "I don't even know how to think things through."

"You're thinkin' fine, or you wouldn't be askin' questions."

He kept right on working, and I tried to. I didn't say anything more for several minutes. Rachel's prayer was occupying my mind again, and I don't know why I didn't come right out and ask him what I'd wanted to all along.

"Frank?"

He was slicing sickle through hay in a fluid motion, on and on, back and forth.

"Frank? Do you understand God better than you used to?"

He stopped cold.

"I mean, are we supposed to?" I asked on. "Are we supposed to know him better than we did at first? I always thought it was all the same. You believe or you don't believe. You know?"

"I think you better ask your pa to have the pastor over."

I almost dropped the rake. "I don't know if I could ask him, Frank. It's like when you said you wanted me to be your friend. And you told me things you couldn't tell anybody else. I get nervous with the pastor. I feel foolish talking to anybody else about some things. But I knew you'd understand and that I could talk to you. Please."

He looked perplexed. "I ain't sure what you're wantin', Sarah."

"I want to know if I'm missing something, if I'm supposed to understand things better by now and know what I'm talking about and what the preacher's talking about and everything else."

"Nope," he said flat out, much to my surprise. And then he continued. "If I understand you right, there's two ways I can answer that, an' the most important one is nope."

I dropped my rake completely that time. "What do you mean?"

"You wanna know if I understand God better? The answer is nope. If you're talkin' 'bout my head, I don't understand him at all. I don't know half what I used to think I did. Sometimes I just got to shake my head and ask him what in the world he's doin'. But the heart's different. Maybe my head's all turned around, but my heart knows he's got us in a good place, and we're gonna be all right one way or another. He's bringin' us up through things the way he does so we'll question, and look for him, and find peace. He keeps drawin' us closer, so we grow up like the Word says and not be babes anymore. Does that make any sense?"

"I think so." He'd given me a double answer. Can we understand God? No. Can we grow in understanding? Yes. At least that's the way I understood it. I picked up the rake.

"You're somethin' special, Sarah Jean," he said suddenly.

"Why? Why do you think so?"

"'Cause you wanna know, that's all. That's somethin' special."

He went back to his work, but I had a hard time concentrating on the haying. I kept thinking about Frank on the Ferris wheel looking out over the blue sky and talking about mountains and hills breaking forth in song. I knew it was Psalms he'd been quoting, or at least I thought it was now, but it stuck in my mind like a gift. *Frank thinks I'm special? Frank, who understands temptations and distractions and being drawn closer into the peace of God?*

I felt like writing my brother another letter. I felt like asking him, *Did you know? Did you know when you told me to help Frank that I'd be doing my own wandering mind a favor?*

That night, when everything was quiet and I was supposed to be in bed, I tiptoed down the stairs and found Mom awake in the sitting room, on her knees in front of the rocking chair.

"Are you praying for Robert?"

"Yes, honey. And Joe and the rest. And you. All of us."

I went and sat beside her. "Something's happening to me, Mom."

"What do you mean?"

"I'm looking at Frank different. I think he's looking at me different."

She was quiet. I hadn't expected that.

"You're not going to ask me any questions?"

"I don't know what ones to ask yet. Would you like to tell me more?"

"I wouldn't say anything to anybody else. I'm probably

just being silly. But we've been talking kind of deep. We don't talk like kids anymore. But that's how I used to feel. Like I was just a kid, and he was just a kid. Rorey's brother."

"I guess he's more than Rorey's brother to all of us by now."

"You really like him, don't you, Mom?"

"He's a good man. One of a kind, I think."

"We've been talking about God."

She smiled. "I'm glad."

"I've been talking to Robert about God too. In my letters. He says he's called. But I think we all are. Frank and me just as much as Robert and Rachel. Just in our own ways. Does that make sense?"

"It makes plenty of sense."

"I'm not as scared about things as I was. I mean for Robert. There's plenty of other things to worry about, I guess, but I think Frank's right that Robert's going to be okay."

She hugged me. And I didn't feel like I needed to say anything else. Mom had heard what she needed to hear. And whatever she thought I meant about Frank was all right with her. She trusted me. She trusted him. Most of all, she trusted God.

# 22

## *Julia*

A year ago I wouldn't have imagined so many changes. Both of the girls out of school. Robert overseas. And Samuel working in town, of all things. I wondered at Sarah a little, because she worked like she was trying to take her brother's place. But rather than wearing her down too much, she seemed to like it. And Katie helped me all she could when she was home. Things were a little better than I expected, but that's just like God to work things out better than we know to plan.

In the back of everyone's minds were the unanswered questions about Joe. We hadn't heard anything at all from him or from the war department, and it was hard on all of us. Especially George, but he seemed to be doing all right now. He worked his farm like he had been before and was right in the middle of everything going on with his family again. Many times he sat back and listened to Rorey go on and on about what she wanted at her wedding.

"You can have what you fancy if you save your money, girl," was about the only thing he had to say about it.

Harry, Bert, and Emmie were back to school in September, but George let Harry skip a lot of days to help with the farm despite Franky's objection. I could see both sides of that issue and didn't offer my opinion at all. Emmie came telling me that their teacher was starting a drive to collect cards, games, and records for the USO. We didn't have much to give of that kind of thing, but Katie bought a box of cards, a jigsaw puzzle, and a checker set from the five-and-dime for her to contribute. Sarah and I started spending an hour in the evenings knitting sweaters and headwear for the Red Cross. We knew that what we made would go to military camps and hospitals, so I prayed for the soldiers as I sat knitting. Emmie liked to join us at that when she was at our house. She said she'd like to be an army nurse some day, or better yet, a cook to feed all the men.

"Girls can't be army cooks," Bert told her with a scowl.
"Some of the men do that."

"They'd sure let me once they tasted my cooking," Emmie insisted, and nobody argued. For a little girl, eleven now, she did a fine job in the kitchen.

Rorey's plaster cast came off, but she still treated the arm gingerly. She liked her new job better than the five-and-dime, but for some reason acted like she still resented Katie over what had happened. But most of what we heard from Rorey was talk of Lester and the wedding. She had hoped he might be home on leave for Christmas. It didn't look that way now, but they wanted to marry at the next opportunity and not wait. She thought that might be next summer, and she wanted to be prepared. They'd have roses. They'd have red boutonnieres, they'd have crepe paper streamers, and rice for the guests to throw.

Rorey had her eye on a store-bought dress on display in the dry goods store, but it was very expensive, so she thought she might make her own. She decided pretty quickly on a pattern, and one day came home with yards of white fabric and French lace.

"I'll hafta start right away, Mrs. Wortham," she told me. "A dress like this takes time."

I promised to help her, but it would have to wait until after the harvest. We'd have our hands full on both farms till then.

Rationing had started across the countryside, of coffee, sugar, and such. That didn't affect us as much as it did some people because we were used to not buying much anyway, but I feared the rationing of tires and gasoline would make things slow for Samuel at the station. I wondered whether Charlie could continue to pay his full wage. But Samuel said there was always plenty to do, and Charlie felt he was doing the community a service by keeping the place open. He must have been earning good money with the oil driller. There were several wells in our area and something or other in the news about them nearly every week.

Sam and Thelma spent quite a while hoping I was wrong in my concerns for Albert's hearing, but eventually they decided they had to know for sure. They took him to see Dr. Clyne, who sent them to a special doctor in Mt. Vernon. And the news they got was bad. Albert's hearing was extremely poor. There was no explanation, and there was nothing they could do for it. He might have been born that way. They weren't really sure. But he wasn't expected to learn to speak without special instruction. And he wouldn't be able to go to regular school either.

Sam took the news better than Thelma did. "He'll be good at somethin', like Franky's good at somethin'," he said.

"That's a lot different, an' you know it," Thelma la-

200

mented. "Franky don't have no real handicap! He can talk an' listen better'n most folks even care to!"

She wasn't easily consoled. But little Albert was as cheerful as ever, unstacking and restacking the wooden salad bowls I'd let him play with. He even tried leaning them against one another so they'd stand on their sides. And then he merrily plunked one on his head and greeted his mother with an angelic smile. She very nearly cried.

"He don't understand, Mrs. Wortham."

"I wouldn't say that," I tried to encourage. "I think he's remarkable. To understand as well as he does, and do all that he does, without hearing us. I expect he's very bright."

I meant what I said, but I think Thelma thought I was only talking to make her feel better.

About the first of October, we started planning Christmas gift packages. There'd been a notice in the paper to mail by the end of October to be sure the packages would reach the boys overseas before Christmas. Having four boxes to pack was difficult, not because of buying or making the things to put in them, but because of missing our boys so much. Especially Robert. And Joe.

We didn't know whether to pack Joe a Christmas box or not. We didn't know where to send it. Emmie came over one day after school, and I expected she'd help me wrap some of the boxes to send. But she ended up just sitting and holding Joe's box with big tears running down her cheeks.

"Mama," she called me. "Mama, I already filled it with prayers."

I think we all did.

Frank had carved little wooden crosses to go in the gift packages. They were cherrywood with designs on the sides. On a stand, so they'd stay upright on a table or a shelf. He made Joe's different than the others. It was beautiful, with what looked like angel wings behind the cross and curved around its sides. He also had Sarah write out two Scripture verses to put in the box. John 3:16, and the passage in the book of Revelation that says there shall be no more sorrow or pain.

We sent all four boxes, with Joe's going to the last known address we had for his unit. I knew it might come back. But I prayed it didn't, especially for Franky and Emmie's sakes.

That harvest, Frank was in the fields from sunup to sundown, and Sarah was most of the time with him. Harry took off from school, and Samuel got Charlie's permission to hire Oliver Mueller to stay at the station so he could be home a few days when we needed him most. Thelma's Sam came out to help. And George worked along with everybody else, at least most of the time.

We'd had plenty of garden harvest too. We put up twenty-six quarts of bread and butter pickles and seventeen quarts of piccalilli relish. Seventy-nine quarts of green beans, eighty-two of tomato juice, and forty-seven of corn. Plus peaches, applesauce, sauerkraut, and all the rest. We gave a share of everything to the food drive our church was sponsoring for the needy. Katie, who had money of her own for the first time in her life, said the Lord was blessing us and our country for the sacrifice we were making.

Emmie asked me to help her put together a "Food for Freedom" scrapbook for a contest at school. She was excited about that project and drew a lot of her own pictures or cut them from the newspaper and colored them with Crayolas. We didn't have any glossy colored magazines at our house, so Emmie was thrilled when Katie brought her copies of *Harper's* and the *Saturday Evening Post*. She said she'd let everybody read them who wanted to before she cut one thing out.

202

Bert spent every bit of his free time studying books with information about all the places war reports were coming from. Philippines. Savo Island. Tulagi and Guadalcanal. He wrote a letter to the *Times Leader* telling about his brothers and urging everyone to pray daily and contribute to the war effort in every way they could. The editor printed his entire letter with a heading calling him a "fine, brave boy doing his patriotic duty." Then, after Bert followed that letter with another letter two weeks later, a man from the newspaper office drove out from Mcleansboro to meet him and his father. They asked if Bert might be permitted to write every week with updates about his brothers, or calls for people to participate in the local war drives, or anything encouraging he should choose to include.

Bert was glad to do it. And he got the school involved, using short pieces from other students in some of his articles. Kirk was writing to us more regularly again, and sometimes Bert shared bits of his letters too. The editor at the *Times Leader* called Bert's articles "Letters from an American Boy" and put them on the same page of the paper every time. George took the whole thing rather sourly. He said he was proud of Bert, and yet he didn't like the well-meaning inquiries he got from people when he went to town. He didn't want to talk about the war. He didn't want to talk about his boys who were in the war. He just wanted to be left alone.

November drifted in cooler, and Samuel and George started making plans for butchering time. Sarah put in applications at a couple of places of business, but even though Katie and Rorey had had no trouble getting jobs, Sarah wasn't hired. Samuel wanted her to think about attending the teacher's college. She wasn't sure what she wanted to do, but she went with her father to inquire about classes beginning with the spring semester. She'd been a fair student, but I think she was worried about being able to handle the college material. One day she hit upon an idea and told me about it, but I wasn't quite sure whether she was serious.

"I could read the textbooks to Frank," she said. "And then have him explain it all to me. I think I could make a passing grade then."

"Sarah," I tried to tell her. "You've always made passing grades. You were a good student in school."

"But college will be harder, and I doubt I'd understand half of what I read about, or remember it, either."

I don't know why she was doubting her own ability to such an extent, but I didn't have any problem with her asking Frank for help, if that's what she wanted to do. I thought Frank might like the opportunity to hear college textbooks. I even asked him if he might want to consider attending the college too. I had no doubt he'd do well hearing the lectures, and Sarah could help him with the written material.

But Frank thought the idea completely unrealistic. "You know they'd never take me, Mrs. Wortham. Besides, I'm needed too much on the farm right now."

I almost argued that perhaps his father and younger brothers were more capable than he thought, especially with George doing well again lately. But there was a cloud of doubt edging the back of my mind, and I let the matter go.

Sam and Thelma surprised us considerably by saying that they were considering moving clear up to a town called Camp Point, where Thelma's Uncle Milton had offered Sam a job. "We'd have a little more money for a bigger house," Thelma told me. "And we'd be closer to the deaf school that's up that way."

Camp Point was still in Illinois, but it seemed like a very long way, and they'd be almost fifty miles from the

204

school for the deaf one of the doctors had mentioned to them. But that would be better than the hundred and eighty or so from here. Even though Albert was much too young for school now, I was glad they were taking his needs seriously. Still, I was concerned about how the rest of the family might react to the idea of them being so far away.

"That's why we're telling you now," Sam said. "If we go, it won't be till spring, and by then everybody'll have time to get used to the idea."

"Children grow up and move on. That's life for you," George said. If the idea of his oldest son moving more than two hundred miles bothered him, he didn't let on about it, much to Thelma's relief.

"I feared it would upset him terrible," she told me when we were alone later. "I think that was worrying Sammy a little too."

But the one who was upset the most was Emmie. She absolutely loved having Georgie, Rosemary, Albert, and baby Dorothy around us all she could.

"It ain't fair to think that after they have the new baby, they might be takin' it far away from us," she complained.

"They'd visit," I assured her. "And we'd find a way to visit them too."

"Would you really, Mrs. Wortham? If your family was to go an' visit Sam an' Thelma, would you take me?"

"I imagine we'd take whoever wanted to go. We've operated like one family for so long, I don't see why we would change it now."

"Thanks," Emmie told me with a hug. "I wanna be able to call you Mama forever."

We were very glad to get letters from Kirk, which were coming from England now. But he told us almost nothing of why his unit was there or what he expected next. He spoke angrily against the Germans, the Italians, the Japanese. And he spoke mournfully of loneliness for home.

"I can't wait to get hay in my hair again," he wrote. "I think our blackberry-lined creek and plowed fields is the prettiest place in the world."

I wondered if Robert, somewhere in the Pacific, thought so too. It bothered me considerably not to have gotten a letter from him since early August. Unless there were letters on the way, he hadn't written since July. But I knew he couldn't write every day. And when he did write, the letters now would be a long time reaching us.

I prayed for him daily, but it seemed increasingly to be at night when I felt I had to pray the most. I would find myself waking at all hours, unable to rest again until I got up to pray. Sometimes I would go to his box of letters and pull out the latest one or one of the many beneath it and read it by a candle's light, lingering over every word and then returning to prayers again. Sometimes I was driven to the mantelpiece in the sitting room, just to take his picture down and hold it a while.

Samuel caught me at it more than once, and at those times I felt a little foolish, but Samuel said I wasn't being foolish at all. Looking at me with his tired dark eyes mirroring my cares, he would ask me one simple question.

"Why do you think *I'm* not asleep?"

# 23

## Sarah

Thelma and Sam's fifth baby was born one year from the day that Pearl Harbor was attacked. Because of that, they changed their minds about calling her Irma Lee and instead named their little girl Pearl.

Mom was really, really glad that we got word of the birth after it had already happened. Thelma's aunt Dina was visiting, and she and Thelma's mother were the ones to deliver the baby. We drove into Dearing to see them that afternoon. Mom had made a pretty new baby blanket, and I made a bib like the one Mrs. Graham had made for Emmie when we were little kids. Katie brought store-bought baby booties that had been in the window at the five-and-dime. And Emmie, who liked cooking better than sewing, brought a big pot of chicken and dumplings to feed everybody. Thelma's mother just couldn't believe she'd made dumplings by herself.

The very next day we got letters from Robert. Two of them, but they'd both been written in October.

Mom was thrilled, even though the letters had taken so long. Robert was fine, and he said Willy was too.

They were on Guadalcanal, the American stronghold in the Solomon Islands. We were glad because we'd heard that a war correspondent named John Hersey reported such overwhelming American superiority there that the Japanese offensive was doomed.

Robert didn't say anything about doing any fighting. He did say he missed us very, very much and kept praying Rachel's prayer every night for God to make us stronger in this time of being apart. "Pray for me when you think of it," he said. "I don't get to sleep as easily as I used to." We wrote back to tell him that we thought about him all the time and were praying for him every single day, morning and night.

Christmas was strange without him and the older Hammond boys. We made cookies like we usually did, and I hoped the Christmas boxes had all been delivered and that Robert and the others were enjoying the things we'd sent. Joe, too. Our letters to him were not coming back, and neither had his Christmas box. We were all hoping that meant he'd been found somewhere and surely we'd be getting word soon enough.

On Christmas afternoon when Ben and Lizbeth and Sam and Thelma and all the kids were over, we played out the story of Christ's birth with our little nativity set like we'd been doing for years. But Emmie and Georgie had the angels flying not only to the shepherds at Bethlehem but also to Kirk in Europe and Willy, Robert, and Joe in the Pacific islands, because they couldn't be with us.

Just about everybody wrote all of them a Christmas letter or drew a picture to send. Frank told me what he wanted to say, and I wrote it down for him. He had good ordinary letters for the rest, but for Joe it was the whole Ninety-first Psalm.

"Are you sure?" I asked him.

"'Course I'm sure," he said. But he didn't give any explanation.

I just about cried when I was writing it down. All of the wonderful promises of protection in that chapter made me think that Frank surely had renewed hope for Joe, and I was very glad. "There shall no evil befall thee," it said. And "he shall give his angels charge over thee, to keep thee in all thy ways."

I liked those words, and I kept them turning around in my mind in the next few days. But I couldn't help wondering more about Joe. If he could, he'd have written to us by now, I was sure of that. So he must be somewhere where he couldn't write. But if the army knew where he was, they'd surely have told us he wasn't missing anymore, and they hadn't done that. So where were our letters going?

We'd heard about the Mcleansboro boy who had been declared missing after Pearl Harbor. Everybody'd thought he was dead; only he was found later alive and well. Such confusion could definitely happen. So I wondered if maybe Joe hadn't already been found and there'd been confusion about getting word to us. Maybe a letter had been sent and gotten lost somewhere.

Rorey had several days off over the holidays, and she made good progress on her wedding dress. Secretly I was still hoping she'd change her mind about marrying Lester, though it didn't look like that was going to happen. I tried to tell myself maybe the service would change him a lot and he'd come back a lot more well-mannered than he'd left. She was still hoping they'd be married in the summer, though nobody knew for sure when he might be coming home.

Kirk was now in North Africa. We learned that when we got his newest letter the first week of January, and it came as a complete surprise. He said mail from us was always encouragement right when he needed it. And he asked if one of us could please write to a friend in his unit who hardly ever got any letters. Katie said she'd been thinking about writing to more servicemen anyway, so she sat down and wrote a letter that night. She ended up writing that young man, whose name was Dave Kliner, every week.

Hearing from Robert and Kirk again and not getting Joe's Christmas box back had made me feel better about everything. Dad said Oliver Porter had heard a report that the Germans were losing ground in Europe and the Japanese were backing down in the Pacific. Maybe the war would be over soon after all. I hoped it'd be over by Valentine's Day because that was plenty long enough for our boys to be away from home. And when they got back they'd be glad to see that the whole country was doing better because of their efforts. There were jobs now. We had some money.

I was so hopeful. I wasn't feeling the heavy weight that I'd been feeling before. I was just sure everything was going to be all right.

But the next week changed everything. January twelfth my parents got notification that Robert had been wounded. That was hard enough, but it had happened almost two months ago, and we didn't even know. He'd been put on a hospital ship that was docked in Hawaii now. And they said he'd have to stay in Hawaii until he was well enough to be moved to the continental states.

Mom tried not to, but she cried. I know it was hard, thinking of Robert two months hurt with none of us by his side. If there'd been any way, she'd have taken off for Hawaii that very afternoon. But there was no way. I cried too. I prayed and prayed that he'd be able to travel real, real soon. That it wasn't so bad and he'd be home.

But we didn't even know how bad. I guess that was the hardest thing. Two weeks passed before we had any more details. Dad had gotten a man from the war department to help him get in contact with the hospital in Hawaii,

210

and he found out that Robert had four bullet wounds across his back and one leg. It would be a while before they'd be able to move him again. Dad came home that day looking like I'd never seen him look, ever. It scared me. It scared Mom. He told us everything he knew, and Mom and Dad hugged each other for a very long time, and then they both got on their knees and prayed.

That night Rachel came to our house. She cried, and we hugged her, and she cried some more. She said she'd sell everything she had to get to Hawaii, and Dad told her he felt the same way, but so far nobody could go. The very same day Eugene Turrey came looking for Rorey in the drugstore to tell her that Lester had been wounded too.

It felt like the whole world was coming to pieces. All of my fears about Joe were back again, plus heaps of extra fears for Robert. Rorey was so frazzled she couldn't hardly work. They hadn't been able to find out anything about how Lester was doing.

I worried terrible. So many things could go wrong if someone was shot in the back. So many vital parts were packed inside us there. I almost got mad at God because we'd been praying all along. But Mom reminded me that the Bible says "many are the afflictions of the righteous, but the Lord delivereth him out of them all."

"I don't understand it," I told her. "Robert was getting closer to God. Why didn't God protect him?"

"I'm sure he did," Mom answered me. "I'm sure he's with him. But, honey, it's a sinful world. Painful things happen."

I felt bad to be talking to her about it. I knew she was hurting too. But I couldn't quite let it go. "But, Mom, it shouldn't be like that."

"It won't always be. One day he'll set things in order with his coming. There may be no way to understand it all until then, but God promises to bring us out of

Rachel's Prayer

every affliction and trial. He's with us, and he makes us stronger."

I could see the tears in her eyes even while she was trying to encourage me. And I knew God was making my mother strong. I didn't think I could ever handle something like this so well as she was handling it. She cried, sure. At the strangest times. Stirring a supper pot or fixing a steam treatment for Berty's awful cold, she might suddenly be wiping away tears. But she was strong enough to help all of us and not get mad at God even one little bit. So I didn't let myself get mad at God either.

But it was hard to pray. It was hard to put together any words at all except "Heal my brother. Bring him home." So I kept praying that. But it seemed like there ought to be something more. I prayed for Joe and Kirk and Willy, of course. I prayed for Lester. But besides that, I couldn't seem to manage anything else. So I pulled out one of Robert's old letters, and I prayed Rachel's prayer again, over and over.

*God give us peace in this time of being apart. Make us stronger . . .*

Rachel came over a lot now, hoping we'd heard more word about Robert. But usually we didn't have anything new to tell her. She started sewing him a shirt. And knitting socks. And a wool hat. All presents for when he came home.

She and Katie and I got really close, and I kept trying to include Rorey, but she would pull away from us half the time and go to see the Turreys.

I kept hoping in that time that Willy would write to us and give us details, if he knew them, about what had happened. But Willy didn't write. I guessed he was just used to Robert adding in messages for him at the bottom of his own letters. He'd almost never written anybody. And then I thought how awful William must feel about Robert and Lester. So I wrote to him, hoping it would

212

help him feel better. I included the best assurances I could that they'd surely be all right.

I mailed that letter on January twenty-eighth. The next day, Mr. Hammond got a letter saying that William had been wounded in action. Apparently it had happened the same day as Robert. The letters were even dated the same. No one knew why Mr. Hammond's letter had taken so much longer getting to him.

He didn't take the news like my mother had taken the news about Robert. The day the letter came, Mom had sent me over to the Hammonds' with chicken soup for Berty because he was still home from school not feeling very well. I'd been crunching through the sparkly frozen timber, walking fast because of the cold, with my mind lost in my thoughts. But I heard yelling when I got close to the Hammonds' house, and I knew something was wrong.

Frank and his pa were outside when I got close. They were both upset, especially Mr. Hammond. He was screaming at Frank, words that didn't make real sense to me yet.

"I tol' you an' Lizbeth this was gonna happen! God's punishin' me for somethin'! He's gonna take every one of 'em!"

"No, Pa," Frank was trying to calm him. "Maybe it's not so bad. And Willy's strong as an ox. He'll be okay. This prob'ly just means he'll be home quicker'n we thought."

"You don't know that. You don't know nothin'!"

Mr. Hammond started moving quickly for the barn, and Frank got in his way. "Pa, don't ride off. Please. It ain't gonna help things."

"You know somethin' that will? Huh, boy? You gonna tell me some Bible words that'll do me any good right now?" He tried to go around him, but Frank just got in his way again.

"I could tell you words," Frank tried to tell his pa. "About love and protection. About God bein' with 'em in time of trouble. They'd be comfort if you'd hear it—"

"Get out a' my way!"

"Pa—"

Before Frank could say anything more, his father grabbed him by the arm and shoved him so hard he very nearly lost his balance. I was so startled I almost dropped the soup. The warm pot jostled against my coat, and it was all I could do not to lose the whole thing on the ground.

Frank saw me. With a quick wave of his hand he told me not to come any closer. His father was moving fast, already to the barn door and shoving it open.

"What do you think it's gonna solve, Pa, you goin' to get drunk again?" I could hear Frank trying to reason. "Harry and Emmie are gonna be home pretty soon. Rorey too, and when they hear this they're gonna worry. Berty's already worryin', and we ought to be in the house showing him somethin' solid instead a' this!"

"Shut up!" his father yelled back. "Just shut up an' leave me alone! You wanna be solid, you go be solid, Mr. Wise-mouth. Tell 'em all the Bible words you want to."

The next thing I knew, Mr. Hammond was riding out of the barn on their horse Star, and Frank was standing there helpless. I don't know if Mr. Hammond saw me at all. He didn't act like he did. He just rode off into the trees without looking back.

I turned my attention to Frank. He looked so sad, so defeated, that I didn't know what to say.

"He's gonna be plastered drunk before suppertime," Frank told me. "Lord knows what he'll do after that."

"He'll just come home, won't he?"

"I don't know. Sometimes I think he's right that I don't know nothin' no more."

214

I'd never heard Frank talk like that, and it bothered me terribly. "Is Willy hurt?"

He nodded. "Maybe he's with Robert. I hope so. That'd be some comfort to 'em both, t' at least be together."

"I'm sorry."

He didn't say anything, just walked up and took the soup pot out of my hands.

"Are you all right?" I asked him. "Your pa was pretty rough."

"I just don't know what he'll do, Sarah Jean. And that ain't helpin' nothing."

He started for the house, and I went with him, wishing I knew something to say to help take the load off his shoulders. "I'm sure Willy will be fine. We've all been praying for Robert, but I prayed for Willy too, and I will even more now. He's strong like you said. I'm sure he'll be fine."

"Thanks." He opened the door and held it for me even though he was still holding Mom's soup pot. Bert was sitting inside at a kitchen chair, coughing and looking miserable.

"Pa's gone, ain't he?" Bert asked us, and Frank nodded.

Bert hung his head. "Why's he always have to think the worst? An' then run off an' drink like a fool?"

Frank sighed. "Don't call Pa a fool, Berty. That don't help nothin' neither."

"You know what I mean! This ain't so bad as the news about Joe. At least they know where he is! At least he's prob'ly gonna be all right!"

"Sarah brought you some soup." Frank took the pot to the stove and put another chunk or two of wood in the fire. "You keep them thoughts, Bert. That this prob'ly ain't so bad. That Willy'll prob'ly be home 'fore long just fine. Emmie an' Harry's gonna be home from school, and we don't need to act like somethin' real terrible's goin' on. No need to get 'em more upset than they oughta be."

"But when they know Pa's took off, they'll be frettin'," Bert said with a worried look.

"Then we don't wanna say nothin' to make it worse."

I looked at both of them, unable to understand what it must be like to live with a father like George Hammond. They shouldn't have this kind of weight on them. Frank was barely grown, and Bert was still a kid. Mr. Hammond ought to be here to take care of things. He should be comforting them, instead of leaving them to tell such news to their siblings.

"I might've followed him," Frank said. "Except it wouldn't be right to leave you to handle this. Be prayin' he comes home."

He sat down like he was too weary to do anything else, and I wondered if I ought to go straight home and tell my mother the news they'd gotten. But I didn't feel right about leaving yet. They both looked so glum.

"Have you been feeling any better, Bert?"

He looked at me funny, like he thought it was the last thing I ought to be wondering about. "I don't know."

"I'll scoop you some soup in a minute," I volunteered, moving to stir the pot.

"Don't think I want any right now."

"Mom said you should. She might even think you ought to be in bed."

"I ain't that sick."

I nodded to him. "I'm glad. But the soup'll do you some good anyhow."

He shook his head. "You act just like your mama."

I served him some soup before long, and I put some in front of Frank too, but he didn't touch it. And then I started sweeping because it was something to do, and with Emmie in school and Rorey working, I doubt it got done every day. Bert just sat, still coughing, but Frank

216

got out some leather scrap and started patching a hole in his glove. When he finished that, he started carving on a little piece of walnut wood. Over a bucket, so he wouldn't get shavings on the sweeped-up floor.

It wasn't long at all before I heard sounds outside. Harry came bursting through the door first because he was always moving pretty fast. Emmie came behind, a good deal slower.

"You picked a good day to miss school," Harry complained to his younger brother. "Teacher was quizzin' on just about ever'thin'."

"Ah, shoot," Bert declared. "I didn't pick. I wouldn't a' picked if she was quizzin' in history."

"She was."

Bert looked genuinely disappointed, which perplexed Harry to no end. Harry'd always liked baseball, or any other sport, far better than any kind of book learning.

"I did pretty poor," Emmie said sadly.

"Oh, Emmie, I bet you're the only fifth grader that can make a cheese chiffon cake," I said, trying to perk her up.

"That's true," she acknowledged. "But Teacher don't quiz on that."

I'd been wondering if staying was the right thing, but when I saw her face I was glad I had. Without Mom or Dad here, it was right that I should be. Because I could at least help Frank talk hopeful words. And they'd need that, sure enough.

"We got news today," Frank started kind of slow. "Seems like Willy's in Hawaii with Robert. He was wounded too, but there's no reason to think it's so bad."

"Did they say?" Harry asked immediately. "Was he shot?"

"Don't know," Frank said. "But you know Willy. Ain't never been much of a scrape that could knock him down, nor keep him down any time at all. If he ain't out a' the hospital already, he's prob'ly itchin' to be."

"That's right," Bert added, trying to look on the bright side. "He'll be all right in no time. He may be fine already, seein' it's been some time since the letter was sent."

"Why don't he write us then?" Emmie asked.

"He don't like to," Frank told her. "An' maybe he's busy bein' help to Robert. In a way, I'm glad they was both sent to Hawaii, so they ain't left someplace alone."

Emmie teared up suddenly. "But that makes me think of Joe."

I went to her quick as I could and hugged her close. I didn't know what to say. All I could do was let her cling to me and cry a little, and then hope it made her feel better.

"When can we find out for sure?" Harry asked. "Is Robert an' Willy gonna be comin' home together 'fore long, then?"

Frank set his piece of wood on the table. "I expect we'll find out soon enough."

"Well, where's Pa?" Harry asked then.

Emmie dried her eyes and looked up at me.

"You know Pa," Frank answered more honestly than I expected. "Some news don't set well with him. He's gone to town near as I could tell. We'll have to give him some space when he gets home. He won't be all hisself."

"I don't get it," Harry said with a shake of his head. "If he wants to drink, why don't he just drink? Why does he wait till he thinks he's got an excuse an' then let it make him half crazy?"

Frank drew in a deep breath. "Long time ago, he promised Mama he'd quit his drinkin'. Since then, he's promised the pastor and Mr. Wortham the same thing because it ain't doin' him nothin' but hurt. I reckon he knows it's wrong. An' most days he's got the strength to turn away from the temptation. But when somethin'

218

happens, he lets hisself get weak. He gives hisself an excuse, just like you said."

Harry looked mad. "You gonna go after him?"

"I don't know. Maybe now that you're home I should."

"I think you oughta just let him alone if he's gonna be that way," Bert said suddenly, and the bitterness and resolve in his voice surprised me. "Wouldn't do us no good to have him here anyway. Not till he's sober."

"That'd be the easiest," Frank agreed. "If I could be assured he'd find his way home."

But I knew just looking at Frank that right then he didn't feel very assured about anything. He got up and got his coat from where he'd hung it on a hook by the door. "If you don't mind stayin' till Rorey's here," he told me, "I think she'd appreciate it. I sure do. I'm gonna ride in an' tell Lizbeth and Sam what happened." He looked at me direct for the first time since I'd gotten there. "Then I'll go by Buck Fraley's so if Pa's there I can encourage him to get home 'fore too late. Thank you for lingering, Sarah Jean." He turned and started out the door. "Harry, I'd appreciate it if you'd feed the stock an' start the milkin'."

I looked after him for a minute but then turned my attention to his brothers and sister. Bert took another sip of his now-tepid soup broth. Emmie turned from me with a sigh and reached for the potato box. "We always eat early. I guess I'll get things started."

Harry left a short stack of books on the table next to Bert and headed back outside. And my eyes rested on the little chunk of walnut Frank had left behind. It was a tiny, long-robed angel, not near so detailed as some of his work. But its wings stretched out almost like a cross, and its hands were folded together in solemn prayer.

# 24

## *Frank*

Sam and Lizbeth both appreciated me comin' to tell them 'bout William. Thelma was real upset, but Lizbeth took the news pretty calm. "He'll be okay," she assured me. "We've been prayin'. He'll be okay."

Ben offered to go with me to check on Pa. I didn't think it'd work out very practical since I'd come in all the way to town on Tulip, and he was wantin' to take me in his car. But he said he'd meet me over there. He just thought I hadn't ought to be dealin' with this alone. And Pa was at Fraley's, all right. Star was outside lookin' impatient, and Pa was inside sitting at the bar counter. From the looks of him, he had more than one of whatever he was drinkin' down him.

"Don't you s'pose you oughta come home now, Pa?" I asked him.

He turned and stared for a minute, lookin' angry. But then he saw Ben behind me. "Sit down. Have a drink," he told him, choosing to ignore me completely.

"You know I don't drink," Ben told him.

"Yeah. Yeah, I guess I know that," Pa said with a disheartened sort of sigh. He turned around again and slumped over the glass in front of him.

"Pa—" I tried to get his attention.

"Ah, go home. You ain't helpin' nobody."

"Maybe not," I said, tired of arguing with him. "But you ain't either. Least of all yourself."

"Don't even start," he warned me. "Don't you be throwin' them preachin' words at me. I can't help it, Franky. I got me one boy missin' an' another one hurt. There ain't a soul in here to blame me. I ain't even had to buy a drink since I come in. They understand, that's what it is. They 'preciate what me an' my boys is goin' through."

"What about your girls?" Ben asked him. "And the boys at home? Are you and your buddies thinking about them?"

Pa didn't answer. He just picked up his glass and drained the rest of it down. "What do you wanna be here for?" he said suddenly. "This ain't no kinda place for you."

"Lizbeth worries," Ben went on. "She's afraid you're going to get so beside yourself one of these days that you don't get home. That's why I came. To set her mind at ease."

"Tell her she's got enough to think about, with you an' that Mary Jane. What's she gonna do if they start callin' up men with young'uns? They'd take you over Sam, on account a' he's got five already. Liable to be another'n on the way 'fore the year's out too. Makes 'em right tiring to be around, what with the babies cryin' and all the other racket all the time—"

"Dad Hammond," Ben said with a sigh. "I'm thinking to send Frank home with the horses. I think I'll just sit here till you get tired of this, and then drive you home. Maybe that's the surest way."

"Horse knows the way home," Pa growled in response.

"I suppose so," Ben told him. "But Lizbeth'd feel better about it just the same."

I wasn't expecting that from Ben, but he was serious. With a hug and a word of assurance, he sent me home with Tulip and Star and promised me that he'd stay. "If I don't get him home tonight, he'll be at our house," he promised. "You just let the rest know not to worry for him, and that we're praying for William. It'll be all right, Frank. And we appreciate you taking care of things like you do."

I hardly knew what to say about Ben being so helpful. There wasn't anything more to do but thank him and head for home. Not having to deal with Pa by myself was something I hadn't expected. It was better this way. Pa wasn't so likely to cuss Ben as he was me. An' he wasn't so likely to bust him out of his way, neither.

I rode Star comin' home because he was the stronger of the two horses and he liked to get a move on when I wanted him to. Tulip just wanted to mosey most of the time, and I was hardly ever in a moseyin' mood.

My head was full of all kinds of things. Mostly William. Fearless, reckless, carefree William half a world away and hurt somehow when we didn't know how bad. I prayed it weren't near so bad as what it sounded like with Robert, and then I prayed for Robert again too.

I thought about them over there, still almost wishin' I could have been there too. Maybe I'd have been wounded too if I was. Maybe I'd be dead by now. Or maybe I wouldn't be hurt at all, and they'd let me stay with William and Robert, right by their sides, to pray and give 'em words of comfort.

I thought of Lester and prayed for him too because he was sufferin' for his country and my sister cared so much about him. I prayed he'd be all right. I prayed he'd come to know the Lord. But I didn't pray they'd go ahead and get married according to their plan. I wasn't so sure about that.

Kirk seemed to be doing all right, and I prayed it would stay that way. He was facin' a different kind of battle where he was, and it was hard not to worry a little. And then my thoughts turned to Joe again, and that was still the hardest of all. I knew by now that if he wasn't dead, he must be captured or hurt so bad that they didn't know who he was and he couldn't tell them. It was hard to swallow down that kind of thing, and I still wouldn't speak it out to anybody except Sarah Jean. I kept hopin' everybody else could just believe it was all some kind of mix-up.

It had been goin' around in my head for quite a while to wonder why God lets this kind of thing be in the world. All the pain and hate and killin'. None of it made much sense to me, especially since God is good. I knew he was good, and there was no way my heart could doubt that. But my mind was strugglin' over all the bad in his creation. Why was that? He's God, after all. He knew what was gonna be. He knew what people were gonna turn out like. Why did he put up with it?

I guessed the pastor would say that God puts up with the world because he loves us so much. He wants to give us a chance to reach our hearts to him so we can be with him when we finally enter eternity. Pastor'd probably even say we can understand God better when there's trials in life because otherwise we wouldn't know what it was like to need him, and to be rescued, comforted, and healed. Everythin' that happens shows us somethin' else about the love and the good of God, if we know how to see it. I guess I knew all that, but it was still hard to take the bad things.

I stopped for a minute in the timber when I saw Mama's grave in the growing moonlight. I wondered what she'd do in times like these. Try as hard as I might, I couldn't remember so much 'bout her anymore, and that made me sad. It wasn't right that anybody oughta be even partly forgotten.

"I love you, Mama," I whispered into the wind, hopin' the Lord in heaven would relay the message for me. And then I was suddenly picturin' Joe being with her again, and I had to shake that thought away because it made me angry.

*Lord, it ain't always easy to keep my thoughts straight. I don't even know anymore which way faith oughta be reachin' sometimes. Is it all right to wish somebody was in heaven? Because in some ways I think that'd be better than thinkin' of 'em sufferin' awful at the hands of an enemy. But at the same time, I wanna believe the best. I wanna believe that there's nothing so awful, and my brother'll be comin' home.*

I took a deep breath, thinkin' I better get ahold of myself better than this before I got home. I'd let my thinkin' move me almost into tears again, but I knew that wasn't going to do any of the rest of them any good. They sure didn't need me mulligrubbing around like the world had come to an end. I had to think hopeful, to help them be hopeful. I didn't want 'em worryin' too much about Willy, or Joe.

I wondered if Sarah Jean would still be there. Probably not. I'd asked her to stay just till Rorey got home after all, and since her father would be bringin' Rorey on his way home from work, I figured Sarah would just go ahead and ride home with him.

But I was glad she'd been there when she was. She was good for Emmie, and Bert too. She was a lot like her mama, strong to handle the things that come up, and quick to lend a hand. I appreciated that a lot more than I'd told her, and I thought maybe I oughta make a point of tellin' her more plain.

But maybe not. Maybe it would bother her for me

to say how much I appreciated her. I sure didn't want
to do anythin' to make her uncomfortable. She was a
good friend. And I needed that. Ben and Lizbeth were
real good too. They always had been. But they weren't
so easy to talk to as Sarah. I didn't know why.

For some reason I thought of her and Rorey and Katie
runnin' around when they were little, pickin' flowers to
give to Mr. and Mrs. Wortham and even my pa once or
twice. They didn't seem to have changed all that much.
Katie was still quiet, and never, ever did anything to get
in trouble. Rorey was still a little loud, sure to want her
own way if she could get the chance. And Sarah was still
cute as any of the flowers she could pick, and quick as
anythin' to try an' make somebody smile.

I turned Star and Tulip through the last bit of timber
before home, wonderin' how my thinking could have
got off on that kind of track. Sarah was my sister's best
friend. I was her dad's partner at wood-working. It was
uncommon strange for me to be thinking about her runnin' around pickin' flowers. She'd never paid me any
particular mind back then, except to be just as nice to
me as she was to anybody else.

And now, she was her parents' daughter. She was a
Wortham helping Hammonds, just like they were always
doin'. I felt kind of bad about that, to keep askin' it of any
of them. But at least till we got through this, at least till
we knew for sure about Willy and Joe and they all got
home, we were gonna need them sometimes. But maybe
we could help them too. I'd been tryin'. I'd been doin' all
the work I could at the Wortham place because I figured
we owed 'em, and because I wanted to lighten the load
with Robert gone and Mr. Wortham working in town. I
hoped I'd been a blessing. I prayed to be a blessing.

I smelled the wood smoke before I saw the house.
Coming through the trees, I hoped they had supper and
homework done and were all ready to turn in. I was so

225

tired I didn't think I could eat or talk or anything. Rorey was probably sittin' at the table again, or up on her bed, writin' another one of her endless stream of letters to Lester. Emmie probably did most of the cleanup after supper. She usually did. I thought of Sarah again. She might be leavin' one of these days for the teacher's college where her father wanted her to go. I wasn't anxious for that, but I knew it was a good thing. Sarah was smart enough, even if she didn't think so. But more than that, she was good with kids. Real good. She'd make a real fine teacher, or a mother, one day.

I put up the horses, gave them feed, and checked to make sure all the stock had water. I didn't check on the milkin' because I knew Harry wouldn't shirk it if I asked him. He used to be that way, but not since William left. The moon was shinin' bright enough to see my shadow on the way back to the house, and I stopped for a minute and looked way across the field, wishin' I could see all the way to where my brothers were.

*It's a great big world you've made, God,* I prayed. *An' just this piece is too big for me to handle without help. I'm glad your hands is big enough. I'm glad you're holdin' Willy and Joe and Robert. I'm glad you're holdin' all of us because if it wasn't for you, maybe I'd be falling apart. Maybe I'd be worse than Pa right now. Help him. Sometimes he don't even seem to want you, but that's when he needs you most of all.*

I could hear Bert coughing before I even put my hand on the door. Too bad he wasn't over there with Mrs. Wortham, I considered. She'd know just what to do.

I wasn't expectin' to see Sarah Jean when I opened the door. But she was sittin' at the table with Emmie, and Emmie's schoolbooks was spread out in front of them. She looked up at me and smiled. "Emmie remembers almost as well as you do," she told me right away. "She just has trouble reading so much as the teacher assigns and getting all the homework written down."

It was such a strange picture that I had to swallow down somethin' that rose up in my throat all of a sudden. We'd been over to Worthams so many times, and Sarah'd helped Emmie with her homework before, over there. But I didn't think she'd ever stayed here before, past supper and without her parents. She rose up all of a sudden and grabbed the teapot off the stove.

"I'm making Berty some hot tonic before he goes to bed so maybe he can sleep better tonight. And I told Dad maybe I ought to stay over and help Emmie a while because the teacher wants to quiz her again tomorrow on the things she missed."

I nodded my head. "That makes sense," I told her. "It's mighty nice of you."

"You must be awful hungry."

Before I could answer her, Bert asked where Pa was, and Harry dropped down the loft ladder, skipping all but two of the rungs the way he usually did.

"He's with Ben," I told them, knowin' they'd be at ease over that. "He might be home in a while, or else he'll stay with them the night. So there's nothin' to worry over."

Emmie smiled a little. "Oh, good. I was afraid he'd be drunk again."

I just sat down. I didn't have the heart to tell her nothin' more.

"Want some soup?" Sarah asked me. "Emmie made some really good potato soup, and we still have a little of the chicken left too."

"I guess I might could try. Rorey upstairs?"

Sarah nodded. I could tell by her eyes that somethin' about that concerned her a little, but she didn't explain whatever it was, and I didn't think I oughta ask. Rorey was pretty carried away lately with thoughts of Lester, and it'd been a while since she and Sarah had talked so much as they used to anyway. Since the fire, I remembered. Since *I'd* started talkin' to Sarah.

Sarah stirred a generous spoonful of honey into whatever the tonic was she'd made and set it in front of Bert, who looked at me like I might rescue him from havin' to try it.

"Drink it up," I told him. "Time you got feelin' better."

He gave me a funny look but picked up the cup and managed a sip. Apparently the honey wasn't enough to cover whatever taste he objected to, because Bert sure made a face. He drank some more, though, and I was glad.

"What is it?" I asked Sarah.

"Just comfrey and horehound. I'm glad you had some in the house."

"I think your mama left it at Christmastime when Emmie had a scratchy throat, remember?"

She nodded.

"Got any more? I was feelin' a little chilled."

"Sure." She hurried up and poured me a cup and didn't put half the honey in that she had for Bert. Maybe because he was younger. Then she set a steamy bowl of potato soup in front of me, and a biscuit.

"Sarah made the biscuits," Emmie volunteered.

"Looks like you girls is a good team."

It was awful strange having Sarah there. I thought Rorey ought to come down, because they were friends and close to the same age, and girls and all. But Rorey didn't come down. I asked Harry what she was doin', and he said she was already asleep. He helped himself to another big bowl of soup and sat down beside me.

"I'm glad they're in Hawaii," he said to me. "That's U.S. soil. At least we know they's taken care of, and they're gonna be okay now."

"That's right," I agreed, but I saw Sarah lookin' at

228

me with worry for her brother plain in her eyes. *Four bullets*, I thought then. *Lord God, no wonder she's worried. Help him, please.* "Robert's gonna be okay," I tried to assure her. "He's in God's hands, and I just know it's gonna be all right."

Ben brought Pa home in the morning. He didn't want to come. That bothered me, and Ben said it had bothered Lizbeth too. Like maybe Pa just wanted to shut down from everything. He didn't want to see us kids, nor talk about Willy. He didn't want to come home or get any of the work done that was waitin'. The worries were wrappin' him in a fog of contrariness, and he didn't even want to hear encouraging words. He just kept expectin' the worst, thinkin' it was just a matter of time before his whole life came apart.

Lizbeth said he'd talked about walkin' to Marion, where he was born, or maybe to Frankfurt where he knew a man who made liquor from pears off his backyard tree. And when he was drunk last night, he'd talked a lot about Mama. He talked about seein' her in her favorite striped dress and wishin' he could walk right up and twirl her around like they used to do at a barn dance.

"She's waitin' for me," Pa'd told Ben and Lizbeth last night. "She's knowin' it hadn't oughta be long."

Ben wanted me to know all that because he knew we needed to be careful for him. But Pa went straight to his room, and I didn't tell any of the rest of the kids any details at all. I figured I'd talk to Mr. Wortham about it, because he'd been my Pa's friend such a long time, and he'd done more'n anybody to keep him from fallin' apart before this. But when Mr. Wortham came with Kate to pick up Rorey for work again, I couldn't bring myself to say anythin' about it 'cause I wasn't sure the girls ought to hear. Mr. Wortham offered to drop Sarah off by home before they went on to Dearing, but she turned him down.

"Tell Mom I'm going to stay some of the morning," she said. "That way I can doctor Bert again and review Emmie on her lessons before she leaves for school. Then I'll clean a little and walk home."

I hardly knew what to think of her. We needed all she said, sure. I couldn't help Emmie with her lessons very well because so much of it was straight from her books. And Harry and Bert didn't like to take the time. I didn't know the things to do for Berty's nasty cough and fever as well as Sarah'd learned from her mother. And nobody 'round here had taken much thought to cleanin' lately. Still, it felt odd to have Sarah staying and doing for us. I wasn't sure what to say to her.

"It'll be all right about William," Mr. Wortham told me. "I'm going to be speaking to Mr. Winnows of the war department again today, and we'll find out what we can about him. Just believe the best. We're all praying for him."

I thought they were brave words from Mr. Wortham with what we knew of Robert. I appreciated it a lot. And I prayed too, through morning chores, knowing Sarah was heatin' Bert the rest of the chicken soup and quizzing Emmie on her lessons at the same time. I wished Pa had taken what we'd seen from the Worthams a little more to heart over the years. I figured all us kids had, and we was all better off because of their example. And Pa had seemed all right sometimes too. Most of the time, I guess. Till the war. Then maybe worryin' for his boys had turned his mind somehow. I didn't know how else to explain it.

Bert had tried to convince me he was feelin' better—so much better after Sarah's tonic that he wouldn't never need another one, not ever again. But he still felt feverish to me, so I didn't think he ought to go back to school just yet. Harry'd brought his lessons for him, and he could do them at home, and then maybe go back tomorrow. I told him I thought he oughta drink another tonic, for the benefit. I'd drink some with him. I didn't think it was that bad to the taste. But then, I'd been drinkin' coffee strong and black for a while now too, which Berty thought smelled too bad to even bother to taste.

Harry and Emmie left for school. Bert cozied into a sittin' room chair with a blanket over him and his schoolbooks on his lap. I knew the books'd occupy him practically all day, and he'd prob'ly end up ahead of where he was needin' to be with his assignments. Bert was like that.

Sarah was true to her word and started in right away cleanin' up. I told her she didn't have to. She said of course not, but that's what neighbors were for.

"Maybe you oughta be helpin' your mama," I said. "She's over at home all alone right now."

"I'll go pretty soon," she promised. "Dad told me she'd think it fine for me to help here a little while first."

So she swept again, even though she just did it yesterday. I finished up the raisiny oatmeal that Emmie had made, then I fixed the handle on a pair of pliers and set to work sharpening the ax and both hatchets. Sarah started in washin' the dishes and cleanin' off the table and the whole stove, not just the top.

"Sarah Jean, that don't have to be done," I tried again to tell her. "Least not by you right now."

"I know. But I don't work in town like Rorey, or go to school right now like Emmie. I might as well be useful."

I watched her for a minute, not fathoming real clear how she could think herself *not* useful, even if she wasn't doing for us. She was always occupied at somethin'. Just like her mother. I'd always admired Mrs. Wortham for

231

that. The only time she wasn't workin' with her hands was when she was reachin' with her heart, and most times they worked together. Sarah took after her plenty.

"When I'm done with this, I'm gonna start wiping shelves, and then I'll dust and clean up in the sitting room a little before I go," she told me. "I hope that's all right."

I almost asked her why. But I guessed she'd already told me, and I needed to just let it go and let her do what she wanted. But I knew I couldn't stay in the house no longer. She was drawin' my eyes from my work too much, and I wasn't gettin' enough done. "It's real kind of you," I told her, feeling a little awkward. "Thanks."

I took the tools and headed out the door. What in the world was wrong with me? She was just bein' neighborly, like she'd said. She was just following the example given her by her ma and her pa, who'd been more'n willing to help us all the time we'd known them. It oughta be second nature by now, seein' Sarah around. But I was noticin' things like her pretty brown hair pulled back a little different today and Rorey's old apron matching the color of her eyes. That was crazy. She'd think I'd flipped my lid for sure.

And we had Willy to think about. And Robert. All of the horrible war goin' on and the uncertainty about Joe. It was awful foolish of me to let flighty things enter my head about Sarah Jean. She'd be well bothered at me if she knew.

I quick carried in wood to fill the wood box, being careful not to pay her no more mind when I was in the house. I didn't need her mad at me over somethin' like this. I needed her to be my friend. *Lord, help me get my thoughts put together. I don't understand stuff like this.*

The last armload of wood I brought in was the biggest because I was wantin' to have the job done and then stay outside. But I guess I was packing too much, 'cause I lost a top log, and it went rolling across the floor, almost knockin' Sarah in the toe.

"I'm sorry," I said real quick, plunking the rest of the load in the wood box as fast as I could so's I could retrieve that piece and get back outside. But she had a hold of it before I did. She picked it up and give it one little fling, and it landed all neat an' tidy in the wood box like she'd been practicing chuckin' wood across the room all year.

"No problem," she said. "I drop stuff all the time."

"I don't think I ever noticed that," I told her, and got myself straight back outside.

I thought I'd better split some wood. I always got to praying when I whacked wood. I always did a lot of thinkin'. And that'd be just what I needed this morning. Some of the firewood in the shed had been left in pretty big chunks. Bert did some splitting sometimes, especially the smaller stuff, but with him being sick the last few days and my mind on everythin' else, there hadn't none of that got done. It was the perfect time for it now, though. It'd be just the thing to get my head back on straight.

# 25

## *Sarah*

I wasn't really sure why I kept staying. With Emmie gone to school and Bert feeling some better, I knew they'd think I didn't need to. Frank was thinking it already, I could tell. I was sure I was bothering him, and I didn't want to be, but I couldn't feel right about leaving yet, even if I wasn't sure why not. I couldn't do a thing about their father holing himself up in his room again. I sure didn't know how to cheer him. He hadn't even let me give him a cup a coffee.

"Had too much a' that at Lizbeth's," was all he'd say when I asked him.

Frank had an awful load on him, and I was glad Ben and Lizbeth understood that as well as they did. They'd help all they could. But they weren't here now.

I knew it would be hard to be in Mr. Hammond's shoes. With one son missing so long and another son now wounded, it had to wear at him awful. I knew it would wear at me. But I couldn't understand why he didn't seem to see that it wore on everybody, especially

his kids. Especially Frank, who had to shoulder everything all the more because his pa wouldn't.

But Frank kept on, just working, just doing all the
things that needed to be done. I marveled at him this
morning, because I thought if it was me, I'd have had to
take the time by now to sit down for a good cry. But he
was in the yard by the house, splitting more firewood.
I could hear him. There was a rhythm to the way he
worked. *Plunk. Whack. Plunk. Whack.* Steady, without
missing a beat. I thought his whole brain must work
that way.

I glanced out the window and saw he had his coat off
already, his too-loose shirt swinging in the breeze while
he worked. He needed a haircut again. I ought to offer to
do that for him. But no. I stopped myself real quick. My
mom could do it. Or Rorey. He might not like *me* offering. He wanted me to be his friend, but doing something
like cutting his hair might be too familiar. It wouldn't be
a good idea. Thinking about it wasn't even a good idea.
He had nice thick hair with a wave that was cute for a
boy. It wasn't right for me to even have noticed.

I moved from the window and checked to see if Bert
had finished his herb tonic. Almost half. That was all. I
reheated it for him because Mom said it did more good
hot, and brought it back to the little table next to his
chair. He made a face at me, but he took another sip.
Frank was still splitting wood. *Plunk. Whack. Plunk.
Whack.*

But I thought I heard another sound off a ways. I
went back to the window just to be sure. A vehicle, way
down the lane. Except for my father, there wasn't much
traffic by here, especially in the winter, so I watched just
to see if they'd stop.

I didn't think they would. It was an unfamiliar black
car, going slow. But they slowed even more and got as
close as they could on the lane, and then stopped out

front. Frank hadn't noticed. He must be thinking deep again. I imagined he had a lot to think on.

Two tall strangers in uniforms stepped from the car, and for a minute I almost couldn't breathe. *Oh, God, no.*

I didn't say anything to Bert. I didn't call for their father. All I could think about was Frank outside and what he was going to think, how he was going to feel, when he looked up and saw what I'd just seen.

*Oh, please, God,* I cried in my mind as I went for the door. *Oh, please. Not this. Not more bad news.*

I almost tripped coming down off the porch. Those two men had stood for a minute like they weren't sure they had the right place, or maybe were hesitant to face whatever family might be home. But they moved to the house slow now, and I knew I hadn't been mistaken. They wore crisp, neat military uniforms, right down to the hats and gloves. And my heart pounded in my throat, knowing what they must be here to say. *Not William. Oh, God, please. Are they here, after all this time, to tell about Joe? Or even Kirk? That would be just as bad! Help. Oh, please! Help Frank. And his pa. Oh, Lord, what is their pa gonna do?*

I stepped forward, still hearing Frank with his chopping. *Plunk. Whack.* Tears came to my eyes. I wished there was some way to make all the bad go away, to turn the clock back to before the war even started. It was like a bad dream that shouldn't be real. *Please, not this.*

Frank's rhythm stopped. I swallowed hard and moved closer, right beside him, because I thought that if this was my house they were coming to, I'd need somebody beside me. I saw his face change, like a shadow was falling over him on the inside. It scared me. I couldn't hardly stand it, and I didn't think I could bear to hear whatever these men had to say.

"Is this the Hammond residence?" one of them asked

236

as soon as they were close enough. The other man bowed his head, took off his hat, and held it in his hand.

"Yes," Frank answered stiffly. He didn't ask anything else. He just stood there, the splitting maul still in his hand.

"Is your father at home?" The man's eyes were large and sorrowful. He looked as old as my father, and I knew he didn't like the kind of news he'd come to share.

"Yes, sir," Frank said, letting the splitting maul fall to the cold ground. I could see the pain working in his eyes, but he didn't betray it in his voice. He walked tall, leading those men to the steps and then up onto the porch.

My legs didn't want to move. I felt stiff and at the same time somehow spineless as jelly. But I made myself follow them, glad now that I was here even though I was terrified for what would happen next. When Frank got to the door he turned and looked at me for just a second, and I could read his eyes plain as if he were talking out loud. *Hold steady for Berty, Sarah Jean,* he seemed to be telling me. *We're gonna need your help.*

"Pa?" Frank called as we came inside. "We've got comp'ny, Pa."

I heard Mr. Hammond's dull answer coming from the bedroom but wasn't sure exactly what it was he'd said. Bert let his books fall to one side, and he stood to his feet. I went over quick beside him because I felt like Frank would want me to because he was younger. And there wasn't anything else I could do anyway.

"What comp'ny?" Mr. Hammond grouched a little louder. "Who is it?"

I had to work to keep myself from crying in front of Bert. Maybe I was wrong about everything, and everybody was fine. Maybe these men had some other kind of news. We didn't know anything for sure. And even if I wasn't wrong, it wouldn't do to start blubbering. It wouldn't help them any. And I felt sure now that I'd been right to stay, that I was meant to be here. God must have wanted me here to help somehow, because he knew this was coming.

*Give us strength. And peace. Help me, Lord, to have words to say and the sense about me to know how to help when times are hard. Help me to keep my heart close to you so I'll have peace and strength to share.*

Suddenly, strangely, I thought of Rachel. Maybe I'd hit on the gist of her prayer. But that made me think of Robert, and it was all the harder to hold back tears.

Frank went and opened his father's bedroom door because he still hadn't come out. "Please, Pa," he said real soft. "There's men to speak with you."

"What men?" Mr. Hammond asked him bitterly. But then there was dead silence. He was standing in the doorway where he could see them.

"Mr. George Hammond?" one of the soldiers asked. They both had their hats off now, holding them in their hands. The younger man seemed to be squeezing pretty hard at his.

"Yep, I'm him," Mr. Hammond answered, and his voice was angry. I could see the painful understanding in his face. He looked pale as a ghost, and he shook his head, turning his eyes to Frank. "Tell 'em to go away. I ain't wantin' to hear what they got to say."

"I know," Frank said then. "I know it, Pa. But we gotta hear it. We gotta make ourselves, do you understand?"

Bert made a little choked noise, and I took hold of his arm. I thought maybe he'd push me away, but he didn't. He just stood. I thought I felt a shiver run through him.

One of the uniformed men stepped a little closer to Mr. Hammond. "Please, sir. You might want to have a seat."

Frank moved a chair right to where his father stood, but he wouldn't sit.

238

"Just tell me," he said. "Just get it over with an' tell me. My boy's gone. That's what you finally come 'round to say . . ." He stopped. He looked like he could fall.

"Sir," the older uniformed man began with a sigh. "We're very sorry. It is with our nation's deepest sympathy that we must inform you of the loss of your son, Lieutenant Joseph Willard Hammond . . ."

I closed my eyes for just a second. Beside me, Bert started to sob. "Oh, God," he whispered. "Oh, God."

Mr. Hammond didn't move. He just stood there staring. Frank took his arm and tried to prompt him to sit down, but he wouldn't budge.

"You men know I got another boy wounded?" Mr. Hammond asked them, his voice low and strange.

"No, sir," the younger man said. "We're so sorry."

"I didn't know which one you were gonna tell me," he mumbled just enough to be heard. "I didn't know which way it was gonna be."

"Sir," one of the men repeated. "We're very sorry."

"You said that."

But the soldier's sad voice went on to confirm the things none of us had wanted to hear. "On March seventeen of nineteen hundred and forty-two, Lieutenant Joseph W. Hammond was killed in the line of duty as a result of direct engagement with the enemy in the Philippine Islands. Lieutenant Hammond fought bravely and hazarded himself for the lives of his men. His fellow soldiers and countrymen shall be eternally grateful for his courageous and selfless service. Our deepest sympathy, sir, to you and your—"

"You'd best leave now," Mr. Hammond interrupted. "You've done said your piece."

"Your son will not be forgotten, sir," the closest man tried to continue. "Neither will your sacrifice. May God bless and help you."

"Go," Mr. Hammond said impatiently.

I stood tense, my heart pounding, knowing that he wasn't nearly so steady as he was trying to sound. I could see the awful hurt in him, plain as day. But it was just as plain in Frank, who still held his father's arm, his silver-gray eyes looking like storm clouds. *Help them, Lord,* I prayed again. *Oh, God, help.*

Both of the uniformed men put on their hats, but one of them looked straight at Frank before he turned for the door.

"Thank you," Frank said barely loud enough for me to hear it. "Thank you, sirs, for comin'." His eyes filled with tears.

Solemnly, the soldiers turned away. Mr. Hammond stood stiff as a statue.

"Oh, Pa," Frank said as the men went out the door. I knew he wanted to hug his father. I saw him try. But Mr. Hammond only pushed him away.

"I tol' you!" he yelled. "I tol' you they wasn't comin' home!"

"Pa—"

Whatever it was Frank might have said, his father didn't give him a chance. He spun around and shoved Frank so hard that he fell into another chair. "Keep your mouth shut, boy! Jus' keep your mouth shut!"

My insides were in knots, my heart was thumping so hard in my throat that it hurt. I started to move forward, but Frank's look held me back. I didn't know what to do. I couldn't imagine any man coming apart so bad that he'd light into one of his kids at a time like this.

"The Lord's punishin' me," Mr. Hammond said then. "He's gonna take ever' one—"

"No, Pa," Frank stopped him bravely. "The good Lord ain't to blame." He pulled himself to his feet, and I saw him move a little forward, putting himself between his father and the outside door.

Mr. Hammond just stared at Frank. I never saw him

240

look that bad, ever. "If it ain't God, jus' how do you think you can explain this, huh, boy? How?"

"Evil," Frank said in a quiet voice. "The enemy, jus' like the man said." He looked so broken. But he wouldn't take his eyes off his father. "Sit down. Please, Pa. Sarah's gonna make us some coffee. We gotta lot to think about—"

"Shut up." He stood motionless again, still staring at Frank.

Not sure what else to do, I went and grabbed a pot and put it on the warm stove, thinking I'd better help Frank by doing what he said and making his father some coffee. Maybe he'd sit. Maybe he'd calm enough to let everybody grieve instead of holding his boys captive like this just wondering what he was going to do. I prayed he'd sit. I was scared, really scared of what he might do if he didn't, and I knew Frank and Bert were too.

He moved toward the door, and Frank made sure to stay in front of him.

"Don't ride off, Pa. Please don't ride off."

"What difference does it make? Answer me that!"

"Harry an' Emmie'll be home after a while. You need to be here, Pa. Please. Drinkin' ain't gonna solve nothin'."

Bert stood with his cheeks wet with tears. *They all oughta be hugging one another,* I thought. Mr. Hammond ought to hold his boys and comfort them instead of being so hateful. But he answered Frank with a stream of curses.

"Get out of my way."

"Pa . . ."

I saw Mr. Hammond's fist go up, and I knew he was gonna hit Frank again. I couldn't let it be. I absolutely couldn't. Faster than I knew I could move, I ran up and grabbed at that arm, surprising myself with a boldness I'd never known I had.

"No! Frank and Bert's already hurting just as bad as

you are! Don't you go making it worse! Don't you go hitting anybody or taking off and making them fret for you when there's so much else to sorrow about."

He stared at me, and his face was strange, like somebody I didn't even know. "You're your daddy's girl, ain't you?"

Frank came up beside me. He took my hand and moved almost in front of me. "She's just talkin' sense," he said, and I realized that he was so unsure of his father that he was ready to protect me if he had to.

But George Hammond laughed. "Picture the two a' you. I never thought I'd see the like."

He turned around from us, and I could only stare. I could not imagine anyone laughing at a time like this. Emmie had told me months ago that their father was not well. Bad news shook him. Clear off his foundations. I looked at Frank, but he hadn't taken his eyes off his father. Bert stood near his chair, watching just as intently.

"Ah, Worthams!" Mr. Hammond exclaimed. "What would we ever do without Worthams? Now if it don't look like God's done sent a young'un to set me right. I s'pose you'll tell your pa on me, won't you, girl? You might as well tell him that it's jus' like I said. It's all done. Wilametta's waitin' to meet 'em . . ."

He walked back into the bedroom without another word and shut the door behind him. Bert sunk back into his chair. But I just stood there, looking at Frank.

"What are we gonna do?" Bert asked, his voice sounding horrible broken. Frank moved to his side and put his arm around his shoulder.

"We're gonna be strong for the rest, that's what we're gonna do," he answered. "That's what Joe'd want. Don't you think so?"

Berty tried awful hard, but he couldn't stop the tears.

242

He nodded anyway, and Frank leaned into him with a full embrace.

"It's okay. It's okay to cry," Frank told his brother. "The pastor says it is, an' you've seen him at it, ain't you?"

Berty nodded again.

"We ain't gonna be able to help it for a while. We ain't gonna be able to help a lot a' feelin's. But we gotta do the best we can. You're almost a man, Bert. Writin' for the newspaper an' everythin'. I'm so proud a' you I can't even say how much." He stopped a minute, struggling for more words. "I need your help. I know it hurts. It ain't gonna stop hurtin'. But we got Emmie comin' home this afternoon, an' she's jus' a little thing. An' Harry. An' he's like Pa in that he's more liable to hit somethin' than let hisself cry. An' Rorey, an' you know there ain't no tellin' 'bout her—"

"What . . . what can I do?"

"If you can—if you're feelin' better—take Sarah home for me. Tell Mrs. Wortham what happened. I know she's hurtin' too. They got their own problems. But tell her that we need her or Mr. Wortham here for a while tonight, if they can manage it. An' I need 'em to get word to the pastor an' Sam and Lizbeth, or maybe you could go to the Posts an' ask them to go—"

"Frank," I told him then. "I can do all that. Bert can stay here."

"No, Sarah Jean," he said real solemn. "You don't know how to handle the horses. I need Bert to take 'em an' leave 'em there. Please."

His strange eyes were like stormy pools, and I could scarcely bear to look at them. *Oh, Frank,* I wanted to ask him. *What more are you afraid of? If your pa wants to drink so bad, what would be the harm of just letting him go? He'll get drunk. Maybe he'll cry his eyes out. And then he'll come home.* But I couldn't speak those things. There was something about Frank right now that I just

243

couldn't argue with. Neither could Bert. He nodded his head and dried his whole face on his sleeve, and then he got up to get his coat.

"Thank you, Sarah," Frank told me. "More'n I can say. Thank you."

Reluctantly, I left Frank alone with his father and went with Bert to tell my mother the most heartbreaking news I'd ever carried. I knew she'd drop everything to do what Frank asked. She'd do it even without him asking. She'd probably send me to ask the Posts to take the word into town so she could start back here with Bert right away and be here even before the kids got home from school.

Bert was coughing something terrible, but neither of us had taken the time to get the rest of his tonic down him. I knew my mother would handle that later. She would know far better than me what to do.

# 26

## Frank

Bert and Sarah Jean were quick about leaving, and I was glad. But I stood looking around me at our house, and it seemed so empty I wanted to scream. I should've been prepared for this. I'd thought I was. But the news had still come and hit us broadside. Maybe there was no preparing. I felt like I'd been picked up and slammed sideways all over again. I needed to pray, to set my head straight about all this before seein' anybody else, or even talking to Pa again. I knew he'd try leaving. Only Sarah being here and being so bold with him had stopped him, but I wasn't sure anythin' would stop him the next time.

I got on my knees, trying to put my thinkin' together. *Thank you. For Sarah being here. For her to be comfort to Bert on the way over there. For her to help getting us her folks here, 'cause I know we'll need 'em.*

I stopped, thinkin' about Joe's smiling face, about him pickin' up Emmie when she was a baby, racing Harry 'round the woodshed, or even hitching the wagon to take all of us to church. Joe was the big brother I could talk to the best. He was the one who'd stayed with me the most when my leg was broke. He was the one most likely to stand in my defense when all the other boys I knew only gave me a hard time.

It was hard not to cry about all that. It was hard not to be fierce upset at God for all the things that had happened. But it wasn't God's fault; I told myself the same thing I'd told my pa. God doesn't cause the pain in this world. He helps us bear it. He gives us a way out. *Thank you,* I told God, even though the words came out hard. *Thank you that Joe's not suffering. That he's not been months tortured or half starved or laying someplace in pain. Thank you that he's with Mama, and with you. Because he's in the good place. He can't be hurt anymore.*

My eyes filled with tears. I couldn't hold them back.

But then I heard the bed creak in Pa's room, and I knew he was gettin' up again. *God, help me. Help Pa! I can't just let him take off. I don't know what he'll do after all the things he said before. But I don't know if I can stop him.*

Pa's door opened up slow, and he looked out at me. I wiped at my eyes real quick and thanked God I'd sent Bert off with the horses.

Pa looked terrible, like the grief and hard thoughts had already sapped him dry. "I weren't sure," he said kind of low. "I weren't sure they wouldn't be talkin' 'bout Willy."

"Me neither, Pa."

He come walkin' out to the setting room, but instead of taking a chair he went over to the wall for his coat that was hangin' on a hook. "We got that to face eventually, you know."

"It won't be the same," I tried to assure him. "Willy'll be all right." I was surprised he was talkin' as calm as he was to me. But he was putting on his coat, and I knew what that meant. I stood up. "Pa, you can't be goin' nowhere. I sent the horses with Bert."

246

"I know that. You think I care? You think you're clever, boy, but it ain't gonna stop me."

"Pa . . . please . . ."

He looked at me awful hard. "We been through this before. If that Sarah Wortham hadn't a' been here, I'd already be gone. An' I ain't afraid a' walkin'. What do you think you're gonna do? You can't stop me. I can shove you outta the way an' keep on goin'."

I got in his path again, even though I knew he might bust me good the way he would've done if Sarah Jean hadn't grabbed his arm before. But I didn't really care if he hit me. I could see in his eyes that it wasn't his right mind talking, and if there was any way under God's heaven I could stop him from leavin', I'd do it. It was a gut hurt of some kind, a knowin' that if I let Pa go in this kind of state, it'd all be done. I didn't understand it. I could only think of Emmie and the others and what they already had to face. So I stuck myself between him and the door and braced for whatever he might do.

"Pa. Drinkin' ain't never solved nothing."

"Get outta my way."

"I ain't lettin' you go off alone. It ain't right! Just like Sarah said!"

He took hold of my arm. His eyes were crazy angry. But for a minute he just stared at me, and I thought I seen somethin' in him that weren't so angry. Wild hurt. Like a scared critter caught in a corner.

"Pa . . ."

He shoved me, hard. It was all I could do to catch myself 'gainst the wall as he was openin' the door.

"Pa!"

But he was already out. "You ain't stoppin' me, boy."

My heart was thumpin' so fast it hurt, but I run after him because there was nothin' else I could do. He'd talked about being gone from us. He'd talked about leavin' us for good. I didn't know what was in his mind, but I couldn't let it be. Not when everybody was gonna be hurtin' so bad over Joe. It was like the world was rocked out from under us already. They didn't need no other blow.

"Maybe I can't stop you," I hollered at him. "Maybe you won't let me tell you a blame thing! But if you're goin', then I'm comin' too! An' you can't stop *me*, Pa. There ain't no way you can!"

He turned his head. "Doggone it, boy. You're head-strong."

"Just like my pa."

He stopped in his tracks. "You don't wanna come, Franky."

"I will if I have to. If you take off, I swear I'll follow."

For a second, he almost choked up. "Why?"

"Because I love you, Pa. We need you. I gotta see that you come home. What else can I say?"

He shook his head. "You ain't needed me a long time, boy. You work with Samuel Wortham. You make your own money. You do all right."

I'd never heard him say anything like that before, and I wasn't sure how to respond. "Pa . . . there's more to it than that."

"Like what?"

"Like lovin' you. And knowin' that all the rest love you too. Wouldn't matter if we was all rich as Solomon on our own. You're still our pa. And we need you. 'Specially now."

"You're somethin', Franky. You don't never let go."

"I can't. Don't you understand?"

He turned and looked at me. For the first time I saw the tears in his eyes. "I can't handle this. Everybody's gonna be cryin' an' all. I can't do it."

I nodded just a little. "I feel the same way. But we gotta do it. There ain't no choice in the matter. Them younger ones—they ain't got nobody else."

"They got you. An' the Worthams."

"That ain't the same as their pa."

His shoulders kind of shook, and I might have hugged him, but I didn't know what he'd do. "I ain't no kinda pa," he said. "You know that by now."

"You've tried hard," I told him. "Ten whole years since we lost Mama, and most a' the times's been good."

He smiled, just a little, but even that was still sad. "Hard to picture you sayin' that, boy. I'm well knowin' I ain't give you the best a' times."

"It's all right, Pa. I'm just wantin' you to do the best you can now."

He sighed. "That's just it. I ain't got no best. Not for times like this." He started walking.

I followed him. Pa was tall. He was strong and could move pretty fast if he wanted to, but I did my best at keepin' up. "Where you goin'?" I called out.

"You aim to follow me all the way to town?" he shouted back. "It's durn cold out here. Purt' near eight miles too."

"I reckon I can make it if I have to," I answered him.

He shook his head. "Then what? You gonna try a' drink or two?"

"No, Pa."

"You ain't gonna stop me."

"I would if I could. If I can't, I'll just wait. You gotta stop sometime. Then I'll get you home."

He kept right on going, but his voice was different, low and broken, like he was havin' trouble saying anythin' more. "Willy told me once that you was lily-livered 'cause you wouldn't fight at them boys that teased you. I reckon he was wrong."

"Pa. It's all right to be hurtin'. We're all gonna be hurtin'."

He shook his head at me again. "You know I can't take you them places I been, don't you, Frank? Last night with Ben was bad enough. That's why you're followin' me, ain't it? You don't belong there. You know I ain't gonna be able to do it."

"I'm hopin' you change your mind," I agreed. "I just wanna get us back inside. You ain't had no lunch. The kids'll be home after a while."

"I can't eat, Franky. Not right now." He stopped.

"I can't either," I said gently. "And it's all right. Somehow or 'nother, God'll help us, and it'll be all right."

"You really believe that?"

I took a deep breath. "Right now, Pa, it's hard. But I'm gonna believe it anyhow."

He turned and looked at me. I could see something workin' in him, and I wished he'd just come out and say whatever it was, but he almost turned away. "Why don't you go back inside?"

"Not without you."

He sighed. Real deep. "Frank. I just need to be alone. I just need to walk a while. I can't go to town. I see that, all right? I just wanna go by your mama's grave a while an' talk to her. I think . . . I wanna tell her to be watchin' out for them boys—for Joe, an' maybe even Willy if worse comes to worse. I need some time. You understand that, don't you?"

"Yeah," I said. "I understand that real well. I'll come with you."

His eyes turned angry again. "Franklin Drew—"

"I tol' you I aim to follow you." I hoped he could understand. I couldn't let him go alone, not even to Mama's grave, because I didn't know what he'd do after that.

"Weasly cuss."

"I love you, Pa."

"You done said that already."

"It's important. I want you to know. We're all gonna need each other. We're gonna need a lotta love gettin' through this."

250

He started off again, his feet crunchin' into the frozen, icy grass. We got to the timber, and he didn't stop.

It was hard goin'. I couldn't maneuver so good as him on account of my knee that don't bend just right. But I kept at it, hoping he'd quit and go home. I didn't know if he was really headin' for Mama's grave, or hopin' to shake me and take off for Fraley's or someplace else. I didn't try to talk to him. He hadn't wanted to listen. I just kept crunchin' through the frozen timber after him, glad the snow had melted before it got so cold again. He was gettin' further ahead. But I wouldn't lose him. He could get a way off further than that, an' I'd still see him and hear him.

*Lord, if we ain't home by the time the rest of 'em are, give Bert and everybody peace. They know Pa and they know me. They know I wouldn't take off with no purpose. Help 'em understand that I'll be back soon enough. An' I'll be bringin' Pa with me.*

For a minute I wondered if I wasn't being too hard-headed. Maybe I oughta just let him go. But my heart was too heavy to trust him. And I knew there was time before anybody got home. Maybe I could still persuade him. Maybe the good Lord'd touch his heart.

Tears filled my eyes as I made myself keep going. I thought about Robert being shot so bad, and I wondered if Mr. Wortham had found out anythin' more about Willy. Surely they'd been together. I hoped so, because that would have been comfort, not to be alone. I wished there'd been somebody there with Joe too.

I knew Pa was hurtin'. He couldn't help that. Even if we'd known this might happen, it was still about the awfulest thing I could imagine. I thought of Job and what he'd said after everythin' that happened to him. "Naked came I out of my mother's womb, and naked shall I return thither: the Lord gave, and the Lord hath taken away; blessed be the name of the Lord."

251

Those were strong words. Job had lost a lot. All his kids. And the Bible says he sinned not, nor charged God foolishly. I knew that Pa had started to charge God foolishly, when he'd said the Lord was punishin' him, that it was his doing, as if God had caused Joe's death on purpose. I knew that was wrong. It had to be wrong. And yet Job said, "The Lord hath taken away." I had a hard time puttin' all that together in my mind.

Pa slowed down. He knew I was still behind him. I knew that, even though he didn't look back. We were goin' in the direction of Mama's grave, and I was glad. Maybe Pa needed that. Maybe he was right in what he said. *Lord, be with him. Give him peace.*

I watched him slow some more through the trees. We weren't far off now. I thought of Joe in these woods, fishing in the pond or searchin' up crawdads 'tween there and the creek. Pa almost looked like Joe from the back. They were both tall and lanky, taller than me. With brown shaggy hair and shoulders that seemed too broad to fit the rest of 'em, they was built just alike. It'd never been hard to tell whose boy Joe was.

I sighed. It seemed like there must have been some kind of mistake. How could he be dead? Maybe he was still missing, and there'd been some kind of mix-up somehow. He was a good soldier. Smart and strong. With so much ahead of him. He was a good brother too. Quick to take care of us that was younger.

Maybe I had some of the same angry in me as Pa had. I could feel it, down inside. I wasn't sure who I could be angry at. But it helped me understand Pa a little, at least right now. Who could blame him how he must feel? If he seemed a little hateful, how I could fault him, so long as he didn't do nothin' hurtful? Surely he wouldn't.

Maybe he'd need someone when he got done talkin' at Mama's grave. Maybe I oughta give him a little time, like he said, so he could cry where no one could see him.

Then when the cryin' was done, maybe he'd be ready to not be alone.

The timber felt lonely, frigid, with slick patches of ice where puddles had gone solid after a freezing rain a couple of days ago. The wind was stirring the barren treetops, and here and there a tiny piece of ice would cascade down and hit the ground with a soft little plink. We were almost to Mama's grave, where the buttercups and the daffodils and all the other flowers we'd planted so long ago bloomed so pretty every spring. But there was nothing bloomin' now. The woods seemed as lifeless as Mama's weathered stone.

I saw Pa up ahead. He just sunk to the ground in sight of Mama's grave. I stopped, not wantin' to bust in on something I figured he needed. I almost turned back so I could leave him truly alone for a minute like he wanted. I wished I could. I wished I could know that he wouldn't take his chance to get shuck of me in the woods. It didn't seem like respect to be followin' him when he didn't want it, but I could picture Emmie cryin' in my mind. I could picture Bert's sad face, and I knew how it had upset them last night when he disappeared.

This time was worse. This was the worst thing since Mama's passing, and we wouldn't have our pa with us today if Mr. Wortham hadn't found him just in time when he'd took off then. It was a chance I just couldn't take.

Seeing him all humped over made me hurt inside. I wished I could go and put my arm around him, but I thought sure he'd push me away. At least he looked to be prayin', and I figured that was the thing he needed most.

I sighed deep, thinking of our growing-up years, the bad times and good times jumblin' around together in my mind. I thought of Pa sick the first Christmas morning after Mama died, hungover from drinking the night before. He was a mess, weak as he'd ever been. But before the winter was out, he'd recovered himself enough to be some help to us, and he'd saved Mr. Wortham out of the pond ice and made himself a hero.

Surely it could work that way again. He'd recover himself. Somehow. We all would.

I sighed. Pa hadn't moved. When he got ready to, I'd go over to him. I'd offer my shoulder, or anything at all I could do to be some help. I wondered if he was thinking on Joe. It was hard not to. I could picture him in the fields with his hair all sweaty, or strugglin' over his books, 'cause even though he wasn't a very good student, it'd been important to him. Willy used to throw me in the pond, clothes and all, and Joe'd be the only one to help fish me out and scold him for it. Joe was always kind. He'd helped Lizbeth with the little ones when she was havin' to try an' take Mama's place.

With a sigh, I tried to push my mind off those things 'cause I knew I'd end up cryin' if I didn't.

*God, I don't understand it. This world don't make any sense right now. Joe oughta be right here fellin' trees for firewood, or seekin' after a girlfriend, and instead he's just gone, before ever gettin' a chance to see what the rest of life might have been like.*

I felt bad thinkin' a prayer like that. Awful feelings had been tryin' to drag my mind down for months, and even though I guess I'd known right about Joe, I still didn't want to give in to the sad thoughts. I had to be able to be strong and keep up with everythin' that was gonna need done, no matter what my feelings. Because the world didn't just stop, much as it seemed like maybe it should.

All of a sudden a line jumped to my memory from that Hamlet book Mrs. Wortham had read: "How weary, stale, flat and unprofitable seem to me all the uses of this world."

I looked over to Pa and hoped he wouldn't agree with

words like that. It didn't seem like the right attitude to take. But the world made no sense anymore. Maybe it was worth nothin' at all, at least in the eternal scheme of things. And that would make Joe the blessed one, to be gone from here, from an unprofitable, stale, and weary world, and into a better one.

But it'd be foolishness to confuse Shakespeare with Scripture, and if I needed to train my thoughts on anythin' right now to provide any comfort, any answers, it had better be the Word of God. *In this world is tribulation,* I told myself immediately. *But the trials of our faith are more precious than gold.*

There was reason to this world. There was purpose. Because God didn't create in vain. He gives us blessings, he allows us trials, so we can grow and learn and bless somebody else. God's the God who gives rest to the heavy-laden and comforts those who mourn. I thought of some of the words that had caused Jesus trouble when he read them in the synagogue, and words that came right after them in the book of Isaiah: "The Spirit of the Lord is upon me; because he hath anointed me to preach good tidings unto the meek; he hath sent me to bind up the brokenhearted . . . to comfort all that mourn . . . to give unto them beauty for ashes, the oil of joy for mourning, the garment of praise for the spirit of heaviness . . ."

*That's what we need, God,* I prayed. *Beauty in this situation somehow. Oil of joy for the mourning. A garment of praise for this heaviness I feel. Help us.*

I sat on a stump, wishing I knew better what to do. I didn't want to make Pa mad by walkin' up closer after he'd told me so plain he wanted to be alone. But it seemed kind of awful to let him have his way even this much. It didn't seem right for him to be kneeling there alone.

He still had his back to me. The wind was chilly, and I realized for the first time that neither of us had a hat. I started prayin' for him. After Mama died, it'd been

255

hard for any of us to think or do anythin' for days. What would happen this time?

I wondered what Pa would be like when he got up. I wondered if he'd cuss me an' tell me to go home again, or if he'd want to come home as bad as I was hopin' he would. I really did love him. And I wished I knew a way to help him. But I wasn't sure there was anythin' I could do if he didn't want nothin' done.

I prayed again for Pa and Willy, Robert and Kirk and the rest of my family and the Worthams. Then I figured I oughta go over and try to talk to Pa because it'd been a while. But before I got two steps I started cryin'. I knew I was cryin' over Joe, plus Willy and Pa and even my own self about how bad it all felt. I cried for my whole family, because I knew how hard it was gonna be for everybody.

And then I saw Pa turn around. The woods was so quiet I heard the crunch of his boot when he started gettin' up. And I dried my eyes real quick again, not sure what to expect.

"Still here, huh, Franky?" He looked pale and lost. He didn't meet my eyes.

"I thought you might need me."

I saw him fix his eyes on a icy wild gooseberry bush that was still holding a dried berry or two. I sure wished I could read what he was thinkin'. "Was hopin' you'd give up an' go home," he said sorta low.

"Well, Pa. It's cold. I didn't feel right about leavin' you to walk home alone."

"Maybe it's just as well, boy," he said without lookin' up. "'Fore I get shuck a' you, I'm gonna have to talk at you. I guess it ain't gonna leave me alone."

His words left me cold inside. He was still planning on leavin'. What would he say? Did he think it would help matters to tear me down first? I just stood, unable to answer him. No matter how badly he might think he needed to sound off at somebody like he'd done so many times before, me listenin' to his hateful words wasn't gonna bring my brother back or bring any comfort to our family. Didn't he see that?

"You're botherin' my mind, Franky," he started. "Ever since that night in the schoolhouse."

He paused, and I forced myself to answer him. "I don't understand."

"You remember what you told me then? Same thing you said a little while ago."

I nodded, my heart poundin' furious in my chest. "I love you, Pa."

He kept starin' straight at that bush. "Maybe you do. Maybe that's why you keep after me. An' Lizbeth an' Emmie've tol' me they love me. Rorey too, once or twice."

"I'm sure they do. We all do."

"Ain't but two a' you boys ever said it, though. You an' Joe. Why do you think that is?"

I hung my head. Just thinkin' 'bout Joe made my insides feel like they were being squeezed. "I don't know. Maybe him an' me failed at learnin' by example."

He laughed. Just one short burst, but it cut at me something awful. "You're right there," he said. "Don't guess I've said it much, have I?"

"No, Pa. You haven't."

"Well. Maybe that's why you been botherin' me."

He was still staring at the same bush, lookin' almost like he had in the schoolhouse, like a specter even though it was daylight this time.

"Can we go home, Pa? Please?"

"Hang it all, Franky! There you start in again, when I'm tryin' to tell you somethin'! Why don't you just shut up an' listen?"

I closed my eyes, not sure what to expect. And I could hear the hesitation in what he said next.

257

"You tol' me in the schoolhouse that you love me. You said it twice, an' again today. I know real well that I ain't never said it to you. I ain't never tol' none a' you. Never thought I oughta need to. But you don't know it, do you? An' I got a boy gone . . ." His voice broke. "Maybe two, that never did know . . ."

He stopped, and tears filled my eyes so quick there weren't no holdin' them back. "Oh, Pa—"

"Don't say nothin'. I gotta talk. I gotta tell you somethin' I can't say but once. You're gonna have to tell the rest. You can do it. You're better'n me at talkin'. And you's the one I gotta tell face to face 'cause I reckon I give you cause to doubt it the most. I love you, son. I love all a' you. Ever' single one . . ."

He couldn't go on. Suddenly, my pa was cryin'. I stood stiff for a minute, not knowin' what to do. What would he want me to do?

But then I couldn't wait any longer. I went to him. I held him. He put his arms around me too, and we both cried. I used to dream of Pa holdin' me this way, but I never thought it would ever happen. I'm sorry for both of us that it didn't happen until somethin' so bad come along that we was too weak to do anythin' else.

"Pa—"

"It ain't your fault, boy. I don't want you to go blamin' yourself for no part a' nothin' in this, do you understand me?"

I tried to nod, wonderin' why he felt he needed to tell me that. How could anyone think of blame for anyone but the enemy? Joe'd been so far away in the war.

"You tell the rest of 'em ever'thin' I said."

"Pa, you can tell 'em—"

"Nah. I tol' you I can't say it but once."

"But Pa—"

"I'm wantin' to go to town now."

I knew he didn't want me to argue. He wanted me to

accept somethin' I'd never gained from him in my life and go home thinkin' that was enough. But I couldn't. "Pa, I meant what I told you. I'm comin' too."

"An' I tol' you I can't deal with no more." He pulled away and started toward the trees.

"Pa—it's crazy! We oughta go home! If you wanna walk eight miles in the cold, then we'll go, but we belong at home where they're gonna need us. This don't make no sense—"

"There ain't no sense to nothin'. Wouldn't be no sense me sittin' 'round home."

He was getting further away, and I ran after him. "This won't help, Pa. Drinkin' won't bring Joe back. It don't make nothin' better."

"An' you know somethin' that does? Huh, boy? You got a Scripture for this? Do you? Let's hear it."

He stopped and stared at me, and I longed for words that would be some help. "I can tell you Scriptures 'bout how much God loves us, Pa. That's the important thing to remember. Despite all the trouble in this world, God loves us so much that he saved us. He promised eternal life, where we can be with him and see our loved ones again."

"You reckon Joe's in heaven, do you?"

I sucked in a deep breath. "I believe it. I ain't got no doubt. I know he prayed plenty a' times, 'specially that time our church had the outside meetin' when he was fourteen. You remember?"

"Yeah," he said pretty solemn. "What about your mama? Got any doubts 'bout her?"

"No. I don't have no doubts."

"What about me, then? Will I see 'em when I die?"

He stood lookin' almost like a child. But his words chilled me deep anyhow. I used to pray for Pa to ask questions like this, to be hungry to know that he was saved. But now my heart was poundin' in my throat, and

259

it was hard to talk to him. I didn't like him asking about his own self dyin'. I didn't like him thinkin' on that. But I had to tell him something. He needed to know, and so did I. "Pa, I can't answer that so well as you can. I've seen you praying. But is it true in your heart? Do you believe what Jesus done for us?"

"I heard the words plenty a' times," he answered me. "An' I said the words the pastor tol' me."

"But do you believe it?" I asked him, my eyes fillin' up with tears again.

He bowed his head. "Yeah. Yeah, boy, I reckon I do."

I hugged him again, but this time he stood stiff and didn't hug me back. "Then you can be sure, Pa," I told him. "If you prayed and you believe. We're gonna see 'em again someday."

He nodded, and he talked just as stiff as he'd felt. "Get back home. You oughta be there. You can tell 'em what I said." He turned around.

"Pa?"

"Don't fret. An' don't follow me. I ain't gonna be out all night. It's gonna be too blame cold."

I didn't want to disobey, but I still couldn't let him go. "I'll come with you. It'll be all right."

He glared at me. "There ain't nothin' all right about it, boy. An' no way to make it better."

I took a deep breath. *Help me, Lord. I'm scared of what I'm still seein' in him. Even after he says he's prayed.*

He turned from me and went walkin' into the trees. The things he'd said might seem good, to tell me after all this time that he loved us. But it made me wonder at him, like maybe he was just settlin' things in his own mind so he wouldn't feel guilty if he left us at a time like this. So I started walking, resolvin' in my mind that this was just the way it was gonna be. Pa too hardheaded to stop, and me too hardheaded to go back without him.

"You're acting a fool, Franky," he told me.

"I'm finally learnin' by example," I answered him back.

He turned and eyed me coldly. "What's the matter with you?"

I was careful not to back down from his gaze. "I thought we settled that already. We love you. We need you. An' you ain't gettin' shuck a' me."

"So what if I'm gonna get me a bottle?" he suddenly demanded. "What's so bad about that? I've done it before. Can't you let it be?"

"This ain't like before. You ain't lost a son before."

He took a deep breath, and it seemed like the weight of it was taking extra effort.

"I'm scared for you," I told him flat out. "You tell me you can't handle no more. An' you been thinkin' a' leavin'. Pa, I know what things was like when we lost Mama."

It was hard to see him clear; my eyes had suddenly got so damp and blurry. But his look had somehow softened.

"Franky. I shoulda knowed better. There ain't much use tanglin' with you. I figured I could get ahead a' you out here. But I shoulda knowed you'd keep up till you backed me down."

"Pa—"

"You don't have to say nothin' else. I'll come home. You're right anyway. Drinkin' don't solve nothin'. It just gets in the way a' thinkin' 'bout it for a while."

I hardly knew what to say. For him to back down was what I'd prayed for, but I still wasn't sure of him. He still looked wild. We walked side by side back through the cold timber, and he told me he didn't want to talk to anybody else. He just wanted to be left alone in his room a while. That bothered me. But just havin' Pa home, silent or not, would be better than everybody frettin' over him being gone. They didn't need no more worry, that was

261

for sure. And surely he'd be better after a while, like he was before. Surely he'd be okay.

We didn't say nothin' else on the way. But at least he was sober. At least he'd be home. Bad as everything else hurt, havin' that much seemed like a victory.

# 27

## *Sarah*

I wanted to get back to the Hammonds' house so bad it hurt. And I knew it was for Frank. I couldn't shake the thought of him getting knocked into a chair and then just minutes later taking my hand and stepping up to protect me from his father, when it was his father who had knocked him down. What would happen now that they were alone? Mr. Hammond flew apart in the bad times, and he was way too quick to take it out on Frank.

It was hard to breathe, all of this hit me so hard. By the time we'd got home, Bert was so upset he could hardly talk. He cried, and I knew he was still feeling sick. Mom hugged him and then said that he and she ought to ride back to be there for Frank and their pa in plenty of time before school got out.

"No, Mrs. Wortham," Bert said. "We can't ride back. Frank said to take the horses an' leave 'em here. I know what he's thinkin'. He don't wanna give Pa no easy way to leave."

My mother nodded, the tears working in her eyes. "But I don't want you walking back through the cold,

Bert. We can't have you getting worse. Sarah, I'm sorry
to send you out again, honey, but you're going to have
to go to the Posts. I'd go myself, but I think I'd better
stay with Bert."

I nodded. She hugged me, and suddenly my faithful,
strong mother wept. I didn't know what to do but help
her to a chair and hug her back, fighting my own tears.
"I'll go, Mom. Don't worry. It's really not that far."

I could feel her taking in a deep breath, steadying
herself. She nodded and pulled away a little. "We need
Mr. Post to come by here, if he will, and take Bert and
me back over to the Hammonds. We need to be there
when the other children get home. And I expect that
Frank and George could use some help. Then if Mr. Post
would go to town—he needs to tell Samuel. That will be
enough. Samuel will get word to Sam and Lizbeth, and
the pastor. And probably tell Rorey and Katie on their
way home . . ."

She took another deep breath and rose to her feet. I
could see the pain seething raw in her eyes, worse than
I'd ever known it, and I knew that this news on top of all
the heartache for Robert was weighing her awful bad.
But she went straight to the stove and put on water to
heat. "While we wait for a ride, I'm going to make Bert
some tea for that cough. Put my coat on over yours,
Sarah. I want you to stay warm. I'm sorry . . . to have
to ask you—"

"It's okay, Mom. It's okay."

She nodded, already pulling something down from the
cupboard. Bert had leaned his head and arms down on
to the table. I hurried. I grabbed Mom's coat like she told
me and buttoned it quick as I could. I went running out
the door and kept right on running down our icy lane.
The Posts' house was only a couple of miles. I'd walked
there before. But not for anything like this.

I slipped once. I didn't fall all the way down, because

I'd come close enough to a pasture fence to catch myself first. I kept right on going. I could almost see Mr. and Mrs. Post opening the door of their big, fine farmhouse to me, wondering why in the world I'd run myself practically out of breath. What could I tell them? That Joe was gone? The honored soldier, brother, and friend. So soon. Way too young. And we needed them to rush into town and spread the horrible news.

My eyes filled up with tears, and I had to brush them away to see to keep going. This was all like some awful dream. Not real at all. *God give us peace!* I prayed as I ran. *God give us strength! Be with us. Help us understand. Help us make sense of all this.*

Mrs. Post was outside when I got close, on her way back to the house with a skillet in her hands. She must have just dumped kitchen scraps out someplace. She saw me right away and first waved in the yard but then stopped and waited when I hurried her way instead of waving back.

She called for her husband as soon as I told her what had happened. They both had aged so much. Mrs. Post was getting a little stooped, and Mr. Post wasn't as spry as he used to be. But they'd always been good neighbors. And they were quick to be good neighbors now.

"Climb in the truck," Mr. Post told me. "I'll take you home before I head to town."

"Mom wants you to take Bert home from our house once you get there," I told him, almost forgetting that part of the request. "And Mom and I might want to ride along too, to be there for the rest of the Hammonds when they get home."

"That's the neighborly thing," he told me solemnly. "God be with them."

It wasn't a very long drive between the Posts and our house, but my mind was so taken up with awful questions that I hardly noticed the distance at all. Why Joe?

265

Why did he have to die? All this time we'd prayed and cried. But he was still gone. And Robert and Willy were hurt bad too. Even Lester. What if Rorey's awful dream had been true? What if none of our boys were coming home?

Getting out of Mr. Post's truck to get Mom, I found that I was shaking enough to make me feel unsteady on the frozen ground.

"You all right, Sarah?" he asked me.

"Yes." But I couldn't take my mind off things. I couldn't stop thinking of Frank's face, and Bert's face. We still didn't know for sure how bad Willy was hurt. And now this. How could the Hammonds manage it all? How could they be expected to bear it?

I wouldn't have had to get out of the truck at all. Mom had been watching, and she and Bert hurried out of the house so Mr. Post wouldn't have to wait. I gave her back her coat first thing, because she hadn't thought to grab a quilt or anything to put around herself. But she'd left Dad and Katie a note to tell them where we were in case they got back before Mr. Post found them.

"Don't have to worry about that," Mr. Post said. "I'll be going straight to Samuel at the station first thing."

I thought I'd have to ask Mom about me going back to Hammonds with her. She hadn't said a thing about it, but it seemed like the most natural thing for me to climb back into Mr. Post's truck and go with them. Mom seemed to expect it from me.

"How was Mr. Hammond?" she asked me for the first time when we were on our way over there.

"Not very good, Mom," I told her. "I'm glad you're gonna be there."

"I hope Franky's all right," Bert added. "Havin' to deal with him alone."

None of us were too surprised to find that Mr. Hammond was in bed by the time we got there. Mom hugged

266

on Frank and then sat Bert down and started heating his abandoned tonic and trying to make some lunch. They didn't feel like eating it, but Mom said they ought to at least try, at least Bert ought to have a little and then maybe go back to bed till he felt some better. He did what she said, because he knew my mother was wise and there wasn't anything else he could do. His schoolbooks were abandoned by the chair. I offered to bring some of them up the loft ladder to him, but he wasn't sure he could concentrate on them anyway. Mom said it might be better if he could just sleep.

Frank told us he'd walked out to his mother's grave with his pa. I got the feeling there was something working deep in him that he wasn't telling. But he said he was only glad his pa was home, and he wanted to make sure he stayed.

"I'm glad you're here too, Mrs. Wortham," he said. "You're a godsend to us."

He stayed in the house for a while, but pretty soon he headed for the barn to break the ice in the water troughs or fill them if they needed it.

He kept busy. He went from one chore to the next, even things that didn't have to be done right then at all.

"Why don't he sit down, Mom?" I asked.

"Maybe he can't." She sighed. "Maybe he knows the sadness'll catch up if he slows down."

She was the same way herself. She cleaned over things I'd cleaned this morning, and then some. She tried to talk to Mr. Hammond, but he wouldn't have anything to do with that. When it didn't seem like there was anything else to put her hands to, she pulled the last shrively apples out of a bin and started in to make a pie. Not knowing what else to do, I helped her.

After a while, we heard Bert coughing again. "Take him up a drink, will you please?" Mom asked.

So I ladled some water into a cup and started up the

loft ladder. It was all one big room up there, but there wasn't much more to it than a bunch of beds with shelves on the wall above every one.

I brought him the water, and he drunk it down and thanked me. He looked so awful sad I wished I could make it better.

I sat on the end of his bed with a sigh. "Are you all right?"

"I don't s'pose none of us is gonna be all right for a while. Will you get me my notepaper? I oughta write things down. I oughta put it all in my next newspaper article so everybody'll know . . ." He stopped, and I could see him struggling to finish. "I want them to know Joe's a hero."

I nodded, the tears rising back up in me again. "That's a good thing to do."

"Thanks for being here, Sarah. You were brave with my pa this morning. I couldn't a' done that. I don't know what woulda happened . . ."

"It's all right. You're being real brave too. You'll get through this. I think you're all really strong."

"Will you talk to Franky?" he asked me then. "I know he's got Pa on his mind, but I'm afraid he's gonna hold everythin' to himself, an' it's too much for him to deal with alone."

"We'll help him. That's why he wanted Mom here. We'll help all of you all we can."

"I know. But that's not what I mean. Please talk to Franky, Sarah, when you get the chance. He's worryin' over everybody else. But you know him, how he does more thinkin' than the rest of us put together. An' I ain't sure he'll talk to anybody but you."

I was surprised to hear him say something like that. I was surprised that anybody in Frank's family would have noticed him talking to me very much, but maybe I shouldn't have been. Maybe we were more obvious about it than I realized. Maybe some of them even knew the things I tried to hide. That of all the Hammond boys or any other boy I'd ever met, I admired Frank the most. Because he always did what he thought was right, no matter how hard it was, or how ugly other people were being, or how bad life treated him. He'd surprised me again and again. He'd made me respect him all the more, every time something happened. Even this.

"I will," I promised Bert softly. "I'll talk to him."

I went and got him his writing paper. And then I thought I'd go outside and find Frank, but I guess the afternoon was farther along than I thought. He was coming in, and I could see Harry and Emmie coming through the yard.

Mom thought Mr. Hammond should come out of his room to talk to them. But he wouldn't, so she and Frank had to sit them down and tell them that Joe was gone. At first I thought Harry was going to blow up like their father had, but then he just sat and said nothing at all. Emmie started crying right away. Mom held her, and Frank hugged Harry, and I was left standing there feeling completely helpless. It hurt worse than anything to see people hurting and not be able to do anything about it.

*I don't know what to think anymore, God. Instead of understanding you better, all of this just makes me confused. Why would you make a world with so many struggles? I know you made it perfect. But you knew what would happen. Why did you let it be?*

It wasn't long before Dad was driving up the lane. We expected him to have Katie and Rorey with him when he came, but Lizbeth was with them too. She jumped out of the truck first thing with Mary Jane in her arms. She said Ben had gone to help Sam and Thelma get here because they were having trouble with their car.

But Lizbeth hadn't wanted to wait. She tried to talk to her pa, but he wouldn't talk to anybody. Frank told her that's what he'd said he wanted, just to be left alone a while, and if we'd all agree to that, he'd agree not to run off for solace in a bottle somewhere else.

Dad hadn't been able to find out much about William except that he didn't seem to be hurt so bad as Robert was, and they expected him to recover. He told Mr. Hammond, because it should have been comfort to know that much, but Mr. Hammond wouldn't respond to him at all.

I didn't remember very well what everybody did when Mrs. Hammond died, but I knew it was a bad time, and this one was bad too. Mr. Post and his wife brought a bunch of food at about the same time Sam and Ben were getting there, but the Posts didn't stay. The pastor and his wife came pretty soon, and they brought food too.

Pastor prayed, but I guess it was mostly just good to have him there. I wanted to ask him if he could tell me why wars and all their awful consequences had to happen. But I couldn't make myself speak the questions out loud. It got to be dinnertime, and even with all the food sitting there handy, nobody ate very much. After a while, Pastor and his wife had to leave, and when they did I felt kind of empty in my heart even though the house was still full of people.

Lizbeth wanted to stay over, to be here for her father and the rest if they needed her. So Mom and Thelma decided that rather than someone making a trip into town that night to take Sam's family home, they would stay at our house. Emmie was going to go too. Katie helped Thelma bundle the kids while Mom and Sam hugged everybody else.

"I want to stay, Mom," I told her when she picked up our coats.

"Are you sure?" she questioned.

270

"I could help Lizbeth with Mary Jane if somebody else needs her," I said. "Or I could help doctor Bert, or just be here with Rorey for a while."

Rorey looked over at me when I said that. She and I had talked so little in the past few months that it maybe seemed a little different for me to say that now. But I didn't feel right about going home to my bed. And I meant the things I was saying, even though I remembered my promise to Bert too. I needed to talk to Frank. I hadn't gotten the chance. And I felt like Lizbeth did, that we just hadn't ought to leave them all alone. Mom nodded, and Dad kissed my forehead and said he was proud of me for helping. Pretty soon they were gone.

Right away I put on water to heat because I figured that was what Mom would do. I could at least make some more hot tea with honey for Bert, to help his cough in the night. And I thought maybe Rorey would talk to me, but she didn't talk to anybody. When I hugged her, she held onto me a while. But she turned away as soon as she let go and went to her bed in the loft.

Lizbeth went into their father's room, but she didn't stay very long. He wanted to sleep, she said. So she'd hugged him and kissed him and left him alone.

Harry was helping Ben carry in more wood again. Lizbeth was rocking Mary Jane in her mother's old rocker by the fire. And Frank had gone out to the barn. I asked Lizbeth if she thought it'd be all right if I went out just to see if he needed help with anything.

"You do that," she said, and she seemed glad I would want to.

So I bundled my coat back on, and my scarf and gloves and overshoes, glad I'd dressed warm starting out yesterday, because those same clothes were still serving me well. It was even colder now than in the daylight, and I was glad that Frank and his father had come back home from their walk in the timber. There was some-

271

thing about what he'd told Mom and me that I knew wasn't complete. I knew something had happened between Frank and his father before any of us had gotten here, and I couldn't imagine that it could be good. And yet they had gotten back. Both of them, and that was much to be glad about.

The moonlight made the whole farmyard seem strangely unreal. I could easily imagine that I might have dreamed the last few days, or even the whole last year, except that the hurt in everybody's faces still pressed upon my heart. It was far too deep not to be real. I opened the barn door slowly and stepped inside, trying to see in the dimness.

"Frank?"

I didn't know if he'd hear me. I wasn't completely sure if he was here or in one of the other outbuildings. But if he was here, he might not hear me anyway. He might be far away in thoughts of his own.

"Franky?" I called, not sure why I was suddenly using the boyish form of his name I hadn't used in at least three years. I knew I'd find him. I could almost feel him somehow, sending his prayers and his pains upward.

He was kneeling in Star's empty stall. With his back to me, he had his head bowed, and I knew he was praying. I thought of him comforting Bert and the others. I thought of my mother and father and the pastor and his wife and Lizbeth, all of them trying to be a comfort too. But Frank hadn't taken much of the comforting attention for himself. He'd sat quietly in the Hammonds' sitting room and quoted a Scripture I'd been surprised to hear right then, even from him.

"Blessed be God, the Father of our Lord Jesus Christ, the Father of mercies, and the God of all comfort . . ."

Everybody had been silent when he said it, as if there was nothing else that could possibly be said. He'd looked so strong then, like he understood things the rest of us didn't. It seemed like he'd found peace far more than I could attain to. So I wasn't sure why Bert thought he might need my help. Or why Robert had thought it, in his letter so long ago.

Maybe I was only intruding now, walking in to see Frank praying in the barn stall this way. But suddenly he sunk lower, his head almost to the straw. He'd done so much to smooth everybody else's way, but here he was bowed over as though he were carrying the weight of all our pain. "Blessed be God," he'd said, and I swallowed hard, knowing that I came up short compared to Frank. I hadn't given the Lord any praise.

His brother was gone. Who knew what else the future might hold? Yet in the face of all that, here he knelt, the strongest young man I could ever meet. He should not be praying alone.

Slowly, feeling unsure of myself, I stepped closer and eased down to kneel beside him on the cold barn floor. I didn't know what he'd think. I didn't know if he'd want my presence there beside him. But I knelt anyway, silent, trying to form halting prayers for Frank and his family in my mind. And slowly, without a word, without looking up at all, he moved his hand to hold mine.

# 28

## *Frank*

I'd felt so cold deep in my spirit. Trying to hold on to faith, and peace, I'd felt like I was fallin' and there was nothing more that could be done. But Sarah's hand in mine was suddenly warm, the only warm thing I thought I could find about this whole situation. But I didn't want to worry her. I didn't want to be weak when she might need me to be strong.

I stood up carefully, helping her to her feet as I went. "You should go back in the house," I told her. "It's too cold to be out."

She didn't move or pull her hand away. "Will you come too?"

"I don't know. Pretty soon, I guess."

I meant to walk her to the porch. I meant to see that she went in where it was warm. I didn't want her catchin' cold like Berty. But it was good she'd been here these last two days. I'm not sure how we'd have done without her.

I was gonna pull away from her hand. I knew I should.

But it was so awful dark in the barn that first I led her out into the moonlight.

"I've been thinking on the Scripture you quoted," she said in a soft voice. "I wish I could find the strength to bless God when I'm feeling the worst."

There was a tiny glistening on her cheek, and I knew it was the moonlight striking a tear. She'd cared about Joe. She loved my whole family, just like her parents did. And of course she was still worried about Robert. She looked so scared and forlorn that I had to put my arms around her just for a minute. "It'll be all right, Sarah Jean," I whispered. "You'll see."

The wind blew some of her long hair across her face, and I brushed it back, wonderin' if she was feeling as cold and empty as I had been just moments ago.

"Maybe you oughta be sittin' by the fire," I suggested. "Maybe Lizbeth would make you some cocoa. That'd warm your insides."

"Will you come?" she asked me again.

I wasn't sure how to answer. "I don't know. Maybe I'm kinda like my Pa in a way. Seems like it wouldn't be right to keep stayin' in there with everybody. I oughta be out here in the cold and let the hurt just hurt as long as it needs to, do you know what I mean?"

She nodded. "I think I do. But I don't think anything will be better that way. There's only one answer to this. You were right that it's God. And he didn't make us to be set off alone in the barn. He gave you your family. And mine."

I just looked at her warm, kind eyes, and something came over me I'd never felt ever in my life. Before I could think twice or realize what I was doing, I leaned and kissed her, real soft, right on the lips.

But the shock of her touch and the look on her face made me jump back. "Oh, Sarah Jean, I'm sorry. I didn't mean to—I ain't thinking right just now . . ."

I figured she'd run for the house, or maybe all the way home. It was a stupid, stupid, horrible thing to do. I started back for the barn. But she surprised me. She took my arm before I could get any farther away. "Franky, it's all right."

I turned and looked at her again. Maybe she wasn't quite herself either.

"We ought to go in and get that cocoa."

I just stared, not sure how to respond.

"It is getting cold," she prompted.

"You're not mad?"

"No. Are you mad that I'm not?"

I didn't know how to answer that. I wasn't sure how she could even turn her thinkin' around enough to wonder about me being mad at her. "Sarah Jean, you're a puzzle sometimes."

"I know. I puzzle over myself probably more than anyone else can think to. I wonder all kinds of things. Like why God made time, and why we're here. And why I'm myself and not Rorey or somebody else. And why God made us with the brains to wonder things we can't get the answers to."

I took a deep breath. "Maybe we can ask him sometime."

"I'd like to ask him about war too. And why somebody like Joe should die so young." She bowed her head.

I quick fetched my kerchief out of my pocket and handed it to her. "Please don't cry out here, Sarah. I'm afraid your tears'll freeze."

"I'll be all right," she answered. "But I came outside because I was wondering about you."

"I wish you wouldn't. Not if it's gonna keep you in the cold."

"Are you doing all right?"

I could hardly believe she was still worried about me. I'd *kissed* her, for goodness sake. It was a wonder she hadn't slapped me. "Yeah. I'll be okay," I managed to answer. "I guess sometimes I just need to put my head back together. I guess I knew this was comin'. But there's no way to stop the hurt."

She took my hand. "Remember what you told me. You can picture Joe already with Jesus. We know he's all right. And someday God will answer the questions and we'll all be together. I can see you hugging Joe and catching up on old times. He'll want you not to mourn him too bad. He'll want to know that you went on with all the things that make you happy, and kept on blessing God through everything the way you did earlier tonight."

For a moment, there was nothing I could say. Sarah Jean stood in front of me like some kind of angel giving me words that could only be inspired by God himself. She looked so pretty in the moonlight. Almost like she had a light of her own. "You're right," I told her. "I know you are. Seems like my heart tells me the same thing."

She smiled. "Does it tell you we're ready for cocoa?"

I managed to nod my head at her. "Yeah, I guess it does. If you'll sit by the fire and let me get yours for you. I don't want to be responsible for you bein' half froze."

We went inside then, and I made her sit by the fire like I'd said. I took off her coat and wrapped her in Mama's patchwork quilt. Lizbeth was rockin' Mary Jane and I didn't want to disturb her, so I made the cocoa myself, but she watched me all the while.

It was hard to get to sleep that night, but Lizbeth made sure everybody was bedded down comfortable where they could at least try. She put Sarah on Emmie's bed, right next to Rorey, but the girls' side of the loft room wasn't all that far from me and from Bert and Harry, and I lay awake a long time, still wonderin' why she hadn't got upset over my foolish kiss.

Finally I dropped off to sleep, dreamin' things like

Sarah'd told me. Of huggin' Joe and tellin' him all the things that were happenin'. And him tellin' me not to be upset. He really was all right. But sometime in the middle of the night, I heard a noise. A voice, I thought. Lizbeth and Ben and Mary Jane were all downstairs, spread out on a pile of bedding by the sitting room fireplace. Maybe they'd woke up for something and were talkin' a little. Maybe Mary Jane had woke up, and they were tryin' to get her back to sleep.

I tried to get back to sleep too. I felt better about Joe than I had before. The worst part now was gonna be helpin' everybody to see that we could be glad he wasn't suffering, and he wouldn't want us to be all upset for his sake.

But behind that peace, there was something, a dark kind of worry that wouldn't let me alone enough to sleep again. What could it be? It didn't make any sense. Pa was home. Everybody was calm. Everything was gonna be all right.

But I couldn't push it out of my mind, for all my tryin'. Something, somehow, was dreadful wrong. Finally I got out of bed and eased down the ladder, hoping I wouldn't be disturbin' Lizbeth over nothing but foolish fears.

"Who's that comin' down?" she whispered.

"It's me. Everythin' okay?"

"Yes. Sorry if we woke you. Pa's just gone out to the outhouse."

Those words—that everyday, anytime part of life—struck at me with a force of blackness. I went straight for my coat and boots.

"Franky," Lizbeth called, getting up. "He said he'd be right back in. He didn't even take a coat."

I swallowed down hard the awful lump in my throat. "He wouldn't care for nothin' in this world if he had his coat right now," I told her. "Nor his boots. Nor the nose on his face."

I run outside. The moon was lower than it had been before, but I could still see at least in the yard where it was clear. I moved as fast as I could to the outhouse, praying I'd get a cussing for followin' him at a time like this. The door was shut.

"Pa?"

No answer. I went and banged. "Pa?"

The door swung open. There weren't nobody inside.

*No! No, Lord! Why would you give me peace before? Why would you let me sleep, and then let Pa, like a sly old fox, get up and take off when no one's the wiser? Oh, God, where is he?*

"Pa!"

I could hear Mary Jane suddenly crying in the house, and somebody—Ben—came runnin' out behind me.

"Did you find him?"

"No! How long since he left the house? Where could he have gone?"

"Not far. It's not been more than ten minutes, I don't think. Come on." He ran to his car. He pulled out somethin' I didn't know he had. A battery light. Flashlight, he called it. He trained the light back and forth across the yard, but I knew he wouldn't find anything. If my pa was determined to go, he wouldn't take no time at the outhouse or anywhere else close in the yard first. He could cover a lot of ground in ten minutes if he wanted to. And he knew this farm and the timber like his own hand. He could have gone any direction at all.

We checked the outbuildings and didn't see no sign. With the snow gone, there were no tracks to make things easier. My heart was heavy, knowing that Pa'd seen his chance and he'd taken it.

Ben seemed to know what I was thinkin'. "I'll tell Lizbeth. Which way do you think we ought to look?"

"I'll go afoot toward Fraley's," I told him. "You get Harry up and go toward Worthams'. See if he's gone to get one of the horses from there. If that's where he went, maybe you can get there first. But if he ain't there, get Mr. Wortham up. You an' him check the roads. Harry can take a horse and circle the timber."

I didn't wait for his answer. I just started off, as quick as I could go. With my head bare and the wind whistlin' past my ears, I ran in the direction of Buck Fraley's tavern, not wanting nothin' else but to find my pa, sober or not, so long as he was still in one piece.

I don't know how far I ran. The trees were all like barren spikes sticking up out of the cold darkness. I didn't hear nothin' but a hooty owl, and I almost screamed at it when I heard it. *Stop mocking me! Devil, get your hands off! Get your hands off my pa!*

My leg got to hurtin' like it does when I've pushed too much, but I wouldn't let up. I couldn't quit. My fingers were getting numb because I hadn't put on my gloves. But I didn't care. "Pa! Darn it all! Why would you go?"

There was nothin' to answer me. I glanced at the ground some as I moved, wishin' there was any snow left at all, just to give me some kind of sign in the darkness, but there was only frozen, weedy grass crusted with ice. In the dimness I couldn't see my own tracks behind me, let alone anyone else's.

For a minute I thought my pa could be any place, even behind the tree I'd just run past, waitin' real quiet till I moved on. Feelin' stupid, I checked, but there was nothin' there. He was like a specter true. In the darkness now, someplace in the timber or on his way out of it, making sure I didn't find him this time.

For a minute I stopped. He didn't want to be found. He didn't want to be run after. He wanted to be left alone. Had I done the wrong thing in the first place, not letting him go in the daylight, when at least I'd known the direction he was headed and had his word that he wouldn't be out all night? Maybe he would have just had a few drinks and then come on home on his own.

But I knew I couldn't count on his word. I knew there'd been no guarantees then that we'd have seen him again, just like there were no guarantees now.

*Fool!* I railed at myself. *He ain't never run off this way before! He just gets drunk as an idiot and then he finds his way home! You drove him off! Makin' him feel like a baby bein' watched over! You drove him off!*

I had to stop myself. It wasn't wrong for me to watch out for him like I'd done. Mr. Wortham had told me once when we were workin' alone in the wood shop how Pa had been after losing our mama. I'd wanted to know the part us kids didn't see, and he'd answered me honest like he would a grown man, even though I was only sixteen then.

"I found him with a rope," Mr. Wortham told me. "I had to wrestle him. He was in a bad way, Franky. He'd have hanged himself sure."

The knowing of that was tearin' at my insides now, and I prayed. Oh, why hadn't I been smart enough to check and see if he'd taken any rope? Where would he go?

He hadn't been in the machine shed. Or the barn, or anyplace else we'd looked. He'd left the farm, I knew that. And he was thinkin' of us kids, at least a little bit. He planned to leave us, I was sure of that now after the way he'd made sure to tell me he loved us. He wouldn't want us to find him. If he was gonna do somethin', he'd want to go someplace else, where it wouldn't be his kin to find him first.

I fell. Right there in the timber I sunk on the ground bawlin' like a baby. What could I do? Where should I go?

I got myself up. There wasn't anythin' else to do. Pa'd said the folks at Fraley's didn't blame him none. He'd said they understood. I didn't even know what time it was.

I didn't know if there'd be much crowd left there. But I had to keep on, in case he was headed that way. If he got as tired as I was, maybe he'd stop and take a break up ahead. If I kept on, maybe I could catch up before he ever got out of these woods. It was the only thing I knew to do. And Ben would make sure they were checkin' other places. Maybe we'd find him. We had to try.

It seemed like forever before I ever broke through the trees. Fraley's tavern was outside of Dearing, where the hard road met the county road that went out to Curtis Creek. I was glad I'd told Ben to check the roads because Pa might have gone that way even though it was longer.

I could see the lights of the buildin' up ahead. Somebody was there, but I saw only one car. I hurried forward, suddenly almost staggering. My leg hurt, but that wasn't the only thing anymore.

The door wouldn't budge when I pulled on the handle, but I wasn't about to give up with that. I pounded with all the strength I could, and my hands were so cold the impact felt more like a bunch of needles hittin' them than one solid whack. When nobody came to the door right away, I started yellin' and pounded some more.

Buck Fraley finally came to the door lookin' sleepy like I'd pulled him out of bed. I'd heard he slept at the tavern a lot, and it sure looked like he'd been sleepin' then.

"Go away," he told me. "Closed two hours ago. It's four a.m."

"Open up!" I yelled at him. "Have you seen my pa?"

"Your pa?" He scrunched close to the window and looked out at me, his head tilted and only one eye open. But he unlocked the door. "You that Hammond boy that was in here the other night?"

"Yes, sir. Have you seen my pa? He left home a little while ago. He didn't have no horse or nothin' else with him." Not even a coat, I remembered Lizbeth saying. Oh,

282

Lord. Where would he go without his coat? If he was still someplace home, and I was actin' the fool, he'd sure laugh at me in the morning. But I knew he hadn't been home when I left. He hadn't gone back in the house, nor anywhere else that we could tell. "Has he been here?" I asked the man.

"No. Not tonight. Are you kidding? All this way without his horse? Don't you live out there by the Curtis Creek school?" He craned his neck out the door and looked around.

"Yes, sir. Not too far from there."

"Land sakes, boy. What'd you do, walk?"

"I run most the way, sir."

"Looking for your pa? Son, he must know someplace open later'n I care to be. He's having a rough time. Let him get his drinkin' done. He'll come home."

I took a deep breath and leaned up against his wall for a minute, I was so awful exhausted. "You don't understand. We're not sure he will come home. Pa's not well. I mean, he just don't manage the way he oughta. He . . . he might be anywhere."

"Boy, you need to sit down."

I shook my head. "I gotta go. I gotta find him."

"Can I get you a drink first?"

I shook my head.

"Coffee, I mean. I got coffee. Warm your insides. Sit and think a minute. You can't be running like a dog chasing its tail. There must be somewhere you can figure he might go."

The words made sense, and I was tired and cold enough that I let him usher me inside for a cup of his coffee while I caught my breath and tried to think what to do next. Where would he go?

The school? He'd gone there once before, thinkin' I wouldn't find him, and I hadn't thought he'd do it again because I knew of the hiding place now. But he was clever

283

sometimes. He might know I'd not expect that. And at least he'd be out of the wind. I should have thought of it before.

I swallowed what hot coffee I could and got up to head for the door.

"You done already?" Mr. Fraley asked me. "Why don't you let me take you home? Don't fret so much. I'm sure your pa'll be all right. I understand him. Lost my little boy when he was just a baby. Never had a well day in his life. Born with a bad heart. It's a hard thing, worrying over one of your kids. An' your pa's got three to be fearin' for. He'll prob'ly drown in a bottle tonight like he did last night. Sure is gettin' a late start, but he'll be home some time tomorrow. Surely he will."

"Mr. Fraley," I told him. "I don't want a ride home. But if you're serious in your offer, I'd take a ride to the schoolhouse."

He was serious. He didn't understand me, but he was willin' not to have me leaving to go so far again on foot. And when we stopped on the lane by the school, I thought he'd turn around and just leave me there, but he waited.

"You sure he'd think to come here?"

"No, sir. But he did once before. I have to be sure."

The building was dark. It stood ominous against the fading moonlight. I tried to tell if there was a window open again, but I couldn't see until I got close.

The first window to the right of the door was broken. Somebody or something had bashed it in. "Pa?"

I was scared, real deep scared of what I'd find. I'd been a long time goin' all the way to Fraley's. And nobody else would think to come here. Pa'd already been a long time alone. And there was a rope in the schoolroom. The teacher used it sometimes to hang a curtain down from ceiling hooks when she wanted to divide the room. But right now it was plaguing my thinking, and I hoped Pa hadn't been mindful of it being there.

"Pa?" The silence was ripping me up inside. I didn't want to go in, but I couldn't stand not knowin'. He hadn't answered me when he was here before. He could be in there.

With Buck Fraley watching, wonderin' what I could be thinking, I boosted myself up and climbed through the broken window. Somebody'd done it before me. Most of the glass was busted and scattered across the floor inside.

"Pa?" I called again. With my heart aching, I looked around and didn't see anythin' at all I could identify as a person. But it was so dark in there. I went to the teacher's desk again for the matches. I lit one and even found the candle in the inkwell right where I'd left it. Its little light spread across the room, but there was nothin' there. I looked by the stove. I looked in the coatroom. Nothin' was different, not even the ceiling hooks. It was almost a breath of relief, and yet at the same time I knew I still had nothin'. Where could I look now?

I was about to leave when I saw somethin' I'd missed before. Somethin' definitely out of place. An overturned bottle lay on the floor beside a student desk. I picked it up. The smell was unmistakable. And it was empty. I hadn't seen him leave one here before. Did he bring it with him, drain it here, and then carelessly drop it before movin' on?

I took it with me when I climbed back outside. "Is this the stuff my pa drinks?" I asked Mr. Fraley.

He gave me a funny look. "It is one of his favorites. But I told you, he wasn't in tonight."

"I know. He wouldn't have had time to get there and back here without his horse. But did he ever take any with him? The whole bottle like this?"

"Sure. Sometimes. He said he liked to keep one set

back for a stash. Hidden, you know. Where he could grab a guzzle if he needed to without his kids knowin'."

It seemed incredible. Would Pa have a hidden bottle someplace and then carry it with him all the way back to the school to drink it down? He wouldn't have had to leave home for that! He could just hole up in the machine shed or somethin' and have his fill.

But he wouldn't want me to find him at it. He didn't want to stay home. And maybe this bottle had never been there. Maybe he'd had it with him the night I found him here. Maybe he'd hid it from me, and then come back for it after all this time.

"Listen, boy," Mr. Fraley said nervously. "I don't think you're accomplishin' nothing out here. I could get in a lot a' trouble, bringin' you an' then you climbing in an' all."

"You can go if you want."

"Let me take you home first. You hadn't oughta be runnin' around like this. Get some sleep. Maybe your pa's home by now."

I didn't like it, but I had to admit he was probably right. I ought to at least go home long enough to see where the others had searched and whether they'd found anything. Mr. Fraley seemed real relieved to take me, and even more relieved to be goin' on once he'd dropped me off. I thanked him, but I didn't take the time for anything else. Ben's car was back, in a slightly different spot. I wanted to know if he'd found out anythin'.

He and Harry, along with Lizbeth and Sarah, were all sittin' at the table when I came in. Sarah and Lizbeth both jumped up right away.

"Frank!" Lizbeth exclaimed. "Lordy, you must be half froze. We were pretty worried. Thank God you got back all right." She hurried to pour me some coffee.

Sarah didn't say a word, but she was the one that grabbed Mama's quilt and pulled it around my shoulders when I managed to get myself to a seat. I must have looked pretty bad. They were all starin' at me.

"What about Pa?" I asked them.

"Oh, Franky," Lizbeth answered for all of them. "There's no sign. But—but I think you're bleeding. What happened?"

I had a cut, just a little one, on my cheek from the schoolhouse glass. And another one on one hand. I wasn't bleedin' anymore. It must have looked like I was still bleedin' a little because I hadn't wiped the blood away. But I hadn't even noticed till now. And I didn't care.

"You didn't find nothin'?" I pressed them, looking at Ben this time.

"No, Frank," he answered me. But he was solemn over something, and I knew he wasn't done. I waited.

"Frank, Mr. Post's truck was stolen a little while ago. It was there when we went by, but Mr. Wortham and Sam stopped when they saw Mr. Post in his yard. He told them he'd heard somebody start his truck and leave with it. He tried to run out and see, but he couldn't get there fast enough. He knows they went up to the corner, but there was no telling which way after that. By the time Mr. Wortham got there, there was no way of knowing which way to go. They're on their way into town now to talk to the sheriff. Mr. Wortham said we might as well be home and let the sheriff handle it from here. No telling which way Dad Hammond could have gone. And we were starting to get worried for you. I was about to go looking."

None of what he was sayin' made much sense to me. "Do you think Pa stole Mr. Post's truck?" I had to ask him. "Why would he do that? He ain't even drove but once or twice in his life! And if he was gonna take a vehicle, why wouldn't he just get in yours? It was right outside."

"We don't know," Lizbeth answered. "Maybe he didn't want to take somethin' that belonged to family."

287

"Mr. Post is a good neighbor," I protested. "That's almost the same thing. And Pa knows stealin' ain't right anyhow."

"I know he knows," Lizbeth said sadly. "But something's wrong with his thinkin'. He's sick, Frank, even if we never heard of a name for any kind of illness like this. It's surely the grief and worry doin' it, but he's still sick."

They didn't have any better answers for me. There was nothin' else anybody could say. And I was so chilled through that I couldn't get warm even with the quilt around me, so Lizbeth and Sarah made me move to the fireside while Harry threw a couple more logs on. They doted on me, bringin' me more coffee when I hadn't even finished the first cup. It bothered everybody about Pa being gone, I could see that. But they also seemed to be bothered for me, and I didn't like that one bit.

"I'm just warmin' up a minute," I told them. "I can go right back to searching—"

"Frank." Ben shook his head. "We can't do any good if we don't know where to go." He looked so weary when he said it that I felt sorry for him.

"I know," I answered him. "I just don't wanna give up."

"We have to," Harry said gravely. "We shoulda known all along it wasn't no use. We shoulda just let Pa do whatever he wants."

But Lizbeth disagreed. "We can't do anythin' to help what he does now. But when he was here, you did right to look out for him. He hasn't been himself for a long time. I should have known better, when he got up tonight. I should have thought this through and been more watchful."

Pa's words from the timber came back into my mind, and I knew I should tell her what he'd said. It occurred to me now that despite whatever was wrong with him, he'd had a lot of things all thought out. "Lizbeth, Pa told me today that there was none of this that was my fault, that I wasn't supposed to blame myself for anythin' that happened. I think that was a message for all of us. For right now."

She looked at me with tears in her eyes, and I had to go on.

"He also said he loved us. Every one of us, and I was supposed to tell you all, because he couldn't say it himself."

Lizbeth lowered her head to her hands. "Oh, Lord."

Sarah reached and touched her. "Why does that make you more sad?" she asked innocently. "Maybe he's doing the kind of thinking that he needs to. Maybe he's going to try to be closer to you all."

But Lizbeth wasn't comforted. "Pa's different than that, Sarah," she said tearfully. "I'm afraid it was his way of saying good-bye."

# 29

## Sarah

I'd wondered if Lizbeth and Frank were worrying too much about their father. Surely he'd just come home once he'd gotten his fill of his foolish drinking like usual.

But this time they were right. Sheriff Law found Mr. Post's truck overturned in a ravine near Rend Lake. Mr. Hammond's body was beneath it. No one knew whether drunkenness, his driving inexperience, or something else had caused the wreck. My father came with the sheriff about midmorning to tell us.

Harry shoved his chair hard against the kitchen wall. A metal bowl fell from a shelf with a clang, but nobody moved to touch it. Dad and Ben had to sit Harry down to calm him. Lizbeth fell apart in tears. Rorey cussed their father, yelling that he'd probably done it all on purpose, and that made Berty yell at her. Only Frank was quiet. He sat for a long time like he didn't even hear what was going on around him. In a little while the sheriff left, and I was glad that Emmie was with my mother. It would be hard enough when she was told, but I didn't think she could have handled it very well over here right now.

"Mr. Wortham, what are we gonna do?" Bert asked.

Dad sighed. I knew he didn't know how to answer that. Frank stood to his feet, and I hoped he would quote a Scripture. I wanted him to so badly, because I knew that Frank's spirit as well as mine and everybody else's could latch onto one of the Scriptures and find some kind of foothold. But he didn't say anything. He just walked to the window and stared outside.

"We'll help," Dad finally said. "We'll work things out."

"Does the pastor know?" Lizbeth asked gently.

"We asked the deputy to tell him," Daddy answered her.

"Didn't he think of us?" Harry raged. "How could he do this?"

"Maybe we won't ever know that," Lizbeth answered quietly.

I was watching Frank. His eyes seemed to be focused on something far away, but I had no idea what it could be. *Touch him, Lord God. Help him. Everybody looks to Frank around here, maybe more than any of us have really known. We need him to be all right.*

"Sam's still at our house with his family and Emmie," my father said solemnly. "They don't know yet. Do you need me to stay? Or would you rather I take them the news?"

Ben was the only one who knew how to answer him. "Maybe you'd better stay here, Mr. Wortham. I can go tell them."

Lizbeth nodded and hugged her husband. Mary Jane was playing on the floor like she knew nothing of what was happening. My father hugged Ben as he was leaving, and then sat down to pray with Bert and Harry. Bert was still sick, coughing some, but I knew it wasn't the cold now that was making him shake. And Harry was still angry. With one fist doubled, he looked like he'd like

291

nothing better than to find somebody to blame and then whale into them for all he was worth.

Rorey went up the loft ladder, and I could hear her upstairs crying on her bed. I prayed that Frank would cry. Or talk. Or get mad, or something. But he just kept staring out the window, until finally he turned. Without a word he went past everybody and walked outside.

"Daddy," I said. But I couldn't wait for his response. Something was moving my feet without me hardly thinking about it. Frank hadn't spoken to anyone, hadn't given his hand to comfort any of the others. He hadn't even looked at me, or at my father, who was the friend he'd shared work and wisdom with for years now. For him to close us off scared me because it seemed like Frank always coped best by first helping someone else cope. I didn't know what I could do. But I couldn't stay still. Without waiting on anybody else's word, I took off out the door following him.

He was limping straight out across the yard, I didn't know why, or where he was headed. I ran up behind him. "Frank?"

To my surprise, he spun around and answered me more harshly than I'd ever heard him speak. "Leave me alone! I'm not like my father, do you hear? I don't need you runnin' after me! I don't need you to say nothin'! Go away!"

I just stood for a moment, seeing the pain working deep in his eyes. "All right," I answered him softly. "I just wanted to be here—in case you need anything."

"Like what? Huh?" he shot back. "What could you do if I did need something?"

His words were like a slap. My eyes filled with tears. "I'm sorry. I'm just so sorry about all this." I stood watching him, wondering if I should turn my feet back to the house. But I couldn't make them go.

And suddenly his face changed. "Oh, Sarah Jean. Oh, Lord, I'm sorry."

"It's okay," I told him.

"No. It's not. I can't be yellin' at you."

"You're just upset."

He struggled to say the next words. "But . . . but Pa used to do that! He always used to . . . to take things out on me . . ."

He did indeed look like his father then, more than I'd ever seen, his gaunt face drawn tight with strain.

"You didn't do anything wrong," I told him.

But he bowed his head. He almost walked away from me. I could see that he wanted to. "I was leavin'," he said with tears in his eyes. "Just straight into the trees or somethin', just to get some distance from the house—"

"That's all right for a little while, Frank. You told me before that sometimes you need time to think. I understand that. Especially now."

"But I wasn't thinkin'. I was just walkin' away."

"You're not like your father," I said, not sure what else to tell him.

He took a deep breath, and the weight of it seemed to press him down. "He planned this, Sarah Jean. Whether it was an accident or not. He meant to get away from us."

"Oh, Frank."

"I used to think he hated me. But I was wrong. I can see now that he counted on me. He counted on me to find him, to keep a jump ahead and make things okay. But this time, when he needed me most, I failed him."

"You can't blame yourself. Remember what you told Lizbeth."

"I know." He bowed his head. "I know Pa meant those words for me. For this. But it don't help. Not one bit." He turned away.

"Blessed be God, the Father of our Lord Jesus Christ," I said softly. "The God of all comfort . . ."

"Oh, Sarah." He sunk suddenly to his knees. "Help me. I feel like I ain't got nothin' left. I oughta be inside helpin' them. I oughta be the one speakin' God's words of comfort . . ."

I knelt beside him. "It's all right. You don't have to be strong. Not right now—"

"You don't understand. If I ain't that, I ain't nothin'." He stood to his feet again. "He counted on me. He . . ."

Frank couldn't finish. He turned away again, and I knew he was in tears.

"Do you want me to leave you alone?"

I barely heard his answer. "No."

He stood crying, staring out into the clouds. I rose and put my arm around him. There wasn't anything else I knew to say. Maybe he just needed me to be here beside him, quiet as the trees, just so he wouldn't feel alone.

"Thanks for stoppin' me, Sarah Jean. It don't do no good to run."

My father came out on the porch. I heard the door and turned my head enough to see him. He only stood watching for a minute, as though he were wondering if we needed him to come closer.

"You can't be strong all the time," I told Frank. "Sometimes life can knock you flat."

"Yeah," he agreed solemnly. "But why art thou cast down, O my soul? And why art thou disquieted within me? Hope thou in God: for I shall yet praise him, who is the health of my countenance, and my God."

I smiled. "Is that from a psalm?"

"Forty-two. Maybe we should go back in. I'm glad Emmie's not here yet. But she prob'ly will be soon. And Sam. And your mother. We're gonna have to talk some things through, about what happens next."

294

"It doesn't have to be right away. You can give yourself time . . ."

"I'm of age, Sarah Jean. But the younger ones is orphans. Whether Pa thought that much through or not, we need to decide some things today, for their sake. I can't be runnin' off, nor knocked flat for long. I gotta take my part."

To my surprise, he took my hand as he turned back toward the house. My father was just turning to go in.

"Mr. Wortham," Frank called.

Dad looked back at us.

"If you could, I want you to help me do what we did for Mama, to make the coffin ourselves. Do you think that would be all right?"

"If you want it, son."

"Thank you," Frank told him then. "For being here for us today just as much as always. I promise you, it ain't gonna be left on you to see to things for us. We're not so little anymore. It won't all be on your hands."

My father and Frank hugged each other, and I felt at least a little more warm and solid inside. We'd all be okay, I felt sure now. Even the Hammonds. Even after this.

"It's never all been on me," Daddy said then. "We've been in God's hands all along. We're one family. And he'll continue to take care of us. Together."

That understanding was the Hammonds' foundation after that. We really became one family. With two farms and one heart.

Because of the paperwork signed years ago by Albert Graham, Emma's nephew, their farm was to remain in the hands of the oldest child willing to live on it and work it, and that meant it fell to Frank, at least until one of his older brothers came home.

They buried their father beside their mother in the plot across the timber, and Frank and Sam worked tearfully to put up a nice little fence and prepare a place for Joe's body when it came home. I didn't think that if I lived to be a hundred and ninety I'd ever see such strength, to do what they did and go on with life. But it wasn't easy for them. The younger four Hammonds especially had trouble. Who could understand a man like George Hammond? If treasure were counted in the hearts of children, then he'd been rich. But he'd also been blind, to all that was in them, and all the rest of living he could have known.

No one ever did know what caused his wreck. I know they thought that Rorey might have been right, that he might have met his end by his own purpose and plan, but I think it was a relief at least for Frank not to know for sure. And Mr. Post himself offered an explanation about why Mr. Hammond might have chosen to take the Posts' truck and not one of his own family's vehicles, or one of the horses that could easily have been found in our barn.

"He told me more'n once I was the only farmer 'round here that could afford a loss," Mr. Post said. "He knew it wouldn't hurt me so bad as it would somebody else. He couldn't take a horse and leave you without a pair for the wagon. He couldn't take Ben's car without hurting family."

It was sad to think that Mr. Hammond hadn't had a chance to learn that Willy wasn't wounded all that badly. I wondered if things might have been different if he had known, but there was nothing that could be done about it now. Willy and Robert were coming home. Robert to stay. Willy was going back, of his own free choice, once Robert was here and he had the visit he wanted.

I worried about Rorey more than ever, and more than the rest of her family, even when things were so hard for all of them. She talked bitter words nearly all the time, and the only bright thoughts she seemed to have were about marrying Lester and expecting he'd be home too, since Robert and Willy were coming. But life can be cruel. Too cruel for any kind of explanation sometimes. Lester died on a military hospital ship. Lester wasn't coming home. It was one blow too many for Rorey. She threw the wedding dress she'd made such beautiful progress on into the fireplace and started running off at night with a crowd of boys we knew to be trouble.

I felt horrible. I wished to goodness I'd been far kinder, far more open to her feelings for Lester so she'd listen to me now. But she wouldn't listen. Not to me or my mother or Lizbeth or anyone. Finally, she got tired of being talked to, and she ran off to St. Louis with Lester's brother Eugene and a friend of his that we didn't even know. They said they had jobs. Rorey wrote and told us they'd gotten an apartment, and she had a job. But it felt like a hole in my life to have her gone.

I kept praying Rachel's prayer because it seemed like it had extra meaning now. We needed strength. We needed peace. In this time of being apart from our loved ones, whether in St. Louis, or across the ocean, or already waiting on heaven's golden shore. *Help me understand you better, God,* I prayed. *Help me understand the mysteries, the struggles of life. Because everything you do, everything you lead us through, has a purpose, a significance, if we can see it. Trials can shake us apart from you and each other, or draw us closer. Help us, Lord, to be knit together in one strand.*

Mom and Dad spent what they had to for the train to St. Louis to meet Robert's airplane. We knew by then that he wasn't walking, that he wasn't expected to walk for months yet, and he was coming home more because he'd insisted on it than that they were really ready to let him go. But there wasn't much to be done except to let the healing progress and to work what muscles he could, so they let him go. We were still worried for him but excited that he'd be home.

Rachel wanted to go to St. Louis with my parents. She could hardly wait to see Robert again. The strain had been awful for her. I could tell that, despite the calm she tried to maintain on the outside. But her father made her wait. He said they weren't engaged, and it wasn't right her being there when Robert's parents ought to be able to joy in their son first.

So she waited at home with us. She cried just thinking about what Robert had been through and how he might react to all that had happened at home. But I think mostly she cried because Robert was alive. We'd come closer to losing him than any of us wanted to think about, and now at last he'd be with us again. Rachel was hopeful, I knew she was, that Robert still felt the same way about her as he had when he left. That he'd look at her the same, and not be so changed that he didn't want to be together.

The day they were due to be home, Frank drove us all to the train station and we waited, all of us so anxious that we could hardly speak. It would be so good to have Robert home. To see Willy safe and sound. But things were still hard for the Hammonds with grieving that seemed to never stop. And I fretted for Robert's struggles. I worried about the challenges he would face. Would he have to be in bed a lot? Could he get up at all?

The train was fifteen minutes late, but it seemed like an eternity. Emmie started crying. I took her hand, only to realize that Frank had reached for her other one.

"What's wrong?" I asked her.

"Rorey's not here," she said in a solemn voice, and then the tears got worse. "Nor Pa and Joe."

"Rorey's gonna sow her oats till she can get things settled in her heart," Frank answered quietly. "But Pa and Joe are with us. They always will be, Emmie. You remember that."

Rachel joined us, her gloved hands nervously crumpling a wrapped package for Robert. The train thundered into the station. Rachel wiped away tears. *Oh Lord*, I prayed. *Let Robert be Robert. Let him be all right, and look at Rachel the way he did when they were dancing. Bring their hearts together. He needs her right now. They need each other.*

I felt almost weak with the anticipation. Two people we didn't know got off the train and met the Clarkson family that lived east of town. But it was a while before anyone else got off. We just stood, nobody daring to ask anything, everybody just standing, just waiting as long as it took. Finally Mom came to the platform. She was smiling, but I could see the strain in her face, some of the worry still in her eyes. Behind her, slowly, came Dad and then Willy bringing Robert with them in a wheeled chair that was a little bit like the one Daddy had put together for Emma Graham so long ago.

Robert looked so fine in his uniform. So handsome. Even strong. But far, far, thinner, with something different in his eyes that I had no way to describe. Rachel stood for a moment, a bright smile and new tears meeting her face at the same time. And then she hurried forward as Dad and Willy lifted Robert down. We all gathered around.

This much closer, I could see the weariness in Robert. I knew the trip had exhausted him, and he was far weaker than he was willing to let on.

"Looks like you've all grown up," he said.

Emmie hugged on Willy, and I leaned forward to hug Robert a little, gently, not sure how much he could take. But he grabbed me and gave me a squeeze.

"Don't be afraid of me, Sis. Are you all right?"

I nodded, amazed that he would ask me that. Everybody hugged him, and Willy too. Except Rachel. She'd moved to the side just a little to give our whole family room. But I reached for her hand and drew her close again.

Rachel couldn't seem to say anything. She only stood with the package in her hands, all dressed up the prettiest I'd ever seen her, with hope and maybe a little fear mixed up in her eyes. Finally she managed to put her bundle in Robert's hands. He looked at her as though for him too, words had failed. And then she leaned forward and gave him a little kiss on the cheek. She took his hand and kissed that too. But she didn't let go. Even though neither of them spoke, she stayed beside him all the way to the truck as Daddy and now Frank maneuvered the chair down steps and over the rough ground to where we were parked.

I felt like singing, I wasn't sure why. It was still a sad time, despite the happiness. I took a deep breath, with a hymn already circling my mind, and with a faltering voice I did my best to try to sing. Katie joined me, and her beautiful voice seemed to make it all right. Mom hugged us both and then joined in too. Pretty soon Emmie was singing, and even Bert. And beside the truck, Rachel finally found her voice.

"I love you, Robby. I thank God you're home."

He hugged her. And then my big brother cried. We all just waited there in the parking lot while he held her. I cried too. So did Mom.

*Ask her to marry you,* I urged Robert in my mind. *Right here and right now.*

But he didn't. For some reason he probably couldn't. He pulled away a little from the embrace and said he was tired. He was ready to go home.

"Can I come and see you?" Rachel asked him.

He nodded his head, but he didn't say anything else. Daddy lifted him into the front seat of the truck and put

300

the unwieldy chair with us in the back. Rachel went to her father's car, and then Robert sat in the front of our truck and cried. *What's wrong?* I wanted to ask him. *Oh, please, Robert. Please be all right.*

Willy told us that they'd been sent into the jungle around Henderson Field on Guadalcanal to search for any Japanese holdouts in the area. He and Robert and Lester and two other men were separated by not more than a few yards from the rest of their troop. They didn't see the Japanese soldiers hiding in the underbrush until it was too late. Machine guns did their grisly work, and all five men had been hit before the remaining Americans opened fire and killed every one of the Japanese assailants.

It was a horrible story, and I hated hearing it, even while I was glad to know what had really happened. I worried about Robert. I worried once we got home that the farm would be hard for him. Things were too different.

The Hammond kids were with us even more than they had been, because even though their farm was still theirs and they could stay there because Frank was an adult, we pretty much took them all in as ours. They ate here a lot, slept here a lot, because it was just easier that way. But their presence made the loss very clear to Robert. And he couldn't move around very well on his own, even when he felt like it. There were steps to the house in the front and back, and no real sidewalks. His old room was upstairs, so Mom and Dad gave him theirs, but he didn't like that. I know he didn't.

He had to sleep a lot. He had to rest a lot even when he wasn't sleeping. Sometimes he had to go into the hospital with Dad to see the doctor again. Sometimes the doctor came to us, and his words were always encouraging.

"He's doing amazingly well. He's coming along fine."

Sometimes one of us helped him pull up out of the chair and lean into a pair of crutches. Robert practiced on the crutches every day. But he didn't do very well, and he got mad about it every time.

Rachel came over. Again and again. But he didn't talk to her very much or seem to want her to stay very long. When that hadn't changed even after Willy went back, she finally pulled me aside tearfully to ask me what was wrong.

"I don't know what to do, Sarah. I don't even know if he wants me here."

*Peace, Lord. Strength.* I prayed that way a lot now. Just one word or two at a time, knowing I'd prayed her prayer so often that the good Lord knew exactly what I meant.

Even now, with Robert with us, he still seemed to be apart from us. And he and Rachel were apart somehow in ways we couldn't understand. *Help, Lord. If Robert needs your healing on the inside, touch him. Help him open up again and let Rachel into his heart.*

I went to talk to him. Spring was just beginning to warm the world around us, and Mom and Katie had gotten Robert situated on the porch with a cup of tea, hoping the fresh air would do him good. He'd been sitting there when Rachel left, but he wouldn't even watch her go.

"Robert, you need to tell me what's wrong."

I could see the angry look in his eyes, but he didn't let his voice reflect it. "I guess I'm not patient enough, Sis. They say things are supposed to get better."

I sighed and moved a chair so I could sit down in front of him. "Robert, Rachel loves you."

He looked away.

"I know you love her too. What's wrong? You told me you were going to propose to her when you got back.

302

Don't you know she still wants that? She wants to be with you."

He shook his head. "I know," he said so quietly. "I just wish it wasn't that way."

"Why? I know you love her."

"Sarah, I had plans. Farming. Working. Even dancing with her again. I can't do that. I don't know when I will. Even when things are better, I might still need the crutches, that's what they say. Or at least a cane. And I don't know how long before I can get a job. I can't do for her, Sis. I wish she'd see that and go someplace else."

"I'm glad she left," I said with a sigh. "I wouldn't want her to hear that. You'd just make her cry."

"I know! But I can't help it! I *do* love her! That's why I don't think it's right—"

"To let her be so strong and steady that she doesn't care whether you can dance or not?"

He looked at me.

"Robby, she's got faith stronger than wondering when you'll have a job, or what kind it'll be. She loves you like she's married already, trying to be what you need for better or for worse even before you've asked her. You can't push her away. Because she won't be able to take her heart someplace else."

He took a deep breath. "You really think it's fair?"

"No," I told him. "The whole war isn't fair. For you to get hurt, and Joe—oh, Robby, none of that's fair, but it wouldn't be right for you to act like Rachel shouldn't be with you. You're not doing either one of you any favors."

I took his hand. He just held it, and we sat quiet for a long time. "Thanks," he said finally.

I smiled. "Are you gonna propose?"

"Sarah, if I do, at least act like I can make it a surprise."

He truly did. And it was just three days later, on the fourteenth of March, when Rachel had come over bringing him a batch of brownies. He'd picked that day to wear the shirt she'd made him. For the first time. She nearly cried when she saw that he had it on.

"Put me on the floor," he suddenly told Harry, who was across the room cleaning ashes out of the fireplace.

"What?"

"Help me get down on the floor," Robert repeated impatiently, though nobody knew at that moment what he had in mind.

Harry helped him. I did too, and then he motioned us away, but he couldn't wait till I was all the way out of earshot before saying what he had to say.

"I can't kneel," his quiet voice was telling Rachel. "Not yet. So this'll have to be good enough. If you think you can handle all of my ways plus an ugly chair and some crutches, would you be my wife?"

I ran to get Mom. She got there in time to see them hugging on the floor and thought maybe Robert had fallen. But she knew soon enough that it was happy news that had Rachel crying in his arms. Robert and Rachel were getting married. June first, they decided immediately, which didn't give anyone very much time, especially Robert.

"I'm going to walk in," he said. "I'm going to marry you standing up."

In the days that followed, he worked and he worked with the crutches. He got mad. He got tired. But then he worked some more.

Sam and Thelma packed all their things and moved up to the town of Camp Point late in April, promising they'd be back for the wedding. We sent word several times to Rorey about it, but she wouldn't promise a thing.

When the day came, Robert, in his spiffy marine uniform, maneuvered our church in Dearing on his crutches.

304

Even the steps outside. He sat for a while because he had to rest, but when it was time for the wedding to start, he stood up front with only one crutch to support him, so he'd have one hand free for Rachel.

They moved into what had been Sam and Thelma's house in Dearing. But we were there several times a week. Robert got so he wouldn't use his chair at all, but there'd been so much damage to his back and one leg that it wore him out, even months later, to be on his feet very long. He got a job at the bank, and they were glad to have him, but he wasn't satisfied with that. He wanted to help with the farm work, but much of it was too tiring for him, and that didn't satisfy him either.

In the summer of the next year, Ben was called into service overseas. While he was gone, Lizbeth and Mary Jane moved out to the farm to be closer to the rest of us.

We didn't see Kirk for the duration of the war, but he kept on writing whenever he could and we wrote to him. Katie kept writing to his friend Dave too. She liked to be the one checking the mailbox, and her eyes would always look so perky bright whenever a letter came from him. His family was in Brachett, Wisconsin, but he promised that when he got back to the states, he would come and meet her.

Frank kept busy constantly, insisting on helping with our farm, even though he had so much work on theirs. And he kept up with the wood shop too. He was always making something, even when Dad didn't have time to help. He made a beautiful oak bed for Robert and Rachel with a dove carved into the headboard. Rachel loved it, and I think that was what prompted Robert to try his hand again at carving too. He'd done a few things with Frank when they were younger, especially Christmas presents for the other boys. And now Robert started doing woodwork for the shop when he wasn't busy at the bank.

The Hammond kids seemed to be adjusting all right. Emmie was improving in her schoolwork, though it was still an awful struggle. Harry was a lot of help on the farm, and Bert too, when he wasn't writing. The Mcleans-boro paper hired Bert regular even though he was so young, and he kept up a column every week.

I never forgot Frank's kiss. Neither did he, because I caught him looking at me funny a few times, and acting odd once in a while, like he thought he had to be careful not to put himself in that position again. But he was my friend, just as much as ever. I didn't go to the teacher's college because I wanted to stay close where I could help everybody. I spent a lot of time with Robert and Rachel, or babysitting Mary Jane when Lizbeth got a part-time job. And I got a job too, without even trying, when I stopped in the McCoy Library in Mcleansboro to ask about borrowing a book or two for Frank. He wanted to hear more Shakespeare. And *Oliver Twist*, by Charles Dickens.

One of the ladies thought it was me who knew so much about books, and she told me they had an opening and I ought to apply. I did, never expecting to get the job. But I got it, and Frank loved it because it wasn't in Dearing, where Dad and Kate worked. He had to take me to Mcleansboro in Ben and Lizbeth's car, and I read to him all the way there and all the way back.

Once when Frank was driving me home from work, the car quit and we were stuck alongside the road. He got out and started tinkering. He didn't seem quite so skinny anymore, his hair was nice cut, and I considered it pleasant to be out on a pretty, sunny day, even if we were stuck two or three miles from home.

"Do you have to fix it?" I asked him.

306

He looked at me like I'd left my senses back in Mcleansboro. "You wanna walk home?"

"No. I just want to sit a minute in the grass and read you the next chapter of *The Merchant of Venice*."

He smiled.

"Do you even like that story?" I asked him then. "Because I don't."

He really gave me a funny look. "Well, what in the world do you wanna read it for then?"

"Because it's a beautiful day. And I like the way your eyes look when you're far off in a story. Like you're almost part of it, feeling what's going on."

He turned his face back to the car engine. "Did anyone ever tell you that you're peculiar, Sarah Jean?"

"A time or two. I guess I've known it all my life."

"Well, I don't like that story as much as some," he admitted. "But I like listenin', because you make it seem real."

I scoffed. "I trip over half the words. That must be frustrating to listen to."

"No," Frank told me. "You do real well. An' I like it when you trip a little. That's part of what makes it real."

He turned to look at me with his silvery eyes almost seeming to dance in the bright sunlight. I felt something tingle clear down my spine. He had a grease smudge on his cheek and an oil can in his hand, but he looked more handsome to me than if he was all dressed up for a party.

I swallowed, feeling flustered. "Frank . . . I think maybe . . ." I had to stop. His merry eyes held me, and I couldn't say another word.

"I'm gonna get a truck of my own when the war's over," he said. "Maybe move the shop to town and get a house when Kirk and Willy get back, if they wanna take the farm on. An' I think Kirk will. He misses it awful bad. 'Specially the horses. He's always loved horses."

"I think I'll just work at the library. I like it. I like getting you books."

He leaned closer, and my heart skipped a beat. I thought sure he was going to kiss me again. And he did, but it was just a teeny peck on the cheek. "You're real nice to me, Sarah Jean. The best friend I ever had. But I don't think I better linger too long on the grass out here. I got milking to do. And I promised Mary Jane a story when I got home. Could you just read to me while I finish this up? If it's still nice when we get back, maybe we can pull a blanket outside and sit out then. Okay?"

"Okay." I watched him for a minute, leaning over the car engine, his strong hands on one part or another that I didn't even know the name of.

"Do you wish you didn't have to haul me to work?" I asked.

"No," he said without looking up. "I believe if you quit, I'd be missin' the highlight of my day."

"I should have read to you a long time ago, if you like stories that much."

He still didn't look up. "It'd be the highlight if you never read at all."

I opened the book to the place I'd marked. I wasn't sure how to respond. After a moment of silence, he looked my way. "I hope I didn't fluster you, sayin' something like that."

"Oh, no," I stammered. "Not at all."

"To be plain honest," Frank admitted, "I been worried quite a while about flusterin' you. I been thinkin' you oughta be mad at me, but you don't never seem to be."

"Why would I be mad?"

He lowered his eyes a moment and took in a deep breath. "I'm not feelin' very brotherly to you, Sarah Jean. Nor neighborly neither."

308

I stood with my heart doing flip-flops as his meaning sunk in. Of course he couldn't feel like my brother. Or just a neighbor anymore. There'd been moments between us different than that for quite a while if we chose to admit it. And it must be time. I laughed. "That's good. Because I don't feel sisterly to you. Or neighborly either. Not a bit."

He stared at me for a minute. "That's good," he finally said, and turned back to the car engine. "That's real nice to know."

Things were not the same between us after that. We did things together that had nothing to do with his work or mine. I never even considered dating anybody else. Neither did he, so far as I could tell. We talked a lot, about our blended-together family and what the future might hold. By the time the war was over and we heard the blessed, glorious news on the radio, we were so used to each other and everybody seeing us together that we kissed in celebration, right in front of everybody.

About three months later, we got a letter from someone in Rochester, Minnesota. There was no name on the outside of the envelope, but we all got a start looking at the inside signature. Joseph Earl Hammond the third. Mom read the letter out loud to everybody.

*"I've been owing you this letter for a long time,"* the other Joe Hammond wrote.

*I did you wrong, and I hope you'll forgive me. I knew your Joe. We both thought it was funny finding somebody that shared our name. We hit it off right away. Then just two weeks after I met him, he went missing, and it hit me hard. I didn't mean to steal your letters. The first time was an accident. They just handed me a letter that was meant for him. I told myself I'd save it for him. I shouldn't have read*

309

*it, but I was so lonely for home I was almost out of my mind. I was sick with malaria, thinking dying would be better, and your letter picked me up even though it wasn't for me.*

*I kept on claiming the mail for Joe Hammond. I kept the carved wooden cross with me, thinking someday I'd send it back, but I finally gave it to a Filipino family that had almost nothing but the shirts on their backs. They called it the peace of angels. But it wasn't mine to give, and I hope you can accept my feeble apology.*

*I couldn't eat your cookies. I gave them to my friends. And then I felt like I was a miserable cheat to be doing what I was doing. I knew it was all because of a mix-up or my company clerk would have caught on by then. When your Joe was confirmed to be lost, I knew the letters would stop. And I felt too guilty to write to you.*

*You have every right to resent what I did. I was a thief of the goodwill that should have been his, and I don't deserve anything now but your contempt. But I want you to know that the 91st Psalm you sent in your Christmas box saved my life. I would never have made it without that little piece of hope. I kept it pinned to my shirt wherever we went. I still carry it, in my wallet now. I think I always will. Your Joe was a good man. I never meant to do anything disrespectful of his memory or of your love for him. Forgive me. But I had to thank you. Because I owe you far more than these petty words can describe.*

Mom's hands were shaking by the time she got done reading. Everybody was quiet. Hearing that letter was like revisiting all the sorrow we'd worked through after being told of Joe's death. Even Frank cried. But then it was peace, knowing we'd ministered to a need. After so much time, none of us were upset with that man. Instead, his letter left a good feeling because it seemed that Joe had managed to give his friend, and us, one last gift. We wrote back so the Minnesota Joe Hammond would know that we weren't angry, that we were glad God had used our letters to help him through a terrible time. "Our Joe," as he called him, would not have minded that.

"God works in mysterious ways," Frank said, "his wonders to perform."

Eventually, we learned that Joe was to receive the Bronze Star military award for distinguished service. And it made us proud, though nobody could ever really quit missing him. Things weren't the same without Mr. Hammond, either. Frank said that if our life was a book, his father's absence was like pages torn out and thrown aside, whole sections of the story lost and never to be recovered. Who knows what we might have missed? The rest of the story was a good one, though. Kirk and Willy came home all right. Robert kept getting stronger. Even Rorey seemed to be okay, though she decided to stay in St. Louis.

So many things had happened in the war years. Some awful, awful things. But in everything, God brought good. It seemed like we were stronger than we'd ever been. And not just us. The whole country was stronger. Because we'd pulled together, we'd picked up hammer, or plow, or gun, to do what had to be done, whether in the Pacific, in Europe, or at home.

I felt closer to God than I'd ever felt in my life. And I wasn't alone in that. Robert went forward to talk to the pastor one Sunday and tell him he'd finally realized why nothing around could give him the kind of satisfaction he thought he needed. He was called to the mission field. And Rachel was in agreement. They wanted to go back to the Pacific islands and preach the goodness and love of God.

That scared Mom some, because Robert still needed his crutches most of the time. And the Pacific was so far away. But she was proud too. She knew it was right.

"Sing unto the Lord a new song," Frank quoted to them from Isaiah. "And his praise from the end of the earth, ye that go down to the sea, and all that is therein; the isles, and the inhabitants thereof."

We went home from church that day happy. We had a picnic among the flowers in our yard. Frank was relaxing on a blanket with Lizbeth's Mary Jane next to him. And I was sitting close by, just glad we were together. Emmie watched us for a while and then asked if we would be going to the mission field too.

"Whither we go, or stay, tomorrow or the present day, is all in the hands of God," Frank answered her. "For to will and to work we do his pleasure, so long as our hearts seek his treasure. This day and the day to come, till we meet Christ here, or he calls us home."

He reached and took my hand. I wasn't sure I understood all of what he meant by what he said. Or what he was quoting from. But I didn't ask. It seemed to me a good thing to let my future, my heart, and his, rest where he said they belonged: in the hands of God. No other hands could be so capable. None could be more generous, more able to give peace in trials, strength in despair, and understanding in the midst of a confusing world.

Blessed be God, the Father of mercies, the giver of peace. Now and forever. Amen.

**Leisha Kelly** is the author of two inspirational fiction series. She and her husband live in an old house in small-town Illinois where they are busy with the ministries of their church and the education of their two children.

For more information on Leisha and her books, go to www.leishakelly.com.

A devastating fire. A troubling secret.
*Another adventure for the Wortham family.*

Don't miss book 1 in the Country Road Chronicles

ℛ Revell

# The books that started it all!

LEISHA KELLY

*Julia's Hope*
A NOVEL

LEISHA KELLY

*Katie's Dream*
A NOVEL

LEISHA KELLY

*Emma's Gift*
A NOVEL

Don't miss the beginning of the Wortham story

Available at your local bookstore